TOMORROW'S MAGIC

TOMORROW'S MAGIC

PAMELA F. SERVICE

Random House　New York

Copyright © 2007 by Pamela F. Service
Cover illustration copyright © 2007 by James Bernardin

www.randomhouse.com/kids

Educators and librarians, for a variety of teaching tools, visit us at
www.randomhouse.com/teachers

Library of Congress Cataloging-in-Publication Data
Service, Pamela F.
Tomorrow's magic / Pamela F. Service. — 1st ed.
p. cm.
First published: New York: Atheneum Publishers, in two volumes:
Winter of Magic's Return in 1985, Tomorrow's Magic in 1987.
SUMMARY: Two novels in which a young, resurrected Merlin and two friends attempt
to bring King Arthur back to Britain, then struggle against
the evil plots of Morgan Le Fay to build a new and better
civilization in the wake of a nuclear holocaust.
ISBN: 978-0-375-84087-6 (trade) — ISBN: 978-0-375-94087-3 (lib. bdg.)
ISBN: 978-0-375-84088-3 (pbk.)
1. Merlin (Legendary character)—Juvenile fiction. [1. Merlin (Legendary character)—
Fiction. 2. Arthur, King—Fiction. 3. Morgan le Fay (Legendary character)—Fiction.
4. Wizards—Fiction. 5. Fantasy.] I. Title.
PZ7.S4885Tom 2007   [Fic]—dc22   2006016131

Printed in the United States of America

10 9 8 7 6 5 4 3 2 1

First Edition

BOOK
ONE

WINTER OF MAGIC'S RETURN

1

SUMMER THAW

Wellington Jones awoke to the sound of dripping water. Drops fell from the eaves, then a whole patch of snow broke loose and rumbled off the roof. His eyes snapped open in excitement. They were having a June thaw!

He sat up, and the covers slid from his plump shoulders, letting a whoosh of cold air invade the bed. Hastily he pulled the coarse blankets around him and squinted across the small room. Of the two narrow windows set deeply into the stone wall, he looked eagerly at the one covered with real glass. The ice crystals that patterned it most of the year were gone.

If it was a real June thaw, this might be another mild summer. There had been one just four years ago when he first came to Llandoylan School, though he'd been too upset at the time to appreciate it.

Maybe Master Foxworthy was right. He'd said in geography class that in the five hundred years since the Devastation, the climate had been slowly warming again. Wellington had doubted, feeling that in his own twelve years he had seen no change worth noting. But if this summer proved like that other one, there might be another August with no snow on the ground.

Slipping a hand from beneath the blankets, he fumbled along the cold stone wall for the niche where he kept his glasses. Pudgy fingers grabbed the icy metal frames and yanked them into the warmth. He scowled. He wanted to see if the icicle hanging outside his window had shortened any. But, as every morning, he didn't want to give in to these glass tyrants and put them on. They were responsible for so much of his misery.

If his eyes had been stronger (and he had been a little thinner and faster), he would be at the Cardiff Military Academy now, learning to be a warrior, as the son of a noble Glamorganshire family should be, as his parents had expected him to be when they named him for the ancient hero Wellington. Not that anyone called him that now. He was just "Welly," like the name of high boots for slogging through mud.

Angrily he jammed the glasses onto his round face and glared around the bare room. So now instead of the yearned-for academy, he was at Llandoylan School receiving a "well-rounded" education, when he wanted to be learning to fight boundary raiders from Gwent or Angelsy pirates or perhaps the rumored hordes of muties from the South.

Of course, he'd been told often enough, he was lucky to get any education at all. Children of herders or farmers generally got none.

The muffled clanging of the ten-minute bell startled him. Hurriedly Welly slipped out of bed, yelping as his bare feet slapped against the cold flagstones. When he was an upperclassman, he'd at least have a rug in his room. He tugged on a pair of socks. Then, rushing to the washbasin, he broke the ice crusting its surface and splashed his face perfunctorily with water.

Anyway, he thought as he hastily pulled on his long underwear, this was an early thaw—a time for exciting things to happen. And this time, he would make the most of it.

Trousers and shirt on, he slid into his boots and, grabbing his fleece-lined jacket, rushed out the door into the narrow hallway. Still struggling with one sleeve, he rounded a corner and smashed into another hurrying body. Adjusting his skewed glasses, his heart sank. It was Nigel Williams, accompanied by several of his cronies.

"Watch yourself, Frog Eyes!" Nigel snarled. "If you don't know how to act in the presence of your future duke, I'll be glad to show you."

"Aw, later, Nigel," drawled Justin, the young lord's chief lieutenant. "The pleasure of whipping a worm like that isn't worth missing breakfast for."

Nigel snorted agreement, and without another word, he and his companions turned disdainfully and descended the stairs. Welly, pale and shaking, stood on the landing until they were out of sight. Then he hurried down, slipping into the great dining hall as the final bell sounded and the ancient wooden doors closed ponderously behind him.

Hazily lit by narrow windows, the hall was noisy with pre-mealtime chatter. Welly scanned the long tables and benches for a free place, finally sliding into an empty seat across from one of the younger students, not a friend but at least one who hadn't made fun of him yet.

Not, he thought glumly, that he had any real friends here. Except, perhaps, Heather McKenna. But he wouldn't sit next to her here. Nigel or his sort might trot out one of their taunts: "Horseface Heather and Frog-eyed Welly, ugly as muties and equally silly." When they did, Heather usually pointed out that the rhyme stank and that, anyway, frogs were extinct, so how did they know what frog eyes looked like?

At last, bowls of steaming porridge were being passed down the long wooden tables. When Welly's bowl reached him, he clamped his hands around its rough pottery sides, letting the warmth seep into them. Up and down the table, the students' breath rose in white puffs.

At the head table, old Master Bigly rose and mumbled the usual invocation. "We remnant of Man thank the Creator for his mercy. As life is preserved and sustenance preserved, so hope is preserved. World without end. Amen."

Welly began eating in silence and avoided looking at his tablemates by staring into the dim cobwebbed recesses of the vaulted ceiling. His thoughts were on how to avoid Nigel's promised punishment, though he might forget. The bully probably made too many threats in one day to keep track of them all.

Nigel had been here for less than a year and would return to the Cardiff Military Academy after a stint at rounding his education. But already the big, hulking boy had made his mark at Llandoylan. Welly wondered if Nigel's boast was true, if when he became Duke he'd change the title and declare himself King. Dukes of some of the larger shires had done that already. It added zest to the regular border clashes. Not that any of the shires had populations big enough for real wars. But it sounded better to fight for a king than a duke, even if Britain had a dozen of them.

After breakfast, Nigel sailed out of the hall along with

the other upperclassmen, not casting Welly a glance. On the other side of the hall, however, someone was waving at him energetically. Squinting, he recognized Heather and waited while she threaded her way between the benches and departing students, light brown hair swinging in two thin braids. Her long, narrow face, though not quite pretty, was lit in an eager smile.

"Welly," she whispered conspiratorially, "I've really come across something good this time. Don't dare talk about it now, it's too big. But I'll . . ." She stopped and looked with exaggerated caution around the near-empty hall. "I'll come to your room tonight. Usual signal." Then she whisked out of the room to her first class, and prickling with curiosity, Welly headed to his.

Ancient Written English was not his favorite class, but it was necessary if he wanted to read writings that had survived from pre-Devastation days. Not that Welly was anxious to read most of them, unlike Heather, who read every printed word she saw. He simply reasoned that if he was too fat and blind to be a warrior, perhaps he could learn about ancient strategies and battles and be some general's clever strategist.

The morning's second class, geography, he enjoyed more. For the last several months, they had been studying the pre-Devastation world and the nations that had flourished before the nuclear war and cold darkness that followed wiped out most life on the planet.

Welly had been interested, partly because Nigel and his followers had loudly voiced their disinterest. They considered unimportant the layout of extinct nations, most of which were now poisonous, glassy plains, peopled, if at all, by sparse bands of mutants.

Master Foxworthy had stressed that the fate of all the earth was interconnected. Britain, he pointed out, had survived the worst of the war because in late pre-Devastation days it had disarmed, ridding itself of its own nuclear weapons and those that allies had placed on its soil. As a result, when war finally came, Britain was a minor target, and only the city of London, the former capital, had been bombed. Destruction from blast, firestorm, and first-wave radiation had been confined to the island's now-desolate Southeast.

But clouds of radiation from the bombed nations had swept the world. Debris and dust blown into the atmosphere blocked the world's sunlight, lowering temperatures and destroying most plant and animal life. The atmosphere's protective layers were thinned, and harmful ultraviolet rays, plus persistent radiation, brought lingering death and terrible mutation to generations of survivors. Civilization collapsed into centuries of barbarism.

Today, Foxworthy was back to the present, showing post-Devastation boundaries by jabbing a pointer into the map drawn on the skin of a large two-headed cow. The colored lines and patches showed the shires, which, sandwiched between the Scottish glaciers and the southern desert, had for centuries operated as independent duchies. For most of those centuries, the boundaries had wavered as shires fought among themselves, nibbling off territory and asserting dominance.

Glamorgan's eastern enemy, Gwent, was the topic of today's class, and for once, Duke-to-be Nigel paid close attention. But partway through the class, one of the older girls interrupted with a question that had been buzzing around the school for several days.

"Master Foxworthy," she said deferentially, "could you

tell us whether it is true that armies of muties from the Continent have invaded the Southeast and are attacking shires fringing the desert?"

"Miss Dillon," Foxworthy replied after a frowning pause, "your question, although irrelevant to the topic of today's class, nonetheless deserves an answer. It is true, as I have pointed out, that with the capture of water in ice and glaciers, the sea level is a good deal lower than in pre-Devastation times. Not only is our coastline farther out, but areas such as the English Channel are narrower. And they present far less formidable a barrier than once they did.

"However, the human population of continental Europe, as indeed that of most of Asia and North America, was largely destroyed in the Devastation and aftermath. Only in the non-glaciated areas of Scandinavia is there any remnant of civilization capable of organizing armies as such.

"Still, bands of mutated animals and humans do reportedly roam the Continent, even as they do here on a smaller scale. And reports have been received of some having crossed into Southeast Britain. But these are isolated incidents and nothing to cause concern."

Master Foxworthy glowered around the room to discourage further rumormongering and then returned to his day's subject. Half of Welly's mind attended to the class, while the other played with strategies for smashing armies of muties on the borders of Northhamptonshire.

After classes in math and culture came the final class of the day, science, which Welly and most of his classmates considered a waste of time. Perhaps the subject could be interesting, but not with Master Quiles pacing about bemoaning the loss of past glories and parroting tales of ancient wonders. And even if the grand old days and their fabulous devices had been that golden, what of it? The knowledge and skills to make those things were long gone.

But finally the intoning ended, and the students were dismissed to a supper of potato soup and barley bread. Afterward, it was still light, and many donned coats and hurried out into the walled school grounds. Usually Welly would choose a game of chess or checkers, but tonight he had other plans. Heather had passed him after dinner with a theatrical wink, and he didn't want to miss her visit. Wild as her ideas usually were, they added some excitement to life.

Leaving the dining hall, he threaded his way through the familiar maze of stairways and corridors that made up Llandoylan School. The venerable building had grown steadily and with no discernible plan since an order of monks had laid its first stones over a millennium earlier. After its monastery days, it had served as a hospital, an insane asylum, a hotel, and several institutes. Each new purpose had brought new additions. Nothing major, however, had been added since the Devastation, and the whole conglomerate had an aura of heavy, well-worn age.

Once Welly reached the boys' dormitory wing, he climbed the narrow back stairs to the second floor. Along his own hallway, most of the rooms were unused. Those that were used had only single occupants, following the school's independence-instilling policies. Welly, an only child, preferred this. Since most people apparently had little use for him, he had decided early not to show a need for other people. This ploy wasn't terribly effective, he realized. The others didn't care whether he needed them or not. Still, it made a defensive wall to fall back to when he was particularly snubbed.

His room greeted him with its familiar smell of cold

mustiness. Gray early-evening light seeped through the windows. Through the glass one, he noted the length of his special icicle, seeing it had melted considerably during the day. Then, pulling out the drawer in the old wooden table, he checked his candles: two fresh ones and three stubs. That was all right, then. They were given only six candles per month, but since he often studied in the library, he usually had spares for needs like tonight.

Sticking a stub into the pottery candlestick, he placed his flint and steel in readiness beside it, then settled himself on the bed. In the growing darkness, he reviewed in his mind the translation he'd been reading of Caesar's campaign in Gaul. Of course, Gaul, or France, was as dead as Caesar, but the military strategies were ageless.

The room had sunk into darkness when he was startled back from Gaul by a rap at the window—one rap, a double rap, then another single. Having a code, he knew, was silly. But Heather liked melodrama. Certainly no one else would come scuttling like a spider over the roofs between the girls' and boys' wings.

Heather scrambled in along with a gust of cold air. While Welly fumbled with lighting the candle, she sat on the deep windowsill, swinging legs that, even padded in their wool-lined trousers, seemed thin and gangly. Then she hopped down, closed the window latch, and perched herself cross-legged on the table.

In the flickering candlelight, her thin face glowed with excitement. Ceremoniously she dusted off a spot on the table and plunked down the package she'd had tucked under her arm. With a flourish, she pulled aside the rag wrappings and revealed a small and very tattered paper book, obviously quite old.

"I found this in the library in the miscellaneous section,"

she announced proudly. "And those snippy 'social' girls say they don't need me or my bookish ways! Ha! I guess I don't need them either!" She slipped off the table and pirouetted dizzyingly around the room, braids standing out like pinwheels.

"Wait till Mabel or Kathleen sees me sweeping into class bedecked with emeralds and rubies! Maybe I won't seem such a washout then!"

"Heather," Welly said, feeling confused, "what exactly do you have there?"

"Treasure!" she declared, one hand held high like a torchbearer. "Treasure that you and I are going to find!"

Welly tried to sound cool and suave, but his "Oh, really?" came out rather high-pitched.

"Indeed!" She slapped a hand solidly on the old volume. "In these pages, we find the true tale of Veronica Hartwell, who, back in the dim past a couple hundred years before the Devastation, was subject to dire tribulation, and in her hour of deepest despair hid her treasures away, where no man has seen them since . . . I hope."

"Where did she hide them?"

"Ah, that's the best part; it was right around here! It says so." Heather picked up the crumbling book and flipped carefully through the pages as she continued. "She was a governess, see. Sent out to wild and lonely country in Glamorganshire."

"There's a lot of wild and lonely country around here," Welly objected. "There was then, too, I expect."

"Yes, but this refers to a grand old estate, Ravenscroft, nestled in wild and windswept foothills northwest of Cardiff. And then it goes on to talk about the ancient battlements where Veronica gazed at the dismal sea."

"You can't see the sea from around here."

"Dummy, you could then. The Bristol Channel ran right up the Severn valley."

"Yeah, that's right," he muttered. "But that description still fits a lot of territory."

"Naturally. But the best part is . . . we have a picture!" She shoved the book toward the candle, revealing a cracked and faded paper cover showing a lovely young lady with wind-tossed hair and disheveled gown running down a path from a gloomy castle-like building. A dark caped figure pursued her, and in the background was a glimpse of cliffs and distant sea. Above it all, in barely legible scarlet letters, were the words "Desire at Ravenscroft."

"All we have to do now," Heather said triumphantly, "is find a place that fits the description and the picture, and we'll have it."

"Heather," Welly ventured after a long examination of the cover, "are you sure this isn't a work of fiction?"

She gave him a long, withering look. "I'm not that gullible. I am eleven years old and exceptionally well read. Besides," she continued as she thumbed through the old book, "I still don't believe what Master Gallowglass said about Holmes. I think he misread the historical evidence. Arthur Conan Doyle was clearly only a pen name for Dr. Watson. Anyone can tell those stories are factual accounts."

With mixed emotion, Welly recalled Heather's enthusiasm of the previous year after she'd discovered the recorded investigations of a nineteenth-century detective named Sherlock Holmes. She had even involved him and a few of the younger children in a New Holmes Detective Agency to study the great man's methods and solve local mysteries. They'd had a splendidly exciting time until an investigation of the source of meat for the Sunday stew got them in a good deal of trouble, and Culture Master Gallowglass had disdainfully stated that the Holmes adventures were fictional stories written by an author who had also invented monsters and lost worlds.

"Anyway, this is different," Heather resumed. "It's clearly an historical account—readably written, admittedly, but full of detail. What happens, you see, is that this young woman, beautiful, impetuous Veronica Hartwell, is from a poor but aristocratic family in Oxford. Her father, who was some sort of diplomat, dies in distant India, and she is left penniless. She's taken on as governess for the children of widower Drake Moorgrave, who lives in dark and sinister Ravenscroft Manor in Glamorganshire. Well, he has some mysterious secret in his past, though Veronica is strangely attracted to him. Then she receives a secret message from her supposedly dead father, leading her to a treasure stolen from him by Moorgrave. At last she has it in her room—lovely stuff, emeralds and rubies and a pair of jeweled daggers—when Moorgrave, who for days had been making impassioned advances, is heard approaching. She quickly hides the treasure, except for one dagger, behind a loose brick in the fireplace."

Heather stopped dramatically. Despite himself, Welly was caught up. "Then what happened?"

"Well, unfortunately, the next part of the book is missing."

Welly groaned. "So, if this is the treasure you expect us to find, what makes you sure it's still there? Maybe this Moorgrave character found it."

"Ah." Heather smiled triumphantly. "It's only the middle part of the book that's missing. The last few pages are here, and they say . . . Let me get it here."

She carefully flipped over the final pages. "Here it is. 'Veronica turned again for a last look at Ravenscroft, its sinister battlements darkly silhouetted against a storm-wracked sky. She knew that she would never return there. Better to let its treasure and its painful memories remain untouched until time had cleansed them both. She would never speak of either again. Sighing, she nestled her head against Allen's'—I don't know where he came in—'shoulder, and the two continued down the road toward their new life.' "

"Hmm," Welly said as Heather looked at him expectantly. Then he added, "So, if this story is for real, you think we can go out, find the ruins of this Ravenscroft place, poke around in an old brick fireplace, and find necklaces and a jeweled dagger?"

"Right!"

Skepticism fought with excitement. With this early thaw, it would be fine to get out, out beyond the school grounds and the town itself. And suppose they did find the treasure? That wouldn't be bad—especially the jeweled dagger.

"All right. I'm with you. When do we start?"

"Tomorrow's Sunday. If we leave early, we'll have the whole day to search."

They discussed plans until finally Heather slipped out the window again and headed back along valleys where the slate roofs came together. She could probably have used the corridors just as well. The movements of the night monitors were usually predictable. But that would have lacked excitement.

Once he fastened the latch, Welly blew out the guttering candle and hurriedly undressed. Crawling into bed, he curled up in a tight ball until his body began warming the icy coverings.

His ever drowsier thoughts dwelt on tomorrow's adventure and on his companion. Heather McKenna was his only real friend at the school. They had drifted together perhaps because they were both outcasts. She had been sent to Llandoylan, she claimed, to be gotten rid of when her mother remarried after the death of Heather's father. The aristocratic new husband had no love for this homely girl of Scottish refugee extraction, and her mother now needed to produce male heirs and remove visible reminders of her former lowly marriage. During three years at Llandoylan, Heather had never once been called home for holidays.

But at school she didn't find herself needed any more than at home. Her fellow schoolgirls were there primarily to become refined mates for fellow aristocrats. They felt little need for pure learning, while for Heather, learning and fantasy were what made a parched life bearable. But the more she turned to it, the more the others drove her out of their world and into her own.

When Welly put aside his own reserve and joined Heather, her adventurousness chipped away at his caution. Everything he did with her ran the knife-edge of trouble. She thrust an excitement into his life that he never would have added on his own.

He drifted to sleep dreaming of leading Caesar's armies with a great jeweled dagger held aloft.

In the dead of night, a sound chiseled its way into Welly's sleep. He tried withdrawing deeper into dreams, but it followed and pulled him out. Eyes closed, he lay listening, and despite the wool blankets, he shivered. He had heard that sound before.

The keening wail was faint and seemingly very distant. He'd never heard other boys mention it, but maybe no one else heard it. His was the last tenanted room in this wing. Another older section abutted this one, but its upper floors were abandoned. The cry came again, unearthly and chillingly sad. He refused to imagine what it might be. He just wished it would stop.

Eventually it did. But still he lay awake, nerves strung as taut as bowstrings. He tried to relax, but now something else kept him awake. He wished they allowed chamber pots here instead of stressing fortitude in all things. He tried to go to sleep but was too uncomfortable. He sighed. He'd have to make a trek to the latrine.

Reluctantly Welly slipped from the blankets, slid his legs into icy trousers, and hastily tucked in his nightshirt. Ramming his feet into boots, he pulled on a coat and stepped quietly out the door of his room. The passage was hazily lit with widely spaced candle lamps. He hurried along, listening to the flap of his boots on the flagstones and hoping he'd hear nothing else, particularly that crying. At least he was moving toward the more populated part of the building.

He descended a narrow set of stairs and took several corridors to a small back door. Outside, he hurried through the darkness toward the darker shapes of the outhouses.

On his return, he felt better and was enjoying the relative mildness of the night when suddenly he stepped into a pocket of cold air. Its chill set him shivering—with cold and something else. Then a noise came from ahead, from the front of the darkened school building.

The crashing of wood and glass, a man yelling, and a sound that could not have been a man. Welly stood rooted with fear. A dark shape hurtled toward him. It was large and low and showed the glint of eyes as it swept past. The cold in the air lapped around him like a wave, then flowed away.

The fear that held him snapped. He ran toward the building. Several voices tumbled from the headmaster's office. He wanted to learn what had happened but knew they'd only send him away. And at present, curiosity was not nearly as strong as a wish to be safe in his warm bed.

But once back there, sleep did not come easily. Welly was sure that in the morning, there'd be some reasonable explanation for the disturbance in the school office. But if there was any explanation for what had passed him in the night, he suspected he wouldn't want to hear it.

2

BEYOND THE WALLS

Next morning, the school was alive with stories about the break-in. As the students ate Sunday breakfast of porridge and stewed turnips, rumors flew up and down the tables. It seemed that in the middle of the night, Headmaster Greenhow had been disturbed by sounds from the office adjacent to his rooms. He'd entered and found a dark someone or something (versions differed) tearing through a cabinet of school records. Greenhow had thrown a stool at the intruder, who then leaped back through the broken window.

Several masters had answered the alarm and had immediately checked the records strewn over the floor, but none appeared to be missing. Nor was anything else gone from the room. So the motive for the break-in remained a mystery.

Welly heard no mention of any animal with the burglar and tried to conclude that he'd seen only a man in a heavy coat running low to avoid detection. That explanation did seem more reasonable than anything else, particularly after breakfast when he stepped through the school's doorway into the daylight.

It was a day to banish fears. He looked at the sky with a thrill of excitement. He'd scarcely believed it when he'd squinted through his windowpane before breakfast. But it was true. The sky was blue.

Not the impossible bright blue of ancient paintings, of course. But nonetheless, the sky, which most days was gray or dirty white, today was definitely tinged with blue. His father said that as a boy, he had never seen that. And here he, Wellington Jones, had not only experienced two June thaws but also had seen several blue skies in one year. He hurried down the stone steps, glad that today was Sunday and adventure beckoned.

Heather waited not far from the main gate of the school grounds, offering crumbs to a squirrel. The fluffy black creature stuffed its cheeks as fast as crumbs were dropped in front of it. But at the sight of Welly, the animal scurried onto the high stone wall and chattered down at him.

"I'm sorry, I didn't mean to scare him," Welly said.

"Oh, that's all right. This one's Sigmund, and he's always skittish. His mate, Rapunzel, is friendlier, but she has some new babies now."

"It's wonderful how they come right up to you," Welly said admiringly. "I've never known anyone whom animals liked so much."

"Well, animals are less difficult than people. Maybe they don't exactly need you, but they're willing to let you be friends as long as you're patient enough."

Scattering the last of her crumbs at the base of the wall, Heather patted a bulge in the pocket of her heavy coat. "I've got a surprise for us, too. I talked to Cook before breakfast. You know, she really is a good soul. She gives me scraps for my friends like Sigmund here and likes me to tell her stories. Says they jolly her up. Anyway, I told her we were bound for high adventure today and would miss Sunday lunch, so she gave me some bread and even a bit of cheese. It was left from Master Greenhow's supper, but he had a headache and didn't eat it."

"I don't imagine that ruckus last night helped his headache," Welly said, then immediately regretted bringing up the subject when he saw a gleam kindle in Heather's eyes.

"Now, that's a real mystery, isn't it?"

"Yes, but just let the masters and the constable deal with it. The Holmes Detective Agency is permanently disbanded, remember?"

He decided that, for the moment, he wouldn't even mention what he had seen in the night. He'd much rather spend the day looking for fictitious jewels than tracking down something whose memory still chilled him.

Heather laughed. "All right, one mystery at a time. Anyway, I'm more in the mood for hunting treasure than burglars who don't take anything."

She started for the gate, then stopped as a group of older students came toward it. Nigel was among them, with Melanie Witlow, his latest favorite, draped over his arm.

Seeing Welly, Heather, and the squirrel, Nigel called out, "Do be careful of the vermin, children. They might bite and turn you into muties—but it looks like they have already." The others laughed at this witticism and passed on out the gate.

"As for vermin," Heather snapped, angrily twisting the tip of a braid, "that's Nigel. Sigmund here would make a better duke than that arrogant bully."

Welly shrugged, heading for the gate. "Well, never mind him. We've got a whole day away from his kind."

Once outside the school grounds, they walked along

narrow graveled streets that wound among the varied buildings. A few were old pre-Devastation structures, while others were new, although built largely of scavenged materials.

Since this was Sunday, the streets were full of people
from both town and countryside. Most were heading for
one of the places of worship. There had been several in
Welly's hometown, but he was always impressed with the
variety here. There were Holy Catholics and several old
Protestant sects, as well as Armageddonites, Druids, Is-
raelites, and New Zoroastrians.

Most weeks he went to one or another, always avoiding the New Zoroastrians, the church Nigel's group was
flirting with at the moment. But Sunday was a free day as
long as students were within the school walls by curfew.
Even going outside the town wall was not forbidden, though
few would have wanted to.

The two adventurers soon passed through the north
gate, the one rebuilt ten years earlier after a Gwent raid.
Then, leaving the road, they struck north toward the hills.

Most of the ground was still frozen solid, but the thaw
was softening the snow cover. Scattered around the white
were darker patches where springy gray-green grass curled
close to the ground like coarse wool. There, their snow-
packed boots left inverted prints, compressed white tracks
on the dark earth.

The two walked in silence, enjoying the faint blue of
the sky. The sun could actually be seen as a silvery disk obscured by only a thin dust layer. The air seemed mild, and
soon they unfastened their coats, throwing back the hoods.
A breeze ruffled their hair, but except for its rustling, a vast
silence lay over the world.

In low-lying spots, trickles of melted snow ran together.

Heather in the lead, the two hopped through a network of streamlets, their boots making satisfying squelchings whenever they missed.

Suddenly Heather halted and slapped a restraining hand on Welly's chest. "Stop! Do you see it?"

"See what?"

"Over there. It's a bird!"

Welly looked in the direction of her gesture. Birds were rare sights any time of year. He squinted, then shook his head in frustration.

"There." Heather pointed. "Over by that rock, in the pool of meltwater."

Then he saw it, a large silver-gray shape with a pointed beak and long neck. At their next step, it spread its wings, rattling its scalelike feathers, and with a scolding cry, beat into the air. They watched as it circled slowly overhead, then drifted out of sight toward the northern mountains.

Heather sighed contentedly. "Maybe that's what I really want to be, a naturalist."

As they continued walking, Welly asked, "Do you think there's enough today for a naturalist to study?"

"Oh, I'm certain there is. Wouldn't it be marvelous to study a bird like that? Off on your own, away from people, tracking it for weeks over wild hills until you found its den or whatever. And besides, Master Foxworthy says that with all the mutations, many creatures have never even been named. Maybe that bird could be *Birdus heatherus* or something! That could give you a place in things. It wouldn't matter what people thought of you."

Welly wished she hadn't mentioned mutations. As they drew closer to the hills, he remembered stories about the muties said to roam them, both the animal and the human variety. Unsettling visions from the night before returned as well.

He cleared his throat. "Heather, how much farther do we have to go? Into the hills, I mean."

"Oh, not too much, I should think. In a bit, we should be high enough for that view on the book. Then probably we ought to head west."

Welly was getting hungry. This at least let him turn his thoughts from muties to the food in Heather's pocket. Sunday was the one day the school served lunch, and he was glad they needn't miss it altogether. The thought of the lump of cheese was particularly enticing, and Welly forged doggedly after it up the slope.

He was puffing and panting by the time they reached a level patch. But Heather seemed undaunted. "Ah, this exercise is great! Helps work off the winter fat."

Welly sighed. He knew that exercise wasn't likely to do anything about his fat. He was born fat. He was convinced that when he died, they would cut him open and find that even his bones were fat.

"Think it's about lunchtime yet?" he ventured.

"Yeah, just about. But let's check over there first. Looks like some ruins."

The level patch proved to be the bed of an ancient road. They followed it up the hill toward a cluster of ruined buildings made of the gray artificial stone that was popular, they'd been told, before the Devastation.

"Well, these aren't the ruins we're looking for," Heather announced. "Ravenscroft was real stone, and big. But it's a good place for lunch."

Welly agreed heartily.

They sat down on a dusty slab. Fishing the cloth bag

from her pocket, Heather reverently brought out a small chunk of cheese and generous slices of dark gray-brown bread.

"I wish I had a friend who was a cook," Welly said indistinctly through a mouthful of bread and cheese.

Suddenly they heard a soft thump behind them. A rustling noise prickled the hairs along Welly's spine. Slowly he turned his head.

Something hideous crouched in a broken section of wall. A mutie, the closest he'd ever seen one. Heather, too, was staring at it, her large eyes looking even larger in her thin face.

Another mutie joined the first, and Welly thought for a minute he would be sick. They were both very short, moving with a hunched gait on bowed and twisted legs. Their skin was a mottled purple, and they had no noses, only a damp hole covered by a meager flap of skin. Though one was female, both were nearly bald, with only a fringe of white hair, which on the male spread down into a wispy beard.

It was the male (Welly had trouble thinking of it as a "man") that moved forward, growling in its throat and brandishing a lump of concrete in one hand. Both children jumped up and stepped backward. The female mutie nimbly hopped through the opening in the wall, followed by a child. Heather found the youngster equally hideous, but its eyes were intelligent and wide with curiosity.

"I guess this spot's theirs," she whispered to Welly. "Shall we go?"

"Let's!" he whispered, then raised a tremulous voice. "We're sorry to have disturbed you. We'll be going now."

Both adults growled and said something that sounded

like words, but the children couldn't catch them. The muties continued their slow advance.

"The food," Heather said. "Let's leave them the rest. Maybe that'll satisfy them."

Welly didn't argue as Heather placed the remaining bread and cheese on a section of wall. "Just wanted to thank you for the use of your place," she said loudly while backing away.

After the two children were several yards from the ruins, the muties scuttled over to the food. Welly and Heather turned quickly and hurried off. When Heather looked back, the young mutie was sitting on the wall stuffing bread into its mouth and watching her with liquid eyes. Tentatively she waved at it, and it waved back before somersaulting off and diving for more food.

Hearts racing, the two trotted west over the hillside, putting distance between themselves and the ruins.

At last they slowed, and Welly said between gasps for breath, "Don't you think we should go back now? I mean, these hills could be infested with the creatures. And it's well past noon already."

"Yes," she replied, chewing reflectively on the thin end of a braid. "But you know, this really ought to be about where the old mansion was. Let's look around a little more. If we find something, we can check it out and come back another time."

Welly grunted his assent, and they continued walking west. Dutifully he scanned the slope ahead, but his mind was on bread and cheese and the question of whether muties liked to follow such delicacies with fresh meat.

It had been interesting, he admitted, seeing muties close up like that. But they were certainly awful-looking.

Still, the masters said that if mutations didn't kill or prevent reproduction, they were often adaptive. Everyone whose ancestors had survived the Devastation was something of a mutant, even if only in skin color.

Darker skin kept out more harmful rays, and nearly everyone was darker than their pre-Devastation ancestors. Though, of course, there was a lot of variation. Welly was darker than Heather, and little Zachary Green was as dark as old leather. That older boy, Earl Bedwas, on the other hand, was very pale, like things that lived under stones.

They marched on, but Welly didn't see any grand mansions. "We really ought to turn back soon," he said.

"All right. Let's just go as far as that clump of trees."

This quickened his interest. Silhouetted against the pale sky was a cluster of rare evergreens. They approached with reverence. The trunks were twisted back from years of battling west winds, and on their north sides the dark branches still sagged under dollops of snow. The air about them held a cool, spicy tang.

Welly was so intrigued by the trees, he failed to notice the stones. But Heather saw them.

"Look, stone walls! Oh, maybe we've found it! This could be Ravenscroft Manor."

Welly looked around to see tumbled stones snaking off through the snow. Trees grew up among the ruins, and in spots low bushes half-covered the stonework. The place seemed a haven for plant life. In snow-free patches, the usual coarse ground cover gave way to richer green stuff, and colorful mosses splotched the stones.

"The setting seems right," Heather said a little doubtfully, glancing from the view before her to the book cover in her hand. "Let's look for a fireplace."

Welly was more interested in the mosses and the odd green tendrils pushing up through the snow. Could these be ferns? He stepped over a pile of stones to examine a cluster. Suddenly his foot slipped. He grabbed at a mass of brittle twigs. A whole bush pulled free and tumbled with him into the hole.

For a moment, he lay stunned, liberally covered in loose dirt. Then gingerly he stood up. Little spears of pain shot up his right ankle. Shakily he sat down upon a stone. He should have kept his eyes open! This hole wasn't exactly hidden. The ruins dropped away here, exposing a maze of sunken rooms.

Heather's thin face peered over the edge. "Are you all right, Welly? Oh, look at all you've found! I'll be right down." In an avalanche of snow and dirt, she slid down beside him. "We're bound to find something here."

"More trouble, I expect," Welly grumbled as he stood up again and limped experimentally about.

In an adjacent room, Heather poked around in the rubble, but Welly was rapidly losing interest, even in jeweled daggers. Suddenly her voice came to him, high and excited.

"Welly, come here! Doesn't this look like a brick fireplace?"

He hobbled through the crumbling doorway and over to where a number of bricks were set into a stone wall.

"It might be," he said dubiously. "But how do we tell which is the loose brick for your secret hiding place? They're all loose."

"We'll just have to be thorough," she said, already prying bricks away and throwing them aside. Welly joined in, his interest quickening with the search.

After a few minutes, Heather stopped. "Did you hear something?"

"My stomach growling."

"No. But something was. Sounded like it came from in there." She stepped through a narrow doorway, and cautiously Welly followed.

"Look!" she exclaimed from up ahead. Hurriedly Welly pushed in beside her. The small room was still partially roofed over, but there was enough light to see a pile of branches and what looked like bones. On it crouched a small, furry animal. A pink tongue hung out of its smiling jaws, and bright yellow eyes fixed on them as the creature jumped up and made yelping bounces toward them. It was ash-gray with big paws.

"How cute!" Heather said.

"It's cute, all right," Welly agreed, "but we'd better leave it be."

"But how can we leave the little thing out here all alone?"

"It's probably not alone. It's sure to have family about; this looks like its den."

He glanced around the ruins with new uneasiness, imagining wild animals lurking in the cold afternoon shadows. Again he remembered the encounter of the night before and shivered. Heather picked up a bone and tossed it toward the puppy, who pounced on it playfully.

"Heather," Welly said, "let's start back now. It's awfully late."

A deep growl cut short her reply. They looked up. Glaring down at them from the wall stood a large fell-dog, ears erect, its fur gray and mottled. A limp animal dangled from its jaws. Yowling rose from behind it, and another, larger, dog joined the first. Several answering howls came from not far away.

Fear slammed against the children. Backing away, Welly expected to be leaped upon any second, but the dogs remained on the rim, yapping and snarling. Suddenly he realized these animals were afraid of them. Feral dogs had many encounters with men, usually armed men.

Quickly Welly reached down and grabbed up a brick. "Keep moving back," he whispered. "And arm yourself."

A third dog loped up and, seeing the children, crouched, ready to spring. Welly lobbed his brick, and it glanced off a shaggy shoulder. The dog yipped and slunk back. The others shied away, snarling and pacing back and forth a few feet from the edge.

At the arrival of two more dogs, Heather hurled her brick. Welly followed with another and another. "We can keep throwing stuff," Heather said tensely. "But how do we do that and climb out, too?"

"Maybe there's an easier way out than the one we took down." Welly reached for a stone, since they were clear of the scattered bricks.

By now, seven fell-dogs milled about, clamoring for blood yet hesitant to come for it. But larger numbers increased their confidence, and they moved closer to the edge. As the children retreated, fewer of their missiles reached the pack.

The barking was deafening, but suddenly it stilled. An unearthly howl rose from the other side of the ruins and climbed up and up into a piercing shriek.

The dogs paced about in confusion, tails between their legs. The eerie sound came again, closer this time, and the pack slunk back out of sight. In a few moments, they were yelping some distance away.

The sound that had driven off the wild dogs rooted the children with fear. Dreading what he would see, Welly turned slowly to look in the direction of the sound. A dark shape moved to the rim of the ruins, silent against the pale sky.

"Well met, schoolmates," said a perfectly human voice. "But let's get out of here before your friends return. I can't fool them with that howl forever."

Welly just stuttered in relief, but Heather found the name of their deliverer first. "Earl Bedwas! What a rescue!"

"Here, you can get up this way," the older boy said, and he helped them up what had once been a stairway.

"Now let's go—quickly but calmly," he said when they reached the top.

Following Earl's lead, they moved down the slope as fast as they could. But with Welly's hurt ankle, this was not fast enough for any of them. The dogs, however, did not follow.

"I suppose it's rather obvious to say how grateful we are," Heather said to their new companion. "But thank you just the same. How did you find us, anyway?"

The boy ran a hand through his long dark hair. "Oh, I was out walking around the hills, and I heard the pack up by the ruins. It sounded as if they had some special trouble going, so I thought I'd take a look."

"How did you do that howl?" Welly asked. "It sure scared them."

"Not just them," Heather muttered.

Earl laughed. "I don't know how I first stumbled on it. But I come out to the hills a lot, and I've gotten to know the things that live here. The fell-dogs are afraid of other dog sounds, if you do it right. Maybe they think it's the dog devil or some such. I don't know."

The three walked single file toward the distant walled town. Welly, limping along in the rear, watched the tall, thin boy as he strode on ahead. If Earl did spend his free time wandering alone in the hills, then he was probably as odd as most people said he was. Welly'd never had much contact with the older boy, but whenever he had, Earl always seemed pleasant enough. Probably he was a bit of a loner, and Welly knew that was enough to make some people consider him peculiar.

When they reached the lowlands, Earl stopped and looked back at the hills. "They won't follow us here. Sit down a minute, Welly, and let me look at that ankle." Welly collapsed gratefully onto the soggy grass. Earl, kneeling in front of him, took up the injured foot and peeled back trouser, sock, and boot top. Gently he prodded the ankle while Welly winced. "It's probably just twisted, though it's swelling a little. Anyway, binding will make it feel better, and you'll move faster."

He drew a linen scarf from inside his coat and wrapped it firmly around Welly's ankle. "There," he said when everything was back in place. "Want to rest more?"

Welly swallowed. "Just a bit. It hurt so much for a while, I thought I was going to be sick."

Earl nodded and sank back on the ground, his head cocked quizzically to the right. "Would it be impertinent to ask what you two were doing up there?"

Heather looked down at her hands. "We were looking for treasure."

"In the ruins?"

"Well, somewhere up there. I found a book that talked about it, and that seemed like the right sort of place. But I don't know, maybe the book really was fiction. Anyway," she concluded, looking up defiantly, "it made a ripping good adventure!"

Earl smiled, dark eyes glinting in his pale, almost gaunt face.

Welly glanced uneasily back to the hills. "Earl, are you sure the fell-dogs won't come down after us?"

The older boy shook his head. "They're afraid of people. Unless there's a famine, they don't come close to towns or roads."

"But last night," Welly began, then looked quickly at Heather. "I'm sorry I didn't tell you this earlier, Heather, but I was afraid you'd want to investigate. Last night, I was coming back from the loo at the same time Master Greenhow discovered that intruder, and something big and black and low ran by me in the dark. It was cold and horrible."

Earl raised an eyebrow. "I can't even guess what it was. But no fell-dog would come that near to people unless it was rabid. And a rabid dog would have stayed and fought."

Welly lowered his eyes. "Well, maybe. I just thought that with the cries in the night . . ."

"Cries in the night?" Earl said sharply.

"Yes, that's what woke me first. High, wailing cries. I've heard them before. I just thought that maybe some animal made them, and this thing I saw could have been it."

"You've heard these cries before? Where's your room?"

"At the end of the north wing, near the abandoned part. Have you heard them, too?"

"No, never! It's probably just the wind or something." Earl stood up abruptly, tugging a shock of black hair out of his eyes. "We'd better be going, if you're feeling better."

Earl helped Welly to his feet, then smiled tautly. "From

the look of the sun and your ankle, we're not likely to make it back by curfew. But if you limp impressively into Master Greenhow's study, we mightn't get too grim a punishment."

"You two could go on ahead," Welly suggested unenthusiastically. "There's no point in your getting into trouble because of my clumsiness."

"What!" Earl exclaimed. "And leave you to enjoy more adventures alone?"

"No," Heather said, her back turned resolutely on the rapidly sinking sun. "We all stick together."

3

FRIENDS IN NEED

Earl had been right. The headmaster was impressed with Welly's ankle and the story of the others staying with him against possible perils of the night. (The actual fell-dogs and mutants were judiciously not mentioned.) As a result, the punishment for missing curfew was moderate: they were restricted to the school grounds for the next three weekends and confined to their rooms every evening after dinner.

This penalty, however, proved taxing, since the brief summer was fully upon them. For those three weeks, temperatures were above freezing every day. To miss any of such a golden time seemed terribly hard.

Heather, while refusing to lose the out-of-doors altogether, also sought to avoid those parts of the school grounds where other students might be playing or talking, activities from which she'd be pointedly excluded. Those Sundays she spent in the old orchard, a forgotten spot where the ancient school wall had been joined to the newer town defenses. Most of the fruit trees that had once thrived there had long since died, but a few hardy descendants still remained. During their brief period in leaf, they were the center of much pride and some tourism.

Generally, however, the orchard remained untenanted, and Heather found it a welcome refuge. She played her own games, told stories to occasionally attentive squirrels, or sat in a corner of the wall reading.

Welly preferred to turn a contemptuous back on the weather and passed his confinement in the musty shadows of the library. Earl, too, spent much of his time there. The two boys had seldom spoken before, but now they explored together some of the treasures to be found among the jumbled shelves. The Llandoylan library had, in the centuries following the Devastation, become the repository for most of the surviving books in southern Wales.

Welly soon realized that Earl's interests were wider ranging than his own. In the older boy's seven years at the school, he'd been a voracious reader, gathering knowledge on a variety of subjects. Learning of Welly's interest in military tactics, Earl led him to new sources and helped explain periods of history that had always seemed fuzzy to him. Although neither boy developed friendships easily, there grew between them a tentative openness.

One Sunday afternoon, the two were seated alone at an age-scarred table. Bookshelves towered on every side. The only light came from two high glass windows whose filming of ancient grime gave everything a hazy cast. Dust motes danced in the slanting shafts.

After a time, Earl pushed aside his book on Italian city-states and leaned back in his chair, thin hands clasped behind his head. "Welly, I'm curious. What is it about military tactics that interests you? You don't seem the sort who likes to go out and bash people."

Welly frowned, trying to sort out his thoughts. "No, you're right; I'm probably not. If I'd gone to the Academy,

I'd probably have been a flop. I don't have that leadership stuff." His voice lowered. "I'm not even sure I have the courage."

He blushed at the depth of his confession, then looked up defiantly. "But tactics are interesting on their own, you know. It's exciting to see how things work together, how you can plan many steps ahead and then see it all come out."

"Yes." Earl nodded. "I think I understand. Like chess."

Welly wanted to turn the subject from himself. His old crushed hopes were still too tender. "How about you? You seem to specialize in everything."

Earl chuckled. "I read everything, about anything, and then read something else."

"Why?"

He frowned. "I don't know. It's like always being hungry. I just feel I have to learn things. Maybe there'll come a day when it all falls together and makes sense. I've been like that as long as I can remember. Ever since they brought me here, when I didn't know anything—not the language, not even who I was." He sat forward, his voice tight as he turned to his work again. "But I guess there're just some things one can't learn."

Welly took up his book as well, but his thoughts stayed on his companion. They'd all heard stories about Earl's mysterious background—or lack of it. How seven years ago, raiders from Gwent had attempted to attack Cardiff by hauling in a wagonload of ancient explosives. The wagon toppled off a mountain road and smashed into the village of Bedwas, exploding and killing half the population.

The next day, rescuers had found a boy about seven years old wandering in the ruins, babbling strange words.

They sent him to Llandoylan, where the masters knew exotic languages. But all they could learn was what seemed to be his name—Earl. When he learned English, as he did quickly, it became apparent that in the tragedy, the boy had lost all memory of his life before. So they gave him the last name of Bedwas, after his shattered village, and kept him at the school because, though destitute, he proved an apt and eager pupil.

All this was common knowledge at the school. And Welly realized that though the intense, pale boy would have been considered odd in any case, his strange background set him further apart, as did the fact that this didn't seem to bother him in the least.

Eventually the three weeks came to an end. When the three children had been forbidden to leave their rooms in the evenings, the monitors had taken special pleasure in running room checks. But now that the ban was lifted, Heather wasted no time in arranging another nocturnal visit to Welly's room.

This time when she crawled through the window, she had a battered old metal box under one arm. Into the top were punched several small holes.

"I've devoted the evenings of these weeks to an intensive training program," she announced proudly as she set the box on the table. "I brought Little John because he's a lot better at learning things than Marian or Robin, and Tuck is just hopeless."

First she took some bread crumbs out of a pocket and sprinkled them on the table beside the box. Then she lifted the lid and tilted the box on its side. A huge purplish cockroach darted out, stood still a moment waving its feelers, then settled into eating bread crumbs.

"Well, what do you think of him?" she asked. "I don't think you've met Little John before."

"He sure is big," Welly said, marveling at the four-inch length.

"And he's smart, too. Look at this." She fished around in her pocket and produced a small clay ball. Placing this on the table by the roach's head, she tapped him gently on the back. At first he ignored her and continued munching crumbs. Then, with an annoyed twitch of his feelers, he turned to the ball and began pushing it with his head and front legs. When he reached the edge of the table, Heather rewarded him with a fried potato slice.

"Hey, that's pretty good. Can he do anything else?"

"He can climb through hoops, but you have to put some food on the other side. And he can pull a wagon. I made a little one out of clay with a grass harness and tried to get him to pull Marian in it, but she kept scuttling off."

"Do you think he'd push the ball for me?"

"Probably. Take his chip away first."

Welly snatched away the half-eaten potato, leaving the bug furiously waggling its antennae.

"Now put the ball down by his head. Give him a little tap . . . another. Right, there he goes." At the edge of the table, Welly returned the roach's prize.

Heather sat on the chair and watched her charge proudly. "I wish I could have found Marian tonight. She's a lot prettier, really. More blue than purple and sort of . . . What's that?"

A distant sound cut the air, a thin, high wailing. Welly shivered. "Don't know. That's the sound I told you about. It comes every so often at night. I don't like it."

The sound stopped. Heather waited breathlessly and

scowled at Welly when he shuffled his feet. Then they heard it again, slightly deeper but still very faint.

"Do you suppose it's ghosts?" she asked. "Ghosts of the dead monks who built this place? Or maybe banshees, wailing on the roofs of folks who'll die?"

"Hush up! I'd rather suppose it's the wind or even some wild animal beyond the wall."

"Haven't you ever tried to track it down?"

"No!"

"Let's!"

"Let's not! Suppose it *is* ghosts?"

But Heather had already sprung from the chair and was easing open the door. Silently she slipped out. Welly followed reluctantly and stuck his head into the hall. "There, it's stopped," he said quickly. "Come on back."

"No, there it is again, louder."

Welly had to admit it wasn't as muffled, but that made it worse.

"It's coming from that way," Heather said, pointing left. "Bring the candle."

Welly groaned but went back to the room. He grabbed the candle; then, seeing the potato-eating roach, he steeled his nerves, scooped it up, and hastily replaced it in the metal box. Candle in hand, he returned to the hall. Such an insane expedition was not quite as repellent with company—and light.

Silent as spirits, they slipped along the hall, Heather in the lead. The flickering candle in Welly's hand cast grotesque shadows over the walls. Soon they passed into the older, more dilapidated part of the building. The air was musty, and the empty rooms were festooned with dust. The monk's ghost theory seemed more plausible.

Welly was about to suggest they turn back when they heard the sound again. Closer now, it drifted down a stairwell from the floor above.

An exultant gleam in her eye, Heather hurried to the foot of the spiral stairs and began climbing. The return of Sherlock Holmes, Welly thought bitterly; but reluctantly he followed.

The corridor above seemed even more desolate. The stale air was cold, as though these higher walls were thinner. Taking the candle from Welly, Heather crouched down and examined the floor and its strewing of dust.

"It's more disturbed over here," she whispered, pointing the candle to the left. "Let's go this way."

"Do ghosts kick paths in dust?"

"Shh! Maybe banshees do."

They had taken only a few steps when the sound came again. Much louder now, it floated from around the corner. The inhuman cry bristled Welly's hair. He knew he couldn't possibly turn that corner.

But as the wailing trailed off, it was followed by soft choking sobs. If it was a ghost, thought Welly, it was pretty sorry about something.

They stepped around the corner and saw a closed door. It was clean and straight on its hinges, unlike most of the rest. The sobbing came from the other side.

Welly and Heather looked at each other, then tiptoed to the door. Handing Welly the candle, Heather turned the knob. The door was unlocked. She pushed, and with a faint creaking it swung open.

Something was in the room, something breathing in soft gasps. Welly slipped in, raising the candle high. Its dancing light showed a small room, bare except for a chair and a narrow bed. A dark shape on the bed tossed and moaned.

They stepped forward, and the light fell on a human face, eyes closed, features twisted as though in pain.

"It's Earl!" Heather gasped.

"I didn't know he lived up here!" Welly said. "I guess that school wards get the worst rooms."

Suddenly, eyes still closed, the boy on the bed jerked and began the strange wailing, made more chilling by seeing it rise from a human throat.

"We've got to wake him!" Heather said. "He's having some horrible dream."

She ran to the bedside, grabbed the boy's thin shoulders, and began shaking. With a start, Earl opened his eyes and sat up so suddenly it nearly toppled Heather over. He looked around wildly, snapping out strange words.

"Hold it, Earl!" Welly said. "Calm down. It's us, Welly and Heather. Wake up!"

Slowly the wild look faded from his face. Earl blinked and shook his head. "One of the dreams," he said shakily. "Sorry . . . sorry I disturbed you." He shuddered, then began shaking uncontrollably.

Heather grabbed a blanket that had slumped to the floor and wrapped it around his shoulders. "It's awfully cold up here."

"Yes, but I'm always like this after that dream." His teeth were chattering now. "Sorry. Can't stop it."

"Look," Welly said, "let's get you out of here for a minute. Down to my room. At least until you warm up."

Earl looked up at him searchingly, then nodded his head. "Yes. For a minute. The dreams, they leave a . . . a feeling in the place."

Shakily Earl got out of bed, his bare feet white on the gray stone floor. He stepped quickly into his boots and, grabbing his jacket off the chair back, pulled it over his thin nightshirt. The three left the room and silently made their way downstairs to Welly's, checking at corners for monitors.

As they moved along, Welly wondered over this turn of events. He'd come to think of the older boy as strong and totally in control. Now they found him exiled in a cold, shabby cell and bothered with nightmares like a small child. Welly liked him no less for it, but he hoped Earl wouldn't be uncomfortable at their discovery.

Once safe in the room, they bundled Earl into Welly's bed and piled blankets around him. Gradually the shivering subsided, and his pale face looked less pinched and taut.

"Do you have dreams like this often?" Welly asked hesitantly.

Earl nodded. "Every few weeks. Too often, much too often."

"Tell us about them if you like," Heather offered. "If I talk about nightmares, they start seeming silly and a lot less real."

"These are always just as real." He sat up, but for a minute said nothing more. Then he began talking in a low, pained voice. "It's faces, mostly. Faces and feelings. Horrible feelings. Great forces going through me and around me, and I can't stop them or control them. I should, but I don't know how.

"The faces are the worst, though. Some are beautiful, and some are not; some are very, very evil. And I know every one of them." He looked up despairingly. "But I can't . . . I can't quite remember. They have names, and I can't name them. If only I could, maybe they'd all go where they belong . . . and I would, too. Maybe. But I never quite reach them. I can't remember!"

He shuddered, dropping his face to his hands, struggling to control himself.

Heather turned firmly practical. "These faces, do you think they're people you really knew? Before you lost your memory and came here? Your parents, maybe?"

"Maybe. I don't know. But they are real people, and I knew them. I'm sure of that. Sometimes I see things happening, things that almost make sense, but not quite. And I never have the words to describe them afterward, even to myself."

He looked up at the two of them. "But I shouldn't trouble you with all this."

"And why not?" Heather said stubbornly. "We're friends, aren't we?"

Slowly Earl smiled, his gaunt face softening. "Yes, you are."

"Well, then, maybe we can help you figure things out."

"No. Nobody can help. The dreams are with me all the time, shoved in the background, maybe, but the oddest things will bring them out: a word in a lecture or a strain of music, a certain view or the way someone laughs. There're answers somewhere; there must be. If I keep looking, maybe I'll find them. But if I don't even know what I'm looking for, I can't ask you to help." He smiled and added, "Any more than you have already."

"Well, one thing we can do," Heather said resolutely, "is provide some light evening's entertainment." She motioned him to the table and opened the roach's traveling case. Soon they were all gathered around, Earl wrapped in a blanket, watching the antics of Little John. They sent the roach through the ball trick several times. Then Heather produced a hoop of braided grass and coaxed him through it.

"Not very impressive, I admit," she said sadly. "Remember that band of traveling entertainers last year? They had real domestic dogs and trained them to do all sorts of things like jumping through hoops. But roaches just don't jump very well."

Earl fumbled in his jacket pocket and pulled out a thin wooden flute. "Let's see how he likes this. I made it several years ago when I had mice in my room. They used to come out and listen."

He settled into the chair and draped the blanket over his bony knees. Then, raising the slender wooden pipe to his lips, he began playing, head tilted to one side.

The music was thin and reedy, rising and gliding through haunting little melodies. It bubbled through the children's blood and made them want to dance. The effect on the roach was striking. At first he sat, twiddling his feelers, then slowly he began swaying back and forth, candlelight gleaming off the shining purple carapace.

"He's dancing!" Heather exclaimed. "He really likes it."

As Earl continued to play, Welly pulled open the table drawer and sorted through the clutter: bits of string and leather, interesting stones, shards of broken pottery. Pulling out a small scrap of paper, he rolled it into a cone, crimping the edges to hold the shape.

Carefully he balanced the conical hat on the roach's flat head. Heather laughed delightedly as the insect continued its swaying dance, hat slightly askew. After a minute, the hat toppled off and fell onto the tabletop. The roach stopped his dance, wiggled his feelers, and with his front feet pulled the paper hat toward him and began to munch it.

Earl stopped playing as they all laughed. "So much for art!" he said.

Suddenly they froze. There was a voice outside in the hall. A monitor!

In a flash, Heather scuttled out the window; Welly blew out the candle and dove into bed. Earl, too tall to hide under anything, jumped into the dark corner behind where the door would open.

There was a solid rap on the door. "What's all the noise in there?" When nobody answered, the door opened. An older boy stood in the doorway, a candle lantern swinging in his hand. By its swaying light, Welly sat up with an imitation of drowsy, newly awakened innocence.

"Whaaa . . . ?"

"I heard voices in here. It sounded like laughter—a girl's laughter, maybe."

"No, sir. It wasn't a girl. It was me, I guess."

"You? Do you often laugh in your sleep?"

"Oh, yes, sir. I mean, not laughing, sort of crying, whining like. It's the dreams, you see. I have these terrible dreams sometimes. With all these faces and people doing things. They really scare me. And I'm told I cry in my sleep."

The boy grunted and stepped into the room. Crouching down with his lantern, he looked under the table and bed. He glanced behind the door where Welly hung his coat on a peg.

The monitor stepped back into the hall. "If you have to be a crybaby, kid, do it more quietly!" He pulled the door closed, leaving silence heavy in the room as his leather boots scuffed down the hall.

When the sound died away, Welly slipped from his bed and, after several attempts, lit the candle. Earl was still standing behind the door, only partially concealed in the folds of the hanging coat.

"Why didn't he see you?" Welly whispered. "He looked right at you."

"I'm thin. And if people expect to see something like a hanging coat, that's generally what they see."

"I wish I was thin," Welly said morosely. "People can expect to see anything they want, but if I'm there, they see a fat boy with thick glasses."

There was an insistent rapping at the window parchment, and its edge lifted slightly. Heather's voice blew in with a gust of cold. "If the enemy has departed, I'll take my roach and run. It's cold out here."

Welly looked quickly at the table and found that the roach had dragged the paper hat into his open tin box and was contentedly chewing. Snapping down the lid, Welly passed the box out the window.

"Thanks for the entertaining evening," Heather said as she tucked the box under her arm and vanished into the darkness.

Welly fastened the window again and turned to Earl. The older boy had opened the door a crack and was cautiously peering down the corridor.

Closing the door again, he said, "I'll head back now. The monitor shouldn't come this way for the rest of the night." He paused, then smiled awkwardly. "I'm sorry I wasn't honest with you the other day. But I just . . ."

"No. It's all right. We understand. I just hope you don't mind my using that . . ."

"No, that was good thinking. Got us out of a bad spot." He put his hand on the doorknob, then turned back to

Welly. "I want to thank you both for trying to help. It's good not having to handle everything alone."

When Earl had gone, Welly blew out the candle and crawled into bed. He drifted into drowsiness, hoping he wouldn't have any dreams, not like Earl's, anyway. Good he'd heard about them, though. It had helped with the monitor. He wasn't much at storytelling, not like Heather.

August that year fulfilled the promise of the early thaw. It snowed only occasionally at night, and the light powdering vanished during the long summer days. The orchard's few gnarled trees were in leaf, and an occasional bird was heard cooing and calling among the eaves. The sun stayed up late, and after classes, all the students were drawn outdoors.

One evening, some of the students put together a loose ball game. Two teams were formed, and a straw-stuffed leather ball was tossed back and forth, players trying to get it over opposite goals.

Welly leaned against a wall and watched. He wanted to play. He wanted to jump and spin and catch the ball in midair. He wanted to cleverly dodge and duck around astonished opponents. But he knew better than to try.

The others jeered at him for never playing, but he knew it would be worse if he did. They'd throw a ball at him, and instead of catching it, he'd duck. He always had and always would. He was terrified that a ball would hit him in the face and break his glasses. Then he'd be blind as a bat.

Blind as a bat. He wondered exactly what a bat was. Surely they must be extinct. But when they'd lived, had they minded being blind? Still, he believed they'd had wings, and that could make up for a lot.

He thought about wings and flying and catching a ball in midair when his reverie was broken. A scream rose from behind the orchard wall. He recognized Heather's voice. Pushing off from his wall, he ran toward the orchard gate.

Inside, Welly skidded to a halt and stared at the scene before him. Heather crouched at the base of a tree with Nigel standing over her. She held the body of a squirrel. It hung limply against her chest as she rocked back and forth shouting at the boy, "Killer! Bloody murderer! You think you're so great, you can kill for fun. You're just a bloody tyrant!"

Nigel laughed, swinging his slingshot casually in his right hand. "Squirrels are vermin and ought to be killed. I'll do it if I feel like it. Same goes for human vermin when I'm Duke. Remember that, Horseface!"

Welly had been standing rigid, fists clenched, eyes hazing with anger. Now a cord snapped, and he leaped at Nigel, flailing the older boy with fists, feet, and knees.

Nigel recoiled, throwing an arm over his face. Then he kicked his assailant hard in the side. Welly staggered back and was socked in the jaw. He sprawled backward in the dust.

With cries of "Fight, fight!" a crowd gathered around them. But Welly saw only his sneering enemy. He launched himself from the ground, driving his head into Nigel's stomach. They fell in a tangle of arms and legs; then Nigel was up, his fingers twisted in Welly's hair, raining blows on his chest and face.

He did not pause until a hand gripped his shoulder from behind, and Earl's voice came cold and hard. "So, that's your idea of being a duke—killing or beating anyone weaker?"

Welly was dropped like an old sack, and he scrabbled

over the ground for his glasses. Nigel straightened, turning slowly to face Earl.

"No, I'll kill or beat *anyone* who gets in my way. Including you, misfit!"

Nigel's friend Justin signaled frantically to him but was ignored. So he slipped up behind Nigel and whispered, "Not him, Nigel. A year ago, he—"

Nigel silenced his lieutenant with a cuff. "If this scrawny babysitter thinks he can tell me how to be a duke, he needs a little lesson!"

Huddled together on the ground, Welly and Heather looked on in horror at what they'd brought on their friend. Earl was slightly taller, but there the advantage ended. He was thin and lanky to the point of frailty, a skeleton loosely tied together with skin. Nigel was compact and powerful. His arms, shoulders, and neck were as solid as stone.

The two crouched and circled each other. The excited crowd of students shrank back to give them room. Nigel made several feints forward, but Earl didn't flinch. Then Nigel lunged to close with him, but Earl was no longer there. He'd slipped aside and now snaked out his foot, sending his opponent sprawling. Nigel bounded back up and swung a fist at Earl's jaw. Again he missed his target. His eyes narrowed to see Earl standing back, head tilted, a taunting smile on his face.

Furious, Nigel sprang, wrapping his powerful arms around the other's thin chest. Earl staggered. Then he brought up his arms sharply and broke the hold, side-stepping the hook that followed. Again Nigel jumped for him. Earl spun around behind him, grabbing his arm. In one smooth movement, he lifted Nigel off the ground and hurled him through the air. He came to earth with a jarring thump. Groggily Nigel struggled to sit up, then slumped back to the ground.

The fight was clearly over. The crowd dispersed, chattering among themselves. "He should have listened," one girl said to a friend. "That's what Justin was trying to tell him. A year ago, before Nigel came, that Earl did the same thing to the strongest boy in the school. Even the tough ones leave him alone now, weird as he is."

Nigel's friends had gone to his assistance, and Earl, breathing raggedly, knelt down by Welly, who was dabbing at his cut face with a sleeve.

"Let's get out of sight," Earl advised. "He won't want a return match for a while, but the less we rub it in, the better."

Heather nodded, looking sadly down at the dead squirrel. "Let's take Sigmund away and bury him. Nigel wanted the pelt. But he shan't have it!"

She gathered up the lifeless body, and the three children headed quickly toward the far end of the orchard, out of sight of the others.

As they walked along, Welly said, "That was incredible fighting; where did you learn it?" As soon as he said them, he regretted the words, but Earl didn't seem to mind.

"I don't know. I've fought like that for as long as I can remember. Most of it's being quick and light. The ones who most pride themselves on their fighting are usually as agile as oxen."

Heather stopped by a stump near the orchard's far wall. "Let's bury him here. Kids never come this far. But Sigmund's family does."

She placed the squirrel on the stump, and Welly found a sharp-edged rock and started digging. The ground was hard, and after a while he stopped. One eye was beginning to swell, and he was having trouble seeing, though his glasses, at least, had been found intact. Earl took over digging.

Heather left them briefly to gather a bouquet of leaves. She would have preferred flowers, like they used in the stories, but there were few flowering plants, even in summer. When the hole was deep enough, she lowered the squirrel into it. Tears streamed silently down her cheeks as Earl filled in the dirt and as she strewed leaves over the little mound.

Smearing tears away with dirty hands, she said, "I know it's silly to make such a fuss over a dead squirrel. But they . . . they made a place for me in their lives. Oh, I know it's not the same as really being needed, but it was somewhere I fit in."

"You fit in with us," Earl said, putting a hand awkwardly on her slumped shoulder. "Come on, let's rest against the wall. There's a bit of sun."

They sat at the base of the old stone wall, its rough surface faintly warm. Peace seemed to seep from the patient stones and the cool evening air.

"You know," Welly said after a while, "that's the second time you've gotten us out of a bad spot, Earl. We're really in your debt."

"Nonsense."

"Oh, but we are," Heather insisted. "If it wasn't for you, we'd either have been eaten by fell-dogs or pounded into footstools for Nigel Williams. We ought to swear you eternal fealty or something. Be your bound knights, as in days of old!"

A look of conviction on his battered face, Welly stood up. "And so we shall! We'll kneel at your feet and offer you our swords!"

"Except we haven't got any swords," Heather pointed out.

"Well, we'll find some!" Welly insisted. Heather jumped up to join him, her grief submerged in new purpose.

The two scurried off to find something suitable, while Earl watched. He supposed this was silly, but it was something they needed, all of them. And it had a rightness that seemed, somehow, to stretch beyond the moment.

The others returned with two short sticks and dropped to their knees in front of the older boy, presenting the sticks to him. Lowering his voice, Welly intoned, "We hereby offer you, Earl Bedwas, our swords and our eternal fealty."

Earl closed his eyes. A feeling of odd recollection swept over him and was gone. He tried to think what he should do next. Then, taking their swords, he tapped the points on each of their shoulders and, with a flourish, handed their weapons back to them. "Rise, Sir Wellington, Lady Heather!"

Heather jumped to her feet, braids bouncing and cheeks glowing with excitement. She leaped to the top of the stump, raising her stick into the air. "From now on, we'll follow wherever you lead and loyally do your bidding. The doers of evil shall be vanquished. Your quests are our quests; your enemies are our enemies!"

Earl looked ruefully toward the orchard gate where Nigel and his friends had disappeared. "That last, anyway, seems likely to be true."

4

SHADOWS
IN THE STORM

The time of cold weather had come again. The leaves on the orchard's few trees turned brown and fell to the ground. And the ground itself was often covered in snow. White feathers and ferns of ice grew on glass-paned windows, while wind from the north carried the raw bite of Scottish glaciers.

The friendship among Welly, Heather, and Earl grew slowly and gently. Despite his accepting their friendship, the other two knew Earl was still a loner. They respected his need to be alone. But when he occasionally sought out their company or offered to help them with schoolwork, they were pleased.

They worried about him, too. Now that they knew him, they noticed there were times when he was clearly troubled. Some mornings he came to breakfast his pale face more ashen than before and dark shadows rimming his eyes. They guessed he had dreamed again.

But Welly heard no more cries in the night. He suspected Earl, trying not to disturb them, had muffled the door with one of his too-few blankets. But he was a very private person, and his friends would not mention it first.

During the icy weather, Heather made few nighttime

excursions to Welly's room. But one night in November, she ventured again over the roofs. She was bursting with ideas, and Cook had given her a rare honeycake, which, after due consideration, she'd decided to share with Welly.

The two sat on chair and table in the candlelit room, savoring every sweet crumb. When at last there was no more to lick off finger or lip, Heather sighed and tucked her legs under her.

"You know, there really ought to be some way we can help Earl."

"What do you mean?"

"Well, here we are, his sworn retainers. He's obviously troubled, and we aren't doing a thing about it."

"But what can we do? The troubles are inside him. They have been for years. If it helps him to talk about it, he knows we'll listen. But if he doesn't want to, we can't make him."

Heather tugged absently on a braid. "No, but the root of the thing is that he doesn't know who he is. If we could help him learn that, we'd be doing a lot."

"But how can we find that out when he hasn't a clue himself?"

"Oh, but there are clues. They just need tracking down. Take that language he was speaking when they found him. There's a fine clue."

"Sure, but the masters didn't know it, and he stopped speaking it after he learned English. Now he says he doesn't remember it at all."

"I'll bet that's what he was speaking when we woke him during the dream."

"A lot of good that does if he can't speak it when he's awake."

"Well," she persisted, "the very fact that he was speaking

a weird language when they found him suggests that he or his family didn't originally come from that village, doesn't it? And if it was strange to the masters here, it's probably not a Yorkshire dialect or anything like that but something really foreign."

"Such as?"

"Well, I don't know. Most foreign places aren't supposed to exist anymore. But there is Scandinavia. Maybe he comes from there."

She chewed thoughtfully on a braid, suddenly almost chomping it off. "Suppose . . . suppose Earl isn't his name at all! Suppose it's a title! Maybe he's the earl of someplace, someplace in Scandinavia. And somehow he got lost over here and was hit on the head during the explosions."

"Well, I suppose it could be, but how would we prove it?"

"Maybe just suggesting it would bring it all back."

Welly only grunted.

"Or maybe it isn't Scandinavian," she ventured, "but Russian."

"Russian? All the Russians died during the Devastation."

"Surely they *all* didn't. I'll bet there were some Russian diplomats over here . . . or spies. And when war broke out, they went into hiding. They were afraid to tell anyone they were Russians. And their descendants didn't tell either, but secretly they kept up the old ways and spoke Russian at home. And then came the explosion at Bedwas, and Earl was the only one left."

"I like the Scandinavian earl better."

"So do I. But being the secret descendant of Russian spies would be exciting."

She resumed chewing her braid, finally sighing and

untucking her feet. "But you're right. There's not much we can do unless he wants us to. He's too good a friend to intrude on."

Earl himself was indeed troubled. Increasingly so. The dreams were coming with greater frequency and strength. Sometimes he was so gripped in horror, he was unable to make a sound. When he finally awoke, he was exhausted and afraid to sleep for the rest of the night.

Increasingly, too, strange feelings held him during the day. His schoolwork suffered, and often his mind drifted off during class. His teachers noticed but had said nothing. For that he was grateful. He was afraid they'd decide he was going crazy. In fact, he almost wished he was. It seemed the less complicated solution. But less complicated than what, he wasn't sure.

By the end of November, the tension was becoming unbearable. Whenever possible, he avoided people, including his two new friends. But when he was alone, he was intensely restless.

One Sunday morning, he awoke with a feeling of enormous pressure, pressure from inside. He felt he'd explode if he didn't do something. There was an acrid taste in his mind, a remnant of the night's dream. Bitter, distorted feelings lingered like smoke in the corners of the room. He had to get away.

Hurriedly he dressed in outdoor wear. Slipping downstairs, he left the school grounds as soon as the gates were opened, not bothering with breakfast. Aimlessly he wandered about the winding streets, hoping to find some relief. Early worship services were beginning, and from various buildings came chants, singing, or ritual music. Standing irresolutely before the Armageddonite temple, Earl glanced up to the town wall, and his eyes fell on the dark smear of the hills beyond. Something inside him settled. He headed down the street toward the north gate.

Once outside the walls, he felt better, no less tense but purposeful. He began walking northeast into the hills.

The snow on the ground was deep, and moving was more like wading than walking. As the morning progressed, the sky thickened. Slowly great white flakes sifted from it. Feathery soft, they fell silently around him. Looking up, he watched them spiraling down from the sky until he grew dizzy. Then he trudged on.

He had no idea where he was going, but he had to go. Stopping for a moment, he experimented. Turning to the west, he deliberately set off in a new direction. Within a few steps, the tension and unease returned. They grew until he could barely force himself on. When he turned back and headed northeast again, the anxiety ebbed away. He shrugged and moved northeast. There seemed little to lose.

He walked for hours. All the while, the snow came more and more thickly. At first it fell in windless silence. But eventually a wind rose, blowing the snow in long streamers past his face. That wind howled with a voice of its own, and it almost seemed he could understand it.

Suddenly a new feeling came over him. He slowed. Nothing looked different. In the blowing whiteness, the sky blended with the earth. Yet there seemed to be a darkness just beyond the white. A waiting darkness, and it was evil.

Very slowly he advanced. The wind howled more fiercely, but he sensed a new sound just beyond hearing. Farther on, he heard it, separate now from the wind. Strange, unearthly sounds, voices and yet not voices.

A speck of light appeared in that darkness, the darkness he felt and couldn't see. And the light was real. Impossibly, a fire burned in the snow ahead. And the voices, for voices they now seemed, came from around it.

He halted. There were shapes moving about the fire, dark and wildly leaping shapes. He crept closer. The fire rose, a tall unquenchable pillar, and around it figures jerked and danced. Some were human; others something else. The voices sang and chanted in a strange language or in no human language at all. Yet the words played on the edge of his mind, almost tumbling into meaning.

Closer now, he picked out one figure among the others: a woman, tall and slender, pale as snow. Her black hair and robes billowed wildly about her. Arms upstretched, she uttered a howling chant. Then she looked down into the fire, and he saw her face.

He screamed! He knew that face! Instantly she looked up. Her green eyes stared directly at him, piercing the glare of the fire between them. Jabbing a long white hand into the storm, she shouted a word full of terrible power. The word went on and on, an endless stream of hate.

Around him the world seemed to shatter, and the bonds that had drawn him cracked. Turning, he ran.

The sound followed him, stabbing at his mind. He must get away from it and from that face! They must not get him!

The horrible sound faded at last, but he knew they were following. He floundered on, every step weighed into painful slowness. Snow clung to his body and blinded his eyes. Was it an enemy, too?

No, it was indifferent, didn't care. But he could use it. He could hide in the storm. They might not see; they might not find him.

He willed himself unseen. To be one with the snow,

part of the storm. Snow swirled into his mind, filled his body with cold. He became the cold, the sharp biting wind. He had no breath but the wind, gusting in and out. He had no head, no legs. Only thin white windblown snow. There was no up, no down, only directionless swirling. Swirling around and forward, always forward.

On and on he went, while a small corner of his mind screamed in fear. He was the snow. Or he was mad. But surely he was dying. No breath, only the wind. He was dying in the storm, as the storm.

He must gain control, fix on something solid, something real. Vaguely his mind saw the stone archway of the school gate. He concentrated on it with all his power. Stone by stone, he built the picture. Every irregular, hard gray shape. He could feel their roughness, the soft crumbling mortar between them. They were hard and real and fixed to earth.

In the morning, they found him sprawled in a drift, outside the school gate. His fingers were thrust into a crack between the stones.

5

THINGS OF NIGHTMARE

For two days, Earl hovered between life and death. They wrapped him in blankets and laid him in a bed by the fire in Master Greenhow's study. A doctor was summoned, but he could say only that the boy was suffering from extreme exposure. Keep him warm, he advised, but only time would tell if he lived or died.

Gradually, however, his breathing became stronger, and faint color returned to his cheeks. The thin hands lying pale against the blankets were no longer clammy and cold.

He regained consciousness but, despite questioning, had little to say. It seemed he had gone out into the hills, as he often did, and had become lost in the blizzard. It was a miracle he'd found his way back at all.

But the recovery was not even. He soon fell into a fever and for several days floated in and out of delirium. Whenever they could, Heather and Welly visited him; but he was always either sleeping fitfully or wracked with fever, tossing about and babbling strange words.

On the fifth day, the fever broke. When his friends came, they found him propped up in bed, gazing into the low bank of flames that flickered in the stone fireplace. He turned his head when he heard them and smiled wanly. "They say you've come every day."

"We have," Heather said as they hurried to him. "And it's about time we found you looking better. You've had us worried, you know."

Welly pulled up a chair for himself, and Heather sat down on the foot of the bed. For a while they said nothing. The firelight played warmly over their faces and on the backs of books on the headmaster's shelves.

Twisting her braid, Heather said, "Earl, the masters are using you as an object lesson against doing stupid things. But you have too good a head on your shoulders to just go out and get lost in a storm. What really happened?"

Earl coughed and nodded weakly. "I *wish* that had been what happened." He looked at the two of them a moment, then back to the fire. "I can tell you, though, as much as I understand.

"I went out because something compelled me. I don't know if it was from inside or outside. But something was going to happen, something that touched on me, on what I am. And I had to be there."

"Did you find it?" Welly asked.

Again Earl nodded. "It was something very bad. Evil. There were things there I almost knew, almost understood. But I've lost the key."

"What was there?" persisted Heather.

"I wouldn't soil words with it, even if I could. But there was someone I knew, a face. The name was just out of reach, but the face I knew."

Heather leaned forward. "A face from the dreams?"

"One of them. A woman, beautiful, and very, very evil.

Once I knew that, I ran. They followed. They were after me, but . . ." A look of pained remembrance clouded his face. "But I escaped."

"Well, that's good, then. You got away," Welly said cheerfully.

Earl's reply was very quiet. "It would be better if I knew *how* I got away."

Heather patted his hand. "That's no matter. You're a skilled outdoorsman, and you made it back. That's all that counts. The doctor says that if you rest and drink that nasty broth Cook makes, you'll be up in a week or two."

"He also said," added Welly, imitating the nasal falsetto of the town's doctor, " 'No more traipsing about in storms for that young man. I certainly hope he's learned his lesson.' "

Earl laughed ruefully. "I didn't learn what I needed. But I'll do my best about the storms."

As weeks passed, Earl recovered steadily. His mind, too, was more at ease. He would gladly have dismissed the whole thing as a particularly dreadful dream if the images hadn't stayed so vivid. He was oppressed, too, with a curious sense of waiting, of suspension between two acts of a drama.

Meanwhile, the year progressed, and Yule was drawing near. This was one celebration all post-Devastation religions shared. It marked the Turn of Seasons or the Savior's Birth or Hanukkah or the Victory of Light. It was celebrated on the winter solstice, December twenty-second.

Earl was now fully recovered but stayed close to home, in the library or his room. The first day he ventured from the school grounds was the Sunday before Yule, when he decided to go into town and buy gifts for his two friends.

Every year, the headmaster gave each student a few coins as a Yule gift. Earl had saved most of his, never finding much he thought worth buying. But having two friends in his life seemed to call for something special. So this Sunday he scooped his little sack of coins into his pocket and set off into town.

He had no clear idea what he wanted, but he figured he'd know when he saw it. Shops were open and temporary stalls set up to accommodate pre-Yule shoppers. Some merchants and customers had come from miles away, and the snow in the streets was churned to dirty slush. Candles burned gaily in windows, colored awnings fluttered, and everywhere people seemed happy and busy.

Earl looked at the candlemaker's stall, the leather shop, and places where they sold woven goods of wool and flax. He wished he could buy Heather some fine fabric. She was, he believed, much less homely than she thought, and maybe a splendid new dress would help her agree. But he didn't have enough coins for anything but undyed browns.

Today the festivities were aided by a traveling fiddler. For a time, Earl stood amid the jostling crowd, eyes closed, listening as the strains soared between carefree dances and melancholy laments. A snatch of tune brushed lightly at a memory but was gone before he could catch it.

He pushed the occurrence aside and continued examining shops and stalls. The wood-carver's appealed for the tangy smell and the feel of its wares. But wood was rare and expensive, as was the glassblower's beautiful work. Both the potters and weavers of grass made things that were useful but of little beauty.

For a while, he was drawn to the hot orange glow of the blacksmith's forge, to the heavy musical clanging of the hammers and the sheer strength of the man who wielded them. Of course, Welly would love a sword, but for that he'd need a true liege lord or at least a friend who was a good deal wealthier.

Earl joined a ragged cluster of children hovering about a booth selling special Yule foods. The spicy odors were painfully enticing, but friendship, he felt, deserved something more lasting.

He was becoming discouraged when, wandering down a side street, he came upon an ancient half-timbered building housing a small antiquities shop. His spirits lifted. Surely he would find something special here.

As he opened the narrow door, setting the bells jangling, a little bald man bustled out of a back room. Wrinkled and bent over, he seemed as ancient as his wares. The man noticed Earl's student garb, which in most cases marked one as an aristocrat, and he became properly deferential.

"May I help you, young sir?"

"Perhaps, but I want to look around first."

"Certainly, certainly. I am at your service." And he began pottering around a relic-strewn table in the back.

The cluttered shop smelled of intriguing, musty age. Earl's eyes wandered over the shelves, tables, cases, and boxes that lay on all sides and overflowed with a profusion of interesting items. On one shelf stood a stack of shiny rectangular trays with raised inside divisions. They were made of the soft ancient metal aluminum. But though attractive, they didn't seem of much use.

There were shelves of antique pottery much finer than anything produced today. And there were even cups of the rare substance Styrofoam. He knew his funds weren't equal to those.

What delighted him most were the items made from

plastic. The ancient material was so smooth and light, and he wondered over the lost process for making it. Perhaps he had enough money for a small item of plastic.

Old fabrics hung in the back of the shop. Some were lovely, with an exotic feel, probably made of artificial materials like woven plastic. Even where faded, the rare colors spoke of ancient wealth and gaiety. But most were mere worn tatters, and all seemed too frail for the modern world.

In one case, in a far corner, were piled trays of jewelry. He had to shove aside decayed shoes and a stack of grooved black disks to see into it.

While ostensibly doing repairs at his back table, the old proprietor watched him keenly. Earl cleared his throat, trying to sound as though he examined expensive antiques every day. "Could I look at that tray, please?"

"Certainly, sir, right away." The man scurried over and pulled out the tray. He hovered like a spider as the boy ran thin fingers through the small glittering treasures. Earl knew that many were beyond his price, but some were not. Perhaps something here for Heather. Wearing some of these could make anyone feel beautiful.

He picked out and replaced several pieces, and then took up a small gold ring. It wasn't real gold, but some gold-looking metal. It had a broad band with spiral patterns around the outside. Set into it was a purple jewel, glass, not amethyst, but it was nicely cut and sparkled in the light. He turned it over in his hand and saw writing on the inside. Holding it up to a dust-filmed window, he made out the words "Cracker Jack."

He wondered what that meant. Some ancient charm or good-luck phrase? He didn't know, but the thing felt right. It seemed bright and cheery, like Heather herself.

"I'll take this," he said firmly. "And I'll need something else." He looked into the case again, squatting down to see the lower shelf. Many small objects were jammed together, including parts of several chess sets. "I'd like to see some of those." He pointed, and the old man bobbed his head and brought out a handful of chessmen, spilling them carefully over the case top.

Some were wood, one was made of stone, and several were metal. But the ones that caught Earl's eye were of plastic. He picked up a black bishop, admiring its cool feel, its smooth surface. Then he put it down in favor of a knight, its plastic the creamy white of fabled ivory. The figure was a horse head, but not a modern horse, heavy-browed and shaggy. This horse had a high, arched neck and delicate face. A proud mane bristled along the neck from its base to the small pointed ears. He would get this for Welly, a token of his friend's knighthood.

At last Earl left the shop, carefully clutching the gifts, which the proprietor had wrapped in a scrap of wool. He was so pleased with his purchases, he wanted to open the package and look at them again, but decided against it for fear of dropping them in the slush.

This visit had almost finished his savings. Back at the town square, he pulled the coin bag from his pocket and stuffed the small parcels inside. Then he glanced up to find Heather looking at a booth, just across the street.

Jumping guiltily, he crammed the bag deep into a coat pocket as Heather turned and waved at him. "Oh, Earl," she said, running over to him, "isn't the town exciting just before Yule? Everything's so bright and happy, and everyone's got their decorations up. You've been window-shopping, too?"

"Yes, I have." His voice sounded uncommonly high to his own ears.

"I've been at it all morning," she said dreamily. "But if we don't want to miss lunch, we'd better hurry back. Cook said there might be something special; Sunday lunch before Yule, you know."

Together they headed up the street toward the school. As they walked, Earl began to feel odd: strangely chilled and out of focus. He wondered if he was ill again. Perhaps he'd eaten something bad at breakfast?

Heather was talking, but he found it hard to concentrate on her words. Then something she said riveted his attention. "Did you see that woman watching us? She's so beautiful. I'd love to look like her."

Earl stood still, started to turn, then stopped. "Describe her to me," he whispered.

"Well, her skin's pale—like yours, really. And she's got lovely long black hair, all tumbling out of her hood."

"And green eyes," he said flatly.

"I can't tell; she's too far. But she certainly seems interested in us. Do you know her?"

"She's the woman in the storm, in the dreams. I must get away, mustn't let her know I've seen her."

They started walking up the street again, Earl trying to hide his tension. "We can lose her in these alleys," Heather suggested. "If that's what you want."

"Yes, let's try."

They reached a corner. The buildings sagged comfortably toward each other across a narrow alley. With seeming nonchalance, they turned right. As soon as they were out of sight, they broke into a run, slipping and sliding over the half-frozen slush. Abruptly they skidded into another alley and, farther on, into another.

At last the maze opened between two buildings not far from the school gate. Looking cautiously in all directions, they saw no cloaked figure and pelted across the last open space and through the gate.

Once inside the school, Heather leaned against a pillar and panted for breath. She'd found the escape great fun and was about to say so, but a glance at Earl's ashen face showed he'd considered it anything but fun.

"Thank you," he said shakily. "I'm glad you were there. Better get to lunch now."

They parted, and Heather was not greatly surprised when Earl did not come to lunch. It was a pity, she thought, because they had meat. Not little bits in stew, but great steaming slices of it on bread. She ate with Welly and in a hushed voice told him about the adventures of the morning.

For two days, nothing happened. They saw Earl only in class, and there he seemed tense and distracted. Dark circles had reappeared under his eyes.

On the afternoon of the third day, they were in culture class, the only period all three shared. The subject for the day was ancient architecture, and the master was extolling structural steel. Halfway through, the class was interrupted by the entrance of a monitor. He went to the master, muttered something, then walked down the benches directly to Earl.

"Master Greenhow wants to see you in his office. He has some strangers with him."

Color drained from Earl's face, and for a moment he looked as though he would faint. Then, woodenly, he stood up and left the room. Welly and Heather exchanged worried glances.

With leaden steps, Earl walked down the corridors.

The ancient stone walls pressed in heavily around him. He was walking into a trap; he knew it. But like a helpless animal, he couldn't understand or prevent it. At the office door, he forced a hand up and knocked.

"Come in," Master Greenhow's voice said through the heavy oak door. Mechanically Earl obeyed.

"Ah, Earl, have a seat." The master waved at a straight-backed wooden chair beside his desk. Earl sat and raised his eyes. Across the desk, seated in chairs by the records cabinet, were a woman and a man. The woman he knew and tried desperately not to show it.

"Earl, let me introduce you to two relatives of yours. Your aunt Maureen and uncle . . . Garth, was it?"

The bearded man nodded. "Uncle Garth," he repeated in a gravelly voice.

Earl turned guarded eyes on the man. He was large and powerful-looking. His skin was darker than his companion's, and under a thatch of coarse gray hair, his eyes were pale and close-set. He smiled broadly at Earl, showing yellowed teeth.

"Little Earl," the woman said musically, "can it possibly be you? I hardly recognize you; you're so . . . changed. But of course you would be, wouldn't you? The magic of time and all." She laughed gaily.

"You really are a very fortunate boy, Earl," Master Greenhow said. "Your aunt and uncle have been looking for you a long time. They tell me your parents were merchants and that you grew up in Denmark. Then, it seems you and your parents came here to Wales to tie in with the wool trade and were never heard from again."

"Yes," the woman continued, "my dear sister and her husband and child. Garth and I searched for them every time we were in this country. Then recently, by sheer chance, we heard of the accident at Bedwas and the poor little boy they found wandering about."

She sat forward, her green eyes studying Earl very closely. "Is it true, then, Earl dear, that you've completely lost your memory? You remember nothing that happened to you before you were . . . seven?"

"That's correct. I remember nothing." He clipped off his words, hating even to talk with her.

"Yes. Yes, I can see that you don't." She sat back, relaxed again. "Dear boy, how very good it is to have finally found you."

She turned to her companion. "You know, Garth, he really does look the same, now that we know who he is. The same intelligent little face, the same mannerisms, the same tilt of the head."

Instantly Earl straightened himself.

"Well, madam," Master Greenhow said, "it certainly is wonderful to find where Earl belongs and have that mystery cleared up. So that language was Danish. Well, well!" He chuckled. "I barely knew there were any Danes left to speak it."

The headmaster leaned back in his chair. "Of course, we'll miss Earl, though I understand your wanting to take him with you. He's a bright boy, and he's been a good student. He would need to be, you know, for us to have kept him at Llandoylan. We are a quality school and don't usually take charity pupils."

"Oh, but this won't be charity now," Aunt Maureen said silkily. "We're not exactly wealthy, but we've done quite well in the import business. We can leave you a little now and send you more later, to help make up for your

years of kindness to our dear boy." She smiled sweetly, and
Earl felt his insides knot.

"Well, that's very generous of you!" Greenhow bubbled. "Very generous. Now, will you be wanting to take
him with you this afternoon?"

Maureen started to reply, but Earl interrupted. "I can't
go this afternoon. I have to pack and . . . and say good-bye
to friends."

"Oh, certainly," the woman said soothingly. "We understand, dear. This all must be quite a shock to you, and with
you recently so sick. Master Greenhow tells us you were
delirious for days after being lost in a blizzard. What a
dreadful experience."

Earl lowered his eyes. "Yes, ma'am. But I'm better now.
I just remember that I was sick."

She smiled. "Poor thing. A bad sickness can be so confusing. And now on top of it we add this big change. One
moment you're a mysterious orphan and the next you
have a past—and a family. Of course we can wait, dear.
We'll stay the night in town and be back for you in the
morning."

After parting cordialities, the woman swept out of the
room, followed by Uncle Garth, who gave Earl a loving grin
that set his spine tingling. The boy looked after the two
numbly, scarcely hearing Headmaster Greenhow's words
of congratulations.

That evening, Welly and Heather were alarmed at their
friend's absence from dinner. As soon as the meal was
over, they hurried up to his room and found him stuffing
his few possessions into a backpack.

"What's all this?" Heather said breathlessly. "There's a
rumor going about that you've found some long-lost relatives. Are you really leaving?"

"Yes," he said coldly. "I'm leaving, but not with them."

Welly plumped himself down on the room's one chair. "What do you mean?"

"Those people aren't relatives, or if they are, I'd as soon they stayed lost. True, I know nothing about my past. But what they said was all wrong. And those two are the most wrong of all."

Earl tied up his pack and leaned back against the wall at the head of his bed. "The woman was very anxious to confirm that I remember nothing about my life before coming here. And I don't! But I do know that whoever she is, she is loathsome and bears absolutely no love for me."

"But still," Welly said practically, "couldn't you use them to find out something more about yourself?"

"Yes, I probably could. That woman holds some of the keys I'm looking for. But I'll find out who I am some other way, or I'll just get along without knowing."

Heather sat down on the edge of the bed, chewing her braid. "So, you're not going with them in the morning, then?"

"I'm leaving tonight as soon as the building's asleep, and going as far and as fast as I can before morning."

"But where will you go?" she asked.

He looked down at his pack forlornly. "I don't know."

Welly stood resolutely. "Well, you can't just go barging off into nowhere, and you certainly can't go alone."

"Right!" Heather agreed.

Welly continued. "The best thing would be for you to find someplace nearby to hole up until things blow over. Heather and I can slip out at night and bring you food and let you know how things stand here. Then when the coast is clear, we'll ferry you off someplace planned."

"He could go to my family's place," Heather said

gloomily, "but they'd probably turn him back . . . or sell him."

"Yes." Welly frowned. "In any case, this will give us time to organize something so he doesn't end up working in the mines or snatched by slavers."

For the first time in days, Earl smiled. "It certainly is good to have a strategist for a friend. I admit I hadn't given much thought to anything beyond getting away. But your slipping out to bring me food sounds too dangerous."

"Nonsense!" Heather said, jumping up from the bed. "We're your sworn retainers, remember? Besides, when have we ever turned our backs on adventure?"

After leaving Earl's room, Heather slipped down to the kitchen to persuade Cook to send him up a meal. It was strictly against the rules. But Cook had heard rumors of the boy's good fortune and was anxious to be part of the excitement and see the reportedly beautiful aunt when she returned next morning.

"No, it wouldn't be kind," the stout woman agreed, "to send that poor quiet boy off without so much as a scrap of bread for his last dinner with us, and him having been so sick and all. You just take this dinner up to him and bring the dishes back when there aren't too many masters watching."

Hurrying upstairs with the food, Heather felt guilty about deceiving Cook. But maybe once Earl had escaped, they could let her in on the intrigue. Maybe she'd even help smuggle out food.

Later, in their separate rooms, the three waited tensely for the agreed two hours after bed curfew. Then Heather stole silently over the roof to Welly's room, and the two met Earl in his.

The three figures, dressed in fleece-lined trousers and hooded coats, crept quietly through corridors and stairways toward the small back door. They reached it, having caught no glimpse of a monitor, and breathed a collective sigh of relief.

Confidently Welly lifted the ancient iron latch. Frost furred the inside of the door hinges, but they opened with barely a protest as the oak doors swung outward. Welly jumped onto the top step and looked directly into the swinging lantern of a monitor returning from the outhouse.

The upperclassman grinned maliciously at the three startled faces. "Well, well," Nigel sneered. "I suppose you are all geared up like that, backpack and all, just to go to the loo?"

"We might be," Heather said, chin stuck forward.

"But you're not, are you? First our precious little foundling discovers some new relatives, then he and the other rejects are slipping off somewhere in the dead of the night. I want to know why and where."

"It's quite simple, Nigel," Earl said, stepping down into the snow beside him. "I'm going away. And if I choose to leave this school tonight instead of tomorrow morning, that's my business. Either way, we're out of each other's lives."

"It's not quite that simple, is it?" Nigel put the lantern down on the steps and crossed his arms. "Everyone knows that aunt and uncle of yours promised Greenhow a bundle of money for feeding your miserable carcass all these years. So whether you want to go with them is irrelevant, isn't it, since they're not likely to give their money if he lets you skip out?"

"He's not letting me; I'm going on my own. And I'm going now. So I suggest you get on with your duties."

"A pleasure!" Nigel yelled, jumping at Earl and toppling him backward onto the stone steps. In a second, he was sitting on Earl's chest, pinning him with his muscular weight. "And one of my duties is keeping upstarts like you in their place."

Earl flailed helplessly. A foot knocked the lantern into the snow, where it hissed and guttered out. Jumping from above, Welly and Heather set on Nigel, beating with their fists. To shake them off, he partway stood. In a flash, Earl brought up his arms. He grabbed the front of Nigel's coat, catapulting him over his head, through the doorway, and onto the flagstones of the hall.

Quickly Welly spun around and shoved the door closed. No sooner had it thudded shut than they heard Nigel's furious yells for help.

"So much for escape by stealth," Earl said, starting at a run for the orchard. "You two had better stay behind now."

"Not us!" Welly said for the two of them as he and Heather raced to keep up. "We're in this together!"

6

CLASH AT SUNSET

The three fleeing figures had nearly reached the outer wall when the door behind them burst open. Lights and angry voices spilled out.

Seeing the high wall ahead, Welly squeaked, "What do we do now? This is a trap."

"No, there's a way over," Earl yelled. "I've used it before."

A dead tree, pale as a ghost, splayed against the foot of the wall. Earl leaped onto its gnarled trunk and reached a hand down for Heather. "There're footholds in the wall, chinks between the stones. Climb!"

He boosted Welly up after her, then scrambled up himself. Crouching on the top of the wall after the others had jumped down, he looked back. Several lantern-swinging figures were coming their way, though clearly they had not seen exactly where their quarry had gone.

Agile as a cat, Earl leaped into the snow beside his companions. "Let's move!" he whispered, then pushed off through the drifts with the others slogging in his wake.

When out of earshot of anyone near the wall, Heather said, "In the morning, even a blind beggar will be able to follow the trail we're leaving."

"That's why I'm heading for the road. The snow there will be too packed for us to leave tracks."

Welly, both shorter and fatter, was having trouble keeping up. "Good idea," he said, panting. "But where to then?"

"Thinking of the old mines. Lots of ruins, good places to hide."

"What about bloodhounds?" Heather asked. "They can follow people anywhere."

"Those are creatures from old books," Welly said confidently. "They don't exist anymore. Besides," he added for effect, not having the slightest idea if it was true, "dogs can't smell in the cold."

They slowed up for Welly. There was still no sign of pursuit. Soon they struck the north–south road and made better time. In the silence of the night, their boots crunched noisily over the hard-packed surface. Perpetual overcast gave a gray tint to the sky. Against it, they saw the dark ruins of an ancient building. Jagged walls jutted like an upward-thrusting hand.

"There's the main mine building," Earl said. "There are house ruins east and south of it."

"Think there'll be any muties or fell-dogs?" Welly asked anxiously.

"Doubt it," Earl replied. "It's too close to town."

"Well, let's pick a house we can find again easily," Heather said practically, "up at the top of the hill."

They trudged up the road until it crested and dropped into a darkened valley beyond. There they left it, striking off to the east along a ridge. To Heather, the mine building seemed an ominously brooding tower. Not that she needed the fantasy, she realized. This adventure was proving exciting enough.

They approached the base of the building. "Careful of the shaft," Earl warned. "The other ruins are this way."

Soon they'd crawled into a refuge. Crouching behind one wind-breaking wall, they discussed plans. Originally they'd thought that once Earl was settled, the other two would sneak back and be innocently in bed by morning. Nobody would connect them with Earl's disappearance. Then the next night they could spirit some supplies out to him.

But now, when they went back, they'd probably be confined to their rooms with extra attention from the monitors and no chance to get out for days. The only alternative seemed to be staying with Earl the following day. Then they could sneak back, raid the kitchen for supplies, and deliver them the same night. After that, they'd have to return and face the consequences; but at least Earl would be provisioned until things blew over.

The night was well on now. The excitement of their flight drained away, and exhaustion took its place. Moving into the back of the ruined house, they found a corner relatively dry and shielded from the wind. There they curled up against a wall, pulling heavy coats close around them.

Sleepily Heather recalled that in most adventure stories, fleeing heroes usually set someone to watch for enemies. But it really did seem a lot of trouble. Adventurers should be flexible, she decided as she drifted to sleep.

When they awoke, it was midmorning. Gray-white daylight seeped through the broken walls. Welly sat up, brushing his coat free of snow. The first thing he realized was that he was hungry. The second was that there was depressingly little he could do about it.

But Earl was already up, rummaging through his pack.

"I brought along most of the dinner Heather got me last night. We'll have some sort of breakfast, anyway."

Sitting in the feeble sunlight in front of their refuge, they shared bread and cold chunks of turnip. When they finished, Earl started repacking but realized he was only putting off what he had to say. He turned to the other two. "I don't know how to apologize for dragging you both into this. I should never have let myself impose on you."

"Nonsense," Heather began. "You couldn't know we'd get caught or that—"

"No. The risk was too great. I had no business involving other people in my problems—particularly friends."

Heather shook her head. "That's the sort of people you're supposed to involve in your problems."

"But now you're both in real trouble."

"That's the chance we took," Welly said. "The times you helped us, you took risks. You could've been chewed up by those dogs or beaten up by Nigel."

"Besides," Heather added, "nothing terribly bad can happen when we finally go back. Not as bad, anyway, as you think going off with that Aunt Maureen would be."

Earl shivered at what the name invoked. "I wish I knew who she really is and what she wants with me. But I don't dare find out!"

He began pacing nervously. "It's as though the answers I want are the bait to a trap. She could tell me, but if I get close enough to ask, she'll catch me."

"Are you sure she's *not* your aunt?" Heather asked after a minute. "I mean, there is a resemblance, same pale skin and dark hair."

"Oh, we're tied up somehow; I'm sure of that. But she's not my aunt Maureen. That's all wrong. And so is that

Garth fellow. Very, very wrong." Sighing, he sat down on a section of the wall, his thin shoulders slumping forward.

Heather stood up and said briskly, "Well, anyway, you're free of them both now. They probably showed up at the school bright and early, put everyone in a dither, withdrew their offer to old Greenhow, and left in a huff. As far as they know, you could be anywhere."

"Tomorrow after we're back," Welly said, "I'll get pen and paper and write a letter you can take to my family in Aberdare. They always need someone to help around the place, and it'll be a good spot to lie low until something better comes along."

Heather nodded. "Good idea, Welly. Your people seem decent enough to take him in. At least they want you back, soldier or not, after your schooling. Mine don't want me, or any friend of mine. They wouldn't care if they never saw me again."

She kicked angrily at a lump of snow. "You know, Earl, you might be lucky not knowing your family. Then you can fantasize anything you want—a home where you're needed, loving people who'd miss you."

"Maybe," Earl said. "But if I'm going to imagine relatives, I'll start with something a lot better than Aunt Maureen and Uncle Garth."

The rest of the day passed in talking, thinking, or dozing in patches of hazy sunshine. Gradually the bright smear of light that masked the sun moved toward the western horizon. Except for themselves, the silence on the hilltop was complete. Once they saw some sinuous animal dart into another part of the ruins. But otherwise they might have been the only living beings in the world.

They'd been sitting in silence for some time when

Heather suddenly jumped up. "I've forgotten about Yule. It's tomorrow. Oh, and I bought you both little bags of candied chestnuts. I wish I'd brought them along!"

"So do I," Welly agreed wistfully.

"Ah, but that reminds me," Earl said. "I did bring your gifts. I never took them out of my coat pocket." He stood up and, after fishing around, carefully pulled out two small parcels.

"I hope you don't mind having them a day early. I probably won't see you tomorrow." He handed Welly his gift. "It's nothing to eat, I'm afraid."

Slowly Welly unwrapped the scrap of cloth and rolled the smooth white chess piece onto his palm. It was beautiful, a figure in rare ancient plastic, its shape delicate yet strong. And it was a knight—as he was in fancy and had hoped to be in fact. Welly was surprised to find his eyes misting. He blinked and looked up, smiling.

"I thought it was right for you," Earl said. "But I've never given a gift to a friend before."

Heather leaned forward to look at and touch the figure, white and cool on Welly's dark palm. Then Earl handed her the other gift. With a delighted squeak, she quickly unwrapped it, then paused as she held up the ring with its faceted gem. Even in the dull light it sparkled.

"It's beautiful, Earl," she said at last. "I've never had anything like it."

Earl smiled with the success of his gifts. "You deserve beautiful things, Heather. Happy Yule."

"Oh, look. There's some writing inside."

"It says 'Cracker Jack,'" Earl said. "Though I'm not sure what that means."

"Hmm, Cracker Jack." Heather mused a moment.

"That's right! I once read an old book where all the kids were always saying it. 'This was Cracker Jack,' or 'Gosh, that's really Cracker Jack.' I think it means 'all right.' "

"Good," Earl said. "Then it is a good-luck charm. Thought it might be. So now maybe all you need do to make things all right is chant 'Cracker Jack.' "

Heather laughed. "Even in books, magic is seldom that simple. I think the real charm is that you gave it to me. Thank you, Earl." She blushed a little as she slipped the ring onto a dusky finger.

It was nearly sunset when Welly stood up, tucked the chess figure deep into a pants pocket, and said, "All right, let's launch this campaign! Now, I suggest, Heather, that you and I leave here as soon as it's dark. We go right past the mine building to the road and along it until we come to the town wall. Then we can just work our way along that until we . . . Earl, how do you know the place to get over?"

"That old tree has roots right under the wall. You'll see one sticking out of a bank. And there're footholds on that side, too."

Earl walked to the house's eastern wall and stepped around the corner. "This house is the closest to the mine building and right in line with the tower, so you shouldn't—"

He froze. Turning to them, his face was drained of color. "She's coming."

The two scrambled to join him. "No, stay back!" he hissed. "They've seen me, but they needn't know you're here."

Heather slipped inside the house and peeped cautiously over the sill of an eastern window. It was the same woman, all right. She recognized the black cape and hood. At first she thought the figure beside her was a dog, and she wondered if she hadn't been right about bloodhounds. But when she looked again, she saw it was a man.

"How did they follow you?" Welly whispered. "They're cutting across country, not even using the road."

"One more thing I don't know," Earl answered tautly. Then he stepped away from the wall. "Seems I can't run anymore. I'll have to face her. But you two stay out of sight, no matter what."

Deliberately he walked away from the house and uphill toward the shattered mine building. Moving quickly to another wall, Heather and Welly peered out a shadowed north-facing window.

Earl stood waiting. At last, two other figures moved into the framed scene. The sunset-tinged sky and blackened ruins hung as a backdrop.

"Well, young man," the woman said as they approached. "You certainly led us a merry chase. Why did you run away?"

"I decided not to go with you."

"That was a foolish decision. Your uncle Garth and I run a very profitable business. Since it's our duty as kin to take care of you, we've decided to bring you into it. Right now we're setting up a new operation in Wessex." She gave Earl a sidelong glance. "You'll like Wessex; it's run by a real king. And you do like kings."

"It depends on the king. Just as liking relatives depends on the relative. And anyway, I don't believe that you are my aunt, for all that you're as washed-out as I am."

"A perceptive boy, isn't he, Garth?" She frowned at her companion, then looked back at Earl. "All right, you deserve the truth. I am not your aunt. But we have known each other a long time. And you're a very important person, Earl. Or at least you can be, with our help. Think of it, Earl, I can help you learn all the things you've forgotten, all the things you've been trying to learn. I can help you find them and much more. You'll have power, and I can show you how to wield it!"

"No! I don't want power—not through you. If I've got things to learn, I'll learn them on my own, or I'll be content to be a shepherd."

"You, a shepherd?" The woman threw back her head and laughed, a melodious, chilling sound. Her hood fell away, tumbling black hair about her shoulders. "Foolish boy, I know you too well. You could never be content with that. You need power, and you need us!"

Earl stepped back, his voice rising in intensity. "No, I don't need you. Get out of my life!"

"But I need you!" Striking like a snake, the woman jumped forward. She clamped his wrists in strong white hands.

Alarmed, Heather and Welly watched the silent struggle. In the deepening dusk, it seemed that sparks actually burst between them, as though steel were striking steel. Garth watched from a distance, crouching, almost growling with excitement.

The two twisted backward and forward as Earl fought to break free. Suddenly he lunged backward, pulling himself away. He staggered, swayed for a second, then fell from sight over the edge of the mine shaft. A terrible, long scream dropped away. Abruptly it ended.

Garth ran up the hill, and the two looked down the dark opening.

"Well," the woman said finally, "that's one solution. And perhaps it's the best, considering everything." She straightened up and turned away from the shaft. "Still, I could have used him."

"If you could have controlled him," Garth added.

She flashed him an angry look, shaking the tousled black hair from her face. "I could have controlled him—as long as his memory was gone. But still, if he ever got that back . . . Oh, well, none of it matters now. It's over. Finally over."

"What about the body?"

"It's safe enough down there. But with him, I should perform some laying rites to be sure."

"Now?"

"No. In this case, the dark of the moon would be best."

"That's the night after tomorrow."

"Good. We can wait in town until then."

The two began walking along the ridge toward the road when the woman stopped and turned. Throwing back her head, she thrust her arms into the sky and laughed. "All this time! All this time, and at long last, I'm finally rid of him!"

Inside the ruined house, the two watchers sat frozen for long minutes after the others disappeared. Then, shaking, they stepped out of the house and walked slowly up the slope. At the top, they knelt in the churned-up snow and peered into the gaping shaft.

"Oh, gods," Heather whispered. "I can't believe it."

After a moment, Welly said dully, "We ought to bury him, you know."

"Yes, I don't know what awful things that woman was planning, but we can't let her have him. Let's go down there now."

"There're some candles in . . . in his pack." Welly couldn't bring himself to say the name. How was it possible his friend was dead?

In the deepening twilight, Welly walked down the slope to the house, returning minutes later with two candles. Lighting them with flint and steel, he gave one to Heather. Together they explored the top of the shaft.

"I think there's a way down here," Heather said after a minute. "It's sort of slumped, and there're old timbers and machinery. We should be able to scramble down."

"It sounded like he fell a long way," Welly commented. "But let's go."

With much sliding and scraping, the two worked their way down, clinging to cold lengths of rusty cables that coiled down the wall of the ancient shaft. The feeble glow of their candles did little to light the monstrous shapes and cavernous holes looming everywhere around them. Dully Heather wondered about goblins and trolls but kept climbing down and down.

Finally, below them, they saw the body. It lay sprawled on a mound of snow and dirt, its dead eyes staring at the patch of sky far above.

Heather's sob echoed through the shaft.

7

AWAKENING

Heather and Welly dropped the last few feet to the floor of the shaft, walked toward the body, then froze. The head turned toward them. Slowly Earl sat up, a calm smile spreading over his face. "Children!" he said.

"Children, indeed!" Heather snapped after a dumbfounded pause. "As if it weren't childish to scare us like that?"

They ran to him. "Why aren't you dead?" she asked.

"Sorry to disappoint you."

"No, I mean . . . You know what I mean!" She couldn't decide whether to hit him or hug him.

"I fell partway and got caught in those rotten ropes and things." He pointed up to where the faint candlelight suggested a tangle of shapes. "Knocked my breath out, but it broke the fall. Then something gave way, and I dropped down here. I hit my head and blacked out." An already purpling bruise on his right temple proved the last point.

"Oh," she said, sorry again, "does it hurt?"

"No. I mean yes, it hurts, but that's not important. What *is* important is that when I woke up, I remembered!"

"Remembered what?"

"Everything!"

"You mean, like who you are?" Welly asked excitedly.

"Yes, everything!" He threw back his head and laughed, a great upwelling of joy and relief. The peals echoed and re-echoed through underground passages.

He stopped and groaned, pressing a hand to his head. "You really shouldn't laugh after cracking your head."

"So," Heather said, sympathy vying with impatience, "you know why that Maureen woman was after you?"

Earl's smile faded. "Yes, all too well. And I also know how lucky we've been to escape her. Afterward, did she say anything about her plans?"

"Yes, she did," Welly said. "They're going to come back and perform some rites over you."

Earl laughed flatly. "She would. Very thorough. But when? When are they coming?"

"It was the night after tomorrow night, wasn't it?" Welly said.

Heather nodded. "That's right. She wanted to do whatever it was at the dark of the moon, and that creepy Garth fellow said it was in two nights."

"Good. Then we've a little time. She won't be happy when she finds I'm not here. So by then I'd better be as far away as possible."

He stood up, suddenly swaying. Welly caught him. "Steady, now. You think you can climb out of here?"

Earl stared up the dark shaft. "Probably. But we don't have to. There's an easier way."

"How do you know?"

"I know a lot of things now."

"So are you going to tell us about them?" Heather asked, exasperated.

"When we're out of here. It'll take a lot of telling." He

stood a moment, as though listening to the darkness. Then he turned to his left. "This way."

He strode off into the gloom, and with candles flickering, the two hurried after him.

Earl led them into a low passageway. In places, the earth was still held by ancient timbers, but in others, soil and rockfall nearly filled the passage. Several times Heather was on the verge of protesting, but whenever their way seemed blocked, Earl considered a moment, then found some gap that just let them through. At one point, the passage divided into two. One way sloped down to the right; the other climbed steeply to the left. Earl stood, eyes closed, then chose the less promising right-hand route. Heather bit her tongue and wondered if they could find their way back again. She thought about the mythical Minotaur and wished she had a ball of yarn.

After fifty feet, the down-sloping passage leveled, then slanted up steeply. The candlelight glinted off curtains of ice clinging to the walls. Underfoot, the ground had the hard crunch of frozen mud. The air was heavy and deathly cold, but it moved faintly, flickering their candles as they continued to climb.

Earl had been walking ahead of them, almost beyond the circle of light. But now they came up to him, at what appeared to be a total blockage of the tunnel.

"Now what?" Welly asked. "Turn back?"

"No, there's space up there," Earl said, pointing upward. He began hauling himself up the pile of timber and rock. The two younger children looked at each other. Heather shrugged and followed Earl.

Welly felt queasy and whimpery. He hated tight, closed-in places. But as Heather's legs disappeared into a dark opening, he knew he hated being left alone more. In panic, he scrambled up to where the passage shrank to scarcely a foot high. Flat on his belly, he pulled himself along with hands and knees.

His candle brushed against a mud wall and snuffed out. Heather's body ahead of him blocked most of her light. He could feel the tons of earth above, waiting to shift and crush the life out of him. He wanted to scream! But noise might loosen the dirt. When he stopped moving, the sense of weight was unbearable. Clammy with sweat, he kept crawling, following Heather's ever receding feet.

Suddenly the feet were gone. Cautiously he stuck out a hand. Nothing but air, fresh cold air. Ahead, the tunnel widened and rimmed a patch of lesser darkness. They had come to another entrance.

Hands reached up and helped him down over a tumble of rock. Heather relit Welly's candle from hers and turned to Earl. "I hate to nag, but while you're explaining everything, you will tell us how you happened to know that simple little route?"

"I'll try," he said. "First let's find someplace to rest. Then you do deserve some explanations."

Not far from this entrance, they found a crude stone shed. Seeing nothing better, they checked the dark recesses for lurking animals and crawled inside. Blowing out the candles, they sat huddled together in the darkness, the doorway a gray patch in front of them.

"Well?" Heather said after a minute.

"I'm not stalling," Earl said. "I'm just not sure how to begin. You may find this a little hard to take in."

"Earl Bedwas, Master of Suspense!" she said sarcastically. "For goodness sakes, will you tell us?"

"All right, let's start this way. Do either of you know anything about Arthur Pendragon?"

"Arthur Pendragon?" Heather thought a moment. "You mean King Arthur? What can that . . . ?"

"Just tell me, either of you, what you know about him."

They were silent. Then Welly said, "Well, he was a king in Britain who ruled after the Romans left. I think he's supposed to have united a bunch of little kingdoms and fought against whoever was invading at the time. The Saxons, maybe?"

"Good. Anything else?"

Heather spoke up. "I read a book full of tales of King Arthur a few years ago. It was pretty good, but I didn't like it as well as *Robin Hood*. The writing was too hard."

"What was it about?" Earl prompted. "Who were the main characters?"

"Well, there was Arthur, of course, very noble and all. And there was his queen, Guenevere. She had an affair with one of the knights and caused a lot of trouble. Lancelot, I think it was. And there were a bunch of other knights, too, having adventures and going on quests. I forget all their names."

"Anyone else?"

"Well, there was some witch who kept messing things up. She had a funny name."

"Morgan."

"Yeah, that's right, Morgan."

"Any other main characters?"

"Hmm. Oh, yes, there was an old wizard named Merlin."

"And what became of him in the end?"

"I don't remember, really. Oh, yes. Didn't he get bewitched by some other lady and shut up in a cave or something?"

"Yes, that's about it."

After a long pause, Heather asked, "So why the folklore lesson?"

"The thing is," Earl said slowly, "I've only been Earl Bedwas for seven years. For a long time before that, I was Merlin."

The two sputtered wordlessly.

"Don't ask any questions. Let me try to get this out first."

They fell into silence, and he began. "I was born about two thousand years ago. I won't go into the details of my life. Let's just say that it was recognized I had a good deal of power. I spent years studying magic and gradually gained some skill in it. Eventually I became adviser to King Uther."

Earl stopped and looked at Heather. "It's funny. I read those same stories, maybe five years ago, and they were just stories to me. Now it's as though there are two people inside me, seeing things from two different places. One of me sees those stories as interesting folktales, and the other sees them as garbled accounts of events I lived through.

"But still, the core of the stories is fairly accurate, though a lot of garbage has been added. King Uther did have a son, Arthur. For political and magical reasons, he was very important and in great danger. I took him away and saw to his upbringing in secret. When he was old enough, he was revealed as heir and King.

"But there were those opposed to what Arthur and I were working for. Some of the British kings were jealous; and, of course, the Saxons didn't want Britain united. And then there was Morgan."

Heather blurted out, "The witch!"

"Heather," he said severely, "*witch* is not the right word.

Magic was more present in the world then. It comes in waves, I believe, throughout human history. Then we were at the end of a strong phase. Even common people had a little magic—skills and sensitivities that tapped into magical forces. Some of these might be called witches. But the term is not right for Morgan. She was a magician, a sorceress of great power. Such power often runs in families, and we were distantly related. Though," he added with vehemence, "she is not my aunt!"

"Maureen! You mean she . . . ?"

"Let me finish, or you'll never make any sense of this. Morgan had her own plans, and they involved gaining control of events by playing sides against each other and keeping Britain disunited. Every step of the way, she tried to thwart Arthur and me. And eventually she won, at least partially.

"For years, Morgan had been preparing an attack on me. Nimue." He paused for a minute. "Even after two thousand years, it still hurts." Sighing, he continued. "It was subtly done. Morgan knew my weaknesses. I didn't realize that Nimue was one of Morgan's creatures. Eventually I shared with her enough of my secrets that they turned my power against me. She and Morgan trapped me in a mountain and bound it about with enough spells to last as long as the mountain did. Which, of course, was the flaw. They didn't expect the mountain to be half-blown away a mere two thousand years in the future."

"But, Earl," Welly interrupted, "Merlin was an old man, and you're fourteen!"

"You've noticed!" Earl laughed. "But think about it. Magicians are mortal human beings, powerful, yes, but not gods. Even with all my powers—and I still had command of most, except those to break Morgan's spells—even with all that, I still aged. Eventually I would die. The path of magic I'd chosen gave me no command over death. That's where evil magic gets most of its strength: it has dealings with death. I imagine that's how Morgan has weathered these years; she's somehow suspended death.

"But in any case, I didn't have that recourse. I did, however, have some power over time. And locked away all those years, I learned to slow it down, or at least slow its effects on life. And then I discovered how to reverse it. When I grew so old that death must be near, I reversed the flow and gradually grew younger. I grew younger until I reached the age when if I went much further, I wouldn't have the skill to stop. Then I reversed it again and gradually aged.

"By the time the mountain was blown open, I had worked through several cycles. I'd gone through a turning not long before and was on my way up again. The explosion tore open the mountain and shattered Morgan's spells. But it also dealt me enough of a blow to completely bury my memory. It left me a helpless seven-year-old, with no idea of who I was."

"And the language?" Welly asked.

"That was just normal fifth-century British. I was always good at languages, so I learned modern English quickly. And since the older language had no memories to stick to, it just slipped away. I remember it now."

"Oh, and your name!" Heather exclaimed. "I bet you tried to say Merlin, and all the masters caught was the 'erl' sound."

"Probably. I'm pretty hazy about those early days."

"Earl . . . Merlin," Welly began.

"Earl Bedwas has been a good name these seven years. Let's stick to that for a while. But before you ask me any questions, let me ask you one. Do you believe me?"

They were silent a moment. Then Heather ventured, "Well, believing things is never a problem for me. But really accepting them is something a little different."

Earl chuckled. "If someone had told me this story a few days ago, I'd have had trouble deciding if this latest fall had jogged his memory or addled his wits. But there were clues, I realize now.

"When I lost my memory, I lost all of it, including how to control magic. The power was still there, but untapped except in stress or danger. Then it came out instinctively. And that scared me. I knew some things happened differently with me than with other kids, but I tried denying it to myself. That time in the snow, though, was the worst. I used the magic instinctively to escape and almost died not knowing how to reverse it. Afterward, I didn't understand what had happened, and it frightened me—a lot."

Welly frowned in thought. "You mean like when you hid behind the door from the monitor?"

"Yes. I tried to tell myself, and you, that he just didn't look carefully. But in fact, I'd wished myself invisible so intensely that I'd become so. It's all a matter of manipulating the forces around you and the other person's mind. And I did it automatically."

"And the fell-dogs and fighting with Nigel?" Heather said excitedly.

"The fell-dogs, yes. There was more in my howling than just noise, though I didn't know it. There was command. But I don't think much magic slipped into my fighting. We were taught to fight well when I was a kid—the first time."

"So what are you going to do now?" Welly asked.

"I don't know. This has all come back so suddenly, I need to do some thinking. But in any case, I have to get away from here, and soon, before Morgan returns. Do you two think you can still slip back to the school and get some provisions for me?"

"You can't just make food, now that you've got your magic back?" Welly asked hopefully.

"Nothing nutritious. I sustained myself in that mountain only through a web of spells and almost complete inactivity. But magicians are just people. Normally we've got to eat just like anyone else."

"Pity," Welly said. "I was sort of hoping you could spread out a banquet here. Sure, of course we'll go back. I think there's still enough night left."

Heather agreed, and soon the two were climbing the hill, past the ominous mine shaft and onto the road. For a while, they walked in silence; then Welly asked, "Do you believe him?"

"Yes, even if that makes me sound as crazy as he does. Remember how that Maureen or Morgan or whoever was talking tonight? All about power and how important he was and how she needed to use him? I thought maybe he was some sort of lost heir, and she wanted to be the power behind the throne or something. But really, this makes much more sense—especially if you remember all the strange things he's done; the ones he's mentioned, and the way he got us out of that awful mine."

"Yes," Welly agreed. "And remember the sparks. When he and that woman fought, it was like two swords clashing."

"So, you believe him, too?"

"Heather, I don't have the imagination you do. I don't

take in weird things easily. But this is too real to be weird. I guess that means I believe."

The night was well advanced when they reached the school wall and the old gnarled roots marking the way over. But there were still several hours before the late winter dawn.

Already aching from their climb down the shaft, every muscle protested as they scaled the wall. On the other side, the two slipped quickly through the orchard toward the darkened bulk of the school. They were almost to the back door when a shadow peeled away from other shadows and leaped at them, gripping their arms.

"I thought you two might come skulking back tonight," Nigel's voice hissed. "I'm not on duty, but I couldn't pass up a little healthy revenge."

"Let us alone, Nigel!" Welly demanded, surprised at his own vehemence. "We didn't do anything to you."

"Certainly, I'll let you alone, as soon as I get you to Master Greenhow's room."

"Well, go ahead, then," Heather said. "You've caught us, and we can't help where you take us. So it'll be *you* Greenhow yells at for waking him to report fugitives who'll still be here in the morning."

Nigel was silent for a moment. "You really aren't important enough to wake anyone for. And you're already in for a delicious punishment. He's furious at that ungrateful friend of yours for escaping. His aunt was beastly mad; scared the daylights out of old Greenhow and didn't leave him a penny."

He jerked the two children toward the back door and into the darkened hall. Immediately Welly's glasses fogged up, and he stumbled blindly as they turned into the girls' wing of the dormitory.

"Let's stable you first, Horseface." Nigel laughed. "I brought along the extra keys."

They were hauled up a flight of stone stairs and along dim, silent corridors. As they neared Heather's room, Welly, who'd been mentally discarding one plan after another, whispered loudly, "This is sure a fix we're in. I'd sure like to see our friends Marian and Robin about now."

Nigel stopped at a door, thrust it open, and pushed Heather inside. As the older boy unhooked a ring of keys from his belt, Welly coughed and said emphatically, "I'd sure like to see good old Tuck right now."

Comprehension dawned on Heather's face. "Oh, look out!" she exclaimed. "My giant roach has escaped! Grab him!" She threw herself on her hands and knees just in front of Nigel. Welly smashed against him from behind, sending Nigel toppling over Heather onto the floor. Leaping onto Nigel's back, Welly pinned him down while Heather whisked a blanket off the bed and wrapped it around his head. Then, snatching a belt and scarf off the back of a chair, Welly tied his prisoner's wrists and ankles.

Nigel's yells were only mumbles through the blanket, but as Heather shut the door, she whispered, "We don't want to smother him. Try a gag." She threw Welly an old undershirt for the purpose. Then, lighting a candle, she hastily stuffed things into a backpack—all the blankets, warm clothing, and candles that would fit.

"Don't forget the candied chestnuts," Welly reminded her.

They dared say little in Nigel's hearing, but as soon as they slipped out the door and locked it behind them, Welly whispered, "I assume you're thinking what I'm thinking?"

They started down the corridor as she replied, "About burning our bridges behind us?"

"Right. Having Master Greenhow mad at us is one thing. But bashing and humiliating the nasty-tempered heir to Glamorganshire—well, this isn't going to be a healthy place for us."

"I was sort of thinking we should go with Earl anyway," Heather said.

"Me too. But this clinches it."

They hurried to Welly's room, where he quickly packed his rucksack. Then they slipped down to the kitchen. "We'll have to hurry," Heather whispered. "The kitchen help will be starting the fires for breakfast soon."

She led them to the pantry, and they began stuffing their packs with bread, turnips, and even several sausages and lumps of cheese. "We'll eat like kings," Welly said.

"If we ever get out of here. That's enough now, hurry."

Welly crammed a heel of bread into his mouth as they slipped to the pantry door and cracked it open. Outside there was a shuffling. Lids clanked, and someone yawned by their door.

Welly's heart sank. He wondered if they'd be trapped in there all day. No. Someone would come into the pantry after something, and they'd be caught. He desperately wished he could do Earl's disappearing trick.

Then they heard a door open and close, and there was silence. "She's gone out to get more water," Heather whispered. "Hurry!"

They shoved open the door and glided like ghosts through the kitchen and down dark, twisting corridors. Once they hid behind a corner while someone sleepily stumbled by. Finally they made it to the back door and slipped into the predawn gray.

Dawn itself was silhouetting the broken mine tower as

they finally crested the hill. Briefly they stopped at the ruined house where they'd first hidden to pick up Earl's pack. Then they worked their way downhill to the small shed.

They found Earl sitting in front, leaning back against the old stone wall. He was staring into the light along the eastern horizon. As they approached, he turned, giving them a blank look which slowly changed into a smile. "You were a long time. Did you have any trouble?"

"Trouble personified," Welly said. "Our good friend Nigel. But we put him in his place."

"Doubtful. There's not a place in Llandoylan bad enough for him." Earl eyed their two packs. "Looks like you've brought enough for an army. I don't know if I can carry all that."

"You needn't," Welly said crisply. "We're coming, too."

Earl sighed. "I was afraid you'd say that." When they started to protest, he continued. "I'll admit, before you left, I almost wished you'd offer to come along. But now I just don't think I can let you."

"Why?" Heather asked. "What's changed? We're sworn to you and mean to follow through."

"I'll tell you what's changed. The world's changed! While you were away, I experimented with some magic, simple stuff. I hadn't really done much since I was sealed away. But things went all wrong, horrendously wrong. And I think I know why."

They looked at him, their expectancy tinged, Earl thought, with skepticism. He sighed.

"Magic is a natural force, with its own laws, like gravity or magnetism. The force lines of what we call magic are part of all things in the universe. People with the power and training can learn to tap that force and use it. But like magnetic fields, it seems magic changes over time. The lines and patterns of force shift."

Heather and Welly both wore slightly confused frowns. Earl continued. "That's the problem, you see. The force lines changed over time; but caught as I was in that web of spells, I didn't change with them. I'm no longer in tune with the patterns. I still have the power, but outside of close personal magic, like protection or finding the way out of that mine, everything I do is off somehow, out of kilter."

"Is that a big problem?" Welly asked.

"Yes, it is!" Earl said, his voice high with frustration. He jumped to his feet. "All right, I'll show you. I can still do personal magic, like changing my appearance, say."

He stood before them, and as they watched with growing amazement, his chin began to darken, and he started growing a beard, a long, wavy beard. It looked a bit odd on a fourteen-year-old face, but it and the mustache were very impressive. Except for the color.

Earl looked down. "Purple! I can see I need to brush up on details. Well, no matter."

The beard shriveled and faded away as he turned and pointed at a good-sized rock some six feet in front of them. "But now let's try this. Ordinary telekinesis is pretty basic stuff. I should be able to look at that rock and manipulate its forces and those around it until it lifts into the air. But watch!"

With his arms crossed, he stared at the rock, head tilted slightly, face taut with concentration. Expectantly Heather and Welly watched, but nothing happened. Then, gradually, they became aware of a faint buzzing noise. They turned to see a huge hornet's nest floating through the air toward them. It was aimed directly at Earl's head.

"Duck!" Welly cried. Grabbing Earl's arm, he yanked him to the ground.

The hive sailed over their heads and smashed on the rock he'd tried to lift. From the shattered pulpy sides rose a cloud of angry hornets. They swirled about undecidedly for a moment, then descended on the three watchers. In seconds, they were swatting, ducking, and waving their arms frantically.

Earl spat out a singsong phrase. The hornets and broken nest turned purple.

"Damn!" he exclaimed. "Purple again!"

"Never mind the color!" Welly wailed. "Just stop them!"

Earl muttered something else, and the smashed hive burst into flames, consuming a number of hornets that hovered about it.

"Ah, that's better," he said, and then groaned as the flames slowly melted down and coalesced into a large cream pie, distinctly purple.

This new arrival, however, interested the hornets. Soon, those insects not destroyed by the fire were swarming over the pie and sinking into its sticky surface.

"Well," Heather commented as the last hornet buried itself in the purple froth, "at least it got the job done."

"I can see," Welly said, "that this is going to be an interesting trip."

8

QUEST'S BEGINNING

E arl shook his head. He looked at Heather and Welly sitting against the stone wall, stubborn looks on their faces and full packs at their sides. "It would be all right," he said, "if it were only a matter of being interesting. But this trip will be dangerous as well. If I had my powers intact, we needn't fear the dangers of the road. Wizards travel in great security."

"But it's no different than if we were traveling with just plain Earl Bedwas," Welly pointed out. "We just have to deal with danger as best we can."

"True," Earl admitted. "And if we only had regular dangers to worry about—animals, brigands, and weather—maybe we could chance it. But suppose when Morgan finds out I'm not lying dead in that mine she sets out looking for me. Suppose she unleashes a man-eating griffin, and I fight back with a cloud of butterflies—purple ones."

"Maybe griffins are allergic to purple butterflies," Heather offered.

"What Heather is saying," Welly said before Earl could sputter a reply, "and I am, too, is that we're coming. So you might as well stop arguing."

Heather smiled impishly. "And if you try to stop us by turning us into rocks, you'll probably get a pair of panda bears as companions, or fleas, maybe."

Earl laughed. "And they'd be purple, no doubt." Running a hand through his hair, he paced in front of the little hut. Then he stopped and looked at them. "All right. Come along. You might be in as much danger if you went back to the school. Morgan probably knows you left with me, and if she learns you've returned, she might pay you a visit." The thought made the two of them squirm. "But remember," Earl continued, "you can drop out of this venture any time. Things may well get over our heads."

The two jumped to their feet. Earl grabbed up his pack and said, "Let's redistribute our gear. But not here; the smell of that cream pie is turning my stomach."

They repacked on a cluster of rocks upwind from the faintly buzzing pie. "Just one question," Welly asked as they shared a wedge of bread. "Where are we going?"

"I was thinking about that while you were gone. And the answer's inescapable. I've got to go find Arthur."

"King Arthur?" Welly said incredulously.

"But he's been dead for two thousand years!" Heather protested.

"Perhaps," Earl admitted. "I don't know for sure. I was entrapped before that last battle, so I wasn't with him. But, if you notice, the legends don't say that he died. They say he was gravely wounded and carried off to Avalon."

"Ah, that's just a fancy way of saying he died," Welly stated.

"No, it's not. Avalon is real. It's part of Faerie, a world parallel with ours and touching it at points. The folk of Avalon, the Eldritch, are interested in our world and occasionally mix in its affairs. And they always had a particular interest in Arthur. They prophesied his birth and kingship and gave him his sword. It seems likely that when all his work was collapsing and he was dying, they spirited him away to heal and wait."

"Wait for what?" Heather asked.

"Wait until he was needed again. Until our world needed someone with Arthur's dream and his skill to bring it about."

Earl finished his packing and sat on a rock. "Maybe that's why I was released when I was. If ever there was a time when Britain needed a man like Arthur, it's now. A world blasted by human stupidity, with petty kings fighting each other and mutants invading its shores. And to add to that, evil magic seems to be loose. So, I'm afraid the answer's obvious. I helped bring Arthur into his kingdom before. That must be what I'm to do again."

A moment's silence. "All right," Heather said, standing up, "where is this Avalon?"

Earl gestured helplessly. "I don't know. The entrances, the places where the two worlds cross, change constantly. Who knows where they are after two thousand years, if there are any left at all? This world may be too dreadful now for Avalon to want any contact with it."

"So where do we go?" Welly asked.

"South . . . south and west. I feel that's the way. Maybe once I'm closer, I'll sense something. But, you see, this is a rather slender set of threads to hang on, so if—"

Heather stood up. "We're going, Earl; no more arguing." She shouldered her pack. "And we're going south."

They trekked off across country, sometimes talking, sometimes in companionable silence. Heather, tired as she was, gloried in every moment of it. This was adventure. This was a real quest. And it was something of her own. She wasn't needed at home; she wasn't needed at school. But maybe, just maybe, she was needed here. The hope thrilled her so much that it frightened her.

Tossing her head, she let her hood fall back. Thin brown hair fluttered in the breeze. The sky was unusually clear, the sun almost a disk. In its diffuse light, the snow sparkled and glittered like crushed diamonds. The white was achingly lovely, and the shadows were a deep cool blue. How she'd love to have a gown like that, glittering as she walked, swirling into folds of mysterious blue. Her hair tumbling about it, pale and gold as the sun. How beautiful she'd be. All the world would see how beautiful. She sighed blissfully.

By midmorning, they were tired and hungry. Under a shelf of slaty blue rocks, they sat down and shared a hunk of bread and tangy sticks of sausage. Ceremoniously Heather brought out the candied chestnuts. "Happy Yule," she said, doling them out. She'd only been able to afford a few, but they savored every crumb.

As they finished the meal, Earl cleared his throat uncomfortably. "I'm not a maker of sentimental speeches. But I want you to know I appreciate your sticking with me."

"But we're friends," Welly said simply.

"That's what I mean—you're friends. I've had very few in either life. I never admitted to myself that I needed them. That was my real weakness, and Morgan knew it and used it. That's what she's best at, playing on people's weaknesses until she breaks them and turns them to her will.

"She knew I needed someone like Nimue, so she trained

her and insinuated her into my life until I was trapped by my own need. But for all that, I don't blame her; Nimue, I mean. She herself was trapped by Morgan. And despite everything, I loved her."

Earl was looking off into the distance, as though seeing over time as well as miles. "During those long years, I often wondered what became of her, once she had served Morgan's purpose. I hope she broke away and found peace somewhere."

He sighed and stood up. The three shouldered their bags and set off over the silent landscape, their breath rising in plumes against the cold air. After a while, Welly asked about Garth.

"That creature?" Earl replied. "He's not from the old times. You can tell by his darker skin, for one thing. His ancestors mutated for survival."

"Oh!" Heather exclaimed. "So that's why you and Morgan—"

"Are so washed-out?" Earl laughed. "Our ancestors lived well before the Devastation. Back then, most Britons were as pale as we are, though people near the equator had lovely dark skin like yours, or darker, to filter out the sun.

"But Garth," he said, returning to the subject, "is of your world, though his mutations may have taken some nasty turns as well. Morgan usually picks deeply flawed creatures for her lackeys. Her evil can get a firmer hold on them."

Welly was frowning in concentration. "Earl, something just occurred to me. Remember the night someone broke into Greenhow's office? Do you suppose it was one of those two looking for your records?"

"Hmm. From what you saw, I think it could have been.

They must have found the mountain destroyed and rumors led them to the school. And . . . and that time in the blizzard. I'm not sure if it was a deliberate trap. I don't think so." He shivered. "If they'd known about my memory then, they could have caught me easily."

In midafternoon, they joined the south-running road and luxuriated in its packed surface. On either side, stone walls snaked over the hillsides in shadow-rimmed ridges. Ancient in origin, they now marked fields where hardy mutated crops grew in the brief summers. Some of the walls fenced livestock whose ancestors had been among those few farm animals which, sheltered during the Devastation, had not died of cold or radiation.

Sunset was still an hour off when Earl gestured toward a cluster of trees and ruins on a ridge to their west. "Let's stop and set up camp. None of us got any sleep last night, and I, for one, am exhausted."

Welly and Heather, who had been walking the last several miles in a mechanical stupor, mumbled agreement.

They struck off along the ridge, on what had once been a road. It led to a grove of dark pines, in the midst of which nestled a ruined chapel. In one far wall, the delicate stone traceries of an arched window were still etched against the shrouded sky.

"We're going to spend the night here?" Heather asked doubtfully, eyeing the tilted gravestones in the low-walled churchyard.

"It's shelter," Earl said. Then, noticing the focus of Heather's attention, he added, "I wouldn't worry about ghosts. I doubt that spirits who knew the old world would bother drifting into this one."

They stepped through the broken archway. The roof

over the back was still intact. Under it, they swept pine
needles into a nest beside the stone altar and spread their
blankets over them. Then, leaving Welly to select provisions, Heather and Earl gathered fallen branches and built
a fire in the roofless space where pews had once stood.

As the sun set, the fire blazed up, postponing the dark,
which Heather still did not quite trust here. Three split
potatoes were stuck into the fire's edge. While these cooked,
they nibbled on bread and turnips.

"We're certainly eating a lot better than at school," Earl
observed, "thanks to our resourceful, light-fingered provi-
sioners."

"We did our best," Heather said. "I just hope Cook
doesn't get into trouble."

"She won't," Welly assured her. "It wasn't her fault the
kitchen was hit by thieves. No, I imagine once the scandal
dies down, the whole place will get along quite well without us."

"Scandal!" Heather breathed excitedly. "Well, at least
I'll have made some impact on those beauty queens. Just
think, someday we may be school legends!"

Welly snorted. "Yeah, the three misfits who forsook
their inheritances and took to the wilds."

"Some inheritances," Heather and Earl said together,
and laughed.

The fire was dying down, and they were thinking comfortably of sleep when a noise outside jerked them alert. A
sound of shuffling. Two ragged figures stood in the doorway.

"Well, well, look what holed up here," drawled one. "It
beats knocking people off on the highway when they just
sit and wait for you."

The other laughed. "Now, didn't I tell you, Tom, we

should bed down here? There ain't no ghosts or Druids, just plump pickings."

They pushed their way into the firelit chapel, followed by three others as ragged and surly-looking. Heather and Welly shrank back, eyes wide with fear.

"That one's nice and plump, anyway," one of the newcomers observed.

"Save that sort of thing for your mutie friends," Tom spat. "We'll go for the clothes and provisions."

"We can take the girl for the slavers," one suggested.

Tom grinned. "Or maybe for us."

Earl stood up, breaking the stunned silence of the intended victims. Something in his bearing halted the bandits' advance. "We have no money and few provisions," he said calmly. "And we are not for sale. So I advise you to leave and find pickings elsewhere."

"Oh, indeed?" Tom said. "Well, I'll tell you something else about yourselves. You're three children, and you're unarmed. Come on, boys!"

The five bounded forward. Earl thrust one hand down toward the fire. It leaped from smoldering embers into tall flames. The sudden new light lit the bandits' startled faces. With another gesture, Earl sent the fire hurtling from the ground.

It shot up like a meteor, but in the wrong direction. The three children threw themselves to the flagstones. The fire hurtled over their heads in a shower of sparks, hit the back wall, and ricocheted off. The brigands yelped as the fireball swooped toward them. Suddenly it jerked upward, slammed into a tall pine, and extinguished itself. The concussion snapped off a branch. This crashed down into the chapel, pinning one of the attackers beneath it.

Amid shrieks and yells, the others ran off, pausing briefly to drag their companion free. For several minutes, the three children heard the highwaymen's cries fading into the distance.

Earl sat down, feeding another branch into the remaining embers. "I'll have to work on that fire trick a bit. But at least it wasn't purple."

That night they set watches. One sat wrapped in a blanket by the fire while the other two slept. The wind wailed forlornly through the darkened trees, and the two younger children kept a particularly attentive watch in the direction of the graveyard. Snow began falling during the second watch, but nothing more disturbed the night except the distant cry of a rare and lonely owl.

9

DRY SEA'S CROSSING

After breakfasting in the chapel on bread and dried radishes, they repacked their bags and set off. Heather hardly gave the graveyard a parting glance. In the light of morning, the gray markers behind the wall were just stones without the slightest mist of menace about them.

Wind had whipped the night's snow into frothy drifts, which, they noted, would cover their tracks from the mine. As they stepped free of the grove, Earl stopped for a moment, looking south to where the land dropped away below them. "We're almost to the shore," he said dreamily.

"Shore?" Welly questioned.

"There used to be a great arm of the sea down there, the Bristol Channel. Now you can't even see it from here.

"It's odd," he continued after a pause. "To Earl Bedwas, that was just another geography lesson. But now I *remember* the Channel. I sailed across it between Cornwall and Wales. I can close my eyes and see the sparkling water, the whitecaps, and blue sky."

"Well, if we're heading that way," Welly said, "I'd rather walk than sail. I've only seen enough open water to wash my face in, and I haven't any idea about swimming."

Heather objected. "Oh, Welly, I can't believe you don't yearn to see the ocean. Why, half the ancient books talk about it! There's always so much adventure there: pirates and smugglers and romantic ladies walking the shore."

Welly grunted. "Well, our romantic lady will just have to be happy with a dry road, because that's all there is now."

They walked on through the morning. Unlike the day before, Earl said very little, answering the occasional question in short, distracted replies. At last Heather asked, "Is there something wrong, Earl? If you're worried about last night, don't be. Your fire business was a little indirect, but it got rid of them."

"No, that's not it. I'm sorry I'm not better company. But seeing that seascape where there wasn't any set me to remembering. This used to be such a beautiful world. So different from now. I can't even describe it to you."

Head lowered, he continued walking. "If our world had been destroyed by a great flood or by a piece falling from the sun, that would be fate. But to find that we destroyed it ourselves, that hurts."

He strode along in silence for a moment, then suddenly turned to Welly. "Remember our talk in the library? Something about it kept bothering me, but I couldn't catch it. Now I know. You said you loved strategy for its own sake. But remember, it's only a tool! I think that's one thing that went wrong. People got so involved with their clever tools and strategic thinking, they were blind to everything else. So they nearly destroyed their world."

The route they were taking was an old one which once ended in the east–west coast road. That thoroughfare could still be seen, but modern tracks ran alongside to avoid its broken pavement. From the intersection, a new road continued south, built over the years more by human feet and carts than by engineers. It stretched before them across the former channel, a gray strip on a white landscape.

Around noon, they passed six merchants on their way north to Wales. The party was armed and traveled with two laden pack ponies. Ignoring the stares of surprise at their own vulnerability, the children warned them of at least one band of brigands ahead. Otherwise, the day was uneventful, and the night was passed among a cluster of large rocks not far off the road.

Earl took the first watch, wrapped in a blanket and leaning back against a boulder. Welly cocooned himself in blankets on the opposite side of the fire, but sleep did not come easily. He lay with his eyes open, watching the thin banner of smoke curl up into the night. Finally he propped himself up on an elbow.

"Earl, I've been trying, but it's hard to imagine what this must be like for you. I mean, it's like every kid's fantasy. I used to think how great it would be to know what I do now and be, say, a toddler again. And now you sort of have that."

Earl grunted. "Well, yes, I know the fantasy. And sure, I remember my life before. But after two thousand years, memories lose something of their immediacy. Besides, what I remember applies to people and situations in the fifth century. It doesn't help much here."

A coal popped and leaped from the fire. Earl kicked it back with the edge of a worn boot. "And there's something else. Age affects more than how your body looks; it changes your thoughts and feelings. In most ways, I really am a fourteen-year-old." He paused, then laughed wryly. "I've been remembering how trying it was being a teenager before. And now I have to go through it all again!"

"Oh, come on," Heather said from the fire-reddened darkness. "Everyone's always moaning about the dreadful teens. Surely it's not as bad as all that."

"No, maybe not." Earl grinned at them. "At least I now know that 'this, too, shall pass.'"

In the morning, a brisk wind had risen in the west, but there was no new snow. Patches of ice were dotted about, rimmed with dry reeds which clattered like bones in the wind. Here and there the ground was blown clear of snow, revealing the coarse curly grass and a new plant—thick, blood-red succulents that grew close to the ground and made wet popping sounds when stepped upon.

Late in the afternoon, a long glimmering line that they'd seen in the distance resolved itself into a river. "The River Severn," Earl announced. "It just followed the retreating sea, cutting itself a new bed in the silt."

As they approached it, they saw that only the river's edges were gripped in ice. The central channel still flowed freely. A bridge had been built a century or so earlier by rolling large stones into the water and spanning these with timbers and scraps from old buildings. The whole structure looked rickety and in need of repair. Earl stopped short of crossing it.

"Do you think it's safe?" Heather asked.

"I'm sure it'll hold us. That's not what worries me."

"What, then?"

"Trolls. Wherever there's a bridge, one has to consider trolls."

"Oh, come on!" Heather complained. "That's only in stories. It's just a bridge."

"The stories of one time are based on the truths of another. And quite a few things seem to be cycling back. Still, we have to cross."

He led the way onto the bridge, but when he reached the first splintered plank, he tromped heavily upon it and chanted, "Troll, troll, under timber and stone, we cross this bridge although it's your own. We cross with your leave and our blessings you'll take; we cross without it and a cursing we'll make."

The two younger children could barely keep from laughing as they followed Earl onto the creaking, sagging span. But they were only halfway across when a horrible little manikin swung up from under the railing and landed squarely in their path.

The creature was small and hunched, with long arms and bowlegs, the body covered with splotchy yellow fur. His head was bald and wrinkled, with a thin yellow beard that began at the huge splayed ears and ran under a receding chin. He glared at them out of small, close-set eyes.

"You take my cursing instead," he lisped wetly. "And me grind your bones to make my bread!"

Earl laughed. "You're new at this, aren't you? Now stand aside; we're going over."

"It's my bridge!"

"Agreed, and we're crossing it."

The troll gurgled hatred and leaped at Earl, its filthy claws outspread. Earl ducked and grabbed the creature around the waist. The troll wiggled like an insect as Earl lifted it over his head and tossed it into the roiling river.

Turning to the other two, he wiped his hands on his coat. "Didn't have to use magic on that one. Good thing, too, or I'd probably have burned the bridge under us or turned it to pudding."

As they continued across, Heather looked back over the rail to see a bald head bobbing downstream. Finally a bedraggled yellow creature pulled itself onto the bank they had left. It shook both fists at them, but its words were lost in the water's rushing. Heather was glad that at least it hadn't drowned.

The cloud-smeared sun was already low above the western horizon. As they stepped off the end of the bridge, Earl stopped and surveyed the barren land ahead. "Let's camp here for the night. It's near water, and this road would be too easy to lose in the dark."

"But what about the troll?" Heather asked.

"I doubt that he'll bother us again."

They built a fire of grass and bits of driftwood as twilight fell about them. The blaze filled the air with a pungent tang and flushed their faces with heat, forcing them to occasionally turn about, like spitted meat, warming one side and cooling the other.

As they ate supper of bread and hard cheese, Heather asked, "Was that really a troll, Earl, like in stories, or just a mutie?"

Earl thought a moment, feeding knots of grass into the fire. "That's not an easy question. Old-time trolls mutated from something, too. They were creatures of Faerie. And I guess that since the Devastation, some doors between this world and the other have opened wider. That young fellow back there may be part of both. He knew some of the traditional forms, anyway."

Heather frowned. "Why didn't those merchants warn us there was a troll at the bridge?"

Earl laughed. "He probably didn't show himself to them. They were six grown men, and armed."

They stacked more fuel near the fire. Then Earl and Heather curled up in two hollows, but Welly, a blanket draped over his shoulders, sat by the fire keeping the first watch. All had passed uneventfully when he woke Earl for the second watch, and after several hours, Earl woke Heather for the last.

With one blanket about her shoulders and the torn half of another wrapping her cold feet, she huddled close to the low fire. To her left, she could hear the steady gurgle of the river. Occasionally over it there were other sounds, ice cracking along the riverbank or the distant cry of some wild animal.

Whenever she heard the latter, she was tempted to drop more fuel into the smoldering fire. But she'd found that a bright fire nearby turned the grayness around her to black. With the glow reduced to a few red coals, she could see farther into the night. She hoped fervently there was nothing out there to see. But in case there was, she wanted to see it at a distance.

Slowly she fed twigs into the embers. The glow spread a soft circle of light just beyond the sleepers.

She looked at them fondly. They were so different. One round and soft-looking, the other all edges and angles. Yet her heart warmed to them both. They were her friends. What did they see, she wondered, looking at her when she slept. Angrily she twisted her braid, dismissing the thought. She knew the answer all too well. But she wished that, lying there asleep in the firelight, she could be beautiful for them.

A rustling noise snapped her back to attention. She stared into the darkness and saw a darker shape, which had not been there before. With flapping and creaking, it moved closer. She was reaching out to wake Earl when the creature spoke.

"It's Troll. Me hungry. You have food?"

"Yes, and it's ours," she replied with more bravery than she felt.

"It was my bridge, and you crossed it."

"You didn't build the bridge."

"You didn't bake the bread."

She paused a moment. "How do you know?"

"Me clever troll. Also hungry troll. You give bread and me no eat your bones."

"No. I might give you bread because you have no bones to eat. But you won't have our bones in any case."

They watched each other for a minute. The troll's beady eyes stared from a face both sad and grotesque. Keeping her eyes on him, Heather leaned forward and fumbled through a sack for a piece of bread.

The other's thin, spindly body hunched forward hopefully in the cold. Slowly she unwound the old blanket from her feet. Wrapping the bread in its folds, she threw the bundle out to him. A squeak and shuffle, and he was gone.

She saw and heard no more of the creature. Soon the sky began graying in the east. When it was light enough to see the bridge, she woke the other two but said nothing about the night's visitor.

The three washed themselves in the river, or washed as much of themselves as they could stand exposing to the cold. Then they ate a light breakfast by the ashes of the fire.

As they were packing up, Earl heard a reedy whistle behind him. He turned to see the troll squatting on a rock twenty feet away. He was wearing an old torn blanket as a shawl. Earl glanced at Heather but said nothing.

Addressing the troll, Earl said conversationally, "Going to be stopping any more travelers today, do you think?"

"Depends."

"On how few and weak they are?"

"Well, me a bridge troll! How else do me make a living?"

"Oh, guarding bridges is fine, if it's your line of work. But there are ways to do these things."

"Such as?" the troll replied sulkily.

"Well, great big horrendous trolls can threaten to grind people's bones. But little ones have to be cleverer."

"How?"

"The usual thing is to ask riddles. That way, if they guess the answer, travelers know they've earned a crossing. But if they don't, they feel you've earned a toll. You'll get more food and things that way, even if you don't grind many bones."

"Hmm. Me like riddles. But don't know many."

"That will give you something to pass the time between travelers, making up riddles."

The troll mumbled and hissed in a thoughtful sort of way, then slid off the rock and disappeared.

Earl stood up, shouldered his pack, and said loudly, "If everyone's ready, let's go."

Welly was down by the river, stuffing his pack with bits of driftwood for future fires. He hurried back to join them, and the three walked off toward the road, followed from behind by a pair of beady eyes. At Heather's sleeping place by the dead fire lay a carrot and the end of a sausage.

That day was like the one before, except that as the morning passed, Earl began feeling more and more uneasy. He kept glancing to either side and behind them but saw nothing. Heather felt it, too, though nothing seemed to be following or watching them. But the feeling grew.

Once Earl noticed a pair of birds circling high in the cloud-layered sky. At one time he would have thought nothing of it, but in this world, birds were not common. He kept a wary eye on the winged shapes floating silently overhead.

The ground began sloping up as the channel road rose slowly toward the former shore of Devon. In midafternoon, they stopped to rest, sharing a handful of roasted barley. Heather leaned wearily against a rock. She'd been walking so long that her legs felt as if they were still swinging and pumping ahead. She wondered dully if they'd ever finish walking.

As she mechanically chewed her barley, her interest was caught by a thin gray line at the edge of the west-sweeping plain.

"What's that?" she asked Earl. "Clouds?"

He squinted into the west. "No, it's the ocean. The Atlantic Ocean."

"Oh, I do hope we get a chance to see it closer sometime."

Just then, Welly called from where he'd been exploring ice-clogged pools on the other side of the road. "Hey, come look what I've found!"

The two pushed themselves off from the rocks and, crossing the road, scrambled down the far bank. There, half-encased in mud and ice, were the rusted remains of an ancient device.

Welly kicked at one pitted silvery strip. "I think it's an automobile, one of those mechanical carts."

Earl poked around, studying the parts. "You may be right. But how did it get out here? This was underwater when those things ran."

"Yeah, I was wondering that," Welly replied. "Maybe it fell off a ferryboat."

"Or maybe," Heather suggested, "after the Devastation, when all the fuel was gone, people hitched horses to it and used it as a cart, until it got stuck out here."

Earl straightened up. "Maybe. But we'll never know. Let's be on our way."

They turned back to the road, but stopped short. Leaning calmly against the rocks where they'd just rested were Morgan and Garth.

"Earl, dear," the woman said, "I'm so glad you weren't hurt by that nasty fall at the mines."

"Cut the charm, Morgan," Earl said flatly as he climbed back to the road. "We both know who we are, so you needn't waste your sympathy."

"Ah," she said, smiling slyly at her companion. "We thought you might be remembering when we heard about highwaymen running into a skinny kid who threw fire."

Heather gasped. She hadn't thought of that giving them away. The sound shifted Morgan's attention to her, and for a moment the woman stared at her with thoughtful green eyes.

"Well, Morgan," Earl said, drawing back her gaze, "if all you wanted was to renew old acquaintances, you've done that. I can't say that even after two thousand years it's been a pleasure. But with any luck, maybe we can avoid meeting again for another couple millennia."

"Dear Merlin, always your same charming self. I can't see how I've gotten along without you all this time."

"Try, because I'll give you another chance." He tried to move past her, but she stepped in his way.

"Blast it, Merlin, let's call a truce. Don't you see? The

world's changed! All the causes and people you fought for are dead. Come with me now, and we can start afresh. We can remake this world the way we want it."

"Any world you made wouldn't be worth living in. No, Morgan, I'm through with that. You buried me away from my first life and destroyed everything I built. Now I don't want any more building. I just want someplace I can be left alone."

"Where are you going, then?"

"I don't know. This world hasn't much left in it. But I'll find someplace." He motioned to Heather and Welly, and the three pushed past the woman and her silent companion.

"You'll regret not joining me, Merlin!" she called after him.

"I've regretted many things having to do with you, Morgan," he said without turning around, "but never that."

Heather felt eyes boring into her back as they walked up the road. But when, at the crest of the hill, she stole a backward glance, the two figures were gone.

"Do you think she believes you?" Heather whispered when they felt safe. "That you're looking for someplace to be a hermit, I mean."

"Probably not. It buys us some time, maybe. But I expect we'll be hearing from her again."

Welly whistled. "I'd rather not, thank you. I've never met a creepier lady."

"Not many people have," Earl said, "and lived."

They continued along the road. The west wind was stronger now, knifing into them with cold and damp. Stormlike, the gray line in the west was moving closer.

An icy wind steadily picked up force, stinging their

faces. The three travelers pulled their hoods tight and staggered on against the gusts. Overhead, dark gray clouds streaked against the lighter sky. In the west, the gray band was much closer. Heather stared at it as they hurried along. From above came the thin cry of a seagull.

Suddenly Heather stopped. Her voice quavered. "Earl, I don't think those are storm clouds. Look at it. That's water!"

The others stopped and stared. The gray line was no longer a distant smear. It was solid and drawing nearer: a great gray wall with flecks of white at its top.

"It's the ocean!" Welly yelled. "The whole ocean pouring back! Run!"

He and Heather bolted off the road, running east as fast as their legs would go. Earl stared at the approaching horror, then leaped after them. "Wait!" he called. "Don't run!"

Wind ripped his words away. The two kept up their panicky flight. He increased his speed, pounding his long legs over the uneven ground. Finally he was up with Welly. Lunging, Earl grabbed his arm. Dragging him along, he tackled Heather.

They all rolled together on the ground. Looking up, they saw the towering wall of water sweeping down upon them, pouring over them. Water was all around, green and deep, pressing down on their lungs. Weird undersea shapes swept past.

I'm dying, Welly thought. I can't breathe! Beside him, Heather was flopping about, gasping helplessly like a landed fish.

Earl knelt between them, his dark hair streaming about him like seaweed. He grabbed them both roughly by the shoulders. "You can breathe!" he yelled. "It's just illusion. There's no water, just air. Breathe! Don't think you're dying, or you will."

Welly stared up at him, eyes wide with fear. Earl thumped his friend's chest. "Breathe! It's air! There's no water. Breathe air!"

Welly gave up and took a deep breath. He wanted Earl to be right. He wanted air in his lungs. And there was. He could breathe, although deep green water lay around and above him.

Earl was working on Heather now, hitting her on the back, urging her to breathe. Gradually she stopped writhing and began to take quick, shallow breaths. Sitting up, she looked wonderingly about her.

"We can breathe underwater?"

Earl replied firmly, "No, it's just illusion. There is no water."

"Are you sure?" Welly said, ducking as a twenty-foot-long finned snake sailed serenely overhead. Smaller fish darted about in the glimmering water. Beside them, on the sandy ocean floor, feathery plants waved in the currents, and shelled creatures scrambled over slimy rocks.

"Look!" Heather said, jumping up, her fear almost forgotten. "A ship!"

They looked up to the light-shimmering surface. A storm raged silently there, and a great ship tossed about on the waves. As they watched, the prow dipped under, and the whole ship upended and began a slow, deathly dive. The delicate shape was all grace and beauty as it spun downward. A few figures swirled from its decks and were carried off by the currents.

"That ship!" Earl yelled. "An Eldritch ship. Quick, run to it!"

He bounded off over the sea bottom, and the other two ran after him, dodging fish and clusters of barnacle-encrusted rocks. As Welly leaped over it, a many-armed sack recoiled and loosed an inky black cloud.

The beautiful ship hung nearly above them. Heather screamed to Earl to keep out from under it, as in eerie silence it settled to the ocean floor. Great clouds of green-gold silt welled up into the water, swirling around them, blinding them and dissolving at last into the wind and the weak afternoon sunlight.

Welly and Heather stumbled to their knees in what had been a cluster of sea anemones. The snow was cold and dry under their hands as they crouched, gasping and shaking their heads. They looked at each other. Their clothes weren't even wet. No seaweed dripped from their hair.

Welly began laughing, and Heather joined him, taking in great beautiful lungfuls of air. When the two finally quieted and dried their eyes, they looked up to see Earl standing above them, a relieved smile on his face.

"Quite an illusion, wasn't it?" he said.

Welly sat up. "I can hardly believe it wasn't real. I mean, it was all there. Did you see any of it?"

Earl sat down beside them. "Oh, yes, I saw it. But if you're trained, there are ways to tell illusion from reality. It was a beautiful job, though, technically superb. She must have been perfecting her talent all these years, because she never used to be as good as that."

"Could it really have killed us?" Welly asked. "Even if it was just an illusion?"

Earl nodded. "If a person's mind believes he's dying, then often he dies."

Heather frowned. "But if Morgan knew it wouldn't fool you, why did she try? Just to show off?"

"Well, there may have been some of that. But basically, it wasn't aimed at me, I'm afraid. It was aimed at you."

The two looked startled. "But she doesn't even know us," Welly protested.

"No, but she's quite astute. She recognized that you two are important to me, so she tried to hurt me through you."

"Oh, that's fine," Heather said dryly. "Then we needn't take it personally that she tried to kill us." She stood up and was brushing snow off her knees when something occurred to her. "Does she know about your . . . your little problem with magic?"

Earl shook his head. "I don't think so. If she did, she'd have gone at me directly by now." He scowled at his boots. "I suspect she's stayed in the world all these years and moved right along with its shifting magical forces. She may not even know that they have shifted. And right now, her ignorance may be our best defense."

Welly stood up and readjusted his pack. "Well, I certainly hope she doesn't try another trick like that. It's incredible that it was all fake. The ship and everything."

"In a way," Earl said, "that part wasn't fake. That's where she went a little overboard, if you'll excuse the pun, in her obsession for accuracy."

"What do you mean?" Welly asked.

"Well, the first part, the returning sea, was all her creation. But the undersea part—I don't think she made that up. Such a complete illusion needs background detail, and Morgan probably hasn't spent enough time on ocean floors to store up all those images. What she did was call up images from the past. She clearly reached far, far back. You can tell by the sea serpent and the ship."

"Yes," Heather said, looking around them suddenly. "Why were you so anxious to reach that ship?"

"Because it was an Eldritch ship. And since those were real images, that ship once actually sank here."

"But so what?" Welly said. "I mean, who are these Eldritch?"

"You probably know the term *elf* better. But they aren't pixies sitting in flowers! They're one of the races of Faerie. When our two worlds were closer, many Eldritch lived in this one. Even later, there was coming and going between them. My own family has Eldritch blood in it.

"I tried to see where the ship sank because I want to find the wreck. Come on. I threw my pack on the spot just before the illusion faded."

The two followed him to where the pack lay on a patch of snow-covered ground, indistinguishable from anything around it. Welly kicked at the snow. "Why exactly do we want to find this old wreck?"

Earl squatted down and spread his hands over the ground. "Because there are certain Eldritch things that would be useful to us now. Many of the materials they used are not affected by age."

He shifted his search to another spot. The others watched as their friend crawled over a large area of ground, face tense, the fingers of both hands spread like questing spiders.

Finally he grunted with satisfaction. "Here, this may be something." He stood up and kicked at the ground. "Wish I could use magic, but I'd probably melt everything. We'll have to dig."

He pried a rock from the ground and began gouging into the half-frozen earth. Heather and Welly did the same.

Welly was thinking they'd been digging forever when his rock struck something hard enough to send shocks up his arm. He poked and scraped at it until a metallic gleam

showed through the dirt. The others joined him, and soon
they'd unearthed the object he'd found and others stacked
under it.

"Swords!" Welly breathed.

"That's what I hoped for. The Eldritch made wonderful swords with their own enchantments forged right into
them."

"Magic swords?" Heather whispered.

Earl chuckled. "Not quite. At least they're not guaran-
teed to slay dragons. But even ordinary Eldritch swords
have certain built-in protections and ease of use. And from
our experiences so far, I'd say we can use some good
weapons."

Reverently he pulled six red-gold blades from the ragged
hole. Brushing away the clinging dirt, he spread them on
the snow. "Choose whichever feels right in your hand.
They serve masters best if the match is right."

Heather ran her fingers over the smooth sunset-
colored metal, and finally she pulled out a short, delicate
blade, its hilt carved like a flower-entwined branch.

Welly knew which he wanted immediately. He pulled
out the sword with the pommel that ended in an arched
horse's head, like the chess piece in his pocket. Earl's choice
had a tapered crosspiece adorned with two hawk heads.

With the point of his blade, Earl poked around in the
empty hole. "Ah, I thought there was something more."

Under the spot where the lowest sword had lain, he
brushed away some of the loose crumbly earth. For an instant, Heather thought she glimpsed a small bag of wonderfully embroidered cloth. But at Earl's touch, it vanished
with a puff of dust. Scattered through the dirt, though, was
a sparkle of colors, a dozen faceted jewels of different hues

and sizes. Scooping them up, Earl held them in the light while the others gazed in wonder. They'd seldom seen real jewels, and these twinkled with a depth of color they'd scarcely imagined.

"These might be useful," Earl said as he fished his old coin bag out of his pocket. In a cascade of color, he poured the jewels into it, then returned the pouch to his coat. The three remaining swords he placed back in the hole and covered with dirt.

"We'll leave these for any who need them. Eldritch hoards don't respond well to greed."

Returning to the road, Earl and Heather gave Welly a wide berth as he swung his sword in great sweeping arches over his head. "Just let that Morgan try again!" he yelled.

"That sword won't be much use against her," Earl cautioned. "Though she may well try again. As soon as she decides what I'm really about, she's bound to."

"Doesn't she have any other hobbies besides harassing you?" Heather asked.

"Plenty, I imagine, and all unsavory. But as much as she hates me personally, I'm only secondary. If Arthur is brought back, it will definitely complicate her plans."

"Well, then," Welly said, brandishing his sword in the air, "let's go complicate them!"

10

MIST ON THE MOORS

The road rose steeply to the old Devonshire shore. In the west, the sun slipped below the horizon. Above it hung the ghost of a new moon.

Ahead, on a prominence, lights shone out from a small settlement that had once been a prosperous fishing village. Tired and hungry, the three trudged up the road past the old stone quay that now jutted uselessly into the dry night air.

With relief, they stepped onto the cobbled streets. Above the door of a large whitewashed building, a lantern-lit sign swung in the evening breeze. "The Rose and Unicorn" was lettered neatly above a painting of the mythical beast entangled in a rosebush.

"Roses and unicorns," Earl sighed. "Both equally extinct."

He looked at his two companions a moment. "What do you say we spend tonight in an inn? One of the jewels should buy a warm meal and dry beds, which we deserve, I think, after our mental drenching."

Heather looked excitedly at the glowing windows. She'd never stayed in an inn, but it was the sort of thing people always did in adventures.

The sign creaked merrily overhead as they stepped through the door. The customers sitting and talking at tables in the firelit common room automatically glanced their way, then continued staring. Even with their Eldritch blades concealed under their coats, they were an unusual sight. With brigands and slavers about, healthy, unmutated children did not travel the roads alone.

Ignoring the stares and sudden silence, Earl strode over to where a stout aproned man was clearing trenchers from a table. The boy felt uncomfortably out of practice but attempted an authoritative manner.

"My good man, we would like beds and a good meal for the night, and breakfast in the morning."

The landlord stopped his cleaning and looked Earl up and down. "Well, young master, you can have 'em, if you can pay for 'em."

Earl lowered his voice theatrically. "I have a jewel that is worth a good deal more than any room or board you could possibly provide. But as we can neither eat it nor sleep on it, we will give it in exchange for the very best you have."

The landlord's eyes were akindle, but he spoke skeptically. "Let's see this great treasure, then."

Earl was prepared with a ruby already in his palm. He opened his hand and tipped the jewel onto the table. With a deft flick of a finger, he spun it like a top on the well-worn tabletop. The facets caught and spun off the firelight in kaleidoscopic flames.

Catching his breath, the innkeeper slammed a palm down on his prey. He held it up to his eye, examined it carefully, and bit it. Then he bobbed his head at Earl and smiled ingratiatingly. "You shall have the best, young sirs and mistress. The very best." And he bustled off to the kitchen.

"That was fun," Earl said in a low voice as they took a table close to the fire. "I didn't have the gall to do that sort of thing the last time I was fourteen."

The meal lived up to the promise. They were served fresh milk and a large pie with both meat and mushrooms in it. At the school on a high day, they might have one or the other, but never both. There was a side dish of fried onions, and the host even brought out a dessert—biscuits with a dollop of rare gooseberry preserves.

Welly and Heather agreed they'd never tasted anything so delicious as this last. Earl knew that he had, but since it was some two thousand years earlier, it hardly mattered.

After the meal, the landlord took them upstairs to their room. It was clean and cheery, warmed by the brick chimney from the common room below. At least half of the windowpanes overlooking the street were of real glass. A small rag rug lay on the plank floor, and the two beds were piled with reasonably fresh ticking and abundant blankets. It was clearly the best room in the house, reserved for travelers of consequence.

Earl dismissed the landlord, conveying that the room was acceptable but certainly no more than their due. Then, as soon as the man left the room, Earl set about defending it. It would clearly need defending. Here were three obviously wealthy children traveling unescorted and apparently unarmed.

Since the swordsmanship of two of the three was untried, Earl decided on a magic defense. If he could make it work, that would at least eliminate the need for setting watch.

A door guardian would be sufficient, he decided, since the windows were reasonably inaccessible. After opening the door and checking to make sure the hall was empty, he tried conjuring a guardian snake to coil about the door handle. What he produced, however, was a vase of daffodils. Heather exclaimed that these were really lovely, but Earl wasn't pleased. The next attempt converted the daffodils into an ostrich, which, though alarmingly large, was not suitably aggressive. Then in rapid succession they went through a tennis racket, a guinea pig, and a potato pancake. Earl was on the verge of hysteria when the next apparition proved to be a dozen large centipedes. He gratefully accepted these and set them about the doorknob and threshold with accompanying protective charms.

The effect, though not as impressive as the five-foot cobra he had aimed for, was nonetheless successful— judging by the yowls and retreating footsteps that disturbed them in the middle of the night.

In the morning, Earl spoke the dismissing formula, and the three children watched their wriggling guardians puff into nothing.

Before heading down to breakfast, Welly said, "Earl, I think I should send some sort of message to my parents. They'll worry when they hear I've left Llandoylan. Even if I can't explain what I'm doing, I can let them know I'm all right."

Earl frowned. "Of course you should, and I should have suggested it. I guess there's not much responsible adult left in me. We can get pen and paper from the landlord, and he can send the letter with the next traveler north. Heather, why don't you write your family, too?"

She snorted. "Those people don't need me. The one thing better than not having me home is not having me anywhere. But I'll write, even if only to make them feel guilty because they weren't worried."

After leaving the inn, they exchanged an emerald for

food and a sack of coins. Earl considered using other gems to buy horses, but neither of the others had ever ridden a horse. And although the shaggy three-toed beasts were considerably lower to the ground than the ones Earl had known, they were also a great deal feistier. So rather than risk broken necks, they continued on foot.

At the edge of town, where an ancient stone pillar guarded the crossroads, they stopped to consider their route. So far, traveling by road hadn't seemed any freer from danger, either natural or supernatural, than traveling cross-country. So they decided to strike off straight southwest.

Not far from the crossroads, they knew they were being followed. Two men were strolling over the open country, parallel with them and keeping pace, although their longer legs could soon have put them well ahead.

Earl figured that one, at least, had visited them during the night; his hand was newly bandaged. Concluding that they might already be wavering in their intent, Earl turned and whipped out his sword. The two men consulted hastily. With casual menace, Earl moved toward them, his bearing suggesting he knew how to handle his sword far better than his age implied. The men turned, and a retreating walk soon broke into a run.

Smiling, Earl rejoined the others and stuck his sword back in his belt.

"Can you really use that thing?" Welly asked in awe.

"Riding with Kings Uther and Arthur, even a bookish wizard learned how to use a sword." He noticed Heather still looked doubtful. "Besides, I wasn't a doddering old man all the time, you know!"

The hillside soon led them onto the moor. With only a light snow cover and the ground frozen hard as stone, they made good time. Their first two days proved uneventful except for occasional glimpses of wildlife: albino deer, birds, and several feral cats.

On the third day, a stiff wind drove at them from the west. By afternoon, it carried a fine dry snow, which sifted into their clothes and rustled over the ground like sand.

Toward evening, they saw through the gusts of snow a cluster of tall stones off to their left. Welly suggested they shelter there, but Earl insisted such places were dangerous, though he didn't elaborate. So they passed the stones by, and looking back, Heather admitted that their stark shapes alone on the moor were vaguely unsettling.

They spent a cold, uncomfortable night huddled against a rocky bank. By morning, the snow had changed to large wet flakes and was falling much faster. Eating a quick breakfast, they hurried on, hoping that movement would warm them. The wind blew with rising force. Snow swirled thickly in the air and piled the ground in deep foot-clogging drifts. Around noon, they stumbled upon a cluster of stone ruins, and Earl suggested they hole up there and wait out the storm.

The ruins were a group of circular stone huts set partway into the ground. Their domed roofs were largely gone, and in some the walls were broken away, leaving nothing but round rubble-filled depressions. The whole site breathed an aura of great age.

When they had crawled into a hut more intact than most, Heather said to Earl, "I thought you warned us to stay away from ancient stone places."

"It was the circles and tombs I meant, the sacred sites. The ancients who built those dealt in powers we'd best avoid. But this was just a farm village."

Next day the storm was worse. It howled and shrieked

outside their refuge, curtaining the air with white. Earl told stories of old kings and warriors and workers of magic. After a while, he wondered if he told them to entertain the others or to comfort himself. Maybe Morgan was right. Maybe he was still tied to the old, dead world and had no place in this.

Angrily he shoved the thought aside. Long storms always depressed him. He brought out his wooden flute and played lively warming tunes.

The next day, the storm subsided around noon, but temperatures dropped rapidly. Cold cut through their heavy clothes like keen-edged knives.

Earl had been struggling for several days to regain control over fire. He still wasn't able to start one from scratch. At times nothing happened, and at others he produced alternatives that were quite alarming. But once Welly had kindling started with flint and steel, Earl could now sustain it without further fuel. It was a small triumph, though, and a frustrating contrast to his former skills. Dejectedly he wondered if his power would ever be realigned with this world.

The following day proved even colder than the last. Every minute outside left skin tingling and painful for hours. Deep breaths drew needles of ice into their lungs.

The incredible cold, however, drove the almost perpetual murkiness from the atmosphere. Through the open roof, they saw above them a clear, icy blue. Heather kept leaning back against the stone wall and gazing up. A wonderful shade for eyes, she thought. Far better than the muddy shade of her own.

Much of that day Earl seemed lost in thought, apparently not cheerful thought. Heather took up the task of entertaining by telling stories she had absorbed in her constant reading.

One was an ancient tale, *How the Elephant Got His Trunk*. None of the three had ever seen an elephant, and they weren't certain if it was mythical or merely extinct. Earl doubted the scientific validity of that method for altering a species' nose. But the story brought him out of his gloom.

Another story was *The Hound of the Baskervilles*. Partway through, however, Heather realized that their setting gave this tale an uncomfortable reality, and she would have stopped if her listeners hadn't demanded to hear how it came out. They were particularly delighted when the great detective, Sherlock Holmes, hid in a neolithic stone hut on the windswept moors. But her vivid account of the chilling climax left them all listening for the sound of distant howling.

After several uncomfortable minutes, they submerged themselves in Heather's verbatim recitation of the tale in which "Pooh and Piglet Go Hunting and Almost Catch a Woozle." The resultant mood was more comfortable.

That night the sky remained clear. For the first time in their lives, Welly and Heather saw a whole sky filled with stars, unobscured by the lingering dust pall of the Devastation. There were more stars than they'd ever imagined. They glinted like chips of ice, crystalline and brittle, set in a bowl of deepest black. Heather thought that this one sight made up for all the hardships and dangers. She could hardly sleep for the beauty spangled overhead.

By morning, the high clouds had returned again, curtaining the sky. The air seemed less bitter. Eagerly the three shouldered their packs and emerged from the ruins, looking about them at the snow-covered world. It seemed criminal to plow into the sweeping drifts and mar the untouched whiteness that spread to every horizon. The fallen flakes, when they did step into them, were distinct and feathery and squeaked underfoot.

Going was slow, and not entirely because of the deep snow. Free from days of confinement, the three were bursting with exuberance. Heather and Earl took to diving into the deepest drifts and cavorting about like ancient sea animals. After carefully tucking his glasses away, Welly joined them. It felt very good.

They hadn't gone many miles from the huts when darkness confined them again, this time to an old stone sheep pen. Temperatures continued to rise through the night, and by morning they were in a midwinter thaw.

The snow became sloppy and less pleasant to walk through. Its wetness soaked their boots and trousers. As the vast fields of snow began melting, mists rose across the moors. That night they were cold, wet, and miserable, and by morning the mists had coalesced into a real fog.

Dank whiteness closed around them. Sky and ground became one. Only Earl's sense of their goal kept them moving in a straight line. At times the wind blew at the fog, tearing it aside for glimpses of bleak, silent landscape. Then formless vapors rolled around them again, deadening all sight and sound.

They trudged on, Earl in the lead, followed by Welly and then Heather. As she forced herself along, Heather tried to keep her mind as blank as the view around her. Otherwise she thought about being cold, wet, and miserable. It was totally expected when a bank of slush sucked at a sodden boot and pulled it off. She groaned and sank into the snow to probe about with chilled fingers until she pulled her boot free. Tugging it back on, she dragged off her wet gloves and fumbled stupidly over the laces. At last she stood up and resumed her march.

But now she couldn't see the other two, not even a glimpse of a retreating back. She wasn't even sure in which direction she should look for them. Panic pricked her stupor, and she cursed herself for not having called out when she stopped.

She called now, but the sound seemed dull and muted, swallowed up in the fog. She tried again, louder, and thought she heard an answering call. Stumbling off in the direction it seemed to have come from, she called again. There might have been another answer, if it wasn't the wind, but it came more from the left. She shifted direction and labored on.

Her heart leaped. She must have been right. Through the shredding fog, she caught sight of a shape, no, two shapes in the mists ahead. She hurried forward, sobbing in relief.

The fog closed, then swirled away again, and the shapes were nearer. Only there were more than two. She slowed down and stopped. They were stones, tall standing stones, jutting from the ground like malformed teeth. Wisps of fog whipped around them, making them vanish and reappear as though part of a dance.

She wanted to turn and run in the other direction, but she didn't know which other direction was right. At least these stones were solid, and if she stayed here, she'd be at some fixed point. If she called, maybe the others could find her.

Hesitantly she passed between two of the looming gray

shapes. She could see now that they were ranged roughly in a circle. Some were tall and erect, while a few tilted at crazy angles, and others lay half-buried in the earth.

She stood waiting, calling from time to time. But the feeble sound didn't seem to reach beyond the stones. A numbing chill slowly spread up her spine. Something, she felt, was behind her. It was not her friends.

Clamminess, like a hand, clutched her shoulder. She tried to scream, but her throat was frozen. Her legs couldn't move. They were pillars of stone like those around her. Weakly she fought against heavy gray thoughts. The thoughts solidified around her, encasing her in their hardness. She would stand here in the cold forever. Millennia would come and go, stars would wheel overhead. She would be untouched, unchanging stone.

11

Refuge

Heather stood immobile, blank eyes staring blindly into time and space. At some meaningless point, she saw a flicker of movement. It was passing, insignificant. There were sounds, too. Words, perhaps. But what did they mean to her?

They came again, incessantly, beating on her. "Move," they said. "Move out of the circle."

Move? How could she move? Her legs were solid pillars of rock. The words were foolishness. But they came again, chipping at her solidity. And slowly her legs did move. They lifted and came ponderously down again. Closer to the edge of the circle. Yes, perhaps the voice was right. Perhaps she should move out of the circle.

The voice beat at her brain, thawing it. Warming blood pulsed through her body. The cold gripped tightly at her shoulder, tugging. But steadily she moved against it, cracking its hold. Another tottering step and another. She fell forward between stones, free of the circle.

Dazed, she rolled over in the snow. Earl and Welly stood over her just outside the stone ring, their swords drawn.

"Now!" Earl yelled, and both of them plunged their blades into a roiling column of smoke that hovered just beyond the gap she'd fallen through.

The blades met no resistance, but the shapeless form suddenly writhed and folded in on itself. A hollow, whispering sound, and the shape swirled away to the other side of the circle. It thinned and vanished on a gust of wind.

Returning swords to their belts, Earl and Welly helped Heather to her feet.

"Talk, sympathize, scold, whatever you want," she said weakly, "but let's do it away from here!"

The fog was lifting now, all over the moor. With the two boys supporting Heather, they moved as fast as they could until the stone circle was hidden behind a ridge. Then gratefully they settled onto a rock—once Earl had satisfied himself that it was a perfectly natural and neutral rock.

After a long silence, Heather whispered, "That was the most evil thing I've ever imagined."

Earl squeezed her arm. "Foul, maybe, but not really evil. Stonewraiths aren't good or evil. They have their own rules. But they are very, very possessive."

Heather groaned.

For the rest of that day, they were propelled by that horror behind. They caught sight of several other standing stones and a huge stone table, which Earl said had been a Bronze Age tomb. These they earnestly avoided. The night was spent in the open, huddled around a magically sustained fire.

Just before morning, it began raining. It rained on and off all day. Their clothes, though designed for cold and damp, were finally overtaxed. Now the children were constantly wet and chilled.

As the afternoon wore on, temperatures dropped slightly, turning the rain to sleet. Liquid ice poured out of the sky, solidifying as it hit. Soon the ground was covered with ice and was treacherously slippery. Finally they took cover under a rocky outcrop where a skeletal bush gave the weak illusion of shelter. The icefall continued through the night, twice almost dousing the fire. Toward dawn, it tapered off.

The sun rose on a new world. Everything was glazed with ice. As far as they could see, the moor glinted and reflected back the light of the sun like a rippled mirror. The bare branches overhead glistened like sun-touched jewels.

This beauty, however, was flawed. Walking was like stepping on wet glass. They could scarcely put one foot in front of the other without falling.

They hadn't gone far from the night's camp when Welly lost his footing at the top of a hill. He catapulted onto his back and, arms and legs flailing, shot down the slope. He reached the bottom and began yelling. Heather and Earl, fearing he was hurt, sat down and deliberately slid down the hill after him.

When they reached Welly, he was near hysterics. They gathered that in his wild slide, his glasses had flown off. Without his glasses, Welly was so helpless he could not even look for them. So he sat miserable and blind while Heather and Earl crawled up the glassy surface searching. At last, halfway up, Heather found them, a glint of metal and glass on a field of ice. They were unbroken.

The rest of the day was spent scrambling over the ice-slicked landscape. As the bruises and cold built up, tobogganing lost its appeal. When in late afternoon they made it to the top of another rise and saw an inhabited farmstead beyond, it was as though they had glimpsed paradise.

Heather stood for a moment gazing at the stone house, a gray column of smoke curling from its squat chimney. "I don't care if the place is peopled by a whole family of stonewraiths. Let's visit."

"Wraiths don't need fires," Earl told her. "But at the moment, I'd hardly care if they did, so long as they shared."

In minutes, three bedraggled children stood knocking on the low wooden door. A shuffling inside, and the door cracked open. A man's bearded face, set in cautious curiosity, peered out at them.

After a second, he threw the door wide. "Martha, John Wesley! Come here; it's all right. It's rare we have visitors, but I can tell children needing a warm fire when I see them."

The three were hustled inside. Their sodden coats were removed, and they were plumped down on benches before the fire. They were just beginning to thaw when mugs of steaming hot soup were thrust into their hands. They drank eagerly while the farm family smiled and watched them.

Earl put down his mug. "Sir and madam, I can't tell you how grateful we are to be taken in and fed like this."

"Well, it's only human charity," the man said. "And you looked like you could use it. But we're not 'sir and madam.' We're the Penroses. I'm Josiah, and this is my wife, Martha, and our son, John Wesley."

After their introductions, Welly's and Heather's eyes widened at Earl's account of how they'd gotten to the Penroses' door. "We all three were students at a school in Glamorganshire, but last month the school had a fire and had to close. Since Heather and Welly haven't any family, they're coming with me to my home in Cornwall. But we ill-advisedly took a shortcut over the moors and have had some rough days of it."

"I shouldn't doubt you have, poor lambs," the woman said. "But you'll stay the night with us now. We've extra bedding to spread by the fire. I don't imagine you've been sleeping too well out there, what with the cold and wet and the strange things on the moors."

"No, madam . . . Mrs. Penrose, we haven't."

The motherly woman was soon bustling about, laying out extra ticking and blankets by the broad hearth. As she helped them out of their dank clothing, she commented, "You may have to stay over with us an extra day just so I can wash your clothes. They're so stiff, they almost stand by themselves."

That night, sleeping dry by the fire, tucked into clean, warm blankets, they seemed, indeed, very close to paradise.

In the morning, Welly woke up hot and shaky. Everything around him seemed oddly distant. Mrs. Penrose proclaimed that he was sick and shouldn't budge from his bed and that, anyway, it was a mercy they weren't all down with fever after what they'd been through.

Welly got steadily worse. For days, his skin was hot and dry, and he developed a wracking cough. He swam in and out of consciousness, always followed by a swarm of images. There were smoky wraiths and trolls dancing on mountains of water, and a beautiful pale woman with black hair and green eyes who alternately offered him gooseberry preserves or ripped off his glasses and stamped on them.

Heather and Mrs. Penrose cared for him, keeping him covered as he thrashed about, bathing his forehead with damp cloths, and making him swallow bitter medicinal concoctions.

Earl was worried for his friend, and he was toweringly frustrated. He had been a fair master of healing magic, but he was afraid to try it now for fear he'd kill rather than cure.

Heather noticed how glum Earl had become, and guessing the problem, she told him over and over again that he wasn't to blame. But he wouldn't be comforted. He was ashamed of his impotence, and for a time tried to avoid her, the one person who knew he should be able to help.

He threw himself instead into helping Josiah and little John Wesley around the farm. The Penrose lands were on the edge of the moor and, except for a considerable kitchen garden, were devoted to livestock. When the snow cover was light, the dark-wooled sheep, shaggy ponies, and shaggier cattle were let out onto the moor. When it was heavy or an icefall sealed off the grass, the stock was kept in pens and barns and fed on the red succulents, or "blood-plants," the travelers had seen on their way.

"These are wonderful plants," Josiah told Earl one day as they shoveled the dried leathery pods into a bin. "The minister calls them 'God's Mercy on the Survivors.' They say that when everything else stopped growing after the Devastation, the blood-plants and moor grass just took over. The stock'll eat blood-plants dried or fresh, and they make fine fuel. When times are hard, people can eat 'em, too, though if you ask me, they taste like rancid pickles."

Working in the stock barn or on the moors, Earl often found seven-year-old John Wesley tagging along. The boy was small for his age. On one side, his arm was shriveled and his spindly leg was too short, giving him a rolling limp. Yet he seemed irrepressibly happy. He had no schooling and wasn't likely to get any. But he understood his world.

When the two were alone, Earl told the younger boy

stories, some from reading at Llandoylan and others well-disguised adventures of his own. In return, John Wesley taught the things he knew, natural things that the wizard Merlin had known but that in this world had changed almost beyond recognition. Earl learned the new weather signs, and the names and natures of those few new plants and creatures that had replaced the many old.

On his bed by the fireplace, Welly lay ill for a week. But at last the fever broke. He was tired and very weak, but the coughing was down to a rasp, and he could sleep without those fever-conjured companions.

His first real food was bread soaked in vegetable broth. Heather brought him a bowl and sat down by his bed to talk. She told him what she and Earl had been doing and about the little newborn lamb John Wesley had shown her.

Welly licked up the last drop in his bowl. "These folks sure have been good to us. Leave it to me to get sick and be a burden." He sighed. "I've held up Earl's plans, too. Is he mad?"

"No, not mad. Not at you, anyway. But he's upset that he wasn't able to help you."

"Well, that's not his fault. He would've if he could. I'm not blaming him."

"I know. But convincing him not to blame himself is another matter."

Welly sighed again and looked down at his hands, plump and dark against the white sheet. "Well, something good ought to have come of this. But look, a week of not eating, and I'm as fat as ever. It's not fair!"

"Welly!" she admonished. "We're so happy you're better; nobody cares what you're shaped like!"

Later that night as Welly was sleeping peacefully by

the fire and Josiah and the two boys were out tending to the stock, Heather echoed what Welly had said and what she had been thinking. "You know, Mrs. Penrose, you've all been very kind to us. There's no way we can ever repay you."

"Lord's mercy, child, you've been repaying us every moment you're here. If the Lord had allowed it, this house would be full of children. But that hasn't been His choice for us. We've only little John Wesley now."

The woman sighed. "I'm sorry you never met our older son, Charles. He was a good lad, and strong. He was born healthy and stayed that way until he got the bone sick and right away died. Poor little John Wesley has had afflictions since he was born. So maybe that's enough; maybe he'll stay with us."

"I hope so, Mrs. Penrose. He certainly is a cheerful boy."

"He is, and he loves your Earl. Follows him around everywhere. Not surprising. That Earl is a fine lad, and very bright. He's sure to make something of himself someday."

"He has . . . I mean, he has been told that."

"And he's been such a help around here. Since Charles died, it's been hard on Josiah, running this place. And you've been a help to me, too, Heather, you know that."

The woman dried the last bowl and put it in the cupboard. "What I'm saying is that we've been very happy having you here. You can stay as long as you wish, and . . . And if any of you wanted to stay longer and kind of make this your home, well, that would be fine, too."

Heather felt her insides knot with yearning. This woman wanted her. She wanted her here to share this home.

Heather closed her eyes and swallowed a lump that had risen in her throat. "Mrs. Penrose, sometimes I think there is nothing I want more than to stay here. But we can't. Earl has things he must attend to, and Welly and I are bound to go with him."

"I know. You three are very close," the woman said with a sigh. "But think on it."

Welly's recovery was steady. After another few days, though still weak, he was walking about. Heather and John Wesley took him to the barn to meet the newborn lamb. Welly, seldom comfortable with animals, had to be coaxed to pat the wooly head. But once he had, the baby was soon licking mashed bloodplant from his hand. Its small pink tongue lapping his fingers was flannelly and warm.

At last Welly was well enough for the three to consider resuming their journey. But it was a decision that day after day they put off. There were things to do around the farm, and Josiah was showing them the basics of horseback riding. Conversation only skirted around their departure.

One afternoon, Welly was outside exercising his new vigor by shoveling manure into trays where it would be dried for fuel. The clouds were swollen yellow-brown with coming snow. John Wesley was in the barn trying to convince the lamb to wear and not eat the braided grass collar Heather had made for it.

Inside the farmhouse, Heather and Mrs. Penrose were rewinding tangled skeins of yarn. Seated on the floor in front of the fireplace, Earl and Mr. Penrose were repairing a broken yoke. As they worked, Josiah told Earl what he hoped to trade for this year when the roads to the market towns were passable.

Suddenly Welly burst through the door. Startled, they all looked up. "There's something awful out there!" he gasped. "It's got John Wesley cornered against the barn!"

Instantly Earl was out the door. He ran into the yard

but skidded to a halt when he saw what waited. The animal was the size of a deer and slender. But its legs ended in wicked-looking talons, and its tail was long and whiplike. Short reddish fur on the body lengthened into a mane. Black eyes glinted from behind a cruel beak.

This was no natural mutation, Earl knew. There was something too bizarre, too intentionally evil about it.

The thing swiveled its head and gave Earl a cold, appraising stare. Then it turned back and continued its step-by-step advance toward John Wesley. The boy stood pinned with terror against the barn door.

Without pausing, Earl hurled a magic attack at the creature. The only effect was a strong odor of roses and a melted patch of snow. The beast kept stalking the boy. Earl tried again, this time producing only a sound—the jangled discord of a falling harp.

He screamed in frustration, and at least the creature stopped a moment and looked at him, beady eyes snapping in annoyance. Well, Earl decided, if all the magic he had left was personal defense, he'd use that as a shield!

Several bounding steps, and he stood between the creature and the boy. The animal crouched and opened its beak. Shrieking, it lunged at Earl. He threw up an arm, and the beast recoiled. Cautious now, it advanced more slowly, making little feints and jumps. Not turning around, Earl grabbed John Wesley's arm and moved backward, always keeping the boy shielded. Hissing in its throat, the creature leaped again. The air cracked, and again it was rebuffed. Earl continued stepping back. The beast kept pace, lunging and snapping, but never closing.

The retreating dance went on and on until, behind him, Earl felt the barrier he sought. A waist-high stone wall ran across one corner of the yard, cutting it off from an old quarry hole.

Still clutching John Wesley behind him, Earl taunted the beast. He poked and kicked toward it. Reaching down, he grabbed a handful of pebbles and threw them at its face.

Its eyes blazed. The creature hissed and rumbled ominously in its chest. Feigning indifference, Earl turned away and looked toward the farmhouse and the four people watching in frozen horror. Out of the corner of his eye, he saw the beast crouch. Muscles rippled under the smooth red fur. With a piercing shriek, it leaped at Earl's head. Instantly he threw himself and John Wesley to the ground.

The animal sailed over their sprawled bodies, its talons missing them by inches. The note in its cry rose sharply. It flailed the air, then tumbled into the rocky pit to lie twitching and broken at the bottom.

In seconds, the others were with the two boys, helping them up. Mrs. Penrose hugged her boy to her, murmuring endearments. Josiah slapped Earl on the back. "I don't know how you did it, boy, but that was wonderful! You certainly had that creature fuddled."

Heather and Welly peered over the wall at the form splayed on the rocks below. Even dead, its strangeness made them shiver. They wondered what it had been or, more disturbing, where it had come from.

Mr. Penrose echoed their thoughts. "No question about it, that's the strangest creature I've ever seen, and we've known some odd things on these moors."

They took the boys into the house and fussed over them some more. John Wesley, rapidly rebounding, chattered about how wonderful Earl had been in fooling the "birdcat." Earl said very little.

After supper, as Mrs. Penrose stood to remove the plates, Earl spoke up. "Mr. and Mrs. Penrose, I think the time's come for us to be on our way again, or at least for me to be on mine. We've been a burden to you long enough."

"Oh, lad, don't say that," Mrs. Penrose said, sitting down. "You've been anything but a burden. Why, you just saved our boy's life!"

"But if I hadn't been here, his life would never have been endangered. You are good people, and this is a fine, peaceful home. But the longer I stay, the more of a threat you're all under."

Mr. Penrose cleared his throat. "Well, now, I can't exactly see how that can be, lad. That mutie beast just chanced upon the place, drawn by the sheep, I should think, not by any of us."

"I can't expect you to understand it. But I attract that kind of trouble the way a lightning rod attracts lightning. Welly and Heather would agree, I think."

The two looked unhappy, but reluctantly nodded their heads.

Earl continued. "So I really have to go. It would be best to leave now, tonight." The others looked startled. "But I'll wait until morning. I think it might be best if Heather and Welly did not come with me, but I'll leave that to them."

"Of course we're coming with you," Heather protested, twisting a braid.

"Certainly. We have to," Welly added.

"No, you don't have to! You would be a good deal safer if you didn't. But you make your own decisions." Abruptly he excused himself to go pack his rucksack.

Breakfast the next day was not a happy meal. Earl was brooding and silent, and Mrs. Penrose seemed on the verge of tears. Heather felt she was tearing down the middle, and looking at Welly, she knew he felt the same. Only John Wesley seemed unaffected, chattering about what he'd do the next time any sneaky old birdcat came their way.

Mrs. Penrose substituted several of the children's old, frayed blankets for warm ones of her own making, and she stuffed food in every cranny the three packs provided. Finally the three stood outside the farmhouse door, coats on, hoods pulled up, and packs once again on their backs.

After Mrs. Penrose had kissed them all and lavished them with tearful good-byes, Earl pulled his hand from a pocket and extended it to her.

"This isn't payment. There's no way to repay your kindness. But it is beautiful."

He rolled onto her palm a large opal the size of a pigeon egg. Holding the stone to the morning light, she gasped. It was alive with fire and color, as though all the world's sunsets were captured in its depths.

John Wesley jumped to see, and his mother brought it down to him. "Oh, that's the prettiest thing in the world!"

"I hope you enjoy it," Earl said, tousling the boy's hair. "Just don't play marbles with it and lose it down a rat hole. Your folks might enjoy it, too."

Together the three children walked out the farmyard gate. They stopped several times to wave, the last as the road topped a hill. The farm seemed small and safe in its little valley. The three Penroses stood at the door, waving.

As they dropped down the crest, Heather whispered, "Perhaps we'll come back someday." Welly swallowed and nodded, but Earl strode ahead saying nothing.

Snow had fallen during the night, dusting the world in fresh whiteness. The road wound through it, a smooth

ribbon of white on white, making its way south to the old
coast. They had walked in silence for several miles when
suddenly Earl stopped and turned back to them.

"No, it's no good. I can't let you come with me."

"What!" Welly exclaimed.

"I'm putting you in too much danger. What I said to
the Penroses goes for you, too. Where I am, there's danger.
And I haven't the power to protect you."

"But that creature . . . ," Heather began.

"That creature was no common mutation. I don't
know if Morgan sent it, but it's odd she's left us alone this
long. It's been a wonderful respite, and I almost fooled myself into thinking it could last. But she'll never rest until
she destroys me and anyone helping me."

"But, Earl," Heather protested, "we have to go with you."

"You do not! I've been too cowardly and self-centered
to say that. Long ago, you discharged any obligation you
had to me. It's I who've an obligation to you, to keep you
safe. I said last night the decision was yours. But it's not. I
knew the decision I had to make, and I didn't want to make
it! Go back; go back to the Penroses. I'm sorry I've dragged
you so far from your homes. But they'll be good to you. If
I find Arthur—when I find Arthur—I'll try to come back."

"We can't leave you," Heather shouted. "You need
us to—"

"I don't need you!" His voice was high and frantic. "I
don't need you. I don't need anybody! I have to be alone.
Always!"

Grabbing their shoulders, he spun them around and
shoved them back up the road. They stumbled ahead a few
steps, then stopped. Heather stamped her foot angrily and
turned back. "Earl, that's not . . ."

She fell silent. There was no one to be seen.

Her shock exploded into anger. "So who cares?" she shouted. "Who cares if you don't need us? The Penroses do! They have a place for us. Go on and be alone!"

The only answer was a vast silence and the whisper of drifting snow.

"What now?" Welly whispered. "Do we really turn back?"

Heather was shaking with misery. "I thought that's what I wanted. But I also thought he needed me, needed us. Maybe the Penroses really do. I don't know. What else is there?"

She turned and walked slowly up the road. Welly followed. They trudged on, heads bowed, silent as the wilderness around them.

Finally Heather stopped and raised her head. "I'm so confused. Maybe we ought . . ."

A dark figure stood on the road ahead. Morgan.

12

Through the Furnace

The woman had an ageless beauty. Raven-black hair flowed free from her hood, framing a pale face and eyes of emerald-green. She smiled sadly.

"So, he left you. That's like him. Always thinking first of himself and his own mad plans."

"No," Heather asserted. "He wanted to protect us."

"He didn't want you tagging along and being a bother. But that's his way, always using people for his own ends."

"That's not fair!" Welly protested.

"Fair? Has he been fair to you? He dragged you away from your home, your schooling. He subjected you to discomfort and dangers, most of which you couldn't understand. Think about it—have you ever been so miserable in your lives? Cold and wet, not enough food or sleep, always afraid?"

Heather shook her head slowly. "He didn't mean to . . ."

"He meant to use you. You were helpful in escaping from Llandoylan, in carrying provisions. You kept him company and amused him. But he's through with you now; you're becoming a hindrance. So he's left you alone in the middle of nowhere, hundreds of miles from home."

Heather stamped her foot, angry at herself as much as at Morgan. "No! That's not true! None of it is! What he wants is right; it's good. When he finds . . ." She stopped short.

"Finds Arthur?" Morgan smiled at Heather's horror. "Don't fret. You haven't let out any secrets. I knew that must be his idea. He has a fixation about it, you know. But Arthur's dead. He died in battle two thousand years ago. His bones are dust, like the rest of Merlin's dreams."

"But he . . . ," Welly began.

Morgan looked down at him, her green eyes wide with sympathy. "It's sad, really. Arthur was Merlin's life. He can't accept a world without him. He wasn't there that day to see him die, so now he grasps at fairy tales. It's a sick, mad obsession, and he'll probably follow it to the end of his days. But he shouldn't drag others with him."

The two children stood silent and confused.

Morgan extended her hands toward them. "Come. I never abandon friends in the wilderness. You have a place with me."

They pulled back. "No!"

"Come, now. You followed him because you wanted adventure, to be part of something grand. You've had danger and hardship, but hardly adventure. Come with me and belong to a noble adventure! Oh, no doubt Merlin's filled you with lies about my evil powers. Certainly, I have power, but power can be used for good! Look at this wreck of a world. Look at the chaos, the stupidity! What is needed is order and direction. I can give it that."

She smiled, stepping toward them. "You two are of this world's elite. Together we have the knowledge to remake this world, to overcome petty objections of the ignorant.

And if you join with me, you can share this power. You can be as you want to be, as you are inside. And all the world will see you like that."

She reached out and took their hands. "Come, let me show you what you can be."

Heather looked into Morgan's green eyes, deeply into those eyes, and saw there her own reflection. It was her, it was Heather McKenna. But there was a difference. It was the real her: She was beautiful. Her hair was soft and thick and flowed about her shoulders, the pale blond of winter sun. And her eyes were the ice-blue of a rare bright sky.

She moved among crowds, and people parted for her, murmuring admiration. She mounted marble steps, and her gown swirled around her, the sparkling radiance of sunlight glittering on snow. As she climbed, it flowed into shadowy folds of deep, cold blue.

She reached the top and sat regally on a chair of stone. The world assembled in awe about her. Surely anyone with her beauty would be given whatever she wanted. But what was it she wanted? Oh, yes, animals. She had always liked animals: deer and squirrels, insects, lambs, and birds. Let them come up. They were there but hesitated, milling about. Animals love her. They will come up to her! How can she go down to them, someone of her beauty, her cool beauty? They need her; they love her. Let them come and show it.

They won't come. They don't need her beauty? They won't give the love due her beauty? Then let them wallow, the stupid beasts. She didn't need them. She had gifts enough. Gifts, yes; she had a gift. She raised her hand for all to see. The jewel flashed purple in her ring.

See, a gift! A gift given for her beauty. No, no, for something else, something when she had no beauty. Given for . . .

friendship. A friend gave her the purple jewel, a gift given for her friendship. A gift for a gift, that was right. Her gift, her ring, was . . . to make things right. It had a charm to make things right.

She wanted things to be right. They were not right now. They were wrong. She was not beautiful; she did not need to be. She had love and gave love. She needed friendship, and her friendship was needed. Things should be right; her gift made things right. She clutched the ring and its purple stone—purple like her poor friend's fuddled magic. Her friend who needed her. The magic, the charm, made things right, all crackerjack. Cracker Jack!

The dais cracked, and the marble stairs crumbled. She fell down into purple, into warmth. She was loved, and she loved. Needed and was needed. And she was free.

Morgan smiled as she took Welly's hand and led him up a green hill. He bounded up easily because he was strong and lithe. He mounted his horse, his tall warhorse; his glasses fell away and shattered, yet he could see!

And below him he saw the plain of battle. He had made the battle plan and made it for himself. *He* would lead; all the troops below knew how clever was his plan and how brave his leadership. They cheered and cheered him.

The clash of battle rose from below. His cunning ambush had come about; the battle cry went up, and they shouted his name. Muscular legs gripping his horse's sides, he called out bold instructions. The slaughter was great, and he exulted in it.

Now the enemy broke through and rushed upon his height. He had no fear. Pulling out his great sword, he skillfully guided his steed and beat the enemy back. Nigel and Justin and the other taunters, they shrank back and cried out. The great dukeling cringed before him, and Welly took his sword and plunged it into his body.

The blood spurted red, and Nigel's face crumpled in pain. The boy's friends wailed around him as he lay small and sad upon the ground, and a girl held his broken body and rocked back and forth, back and forth—as another girl had rocked with another dead thing. She had been his friend, that other girl, and he had fought to help her, as another friend had fought to help him.

All below him now wailed in sadness and loss; his troops and the others, the same. He looked down at their pain and agony, and they called out against the misery he'd brought. They cried against his clever plans. He saw them over the head of his horse. His warhorse, his knight's horse. White and smooth, its neck was arched and its ears pricked forward and pricked his fingers also as he clutched at it in his pocket. His knight, from his friend. He was his friend's knight, his friend who fought for him and knighted him and needed him. His friends needed him. And someone called to him. Called that it would be all right. All right! All Cracker Jack!

The call beat on him, blew at him, swept away the sound of battle. Swept him away, far away. And free.

Masked in invisibility, Earl hurried down the road, ignoring his friends' calls. Every step hurt. But it was hurt himself or hurt them. He had made the choice.

Miles passed as he marched doggedly, fixed on his goal. On his longer legs, he moved faster without his companions. That gave him no pleasure. He strove to keep his mind blank, set only on moving forward. But thoughts kept nibbling at the edges, intruding into the blankness.

He was running. Running from the farm, running

from his friends. Running because he could not protect them, protect them from the danger he brought them.

But what was he running to? He had a quest, a mission. Yet so far he had failed. Would it be any different with Arthur? Could he protect his king, who would surely be in far greater danger? Could he be of any real aid to Arthur in the tasks before him in this shattered world?

Earl stopped abruptly in the middle of the road. Was he of any use to anybody? Even to himself, if he dared not keep simple friendships?

Slowly he walked off the road, noting for the first time that snow was falling. The wind was up, sweeping an empty, mournful howl through the wilderness.

He knew what he must do.

Earl stood in the snow and looked into its spinning whiteness. He let his pack slip from his back. Slowly he took off his coat and cast it away from him, and then his jacket and gloves. He would either become one with this world and learn its rhythms, or he would die in it.

He spread his arms, reaching into the sky, and shouted with his mind, "World of my cold and blasted future, I will be one with you! Either as part of your living pulse, your waves of power and life, or dead as your frozen dust. I will be yours. Take me now!"

He looked up into the swirling snow as he had that day when he'd sought only escape, not knowing the danger of what he did, of losing himself forever. Now he knew. The snow fell lazily from the sky, big soft flakes spinning down toward him. He willed to be one with them, those flakes that swirled down at him, up at him, around with him. His soul thinned into them. He was snow, swirling with snow, swirling on the wind.

Bodiless, he blew on the wind. Blew over the world,

blew over the rocks, rasping against their hardness, blew through the trees, jangling their needles with music. He blew through the thatch of houses and churned the smoke of their fires. He blew over the ocean, caressing the water into billowy waves and whipping the crests with foam. He blew high into the sky above the seas and land. He tore at the clouds, shredding them and seeing beyond.

Beyond were the stars, calling in their splendid beauty. He rose up toward them through eternal emptiness, through endless silence. They glowed with the brightness of beginnings.

Yet embers still glowed on the earth behind him. It pulsed with warmth that pulled at him. Pulled him back, back through emptiness; pulled him deep, deep into its core. Its throbbing heat rose outward. It rose up through the rock, through heavy, patient rock that had known only itself, and through higher stone with sunken memories of the sky.

The pulse of warmth rose to the crumbling surface, to the rich soil. Roots sank into it and drew out warmth and life. Plants raised their heads to the sky, bowing in the wind, weighed by the snow, giving nourishment and shelter to life that huddled among them or bounded over them.

The web closed; the patterns settled into place. The swirling snow and empty wind, the pulsing stars, the answering throbs in stone, and the upward surging of life. All were tied in glowing traceries, in interlocking spheres. The web of force and power and rightness was part of all creation and part of him. Part of his cells and consciousness and joy.

• • •

Heather opened her eyes. She was lying on her side on an empty road. Snow sifted silently from the sky. A hand rested in hers. She recoiled, but it was not Morgan's hand; it was Welly's. She squeezed it.

He opened his eyes with a befuddled smile. "Is it all right, then? For both of us?"

"Yes. Yes, I think it is." She looked down at her hand and its glinting purple ring. "But it may not be for him. That was all rot, you know, about his not needing us. He's just a confused kid like the rest of us." She smiled. "He needs me. I know that now. And he needs you, too."

"Maybe. But not as his general."

"As his friend, then."

"Yes, as his friend." He stood up, surveying the white, swirling landscape. "But how do we find him when we can't even see him?"

"He won't stay invisible forever. Down this road, someone's bound to have seen him. We'll find him. We have to."

They started down the southern road, snow slicing across their path in icy blasts. They staggered on against it until the darkness of the storm shaded into the darkness of night.

Dizzy with exhaustion, they took shelter behind a rocky outcrop and slipped into dream-washed sleep.

In the morning, the snow lay deep and quiet about them, but the sky was hazily clear. A smear of orange spread upward from the east. Hastily sharing some bread, the two donned their packs and stepped from their rocky shelter.

They started back to the road and stopped abruptly. Lying half-buried in the snow, some thirty feet away, was a body. Beside it lay a discarded pack, coat, and jacket.

Heather and Welly ran fearfully toward it, then slowed. The sun, just rising in the east, seemed to catch and play along a web of light, a faint intricate tracery that enclosed the snow-covered body. Then the sun cleared the horizon, and the pattern faded.

They hurried to him and dropped to their knees. Heather brushed the snow from his face. "Oh, Earl," she moaned, and clutched at his hand. It was cold as death. His face was serene and pale as the snow.

The eyelids fluttered, disturbing their fringing of ice. Slowly Earl opened his eyes. "It's all right, then?" he whispered, his voice barely audible.

"Yes, all right," Heather sobbed in joy. "It's all, all right."

13

BATTLE ON THE TOR

Together they helped Earl stand, and, retrieving his things, they led him back to their shelter of the night. Stiffly he pulled on jacket and coat and sat down on a rock. With an easy movement of his hand, he started a fire blazing on the surface of the snow. In minutes, life and warmth were surging through his body.

He spoke little of what had happened. He was again in touch with his power, again in harmony with his world and its forces. That was enough for him to share. But he was interested in the halting accounts of the others' ordeals.

When they'd finished, he sighed. "Once Morgan tapped my weakness and ensnared me in it. And I didn't see until too late. I, a wily old wizard! But you saw her traps and broke them. I'm impressed."

"We had help," Heather said softly.

"The only help you had was in yourselves and what your friendship gave those tokens."

Earl stood up and stretched, feeling every fiber of his being tingling and alive. He extinguished his magic flame with a word. "We've all been through the furnace, it seems. Now, let's see how well we are forged."

They shouldered their packs and set off together. Before long, Earl led them from the road, striking across country to the southwest. "Have you a better idea where we're heading?" Welly asked.

"Not really. But I'm more certain that there is someplace worth heading for."

The snow-blanketed fields dropped into a long valley. Down its length ran a dull silver ribbon that flashed back sunlight like the blade of a sword.

"The River Tamar," Earl announced. "The boundary that divides Devon from Cornwall."

The river was frozen into stillness. They found its valley strewn with debris from summer floods. Heading for the river, they picked their way through bits of tree and brush, rocks, and the occasional scrap of human handiwork. Earl moved more slowly, looking thoughtfully about him. Then he cut off on a tangent across the valley floor until, exclaiming with satisfaction, he bent down and examined something.

Welly and Heather followed to see what he'd discovered and found him kneeling by a young uprooted pine, a few brittle needles still clinging to its boughs. Pulling out his sword, Earl began hacking off the branches. The others squatted down and watched, figuring they'd get an explanation in time. At last, he seemed satisfied. The slender trunk, bare of branches and bark, shone a soft yellow. At one end there remained a gnarled claw where the roots had begun.

Jabbing the thin end into the ground, he declared, "There, a first-class staff."

Welly looked dubiously toward the slope on the far side of the valley. "You need a staff? It doesn't look all that steep to me."

Earl flashed him a look of theatrical scorn. "A wizard's staff!" he said with mock thunder, tossing his work from hand to hand, testing its weight. "I was afraid to use one earlier. It helps concentrate power, and the sort of magic I was producing didn't bear concentration."

Heather smiled mischievously. "You mean we might have had a forty-foot-high purple pie?"

Earl laughed. "Something like."

They walked to the edge of the frozen river. Standing on the bank, Earl tapped the surface firmly with his staff. "The Tamar's a lot more narrow here than the Severn where we crossed it. This should be frozen solidly enough to walk on."

Welly and Heather followed him cautiously onto the ice. Its surface had been roughened by the wind but still produced a good slide. In moments, the two were executing glides, swoops, and occasional spills on the frozen river. Earl joined them, using his staff to vault into acrobatics, sometimes ending in a spinning sprawl of arms, staff, and long legs. The valley echoed to whoops and gleeful yells, until at last the three collapsed, exhausted, on the western bank.

Heather looked at Earl and giggled. "I guess you were right. You're definitely a fourteen-year-old, outside and in."

Laughing, he flopped over in the snow and looked at her. "And you were right, too. There're some very good things about being a teenager."

Awkwardly he placed a hand on hers. "And I've learned some other things. There are mistakes I won't make again. I won't deny that I need people."

She smiled shyly. "And I won't deny that I need to be needed."

Rested finally, the three climbed the opposite side of

the valley. Once on the level again, Earl pointed to a dark table-like rise in the south. "Our route takes us by that tor. It's not the goal; I think that lies beyond. But it's an interesting spot nonetheless."

"It's an odd-shaped hill, all right," Welly said.

"It's an old Iron Age hill fort," Earl replied. "Pre-Roman, but when I knew it, the fortifications were still well intact. I imagine it's weathered a bit since."

Welly was interested now. "I've read about them. Weren't they surrounded by banks and ditches?"

Earl nodded. "Most of the people lived outside the forts, but when enemies threatened, they and their livestock moved behind the walls. There are views in all directions. Very defensible. See a lone flat-topped hill anywhere in Britain, and you've probably found an Iron Age hill fort."

Throughout the day, they trudged on toward the tor. Having a fixed goal that drew closer gave a feeling of achievement. But as sunset neared, they still seemed uncomfortably distant. Earl had been feeling more and more uneasy as the afternoon wore on. Now he urged them to greater speed.

"We know Morgan's about, but that in itself doesn't bother me. She may be content just to watch us. But there are other things, evil, distorted things. I feel them. And her long absence earlier worries me. She was up to something, and it may not bode us any good."

"What you're saying," Welly said, panting, "is that we'd better get to that hill fort before nightfall."

"Exactly."

Night was indeed falling when they reached the tor and began scrambling up its steep side. The sky had been unusually clear all day, and now the full moon shone through a high, thin curtain. As they walked, rocks and humps in the snow cast deep black shadows in the silvery light.

At last they reached the top and passed through breaks in the embankments that encircled the crown of the hill. Not long before the Devastation, restorers had cleared the ditch and rebuilt the walls. But there were still major gaps and sagging spots, the work of both time and scavengers seeking building stone.

Still, any walls gave the travelers some feeling of security. Choosing a sturdy section to break the west wind, they gratefully took off their packs and brought out some food. Earl ignited a small domestic fire while Welly rigged up a blanket lean-to against the wall. The bank of clouds along the western horizon suggested they might be due for a storm.

They dined on bread and strips of dried meat, but throughout the meal, Earl kept getting up and walking to the opposite wall to look east. Again and again the hazy moonlight showed only an empty landscape. But this didn't shake his conviction that something was coming.

At last he saw it. A blackness appeared in the east that was not a cloud. It spread inklike over the plain, and the moonlight did not penetrate it. Slowly it rolled toward their hill.

Noting his suddenly rigid attention, the other two joined him. "What is it?" Heather asked quietly.

"An army of sorts. Morgan's army."

With growing alarm, they watched the advance. This, Welly realized, might be the eve of his first battle. But he feared he wasn't feeling the appropriate sentiments of a warrior. Heroes always seemed exultant, eager for the fray. He felt cold and weak. But he would stick it out. And if it proved to be his last battle as well as his first, at least he'd be spared this wait again.

The black wave flowed closer, lapping around the base of the hill. The moonlight and the glow of their own green torches made the enemy visible. Too visible.

"Well, now we know where Morgan spent last month," Earl said bitterly. "On a recruiting drive among the east coast invaders." The mutant creatures below were men and beast and horrible blendings. Most, Earl imagined, were twisted in mind as well as in body: easy conquests for Morgan, ready to hear a voice like hers and follow. He flinched at the thought of what their progress had been like: the steady ravaging of a land that had little left to ravage.

Standing on the ancient earthen battlements, he scanned the crowd below. His eyes and other senses picked out creatures from a world more distorted even than devastated Europe. They reeked of unnatural evil, beings alien to this world and eager to taste its blood.

Sounds drifted from below. Howls and yapping, inhuman laughter and shrieks. Earl left the others and, chanting words under his breath, walked around the wall's perimeter, moving his hand in quick, decisive gestures.

Now the sounds rose in intensity. From out of the dark, roiling crowd moved a figure edged in fiery green. Morgan's black hair and cape blew wildly about her. At her side strode a huge gray wolf, and she rode a beast like the one at the Penrose farm, yet far larger. Its whiplike tail was split in two, and the mane surrounding its cruel face was longer and seemed tipped with fire. Strange ridges ran down its side, suggesting folded wings. Its cry was terrible.

When its unearthly screech had ceased ringing from the sky, Morgan called out Merlin's name.

Earl stepped onto the wall, his voice rolling down in derisive waves. "Morgan, are you and your friends going somewhere? If so, I suggest you save yourself a climb. This hill just goes down again on the other side."

"Little boy, don't joke with me!" she screamed in reply. "I give you one last chance to join me."

"Join with your netherworld friends and all this world's sweepings? No thank you, Morgan. I choose my own companions."

"Children and dreamers; some companions! You are a fool, Merlin. In every age, you are a fool. And you deserve to live in none!"

She shrieked a command, and the creatures about her answered in deafening response. Like a loosed flood, they surged up the base of the hill. A frontal attack, Welly thought with an attempt at detachment. Very unsophisticated. But with the numbers balanced as they were, he feared that sophistication wouldn't matter much.

He and Heather stood close together, gazing at the approaching horde. But Earl paid it scant attention. Standing alone on the inner wall, he bent low, swinging his staff in a flat arch and snapping out orders.

At the base of the outer bank, a line of purple sparks appeared. Quickly they grew into tall columns of flame. Swaying back and forth like huge snakes, the flames broke loose and began weaving down the slope toward the oncoming army. Some in that force quailed at the sight and ran off into the night. Others held their ground but shrieked when the pillars of fire coiled into their midst. Many were consumed.

Over the land, the night wind was rising. Suddenly the

three on the hilltop were hit from behind by powerful gusts. The storm that had lurked in the west had crept up behind them. With a deep rumble of thunder, the dark clouds cracked open, and rain cascaded from the sky. The columns of battling flames hissed furiously and sputtered out.

A flash of lightning froze the scene before them, showing the dark forces in a new advance. They were led now by a pack of long, skeletal creatures with huge eyes and translucent skins.

"They're coming!" Heather yelled over the crashing rain and thunder.

"Stand back from me!" Earl yelled in return. "When the next lightning comes, keep clear!"

The sky split down the middle and spilled out blinding light. Earl stood with his legs braced apart and thrust up his arms as if reaching into the storm. Lightning jabbed down toward him. Suddenly it swerved and arched away to explode into the masses advancing up the slope. The crash of thunder obscured all but the first screams, but not the smell of charred flesh and fur.

Morgan cried out. From the back of her rearing mount, she, too, reached toward the sky. She seemed to grab at a spear of lightning and send it hurtling off to where the three stood. Earl flung up an arm. The bolt veered aside but smashed into the top of the hill, leaving a new smoldering gap in the walls.

A growling cheer rose from below, and the opponents that remained again surged forward. "Still too many of them," Earl muttered. Head tilted, he surveyed their advance. Then, crouching down, he spread his arms out wide.

In the ditch surrounding the fort, the air quivered and

jelled into a lurid purple mist. It glowed coldly within itself. Pouring over the outer bank, it flowed down the slope, sweeping over the front ranks. From its shroud rose coughs and gasping cries.

A gust of wind from the east smashed into the cloud and pushed it back up the slope to thin and vanish. But where it had lain, the ground was littered with dead or writhing bodies.

A lull descended over the battle. The storm was rolling off toward the north. It continued its sky-bound battle in the distance, one mountainous cloud after another briefly rimming itself in light. It had been a natural storm, after all, Earl decided, not one of Morgan's making. But she had used it well.

The remaining creatures milled about on the slope. Some could be seen slipping to the fringes of the mob and slinking off over the plain. With threatening commands, Morgan urged her troops on. The huge wolf beside her leaped into their midst, tearing at the hesitant until its jaw dripped with blood. Again the attackers moved forward.

They were fewer now, but they were closer. Earl jumped down from the wall into the fort, dropping to his knees by a rain puddle. Dredging both hands into it, he pulled up dripping handfuls of mud. Frantically he patted this sticky mass into a roughly human shape. Peeling a splinter from the base of his staff, he stuck it into the manikin's crudely molded hand.

Cradling his creation in both hands, he climbed back onto the wall to see the foremost of the attackers almost at the outer bank. Shouting a string of rasping words, he lifted his hands above his head and hurled the figure through the air. It shattered on the crest of the lower bank.

The fragments splattered over the hillside. Wherever

one fell, it rapidly grew into a life-sized humanoid: larger, but as lumpy and misshapen as the first. And these new figures moved forward, each clutching a staff licked with purple flame.

Clumsily the creatures lurched down the hill. Wherever one encountered an enemy and swiped it with its fiery staff, the other screamed and burst into flame. But when an enemy struck first at a mud thing, the manikin broke apart into lifeless shreds.

Watching from below, Morgan screamed in anger. She jerked back on the reins of her mount. It squealed with the sound of tearing steel. Rearing back, it spread great coppery wings. With mighty thrumming, the wings beat in the air, and together the creature and its rider rose into the night.

They lifted high above the battle, higher than the hilltop. With a laugh like the cry of night birds, Morgan raised one hand into the air and whirled it over her head. Out from her hand spun a sinuous light. It grew and crackled, and along its length rose a shivering curtain, pulsing and fading and glowing again, an aurora of shimmering greens.

With a flick of her wrist, Morgan sent the glowing serpent snapping toward them. From its tip, great bolts of green fire broke free and showered over the hilltop and into the fort. Whatever they hit burst into flame.

As the firebolts crashed around them, Welly and Heather huddled together, staring in awe at the flying horror. But Earl, his gaunt face glistening with sweat, concentrated on his work. He drove the tip of his staff violently into the earth. As he chanted, purple fire ran up its shaft and spread into tangled branches.

At a word, the limbs bloomed with flame. Wrenching

the fire-tree from the ground, he held it aloft and shook it. Blossoms of purple flame broke loose, arching into the sky. Some smashed into oncoming green fireballs; others rained down among the attackers.

The night air raged with light, screams, and the hiss of falling flames. Heather and Welly were tempted to drop to the ground and hurl protective arms over their heads. What kept them on their feet was a vision of hideous attackers somehow breaking through and jumping on their backs.

They looked nervously about the broken circle of earth and saw that indeed some creatures had made it through. Urgently the two turned to Earl. Lean and pale in the eerie light, he stood on the bank above them swinging his flaming tree. The wind whipped his hair wildly about his face, and all his senses were focused on the battle overhead, meeting volley with volley. Their eyes met, and the two children closed in behind him, holding up their bright Eldritch swords.

The gleaming blades seemed to know swordsmanship, as their wielders did not, and the two thrust and parried with startling effectiveness. Dark blood sprayed the air. Several attackers drew back and disappeared into the night.

A slimy gray creature singled out Heather. Its cold-eyed reptilian head rose from a tangle of tentacle-like arms. It hissed venomously as one arm swiftly coiled up and wrapped around her throat. The thing was cold and slick. Its surface rippled as muscles constricted around her windpipe. With one hand she scrabbled feebly at the tightening coil, while her other arm awkwardly brought up the sword. Several desperate slices, and she severed the tentacle.

The strangling segment loosened and slithered lifelessly to the ground as she gasped for breath. Undaunted, the creature sent forth two more arms to entangle her weapon, but she leaped back and hacked wildly into the writhing mass.

Welly confronted a squat goblin-creature, each of its three hairy arms wielding a club. The thing was clumsy but powerful. The flashing sword splintered one of the clubs, but another broke through the blade's defense and smashed jarringly into Welly's right shoulder. The whole arm went numb. His deadened fingers dropped the sword into his other hand. Wielded left-handed, the sword moved awkwardly, but it came from an unexpected angle and took the slow-witted creature by surprise. With a looping swing, Welly sliced off one of its ears. In an arc of blood, the ear sailed into the darkness, and with a gurgling whine, its former owner followed it.

Welly paused to fight down sickness; then shakily he turned to help Heather. But his eye caught the flicker of something gray rocketing up the hillside. Welly's skin prickled as he watched the thing dart from one concealing shadow to another. It was the huge wolf they had seen at Morgan's side.

Worse than anything from his fevered nightmares, it was three times larger than a fell-dog. And where those creatures had merely been hungry, this beast seemed afire with evil. It slunk on its belly through a still-smoldering gap in the wall. Its hair was brindled and gray, its yellow eyes wicked and close-set. The tongue flicked snakelike between yellowed fangs. And before it there flowed a wave of cold.

The thing stood in a shadow of crumbling wall and looked coolly about the shattered fort and at its three defenders. The jaw dropped open, and there came a low growling laugh.

Hunching down, it began stalking toward Earl, whose whole attention was fixed on the fiery clash with Morgan. Twenty feet from its prey, the creature jumped onto a large rock.

Welly crouched in the shadow of the bank. Numbing cold flowed about him as it had on another night. His hair bristled at the memory, and his hands grew slick and clammy. But slowly he stood up and, stepping out from the shadow, raised his sword between Earl and the huge wolf. The beast glanced down at him, an evil intelligence flickering in its eyes. Then, ears pricked forward, it raised its head and surveyed its goal and the gap between them.

Deliberately the beast crouched down, great muscles bunching and rippling under its fur. A growl rose from deep in its chest. Suddenly it sprang into the air, arching high over Welly's head. Welly yelled and leaped straight upward. His sword point gouged the beast down the length of its belly.

The creature spun sideways and crashed onto the ground. Snarling, it rolled over in mud already bloodied from its long wound. It crouched to spring again. Without pausing, Welly hurled himself at it, thrusting his blade deep into the shaggy chest. The wolf jerked violently and threw back its head. Its jagged howl shattered the night.

The body shuddered, pulled away from Welly's now-smoking blade, and lay still. Its coarse wolf features slowly blurred and changed into those of a man. Garth.

At that dying howl, silence fell like ice over the battle. Earl spun around to see what was happening behind him.

"I should have guessed," he said as even the human form dissolved into dust. "Morgan's consort was a werewolf."

Welly looked down at the smoldering mud where the body had lain. This was his first kill in battle, and it was not the grand thing he'd imagined, even with a victim as foul as this. He felt oddly weak and polluted. Again, he wondered if he would be sick. It would be almost a relief.

Earl had turned back to the battle, but there was little left there. In his brief moments of inattention, Morgan and her mount had vanished. Their snaking green aurora was already fading from the sky. Below, those attackers not dead on the hillside were fleeing in panic into the night. Weary of killing, he let them go.

Heather had dispatched her opponent by finally lopping off its reptilian head. Shaking with fatigue, she joined her companions. Her face was ashen, her thin hair plastered to her forehead with sweat.

The three surveyed the suddenly silent battlefield. It was now lit only by a mist-shrouded moon and by patches of fire, green and purple, that still flickered about the hillside. These burned with cold fuelless flame, except where they fed on corpses.

Heather, her lips pale thin lines, asked weakly, "Is it all over? Is Morgan gone for good?"

Earl nodded wearily, leaning on his now-flameless staff. "She's gone, though hardly for good. But this battle's over at least. I hope she's had her fill of direct confrontation. I certainly have."

He swayed where he stood. Alarmed, Welly caught him and kept him from falling.

"I'm all right," Earl said shakily. "I just need some rest. I can't handle this sort of thing so well anymore. I'm not as old as I used to be, you know."

They helped him over to their camp. The makeshift tent had burned, but most of their other equipment was only scorched.

Earl sank into the blankets they pulled out for him, and in moments he was asleep. Wrapping themselves in their own blankets, Welly and Heather lay down at the base of the wall. Their minds buzzed with sounds and images, but they were too tired to talk or sort anything out. They felt no need to set watch. There was not the slightest whiff of menace left in the air. Exhausted, they drifted into the night's numbing calm.

14

ON MAGIC'S SHORE

Heather's dreams faded into morning mist. She remained curled in her blanket, eyes closed, trying to remember where in their long trek they had camped the night before. She remembered, and her eyes flew open.

The sun was already well up. From beside her, where Welly had bedded down, came the sound of slow, steady breathing. Then she heard another sound and stiffened. Somewhere to her left there was a quiet snuffling.

Images swirled back of the nightmare creatures that had swarmed here the night before. She slipped a hand from her blankets and poked Welly. He snorted and rolled over.

"Hush," she whispered. "There's something over there."

His bleary eyes peered from the blankets, and a plump hand crept out, fumbled for his glasses, and thrust them on his face. Slowly they both sat up and looked toward the center of the ruined hill fort. What they saw was definitely a mutant, but not the sort to inspire fear.

In the weak morning light, its thick coat glowed a snowy white. Its face and long legs were slender, like a deer's, but it was as shaggy as a wild goat, and its tail was long and horselike. Its two horns were separate for only a short distance. Then they became entwined and for several inches twisted together into a single point.

Heather glanced toward Earl's place and saw that he, too, was awake and watching the creature. A bemused smile lit his face.

The animal continued browsing at the grass, which the battle's heat had cleared of snow. Gradually it moved away. Cocking its ears, it suddenly raised its head and looked toward them, its large eyes soft and luminous. The animal and children watched each other for a moment; then it turned and, with a graceful bound, leaped over the bank and was gone.

Earl sighed and sat up. "Mythical or extinct, they seem to have made a comeback. And look at this." Cautiously he fingered some thorny brambles where, in the dark of the night, they had spread their blankets. Nestled among pointed leaves were several tiny pink buds.

"Wild roses," he said softly. "Remember the inn, the Rose and Unicorn? And I thought they were both hopelessly things of the past!" He laughed and climbed out of his blankets. "Maybe there's hope for this battered world yet!"

Over breakfast of bread and cheese, Earl said to the others, "Before I folded up last night, I should have thanked you. Wizard or not, without rear guard, I wouldn't have made it. It was a ghastly thing for you to be subjected to. But . . . I needed you there."

Heather smiled. "Can't say I'd volunteer for that sort of duty every night. But I guess we make a good team."

"We do indeed."

Welly, blushing with pleasure, cleared his throat. "So where to now, Captain?"

In answer, Earl stood up, and they followed him to the fort's south rim. He pointed over the earthen bank to the ocean and both coasts, the new and old. "We're headed there somewhere."

Heather stared at the ocean excitedly. Then she frowned. "Do you think Morgan will leave us alone that long?"

Earl nodded. "She called in reinforcements last night and failed. I suspect she'll bide her time now and watch where we're going. When we're close enough to learn that ourselves, we may hear from her again."

They descended the south side of the hill, where the night's battle was less evident than on the eastern slope. But even so, the grass still smoldered in black patches, and the air smelled heavily of burning and death. They skirted twisted, half-burned bodies. Brief, quickly averted glances showed hideous inhuman forms, made more hideous by death. Furtive scavengers already skulked over the hillside.

The starkness of the battlefield brought a new vision of the battle itself. Then it had been too quick, too appalling and fantastic to be totally believable. Now the reality sank in. They walked largely in silence for the rest of the morning.

By midafternoon, they'd sighted a small village and decided to stop for supplies. Veering west, they picked up a rutted track, which led to the small town square. On every side, stone houses huddled together under heavy turf roofs, and in the center rose a time-battered stone cross. Around it several merchants had set up booths, which were doing a livelier business in gossip than in trade. The sight of children traveling alone with coins for provisions caused only minor comment, for interest was centered on events the locals had witnessed the night before.

Lights had been seen in the northern sky, and outlying farmers near the tor reported weird happenings. Reports of flying monsters were generally discounted. But persistent sightings of other strange creatures throughout the area could not be dismissed, particularly when accompanied by the bloody slaughter of sheep, cattle, and, in one case, a shepherd.

When it was learned that the three young strangers had come from the north, all attention swiveled to them.

"So, lad," a leather worker asked Earl, "what did you see? I'd say you're lucky to have passed through that country alive, judging by what I've heard."

The others in the crowd muttered in agreement and waited for the boy's reply.

"Well, we . . . er . . . didn't see all that much worth talking about. We were camped and slept most of the night, I guess. There were lights by the tor, but then there was a storm, so it could have been lightning or something."

"Didn't you see any strange beasts?" a woman asked incredulously. "Why, my Sam, he saw two this morning!"

Earl squirmed, recalling the dregs of Morgan's forces spreading in panic over the plains. "Yes, there were creatures, very evil-looking things. I think you'd all be wise to stay close to home the next few days and pen up your livestock."

This set off debate over the merits of taking some action, and the three children tried to slip away. But they were riveted by the comments of one gray-bearded farmer.

"If you ask me, it smacks of magic," he said, nodding. "Strong magical doings were going on at the tor last night; count on it. The days of magic are returning to this world. Blast me if they aren't."

"What makes you think that, old man?" Earl asked quietly.

"Why, it makes sense, don't it? There used to be magic in the old, old days, didn't there? Stories say so, before people learned how to do all that nonsense with science. Well, science took over but did no good in the end, did it? What's going to work now? What's going to hold this old world together except magic, I'd like to know. Makes sense, that does."

"Oh, come on, Jeth," joshed one of the younger men. "You'll be giving these kids worse nightmares than they'll have had already. You're always going on about magic and portents. You'd think we were living in some fairy-tale age."

"Well, maybe we are," the old man muttered as he shuffled away, shaking his head, "or soon will be. Maybe indeed."

With refilled packs, the three children slipped out of the village, leaving it to its rumors and speculations. Welly and Heather walked with lifted spirits. Strangers confirming what they'd seen made them feel more comfortably normal. Earl was silent, thinking about old Jeth and his faith in magic and portents. He suspected the old man sensed a truth. The cycles of this world were changing. A time of magic was beginning again.

That evening they stopped at a farmhouse. The family had been reluctant to open the door, with all the rumors of strange creatures abroad. But when they saw it was only children, they willingly offered their barn. They might have offered a place by their fire, had the children tried looking pathetic. But none of the three felt up to socializing.

In the morning, the fresh salt tang of the air spoke of

the sea. Before long, they crossed the broken pavement of the old coast road and stood on bluffs overlooking what had once been a narrow wave-washed beach.

Now a sandy rock-strewn plain stretched out and down toward a distant expanse of water. Overhead, a rare seagull cried shrilly and sailed seaward. Heather tingled with excitement, and even Welly was impressed with the size and power of the ocean, viewed at a safe distance.

To the east, the cliffs curved out in a long arm that eventually reached and jutted into the receded waters. Head tilted, Earl stood surveying this and the rest of the scene: the flat, dark horizon, the white fringe of breakers along the now-distant beach, the wrinkled gray surface of the sea dotted with occasional rocks and islands.

He sighed with mingled satisfaction and sadness. "It's a new landscape for me, but I think I know where we're going now."

"Where?" the others asked together.

Earl glanced uneasily around and shook his head. "Let's just go there."

They searched several minutes for a way down the cliffs, at last finding traces of a path used of old by picnickers and bathers. Once on the ancient beach, Heather and Welly were soon running over the sand, leaping rocks and exclaiming over the occasional weathered shell.

Earl walked more quietly. Nostalgia and regret blew at him like the salt wind. Both whipped his eyes with tears. That descendants of his people should smash their civilization was perhaps their own affair. But that they should maim even its ageless oceans, that seemed a great deal to forgive.

Only a thin veil of snow covered the sand; the sea

breezes swept most of it back against the cliffs. The air was cold and tangy with the scent of ocean.

As they neared the new shoreline, Heather was delighted with the rolling gray-green waters and the luminous curl of the breakers before they crashed into foam and surged up the sand. Welly, recalling Morgan's frightful illusion, was more reserved.

While the two younger children played keep-away with the farthest-reaching waves, Earl set about gathering flotsam from the beach. After half an hour, he'd made a pile of driftwood, seaweed, a few bird feathers, and the jagged neck of an ancient bottle. He looked at his collection with dissatisfaction and called to the others.

"Hey, you two, come and help me or this'll take all day. The oceans don't wash up as much junk as they used to. Less wood to drift, I guess. There're not even many shells."

The two trotted back over the wave-smoothed sand, faces flushed and damp with spray. "Well, give us a clue," Welly said. "What are you up to?"

"I'm going to build a boat," he said simply. "If I ever get enough materials."

The others looked quizzically at the odds and ends piled at his feet. "With that?" Heather asked.

"To start with, yes. If we can get enough natural materials, I'll cement them together into the right form."

The three spread out over the beach, collecting things. Earl had said to take anything, so Welly and Heather, scouting together, picked up slimy shreds of seaweed, a few shells, water-smoothed stones, and an occasional piece of wood, tossed and worn by the waves into bone-smooth whiteness.

In a shallow cove a quarter mile up the beach, they made a discovery. The bleached skeleton of some large sea animal had been washed high up on the beach. Scavengers had removed every vestige of meat, and the bones had finally tired and fallen away from each other. But most still remained scattered about the sand. When they called Earl, he was excited. Gathering up an armload of broad, flat rib bones, he returned with them to his growing pile of junk.

At last he determined they had enough. The others sat on gritty, sand-dusted rocks as he spread his finds over the ground. At first there seemed no order in his work, but finally they made out the rough shape of a boat, its gunwales defined by curving rib bones. Inside these, he arranged the other things, fitting them together like pieces in a jigsaw puzzle until as little space as possible showed between them. The rocks he discarded, saying they had "too many sinking instincts to overcome."

At last Earl stood back and, head tilted, surveyed his work with satisfaction. Welly was less impressed. "If you think I'm going out to sea in that, you're dead wrong," he announced flatly.

Earl shot him a look of scorn. "This is just the first step, ye of little faith. Now we'll see about binding it together."

He dropped to his knees in the sand. Leaning over his strange creation, he began passing his hands smoothly over the individual pieces, all the while muttering words in interweaving singsong. As his hands passed for the third or fourth time over some items, these seemed to blur, their edges to spread and blend into the objects around them.

Gradually the whole became a solid sheet, a flat boat-shaped cutout of splotchy gray. Then Earl changed the rhythm of his chant and began moving quickly around the edges, working them with his hands, pulling them up like a potter molding clay.

Finally a boat rested before them on the sand, fifteen feet long, the shape and color of a fish. Its prow was high and gracefully upturned. Its stern, though broader, also rose above the tapered sides. Down its length ran a knife-edged keel.

Despite their doubts, the two children were impressed. Welly slid off his rock and walked over to Earl's creation. He touched it cautiously, as though expecting it to bite or fall apart. When it did neither, he stroked its smooth sides and even kicked it reservedly.

"Well," he admitted, "it feels real enough, and it looks like a boat. But it has one problem."

Earl frowned at his handiwork. "What?"

"It *is* a boat! I won't go floating out on all that water in any kind of boat, least of all one that's held together by words!"

"Welly, this is very trustworthy stuff. Magic-blended objects are stronger than illusions. They don't have to be tended all the time like creating-spells."

"Maybe so, but that doesn't change the fact that there's a lot of water out there, and I can't swim!"

"There's really not much water to cross. We haven't far to go now." Earl lowered his voice. "We're heading for that rock."

"Which, the big island?"

"No, the cluster of rocks to its left, the far one."

"And you're sure we have to go there?" Welly pressed.

"*I* have to go there. I'm sure the key to entering Avalon is there. You can stay behind, of course, but it will leave you unprotected, and Morgan may still be about."

Welly jumped slightly and looked suspiciously back at the cliffs and long, empty stretch of beach.

Heather spoke up. "Welly, I can't swim either, at least not much. But who knows what Earl's going to find once he gets there or what he'll have to do. He may need us. We've stuck together so far. I don't want to miss what happens next."

Welly kicked the sand at his feet. "Well, I don't either. I'm coming, of course. It's just that I signed on to be a soldier, not a sailor. Water's not trustworthy."

The tide was rising closer to the completed boat. They loaded in their packs and the three paddles that Earl had fashioned, two from larger pieces of driftwood and one from his own staff. Then, with Earl on one side and Welly and Heather on the other, they lifted the boat, finding it surprisingly light, and ran down to the in-rolling waves.

When knee-deep in the cold, foamy water, Earl ordered them to jump in, Heather in front, Welly in the middle. Earl himself took the steering position at the stern. Quickly they grabbed up paddles and dug into the foam. Pulled by undertow and pushed by incoming surges, they moved out swiftly, their propulsion magically enhanced. They needed it, Welly figured, as with fear-widened eyes, he watched great breakers bearing down upon them.

Earl watched these, too, with keen appraisal. Edging the boat up toward the line of water where the crests broke, at the right second, he yelled, "Paddle like mad!" Paddles flashed, and they shot over the next breaker while it was still rising, before it could tumble down in a foamy crash.

They were not long clear of the breakers when the wind hit. Where minutes before it had been only a salty breeze, it now hammered at them steadily, rising almost to a gale.

With Earl's special help, they moved on, but they were definitely slowed. The swells rising and falling under them became mountainous.

Welly's round face was as pale as his dusky skin allowed. To keep from screaming, he clamped his teeth and concentrated on the rhythmic swing of the paddles. Were warriors always this afraid? he wondered. Yet they do frightful things anyway. But then, so did he. Was that bravery? The thought made him grin—briefly.

Only by occasionally looking away from their goal could they tell they were moving closer to the jagged wave-splashed rocks. They saw these now from a different angle than on the beach. Heather was intrigued by their bizarre shapes and watched them steadily. "Hey," she called, her words whipped back by the wind, "look at that fantastic rock on the left. It has a hole in it!"

The others noticed it, too. Among the sky-thrusting fingers of rock rose one with a large irregular hole through it, worn by ages of swirling currents when it had lain just under the ocean's surface.

But now Earl's attention was drawn to something beyond the rocks. A thin gray fringe appeared along the horizon and slowly grew. He said nothing but suggested everyone paddle harder.

In a few minutes, Heather noticed it, too. "What's that out there, Earl? Is there a storm coming?"

"Don't think so; it's too low. Just keep paddling."

They watched it silently as with aching muscles, they rhythmically dug into the dark water.

Finally Welly said, "It's a big wave, isn't it? A whole line of water."

Heather's throat went dry. "It's an illusion, like the last one."

"Afraid not," Earl answered grimly. "She's been busy out there making a real tidal wave this time. Morgan may lack imagination, but she's good at dealing with elements."

"Great," Welly muttered, and paddled until he thought his arms would break off and sink.

The grayness was closer now and could clearly be seen as a gigantic wave. Earl redoubled his efforts physically and magically, but it didn't seem possible that they could reach the rocks in time or even that, once reached, they would prove any refuge.

The wind roared as the wave rolled steadily toward them. With scarcely a flinch, it passed over the rocks and continued bearing down on the fragile boat. A dark, towering wall of water, its top crested into a fringe of foam. In seeming slow motion, the wave broke and began falling down upon them.

Heather and Welly stared upward, voiceless with horror. Earl lunged forward, grabbing their shoulders, and yelled, "Hold on to your paddles! Don't let loose of your paddles, no matter what!"

It seemed ludicrous advice, but they gripped their paddles furiously as the falling water hammered into them, driving them down toward the ocean bottom.

Heather felt the boat dissolve around her. She was tossed over and over with no discernible up or down. The air squeezed from her lungs, and her ears hummed. Then there was a movement she vaguely recognized as rising, and after endless moments, her head burst through the surface. Gasping wildly, she swallowed lungfuls of water and air. She coughed. Her head slipped beneath the waves, and again she was sinking.

Earl was shouting at her, shouting in her mind. "Your paddle! It's wood, old, dry wood! Grip it, concentrate on it, float like it, become like it. You are the wood. Light and buoyant, bobbing on the surface. Up and down over the waves."

Welly, too, heard and responded to Earl's hypnotic words but almost sank again when, remembering his glasses, he grabbed at his face to hold them in place. It took long spluttering seconds to rebuild the illusion. The new mental image produced a stick of driftwood with an armlike branch that crooked up at one end.

Heather, now as buoyant as her paddle, sped along on the surface, and her own mind freely supplied another image. She was like a storm-tossed ship, its carved figure-head bravely bearing down on the rocky cliffs.

And they *were* racing toward the cliffs! Already the long beach they had left so recently was sliding by far beneath them. She could almost feel the tearing hardness of the rocks beyond as she hurtled toward them. They would be smashed!

A grip tightened painfully on her shoulder, moments before a jarring shock. Then blackness.

Welly opened his eyes, a surprising act, considering he was dead. He tried to focus on the cloud-smeared sky above him. He thought about limbs and muscles and tried to twitch a set that would theoretically move an arm. An arm did move in tingles of pain. No, it was asking too much to be dead, to be peacefully, painlessly dead.

He turned his head toward a groaning sound. Beside him, Earl lay facedown in the sand. Feebly the older boy moved a hand. Then slowly he sat up, spitting out sand and coughing.

"Sorry," he gasped after a moment. "I tried to make that landing a little easier."

"May I let go now?" a thin voice quavered above them.

The two boys looked up and saw Heather clinging to her stick of driftwood, which was wedged firmly between two rocks. Earl staggered to his feet and caught her as she dropped. Together they toppled again onto the sand and narrowly escaped falling over a ledge.

Only then did they see where they were: a sand-filled crevasse high on the cliffs that had once marked the ancient coast. Heather shivered and with still-numbed arms pulled herself back from the edge.

Already the incredible wave had slunk back into the sea. The gray depths churned with the huge undertow, while winds beat the surface into froth.

They'd lost their packs and coats in the water, and now, soaked and shivering, they huddled together on the wind-battered cliff, watching the tortured seascape below.

"I conclude," Welly said through chattering teeth, "that this wave was not illusion."

Earl groaned and shook some sand out of his hair. "No. She's good. That was some wave."

"Well, now she's bent on finishing off your rocks," Heather observed.

They looked out toward the rocks, which not long before had been their goal. From all sides, waves tore into them, battering them mercilessly, tearing away huge chunks.

"She's certainly seeing to it that there won't be anything left to find there," Heather said heavily. "There won't even be any 'there' in a few minutes."

Earl stared glumly at the scene but did not reply. He

seemed to huddle into himself, his head sunk dejectedly on his knees. The sun dropped into a thick bank of cloud, spreading a sullen glow over the western sky. Against that backdrop, the jagged pillars and freak window of the battered rock stood sharply silhouetted.

Behind that rock, the cloud curtain tore briefly, and the sun glowed redly through. Its bloody rays shot directly at them through the rocky portal.

Suddenly Heather stood up and looked quickly behind them. "Earl!" she cried. "Look! Look at the light!"

He raised his head and followed her gaze. "Of course!" he exclaimed. "I should have guessed! That rock wasn't our goal at all. Only a signpost—pointing here!"

Even as he spoke, a mighty wave crashed against the pierced rock and toppled it into the sea. Behind it, the sun sank below the watery horizon, but not before its beams had shown them the dark cleft between two tumbled stones, stones still entwined with faintly carved vines.

"Quickly!" Earl yelled. "Before she sees or guesses!"

Grabbing them by their shoulders, he propelled them toward the dark opening. Heather slipped quickly through, but Welly balked at the narrow gap.

"No time for qualms," Earl said, shoving him into the opening.

Three feet into the darkness, Welly stuck fast, wedged between grating rocks. A wave of panic hit him worse than in the old Welsh mine. He felt Earl apply a foot firmly to the small of his back, and suddenly he popped through.

Grabbing up his staff, Earl crowded after him as the wind outside rose to a vengeful shriek. Ahead, they faced darkness more total than any they'd ever imagined.

15

Legend's Return

"Earl." Heather's voice sounded small and brittle in the utter darkness. "Do you think you can give us a light?"

"I doubt it," he said, close beside her. "In Avalon, my puny magic isn't worth a thing."

He stamped his staff sharply on the rock and muttered some words. "Nothing. Here, let's just hold hands and move carefully. We were allowed through the first gate, so there oughtn't be any traps."

Tucking his staff under an arm, he fumbled for their hands, and slowly they shuffled through the blackness. On either side, Heather and Welly felt rough rock walls slip by beneath their fingers. The stone floor was uneven but took no sudden drops.

The walls were becoming damp. Their fingers recoiled at the first touch of spongy moss. Glowing with a faint violet phosphorescence, these patches seemed to swim in the darkness before them. As the moss became denser, the light faintly showed the way and cast an eerie radiance over their faces.

The walls and floors glistened with damp, and here

and there they heard the hollow drip of water over stone. They moved more confidently in the pale violet glow, but the farther they went, the less it felt as if they were traveling in a straight line. The sensation was of curling around themselves in ever decreasing circles—like being trapped in a giant snail shell.

Ahead of them, they heard a faint musical chiming. As they drew closer, it seemed almost to have words interwoven, words they could never quite catch. It drew them on until, turning a corner, their eyes were assailed with light. They blinked in the brilliance. A patch of green-gold shone through a curtain of falling water. The drops, sparkling in the pure sunlight, cascaded over a rocky ledge. With silvery tinkling, they fell into a clear pool edged about with moss and ferns.

The three pulled up at the beauty of the scene. Earl sighed deeply, like a traveler coming home. "Well, no stopping now," he said after a long moment. Tightly gripping their hands, he pulled them after him through the pool and the veil of sparkling drops.

The water was tingling cold, but before they could gasp, they were through and standing on thick green grass. All about them the air was soft and warm, filled with a hazy golden light. Everything was of such aching loveliness, it brought tears to their eyes.

On all sides grew trees such as Heather and Welly had seen only in pictures, great stately trunks with graceful branches that spread into a canopy overhead. Leaves fluttering in the breeze filtered the sunlight in shifting patterns of gold and green. The grass underfoot was thick and soft and scattered over with tiny white flowers. From trees and bushes and the clear blue sky came mingled birdsong.

Earl smiled but could find no words. None of them could. He began walking through the arched trees, and the others followed, bemused with wonder.

On every side, some new loveliness lay casually about, as though natural and not indescribably precious. Undisturbed by their passage, animals rested or fed in sun-drenched glades, animals they'd seen in books or scarcely imagined in dreams. With barely audible whirrings, rainbow-winged insects flitted through the air.

The grass sloped down to a shallow pond, its edge fringed in wind-ruffled reeds. Earl peeled off his travel-worn jacket and flopped down on the grass. Breathing its sweetness, he lay back and looked into the depths of blue sky. The others joined him. There was a gauzy timelessness in the air, as though a single moment had been snatched from some eternal dream.

Sitting up at last, Earl removed his wet boots and socks and dug his toes into the cool grass. Laughing, he jumped up and waded out into the pool, rippling its clear green water.

"Come on!" he yelled to his two friends.

"Are you sure it's all right?" Heather asked. It was so beautiful here that, happy as it made her, she felt somehow out of place.

"Of course it's all right! The water does wonders for sore feet."

Boots and socks quickly discarded, the two joined him. The smooth coolness of the water lapped about their ankles, soaking into travel-weary feet like a healing balm.

Earl waded out farther and then, to the others' surprise, let out a joyous yell and dove into the water. For seconds, the glassy surface closed over him, then he burst through it in a shower of emerald drops. Laughing, he splashed glittering arches of water toward them. They splashed back.

At last, ending the water war, Earl sat down chest-deep in the pond and splashed his arms in great angel wings, watching the cascading drops sparkle in the sun.

"Boys will always be boys, I see," said a soft, musical voice behind them.

Earl spluttered to a stop and stood up in the water, looking embarrassed. Water dripped from his dark hair over his face. "Lady," he said sheepishly.

The woman laughed. "It's a good deal younger you are than when we last saw you, Merlin. But you are unmistakable and always welcome, as are any you bring."

Heather and Welly turned to see a woman more lovely than imagining. Her gown was of sunlight sparkling upon water and her hair an aurora of light caught with shifting rainbows. The delicacy of her face seemed carved from a precious gem, but it was softer and glowed with a golden warmth.

She smiled, her blue eyes bright with laughter, and she held out her hands to Earl as he waded from the pool, dripping water and looking abashed.

"Lady," he said with a bow, "these are my friends and companions, Wellington Jones and Heather McKenna. Without them I would probably not be here."

The woman took them both by the hand. "You are welcome indeed. It is good to know that Merlin has found himself such stout friends. We knew he had awakened but didn't know how he might fare in that world of yours, nor when he would seek one of the few doors left open." She looked at them, a smile playing softly on her lips. "I expect you will all have tales worth telling, and as your friend can tell you, we are very fond of tales here."

Heather and Welly smiled up at her but could find no words that seemed fine enough. Earl, however, said, "Lady, where is . . ."

"Merlin! Two thousand years, and you are still as impatient as ever. One would think your mixed blood might mellow you some. But then, I suppose wizards are a law unto themselves."

Earl hung his head in chagrin, but the Lady laughed and placed a hand on his shoulder. "We wouldn't want you to change, friend; you are needed as you are. Yes, I'll take you to him soon. But first, I think these children can use some rest and refreshment. And as you seem to be a growing boy again, you also might want a taste of the food Avalon offers its guests."

Welly was delighted at the prospect of food, but Heather said, "Oh, Lady, just being here is enough. It's all so lovely!" She stopped, surprised at her own temerity, but the Lady only smiled sadly.

"I am glad it pleases you, child. But it hurts to hear how lovely you find it. Once our two worlds were very close, as close as a mirror and that which it reflects. They grew apart, but even as Merlin first knew them, one could still see the original in the reflection. Now, I'm afraid your world is a pale reflection indeed, and it saddens us."

As she talked, she led them away from the pond to a small sun-filled meadow where other beings as lovely as herself awaited them. Some seemed human or partly so, while others were definitely something else. Several greeted Earl like old friends and led the three to seats of sun-warmed rock. There they were brought food and drink in crystal plates and goblets.

The food was lovely to the eyes, and every bite or sip had its own unique flavor, too fine and rare ever to be repeated. In the air around them was music of wind and pipes and laughter. They relaxed on the grass under the vast blue sky. Golden afternoon slipped into dusky twilight and then into glorious night. The sky glittered with a myriad of stars.

They woke the next morning, or perhaps many mornings after, stretched comfortably on the grass. The Lady was with them and offered to lead them to Arthur.

"He was sorely wounded when he came to us," she told Earl as they left the meadow. "But gradually we healed him, his body at least, and returned him to his youth and vigor. His other wounds . . . they were healed perhaps by time. We didn't wish him to forget, only to rest and wait."

They had come to the shore of a large lake, gleaming like a golden mirror in the sun. The Lady led them into a shallow leaf-shaped boat. Of its own power, it moved out over the water, gliding silently past white swans, who turned their long necks to watch them pass. Heather trailed her fingers through the smooth water, then lifted them to watch the falling drops catch the light. Finally they slid onto the fine white sand of the other shore. There the Lady led them to the base of a high hill, steep and rocky. As they climbed, a stiff breeze played about their hair and over the grass.

At the crest, the air was perfumed by a grove of flowering trees, their silver-gray trunks gnarled with age. Fallen blossoms floated along the surface of a brook, which they followed to its source, a spring bubbling up in a quiet glade. Low in the grass was a moss-softened rock, and on it lay a man sleeping.

He was a young man, scarcely more than a boy. His skin was pale and clear. A shock of golden hair fell over a rough-carved face softened by sleep and by youth. He seemed deeply asleep, as though floating in distant peaceful dreams.

For a moment, Earl stood looking down at him. Then with a sob he sank to his knees. Reaching for the young man's hand, he dropped his forehead upon it.

After a time, the man stirred and opened his eyes. Blue and blurry at first, they focused on the lady. "Ah, Lady, you have such long dreams here." He sighed. "And such rest."

The dark head rose beside him, and the man stared into the gaunt tear-streaked face.

"But who . . . ?" He looked more closely. "Merlin, is it you?"

"One who scarcely hoped to see you living again, my lord."

Arthur laughed and sat up. "I can't say how I knew you, old wizard! Aren't you just a trifle younger than when I saw you last?"

His friend smiled. "Don't rub it in, youngster! Last I saw you, you were a hardened, battle-scarred warrior with streaks of gray in your golden beard."

The two laughed and hugged each other as friends might after several millennia.

Time had little reality there, but in its own way, it passed and was spent renewing old acquaintances and forging new ones. Arthur and several of the denizens of Avalon listened with concern as Earl, Heather, and Welly related the events of their own recent lives.

Arthur's concern deepened as they reconstructed the happenings in their world since he and Merlin had left it. In the end, it was a picture of heartbreaking sadness: great struggle, beauty, and achievement overlain with a wash of hate, stupidity, and inexcusable waste. Afterward, it seemed that not even the beauty and peace of Avalon could raise Arthur's spirits.

But to Heather and Welly, although their own world was harsh, it was something to be accepted, not mourned over. And Avalon was a life apart, a sweetness to be savored: they spent the golden days and crystal nights wandering through its beauties or in companionship with its inhabitants. Waterfolk taught them swimming, and after initial trepidation on Welly's part, it seemed as natural as it would to a fish.

But Earl spent his time with Arthur, and the two wandered restlessly over the Eldritch lands.

The mists of another morning were rising as they walked the rim of a high waterfall. Blue rainbowed clouds rose from the chasm where the slender column of water crashed among the rocks. Moss-hung cypress sighed and whispered among themselves, and the breeze was scented with sage and wild thyme.

Arthur kicked a loose pebble over the edge and waited to hear it clatter and bounce on the rocks far below. "What I don't understand, Merlin, is why they didn't tell me. I wasn't sleeping all that time. And they knew what was happening out there. True, some of them have lost interest; things have strayed so far apart. But the Lady and others, they watch; they know! Why didn't they tell me what was happening, how our dreams were faring—what succeeded and what failed, and how the whole thing drove itself insanely off a cliff? It was my world. They should have told me!"

"Arthur, what good would that cruelty have done?

You, a mortal, were brought here close to death. Their desire was to see you healed, to have you rest as you deserved, and to wait."

"Yes, wait. But for what? Merlin, by some alchemy I'll never understand, you were locked away waiting to be freed. Then, as soon as you were, or remembered that you were, you came looking for me. So, this time of waiting is over. But why? What good can I do? One former king, in a world infinitely more wrong than any we knew."

"That world needs you, Arthur."

"Needs me! That's what you said before. But I was young then, truly young. It was exciting, exhilarating. I was to be King! But, Merlin, I know what that all means now. I've gone through it once. Certainly there was pride and beauty and satisfaction, but there was also pain, failure, and loss. Being king isn't being revered and leading troops to glory; it's taking on other people's pains and problems, being responsible for their lives and happiness and sacrificing your own. Merlin, I loved and was betrayed! I built and saw what I built destroyed! Are you asking me to go through all that again?"

"Arthur, do you really want me to answer that?"

"Yes! I mean, no. Oh, you infuriating old man! You're going to lecture me. I know exactly what you're going to say. And I don't want to hear it!" He yanked a fern out of the dark soil and tore it to shreds.

His companion sat down on a stone and turned his attention to the splendid view across the gorge.

After several minutes, Arthur threw the remains of the fern over the edge. "Your problem, Merlin, is that you haven't the decency to be wrong now and again."

"Oh, I've had my moments."

"But this isn't one of them, is it?" Arthur dropped heavily onto a mossy bank. "You and the folk of Avalon say I'm needed there. I don't understand that now any more than I did before. If it's true, it also seems I can't avoid it any more than before. But you can't blame me for wanting to! This time, after all, I know what I'm in for."

The people of Avalon prepared the four mortals for their departure. New warm clothes were made and spread in readiness under the trees. The hooded fur cloaks seemed alien in this world of perpetual summer.

Earl set about giving Arthur a crash course in the culture of the strange new world he was entering. On the question of language, however, the teacher despaired, and at last complained to the Lady.

"Arthur can talk easily with everyone here but can't seem to grasp that Avalon has its own laws. Out there the language has changed. If he tried to converse in his native tongue, he'd be unintelligible. And, Lady, I know from experience that Arthur's a dunce with languages. He's a fine leader, a great warrior, and many other things. But if I try to teach him a new language, we'll be here another two thousand years!"

She laughed. "It's not that we don't love our guests, but it looks as if I'd better make him a gift of language and spare you the tutoring."

"Bless you, Lady. For me, that gift is beyond price!"

There were other gifts as well. Arthur's mighty sword was reforged and returned to him. But although offered more elegant alternatives, Earl preferred his small hawk-headed sword and the pine staff from the banks of the Tamar. This last, he said, was tied to the world in which it must function.

Welly and Heather also chose to keep their swords from the ancient Eldritch wreck. But sheaths were made for them of soft pale leather worked with designs of twining vines and interlocking spirals.

At last came the eve of their departure. The four travelers sat in the meadow where the three had passed their first night. The Lady was with them, along with others of their new friends. In the center of the meadow, a fire blazed, not for warmth and light but as a symbol of fellowship and belonging that spanned time and worlds.

The Lady looked across the fireglow at the four and saw that all followed their own thoughts. But the young boy and girl seemed particularly troubled.

"Heather, there is something you want, isn't there?"

"Yes, there is." She stopped twisting her braid and looked up. "There were many things I wanted that don't seem important now. And what I wanted most, I never realized—just to be needed."

The other smiled with understanding. "But, Lady," Heather continued, "Avalon is so beautiful. I'm afraid when we go, we'll forget it, like some dream. Our world is different. It is mine and I can accept it, but to carry a small candle of memory would make it easier."

The Lady nodded. "The contrast will be painful. It might be best for you if it did fade. But yes, you may keep it. Like a good dream, let it stay in the back of your mind, to be called on when needed."

She looked at Welly. "And this will be for you as well. But do I sense you need something more?"

He blushed and stared down at his hands. "Well, I guess I understand things better, too. I know what I can do, and maybe something of what should be done. But . . .

oh, it's nothing grand. It's stupid and selfish. . . . But I still wish I had good eyes and didn't need glasses."

She placed a soft hand on his. "I suppose some sorts of magic could do that, but it's really not our way. We don't wish to a make a person other than he is or change what he has made of himself. We can heal a wound or sickness. But, Welly, your eyes are neither. They are part of what makes you. Can you understand that at all?"

Welly smiled weakly. "I guess so."

She put her hands on his shoulders and looked him in the face. "But you needn't be downcast." She laughed. "Perhaps there are a few things we can do. For one thing, I suspect the prescription could be improved. And perhaps a charm to keep you from breaking or losing the things?"

He nodded and saw with surprise that the circles of glass before his eyes were clearer than before, focusing everything in sharp detail. And they rested on his head with a strange new security. He looked up with a confident smile.

Talk in the meadow merged with sleep, ending in the radiance of Avalon's predawn glow. After a final meal, the four, wearing their new warm clothing, hoisted fresh packs on their backs. The Lady alone led them up a pine-clad hill. The ground was carpeted with needles and the air scented with their spice.

Near the crest of the hill, the Lady halted and kissed each lightly on the forehead. They took one last look at her and the beautiful land behind. Then, with Arthur in the lead, they stepped between two tall pines into utter darkness. The scent of warm pine lingered for a moment, then was gone.

This time Welly and Heather walked confidently

through the blackness. Their steps echoed as from high-vaulted walls, and cold began seeping out of the stone around them. At last a patch of gray appeared ahead. They stepped out of an ancient tomb, snow resting quietly in the spirals carved into its fallen stones.

The light was cold and the sky a blank gray. Below them, a new landscape stretched bleak and treeless. Wind whipped over the snow, hurling dry, icy flakes into their faces.

The contrast with what they had left was stark, but to Welly and Heather the air carried a tang of home.

After a long silence, Arthur turned to Earl. "Do you know where we are?" he asked tautly.

"Someplace in Britain. But the Lady didn't say exactly where this gate would lead."

"And the time of year?"

"Time passes differently in the two worlds. But from what she said, I'd guess April."

"April," Arthur repeated. "April in Britain! How can this have happened? There should be trees budding; there should be daffodils and new green grass. We should hear cuckoos in the woods and see larks soaring in the sky—a clear blue sky!"

His face was pained as he looked at his friend. "Merlin, can we really do anything? Is there anything here worth fighting for?"

"There are people left here. People and the glimmer of hope they hold."

He was silent for a moment, then continued. "Arthur, you said you'd been through it before. You didn't relish coming back, because you knew what you were in for. But maybe, because we *do* know what we're in for, we can do better this time. We know our mistakes and the ones made after us. Maybe we can see the danger signals. Maybe we can set things on the right road so this doesn't happen again."

Arthur smiled grimly. "Maybe so. But it's rather an up-hill road."

"Yes, it is," Merlin replied. Then his dark eyes flashed with a smile, and he spread his arms exultantly. "But look what you have to start with! A wise old adolescent wizard and two seasoned young campaigners, dropouts from the best school in Wales! What quest ever began in better company?"

Young Arthur Pendragon threw back his head and laughed. The sound rang like a bell over the silent landscape. "Now, that's a quest I want to be a part of! Let's be on our way!"

Four cloaked figures walked down the hillside as the snow about them turned a soft, fragile pink. In the eastern sky, the veiled sun rose on a new day.

BOOK TWO

TOMORROW'S MAGIC

Nearly three years have passed, bringing Britain more change than it has seen since the Devastation. Slowly the climate has warmed, slowly the power of magic has grown.

In Britain's Southeast, dark forces have gathered behind the sorceress Morgan. In the Northwest, a young-seeming warrior calling himself Arthur Pendragon has won himself supporters, allies—and enemies. Three young people—Earl Bedwas, Heather McKenna, and Wellington Jones—are at the heart of his new court.

16

LEGENDS RENEWED

Heather missed the ball. She leaped, but it sailed over her, inches beyond her outstretched fingers. Her fleece-lined boots thumped back onto the sand, and, laughing, she turned and ran after it.

Already the ball was rolling swiftly down the damp sand toward the ocean. It slammed against a half-buried stone, bounced into the air, and came down on a jumble of dark rocks that jutted out into the water.

Heather's hood was back, and her thin, light brown braids streamed behind her in the cold breeze. They'd just bought that ball, dyed all red and blue, from a leather worker in Ravenglass. She wasn't about to let it get washed out to sea.

Skidding to a halt at the rocks, she stepped onto them cautiously. At high tide they were mostly beneath the water, and even now, their water-smoothed surfaces were damp and slimy. Her boots scraped against crusted barnacles as she stepped around tide pools and slippery patches of green to make her way out to the ball.

It had landed in a pool at the very edge of the rocks. Water surged and boomed in the deep crevasse beyond, while waves regularly slapped against the rock, filling the air with a fine salty spray. Heather licked the saltiness from her lips as she reached down and scooped the ball from the cold, clear pool. Holding it high like a torch, she turned back toward her friends on the distant beach, smiling and waving triumphantly.

She could see the two standing side by side on the dry snow-flecked sand. The veiled sunlight glinted off Welly's glasses as he hopped up and down, waving. Beside him, Earl was also waving, looking tall and thin beside Welly's sturdy plumpness. Both were yelling, but Heather couldn't hear the words over the constant rumbling and crashing of the sea behind her.

They were yelling and pointing; then both started running toward her. Clutching the ball, she began walking back. It was too late. An extra-large wave burst over the rocks, engulfing her in cold, wet foam. In the hammering surge of water, her feet slipped from the slimy rocks.

Suddenly everything was dark, wet, and cold. In panic, she opened her eyes, then shut them against the stinging salt water. The darkness about her surged and eddied. She couldn't tell which was the way up, the way to air. But she needed to find it—now!

Something pulled at her, but not the ocean. An arm pulling her upward. Welly's or Earl's. They'd gotten there quickly. Her head burst through into the air. Another head was bobbing beside hers. But even through the dripping hair plastered to her face, she could see that it was not one of her friends.

It was a young blond man, and despite his own bedraggled appearance, he was grinning broadly. "Excuse the familiarity, miss, but you seemed to need a wee bit of help."

"You'll both be needing that," came a voice from the rocks above them, "if you don't get out before the next big wave. Come on, Welly, let's haul them up."

The two boys soon dragged Heather and her rescuer onto the rocks. "Let's get back to the beach," Earl said, wrapping his dry jacket around Heather while Welly offered his to the stranger. "I'll go start a fire." Picking up his walking stick from the rocks, Earl hurried ahead. By the time the others reached him, he had a good fire going with a few pieces of driftwood.

Heather huddled close to the flames, shivering from cold and from the fear that had suddenly caught up with her. She spoke to the stranger through chattering teeth. "I'm sorry you got soaked, but thanks for helping me. I could have been swept out to sea like . . . Oh, the ball! Our new ball, what happened to it?"

Welly laughed. "Here," he said, producing it from behind his back. "The wave carried it neatly onto the beach. You needn't have risked life and limb for it after all."

"Well, it's new," she said defensively.

Earl grinned, pushing black hair back from his pale, thin face. "And you, of course, are tattered and expendable, being all of fourteen years old."

She kicked a bare foot at him, but he dodged back and then joined the others squatting by the fire. "But as well as thanks," he said, "perhaps we owe this gentleman some introductions. This damsel, formerly in distress, is Heather McKenna. He is Wellington Jones, and I am . . . Earl Bedwas."

Heather raised an eyebrow at that but said nothing. Instead, she studied the newcomer. He was a man and bearded but didn't seem much older than Earl's apparent age of seventeen. His embroidered leather jacket and boots, now drying on the sand, had a slightly foreign look about them.

"I'm Kyle, Kyle O'Mara. I'm a harper, just come this morning from Ireland."

"Ireland," Heather and Welly said together, exchanging excited smiles. Foreign countries always sounded so glamorous, particularly since there were so few still inhabited—at least in Europe and North America.

"Yes, I came to find and join your King Arthur." He looked down, a blush spreading over his already dark face. "You'll be thinking I'm a romantic fool. But over in Ireland we've heard rumors about Arthur's return, about his setting out to unite all of Britain as it was before the Devastation. And . . . and, well, I thought maybe he could use a harper. Kings always did in the old tales."

The three young people smiled and nodded. "I'm sure he could," Welly said. "But if you're headed to Keswick, what were you doing on this beach?"

"Oh, well, I asked a man at the harbor how best to get to Arthur's town, and he said there was a small party from Keswick heading back there soon, and they'd gone off toward this beach. I was looking for them but didn't see anyone except you kids. You didn't notice them, did you?"

After an awkward silence, Earl said, "Actually, it was probably us the man was talking about. We came from Keswick on business and were going to start back this afternoon, except we got a little diverted trying out the new ball."

Kyle's expression wavered between pleasure and skepticism. "Isn't it a little dangerous for, eh . . . young people to travel unescorted all that distance?"

"Oh, no," Welly answered. "Not really. Now that Arthur's

united Cumbria, his patrols keep down the brigands and slavers. And the muties don't cause much trouble."

"Well, that's good to hear. And your, eh, business is all taken care of?"

"Oh, I think so, isn't it, Earl?" Heather said as the older boy nodded in response.

"Yes, we had some people to talk with, and we wanted to inspect the new port. There hasn't been a really good one here since before the Devastation, when the coasts were higher. But the Duke of Ravenglass made an alliance with Arthur last year and agreed to build up the port. What did you think of it?"

"I was impressed, and there seems to be lots of other building going on."

Earl nodded. "These Cumbrian dukedoms used to fight a lot among themselves. But now that Arthur's united them, there's time for building and for trade." He stood up, brushing sand off his trousers. "Maybe we'd better get going. Are you dry enough?"

Kyle felt his clothes. They were stiff with salt, but dry. "Yes, I am. That was a fine fire you built, and with very little fuel, too."

"Eh . . . yes, thanks. I have a . . . knack for that sort of thing. Have you a horse?"

"No. I tried to find one but was told the King was assembling them all in Keswick, at least the tall ones. Why is that?"

Welly spoke up, feeling on safe ground with questions of military strategy. "He's building a cavalry. And he's choosing all the taller horses to breed with each other so we can start getting real warhorses again, like in the old days."

Heather reached for her boots, brushing off the dried sand. "We left our horses up by the dunes. Welly's and mine are probably too small, but there ought to be a little extra room on Earl's. His legs are so long he needs a really big horse." She grinned impishly.

Kyle stood up. "Well now, I would certainly appreciate your company, if I'd not be too much bother. It really is fortunate I fell in with you."

Welly chortled. "I thought it was Heather who did the falling in."

Kyle retrieved his bag and harp from where he'd dropped them on the beach, and together the four trudged through the sand up to where the horses were grazing on clumps of coarse coastal grass.

Soon, with the young Irishman riding on the rump of Earl's black mare, they set off inland. At first the valley of the River Esk was wide enough for several farms. Beyond low stone walls, the hardy short-season grain had just been harvested. It was mid-August, and the first snows had already blown down from the ice-encased north.

Then the fells crowded closer together, and the narrow road rose more steeply. The land, bare of all but coarse gray-green grass, was inhabited here only by dark-wooled sheep. Occasionally shepherds appeared, armed with fur wraps against the cold and spears against fell-dogs and muties. A chill wind buffeted the fells, and the early dusting of snow swirled into the air and snaked in wisps across the road. The bleak stillness was broken only by the sound of their own passage, the bleating of sheep, or the lonely call of some rare fell-land bird.

The road itself was old, having been the main route into the British lakelands since long before even the Romans came to the islands. But now the once-paved surface was pitted and crumbling. Often, despite their careful three-toed agility, the small, shaggy horses were forced to thread it single file.

Throughout the day, the sky remained gray, not as much from cloud as from the high haze of bomb-stirred dust that after five hundred years was only now beginning to thin. Behind it, a veiled sun was sinking into the now-distant smear of the Irish Sea when Earl finally called a halt for the night.

They had already crossed the first pass and dropped into the desolate vale beyond. Where a dark, icy stream gurgled under a bridge, Earl led them off the road to camp within the low stone walls of a sheepfold.

Kyle was content to let the boy take the lead in this. And he'd enjoyed listening to Earl point out features along the way, though his guide persistently sidled away from some of the subjects he'd asked about.

After they dismounted, Kyle set out to collect dried sheep dung for a fire but returned to find that Earl already had an impressive blaze going. They pulled a supper of bread and radishes from their saddlebags, and the young Irishman, burning with questions, could wait no longer.

"Please, now, tell me about Arthur and his court and all. Living in Keswick, you must know something about him. We've heard so many stories, even in Ireland. But I confess it's hard to believe that all of them are quite true."

Welly and Heather took on similar expressions, polite but cautiously blank. They deferred to Earl.

Rubbing a thin hand over his beardless chin, Earl asked, "What have you heard?"

"Well, about how this is the real Arthur Pendragon,

the one out of legends. About how the old wizard Merlin and a couple of warriors battled monsters and Morgan the Enchantress to make their way to Avalon. And how they awakened the King there and brought him back, magically made young again, so he could unite and bring peace to all the fighting shires."

"Well, that's all true . . . enough."

"But what about the magic? I mean, sure I believe in it; there's a lot of little magic these days. Some people can use it to find lost tools or remove splinters or cure sick sheep. But the stuff these stories talk about is high magic, like gray-bearded wizards casting spells and people coming and going into Faerie and talking with Eldritch folk."

The Irishman shook his head. "I mean, maybe it's all true. But doesn't it make you uncomfortable? How can normal people get used to having powerful magic workers just walking among them? I don't know that I could."

Tension tightened around the group like a fist. "You could try," Welly said tautly.

Into the dragging silence, Earl suddenly hissed, "Quiet, something's coming."

Kyle was amazed at how suddenly and silently the fire was quenched. But his attention was quickly pulled elsewhere.

From a small side valley came the sound of horses, many horses. The muffled clicking of three-toed feet, the jingle of harness, the occasional clank of metal on leather. A party of armed men. But whose?

17

THE WAGES OF POWER

Keeping very still, the four huddled together within the stone enclosure. After the sound and the dark shapes had passed down the valley, Welly whispered, "Were they ours?"

Earl answered, "I doubt it. None were wearing the Pendragon badge."

"But it's too dark to be sure of that," Kyle pointed out.

"I have good night vision," Earl answered simply. "But whether they are brigands or others, an armed party of that size should not be wandering around in Cumbria. We'd better follow and see what they're up to."

"But surely that's not our job," Kyle complained.

"Hey," Welly said, "one of the reasons the Cumbrian dukedoms accept Arthur as King is that he maintains order. And anyone who's sworn allegiance to him has to help in that."

"Besides," Heather added while quickly saddling her horse, "wasn't adventure one of the things you came here to find?"

"Well, yes," the Irishman admitted. He refrained from adding that authorized adventure was one thing, but playing around at night with kids pretending to be heroes was another. At the same time, he had no desire to be left in this strange, bleak land by himself.

Soon they were packed up again and on the road, moving eastward. Their quarry was some distance ahead, but although the pursuers gradually gained ground, they were afraid to draw too close and risk being noticed. In the eastern sky, a blurred half-moon cast faint mists of light over the fells.

After threading down the narrow valley, the road rose steeply until there came a brief moment when the armed men were darkly outlined against the gray-black sky. They disappeared over the pass, and the four hurried after them.

When they, too, reached the pass, they saw on the slope below a scatter of campfires twinkling through the dark. Silently Earl motioned a halt.

"There's a second troop camped down there."

"Are they more of the same?" Heather asked.

Earl stared into the night. "No. Some of the ones around the campfires are wearing black and gold badges. It must be one of Arthur's patrols."

"Then who are . . . ?"

Welly's unfinished question was answered by a sudden eruption of sound. Out of the dark, from where they had stealthily circled the camp, the first group of armed men broke into savage yells and swept down in attack.

Instantly all was chaos. Around the fires, startled men jumped up, grabbed weapons, and began flailing at the mounted attackers. Noise of battle jarred the cold, silent valley.

"We've got to do something!" Heather screamed. "Our soldiers are being attacked!"

"What can we—?" Kyle began.

Earl turned in the saddle. "Get off," he ordered brusquely. Startled, Kyle slid off the mare, and quickly Earl unfastened the walking stick that had been strapped to the saddle. Raising it over his head, he spurred his horse downhill toward the fight.

Suddenly it seemed he was holding a torch. From the end of his staff, purple flames soared upward, spewing a cloud of glowing smoke. The smoke pulsed with light and life as it rose higher and higher into the night air. Then it spread out, beginning to take form and solidity.

In moments, a huge purple dragon was hovering over the battle. Its beating wings stirred mighty gusts of wind, and its gaping mouth reeked of sulfur and glowed with the fires of hell.

Below, men and horses screamed in terror. In moments, the mounted attackers were scattering over the hillside. Most of those in the camp hurled themselves to the ground or ran screaming into the night.

After silence began settling onto the hillside, one deep voice rang out from beside a fire. "Look! It's Merlin! Merlin the Wizard! Men of Arthur, that winged beast's only a thing of sorcery—and ours at that!"

The wizard, staff now lowered, rode his black mare up to the large dark-bearded man who was calling back his still-reluctant troops. The big man smiled broadly, but even he stayed a cautious distance from the boy. Overhead, the dragon was already fading to smoke and blowing away on the wind.

"Well met, Merlin lad." The man turned a nervous, scowling face toward his troops, observing their extreme slowness in returning to the camp. Apologetically he glanced back at the wizard. "They're brave boys, really. It just seems that some of them prefer flesh-and-blood enemies to magic, even if it does save their skins. I guess they remember your earlier demonstrations. But me, now, I've never been one to say that magic doesn't have its place in an army."

"Thank you, Otto. But I suggest that from now on, a few more sentries should have a place as well."

The other frowned but held back any reply, and the boy on the black horse continued. "Have you any idea whose men those were?"

"None. But a few got themselves left behind with swords in their ribs, so we should find out something."

Welly, Heather, and Kyle had joined the others around a campfire when a soldier reported to Otto that examining the bodies had revealed nothing. "Well, then, bring me that horse you caught," ordered the commander. "Maybe there's some clue in the saddlebags."

A shaggy bay horse was led up, its eyes and nostrils still wide with fear. Heather got up and walked over to the animal.

"Poor thing, he's even less used to Earl's . . . unusual tactics than our horses are." Gently she patted its nose, then moved a hand up to rub behind its ears and down the long coarse hair of its neck.

Otto finished rummaging through the saddlebags. "Nothing! There's not a clue where they're from."

"Oh, the horse is from Lancaster," Heather said without thinking.

"How would you know?" Otto asked sharply.

"Oh, I . . . ," she stammered. "I just do. I mean, well, horses from different places have a different . . . look about them. This one's just like those Lancaster horses captured after that border raid last year."

"Hmm, maybe," Otto said skeptically.

Merlin looked curiously at Heather but intervened. "If Heather says this horse is from Lancaster, Otto, it probably is. She has a . . . a good feel for animals. However, if a party of Lancaster warriors has penetrated this far into Cumbria, Arthur must be told immediately. I don't know what your original patrol assignment was, but I suggest you detail a contingent to continue it while you and the others set out for Keswick with us by first light."

Otto frowned. "Yes, I suppose that would be best. Come on, let's see how many we lost. Eh . . . will you help with the wounded?"

"If I can. Healing magic is not what I'm best at."

Heather turned to see Kyle staring after the soldier and the wizard. He blinked at her. "You mean Earl . . . he's . . ."

She sighed. "Didn't the stories you heard mention that when Merlin came back into the world, he was a lot younger, too?"

"Well, maybe something of the sort. But he's just a kid!"

"Yes, in a lot of ways, he really is." She could see Kyle was not comforted. As he turned away, she thought she saw him make the hand sign against evil omens.

Shaking her head, she turned to Welly. He shrugged. "Well, it was worth a try. Guess I'll go see if I can be of some help."

Heather looked again at the captured horse. It had a shallow cut on its withers but seemed to be suffering mostly from fear. She tried to soothe it, but her mind kept drifting back to her friend.

She'd known what Earl had hoped to do from the moment he'd introduced himself with that name, the name he'd had in school before he regained the memory of who he was. He must have hoped that this newcomer would come to know and like him as a person before learning that he was also the wizard Merlin.

It might have worked if he hadn't been forced to thwart this attack publicly. But even then, Heather wasn't sure. For though magic was returning to the world, people still found it very unsettling. And the daily presence of magic workers among them seemed the most unsettling thing of all. The greater the power, the greater the fear and isolation it seemed to bring.

She frowned, abruptly forcing her thoughts aside. Strange powers and social isolation were nothing she wanted to dwell on just now. She hurried after Otto and the others, hoping there was some diverting task for her as well.

The next morning, they were all on the road before the dust-shielded sun had cleared the eastern hills. Kyle now rode the captured horse, willingly leaving Merlin alone on his black mare. The route led sunward past a small frozen tarn, then veered north at Ambleside.

Heather felt uneasy but tried to keep her mind firmly on the surroundings. She smiled at the occasional farmer or herder who waved as the troop rode past. She studied Thirlmere as they clopped along its eastern shore. With its long, narrow surface already mottled with ice, it looked like a huge molting snake stretched beneath the fells.

But her thoughts kept sliding back. Finally she faced them. How *had* she known that the horse was from

Lancaster? She had touched the horse and felt its fear and longing to go home. And she'd almost seen the route it longed to take, the winding tracks that led back—to Lancaster.

She shook her head to banish the picture. This wasn't the first time this sort of thing had happened. In a way, it was exciting, like suddenly discovering you had some little skill that others didn't have—like running faster, maybe, or being good at sketching. But this wasn't some ordinary little skill, and when she stopped pretending that it was, it frightened her.

It also made her feel very alone. Maybe this was the time. Maybe she should ride up beside Welly and talk to him about it. But though he was her oldest friend, she knew he wouldn't understand this. And Earl, a friend just as close, might understand too well. Frightened again, her thoughts shied away. Desperately she admired the landscape.

Toward evening, they cleared the final pass and dropped down to Derwentwater and the little town of Keswick. Against the dark backdrop of the fells, smoke from cooking fires was already rising from the clustered buildings at the lake's north shore. Before reaching the center of town, they turned off at the old manor which for five hundred years had been home of the dukes of Keswick and was now headquarters of Arthur, King of Cumbria.

It had not been far from there that, two years earlier, Arthur, along with herself, Welly, and Earl, had emerged from Avalon. At first, the local people had been skeptical of the young blond man and his claim to be *the* King Arthur. But a dramatic and, to many, still-frightening demonstration of Merlin's magic had convinced them on that score. And as the Duke of Keswick had recently died without an heir, the people of the town were willing enough to take on this vigorous, personable young leader. Arthur, through diplomacy and a few strategic battles, had since brought all of Cumbria behind him and this summer had extended his realm beyond the eastern mountains to Carlisle.

As their party clattered into the cobbled courtyard, the sound brought people rushing from the buildings. Soon the air was filled with white breath, eager voices, jingling harness, and the stomping of hooves.

A tall blond man strode out of the main hall, his skin as pale and bright as snow in sunlight. Amused, Heather watched Kyle as with growing understanding, he looked first at the King, then back at Merlin. Both were strikingly pale, paler than anyone could be whose ancestors had survived the radiation rained on the world after the Devastation. But no paler than someone should be who had first walked this world two thousand years earlier.

Arthur slapped Merlin familiarly on the shoulder and listened while he and Otto described the battle on the Ravenglass road. Remembering the horse, Heather said nothing. She started to slip away but decided that might only call more attention to herself. Trying to look small and unimportant, she joined the group around the King.

Arthur was nodding, stroking his short golden beard. "So, the question is, why were Lancaster raiders that far into Cumbria?"

"Spies, probably," said Reginald, Duke of Ambleside.

"Yes," the King agreed, "but would they risk that much

provocation on their own? Up to now, Lancaster's seemed anxious to stay out of our way."

"And you're suggesting . . . ?" Otto asked.

"That they might have formed an alliance with someone and agreed to do the scouting."

"An alliance with Morgan, maybe?" Welly suggested from the sidelines. Arthur frowned, then raised a questioning eyebrow at Merlin, who was standing somewhat away from the others.

The wizard shook his head. "No, there's no feel of Morgan about this. These were ordinary men on an ordinary mission."

Relieved, Arthur nodded. "And we've heard nothing of Morgan or her minions meddling this far north—not yet, at least. No, I was thinking more of Queen Margaret."

"The Queen of Scots?" Duke Reginald said. "That would be awfully bold of her."

"I suspect the new Scottish Queen is a very bold person indeed. Look at all she's done since succeeding her father."

"True enough," the Duke agreed. "But if we're going to debate strategy, let's do it inside. It's starting to snow again." Fussily he brushed snowflakes from his full gingery beard.

The others laughed and headed up the broad steps to the arched entrance of the hall. Welly led Kyle up, but Heather hung back. Then she saw Merlin walking toward her, a questioning look on his face. The fear clutched at her again, and she hurried after the others.

"Come on, Earl," she called tautly over her shoulder. "Let's go hear if the new harper can sing. Haven't you been saying that Arthur needed a bard?"

Merlin's look of concern dissolved into a wry smile. "Yes, but I suspect this one is learning that magic and legends are a lot more comfortable in song than in reality."

Heather shivered and nodded in silent agreement. Behind them, the August snow began falling in earnest as the two walked into the King's hall.

18

STIRRINGS

Whatever his own misgivings, the young harper impressed his listeners with both his voice and his skill at the harp. The background necessary to be bard for this particular king, however, was clearly lacking, and Arthur assigned Welly and Heather to fill the Irishman in on events of the last two years.

For the most part, these sessions were enjoyed by all three, but whenever the harper's questions turned to magic, Heather quickly changed the subject. And although he now knew the story of Merlin's ancient enchantment and his return to childhood in a magical attempt to preserve his life, Kyle did not seem to find Merlin's appearance as a gangly teenager to be the least bit reassuring. Like many others, he gave the wizard a wide berth and spoke to him as little as possible.

One evening at supper, however, Kyle found himself seated beside Merlin. Cold and dark hung among the rafters of the dining hall, but underneath, the air was rich with the fragrance of potato soup and freshly baked barley bread. In noisy conversation, a dozen of the King's closest followers crowded onto benches around an old oaken table, a rare piece of furniture that had somehow escaped being burned for heat in the post-Devastation years.

When, as usual, the subject of next season's battles came up, Kyle hesitantly asked whether they couldn't use Merlin's magic to help plan their strategy.

The wizard frowned at the harper, but when Kyle visibly cringed in response, Merlin softened his reply. "Yes, no doubt it would be very convenient if I could just go into a trance and tell you what Queen Margaret or her allies are planning. But I can't. It doesn't work that way."

"But," Kyle protested, "the old stories say you used to prophesy for Arthur."

The King laughed and passed the tureen of soup down the table. "He's got you there, Merlin. Admittedly, you didn't do it often, but you *did* occasionally come through with some pretty good ones."

Exasperation crawled across Merlin's face. "Yes, but prophecy is not my strong point. Nobody seems to realize that there are many kinds of magic. Prophecy is a specialty, and with those for whom it doesn't come easily, it requires specialized equipment. I don't have that now."

"So you can't even tell what we're having for dinner tomorrow night?" Kyle asked incredulously.

"Not without talking to Cook."

"Then what use is there in being a wizard?"

The large chunk of bread on Kyle's plate suddenly vanished and reappeared on Merlin's. "Oh, it has its uses," he said, taking a leisurely bite. The harper blanched and concentrated on eating his soup.

When the early snow had melted, the second promised consignment of horses arrived from the allied dukedom of Carlisle. The next morning, most of the town came out to the King's horse meadows to examine the new arrivals.

This town of farmers and herders took a proprietary interest in everything their king did. And despite earlier scoffing, they now had no doubt about his ideas for building up the horse population. Arthur's dominion had spread, at least in part, because of his new mobile cavalry.

Heather and Welly joined the others by the horses. In the watery sunlight, the grass glinted silver with frost and crunched underfoot. The air smelled of horse and excitement. Appraisingly their eyes scanned the shaggy beasts, picking out those whose size or other throwback features might breed improved warhorses.

"What do you think of that bay stallion there?" Welly asked as they hung over the stone wall of the corral. "He's almost as tall as Arthur's gray."

"He's a beauty," Heather agreed. "But he doesn't seem very content. Maybe once he gets to know the place he'll calm down a bit."

"Yeah, but whatever their temper, you can bet we won't get tall horses until everyone else is mounted on one."

"We *are* still kids."

"We've seen as many battles as most of the rest!"

"But you don't *look* the part," Merlin said, coming up behind them. "This war business is largely image. Ferocious warriors on big horses scare people more."

"But I can make terribly ferocious faces," Welly said, producing an expression that Heather thought made him look like a demented toad.

Merlin laughed. "As my mother used to say, watch out, or someday your face will freeze like that."

Welly and Heather exchanged startled glances. Somehow, they'd never thought of their friend as having had a mother. But before they could pursue the matter, a commotion arose near the King, and the three went over to find the cause.

"Certainly I can talk with him now," Arthur was saying to one of his retainers. "Didn't he come all the way from Bassenthwaite to talk with his king?"

Though Bassenthwaite was actually no great distance, the statement made the tousled peasant nearby swell with pride. Self-consciously straightening his clothes, the young man walked up to the King. He attempted to bow, looked up, and was struck speechless as he realized the tall, fair man a few feet from him was actually King Arthur.

The King stepped into the spluttering silence. "You have a message from Bassenthwaite?"

"Yes, sire, King Arthur, sir. We lost some sheep, a third of our flock, sire. We're a poor valley, Your Majesty, and it's a real blow. The shepherds lost them in the last storm, and we haven't been able to find so much as a scrap of wool since. And what with the fell-dogs and muties, it worries us, you see, sire."

"Lost sheep," Arthur said flatly. Then he smiled. "Well, young man, why don't you go with this gentleman here. He'll see about getting you some refreshment while I discuss this with my advisers."

"Oh, yes, thank you, Your Kingness." The man bowed and stumbled backward until he was led away.

"Lost sheep!" Arthur exclaimed. "I have horses to work with before the next snow, the couriers from Carlisle brought alarming news about the Scots, and now I'm to look for lost sheep."

"Remember, Arthur," Merlin cautioned, "the first thing any conqueror must do is keep the home front happy."

The King turned on him. "Have you any idea, Merlin,

how difficult it is to take advice, particularly correct advice, from a beardless boy?"

"If you like, sire, I could conjure up a beard until my real one grows in."

"No, please don't. It would look ridiculous. All right, let's get some of those townspeople to form a sheep-hunting party. Make it a prestigious royal commission."

"Could I go, too?" Heather asked. She enjoyed horses but had a special feeling for sheep. They were dumb and helpless, yet hardy and stubborn as well.

The King looked at her a moment. "All right. Several parties would be more efficient, and you're good with animals. And yes, Welly, don't ask. You go, too; you're getting to be a good weapons man. But don't you ask, Merlin; I need your advice on this business with the Scots." He looked around. "Kyle, why don't you go with them. Your songs could use a little more local flavor."

Within an hour, the sheep hunters set out. The largest group headed north with the shepherd, but Heather said she wanted to look west of broad Bassenthwaite Lake.

"Well, miss," the shepherd said, "I don't really see how they could have gone that far. But suit yourself. The more eyes the better."

So the party of three headed where the western fells bore down on the valley, their high peaks trailing thin banners of snow in the wind. Heather trudged along silently, trying to think about sheep, trying to think like sheep. Welly thought more about horses and how he wished he were riding one now, a large white one.

Dutifully Kyle looked around him, trying to find words and feelings for the wild mountain landscape, for the sheets of wind-chopped water glinting like dull silver in the misty

light, for the brave rock-walled fields, and for the high fells
baring the bones of the earth to an empty sky.

Suddenly the sky was no longer empty. Hollow haunting calls fell from it, from the wedge of dark specks cutting
across the expanse of gray. "Look," Kyle called. "Those
must be geese. I read that they used to fly like that."

"Geese," Heather breathed, listening to their wild music.
"Then they aren't extinct. I hope Earl sees them. He gets
so depressed sometimes about the things that are gone."

After a time, staring into the sky, Welly cleared his
throat. "I hate to mention it, but if it's sheep we're looking
for, they'll be on the ground."

"Welly! You have no romance in your soul!" Heather
exclaimed.

"I do too."

"That's true; you want a white charger."

Welly blushed, and taking off his glasses, polished
them furiously on his jacket front. "They don't come in
white anymore," he muttered.

Heather laughed apologetically. "Well, you'd look dash-
ing on one if they did." Tugging thoughtfully on a braid,
she continued. "Let's go that way. I feel . . . I mean, I think
that's a good place for sheep." She pointed to where several fells folded down to form a narrow valley.

"Wherever you say." Welly jammed his glasses back on.

They climbed into the mountains until Heather finally
stopped at the mouth of a small gorge. A frozen ribbon of
water trailed from it into a loudly gurgling beck.

"Up here."

"Here?" Kyle said skeptically. "See any footprints?"

"No. Yes. Come on."

The snow here had melted, and between the rocks the

grass was dry and springy. As they climbed the steep gorge, Welly contemplated the ancient phrase "wild-goose chase." Now that he'd actually seen wild geese, he wondered if "wild-sheep chase" wouldn't be more appropriate.

Heather turned into an even narrower ravine. Welly, puffing up behind her, was about to protest when the cold breeze brought the sound of sheep bleating.

Kyle stopped, bewildered. "How did you know?"

She answered tensely, without turning around, "I just did. Come on, let's try to drive them back to the valley."

After several minutes, they'd had little success. Every time they closed on a dark, woolly animal, it moved off— in the wrong direction.

Suddenly Heather stiffened and spun around, looking at the rocky crags above. "Hurry! We've got to get them away. There are fell-dogs about."

"Nonsense," Welly asserted. "If there were, these sheep would be all worked up."

"Well, there are, and *I'm* worked up. Get them moving!"

Their increased frenzy finally turned the sheep in the downward direction. But they were only halfway to the main beck when the sound of growling rolled down at them from behind.

The sheep broke into panicky flight. Heather looked back. Two grizzled fell-dogs sprang out from behind a rock. Red tongues lolled between bared yellow fangs.

Welly and Kyle pulled out their swords and ran back to her. But Heather just stared at the animals, her gaze intense and cold. The dogs' eyes were locked on hers. The animals crouched for a spring that never came. Slowly the crouch turned into a cower. Bushy tails slid between their legs as the dogs slunk backward into the tumbled rocks.

For a moment, no one said a word. Then Welly whispered, "They'll be back."

"No," Heather said, suddenly relaxing and turning around. "They won't. But we'd better go after those sheep, or they'll run all the way to Borrowdale."

By the end of the day, the sheep were back with their people. Though Heather herself said nothing, the story of the remarkable rescue spread rapidly.

That night, after dinner in the King's hall, Kyle brought out his harp and sang a new song. It carried in its melody the longing call of wild geese and the sound of wind over barren rock. And the words told of a woman of power and her touch with creatures of the wild, her touch of caring and command.

Heather listened, looking paler and paler. She kept her eyes down but could feel the gaze of others on her. A faint noise of shifting bodies told her that the space between herself and those seated near her was widening. Before the harper finished, she slipped out of the room. A minute later, Merlin followed her.

He found her in the old garden below the hall. She was huddled on a stone bench beside a large carved urn. Tears glistened on her cheeks.

Sitting quietly beside her, Merlin reached out one thin hand and touched hers. "This has been going on for some time, hasn't it?"

She nodded, then words tumbled out. "Yes, for months, a year, maybe. Oh, Earl, everything's changing so, inside and out, and it frightens me. Tonight . . . tonight he called me a 'woman of power.' But I'm not! I'm not a woman; I don't want to be. And I don't want any power!"

Sagging against his bony shoulder, she sobbed violently. He looked down at the quivering plaits of her honey-colored hair. His voice was pained. "Heather, in this world, you *are* a woman. You don't choose to grow up any more than you chose these gifts. And power is a gift, though it comes unasked for and often unwanted. You cannot deny it; all you can do is try to understand it and learn to use it, instead of letting it use you."

"Oh, Earl, I don't know. It makes me so . . . different. It cuts me off so."

In the dark, Merlin sighed. "Don't I know that. Magic is the loneliest gift in the world."

"That's what I mean. I don't want that, not now. I mean, when I was at Llandoylan, I was awfully lonely. I didn't fit in. I tried pretending that I didn't care, that I didn't need the others. But now, since we've come to Keswick with Arthur, I do have a place. I belong. How long will that last if people start thinking I work magic, even a little?"

Merlin stared down at his own clenched hands. Then he raised his head, a grim smile on his face. "I understand, Heather. Believe me, I understand. But I don't think it need be like that anymore. The world has changed. Magic is cropping up everywhere now. It might have been latent in your family for generations, and nobody knew because it wasn't the season for it. But the seasons have turned."

A smile quivered on her tear-streaked face. "I don't know. Maybe that makes a difference. I can hope, I guess."

Merlin continued, trying to be cheerful. "Come now. Tomorrow, if the weather holds, I'll take you to a place of power where you can get a feel for what you have and for how to deal with it." He looked at her almost pleadingly. "Is that all right?"

"Yes," she whispered after a silence. "I really can't handle this any longer—not alone."

Hesitantly he squeezed her hand.

That night she lay awake a long while, trying not to think about sheep and fell-dogs and the frightening powers that bound her to them. She succeeded only when sheer exhaustion pulled her into sleep.

19

VISIONS OF POWER

Heather woke to gray light seeping through the parchment-covered window beside her bed. She slipped from beneath her wool blankets, shivering as bare feet touched the cold stone floor. Quickly she padded over to the room's one window, which retained three of its ancient glass panes. Scraping impatiently at its ferns of frost, she squinted out for a glimpse of what the day was like. Nothing but gray.

Annoyed, she unlatched the casement and flung it open. Cold mist swirled in, and with it came recollections of yesterday and plans for today. She slammed the window shut. But the memories remained.

Reluctantly she dressed. Every movement was weighted with dread, with a feeling that she was about to step through a gate, a gate that opened only one way. Thoughts of what might lie on the other side were frightening enough. But what really chilled her was the thought of never getting back.

When she finally dragged herself downstairs, she found Merlin waiting for her by the dark fireplace. It was too early in the season to burn precious fuel, and the hall seemed cold as a tomb.

Heather walked toward him, wondering suddenly if she looked as frail and drawn as he did. Is that what magic did to a person? Did it drain them? Did it eat them up inside? She shuddered with a confused surge of fear and pity—pity for her friend, fear for herself. Somehow she managed a wan smile as Merlin handed her a bowl of warm porridge.

He motioned her to a stone bench and sat down beside her. "Most of the others have already left to work with the horses. I told them we had other plans."

She said nothing, making herself think only of the rough feel of the pottery, of the fragrant steam, and the nutty taste of each mouthful.

But soon they were putting on their hooded, fur-lined jackets and stepping into the cold gray of the courtyard. The mists had risen from the buildings but still shrouded the surrounding fells. Bleakly Heather looked into the grayness.

"It's not far from here," Merlin said as he headed for the gate. "We'll walk. Horses don't like this sort of thing."

They're not alone, Heather thought.

They trudged up the main road out of town. Keswick, always a small town, had not suffered much from the social collapse of the Devastation. The population had dropped sharply, but the survivors had managed to raise the few crops and sheep that had developed resistance to cold and radiation. The mountains were defense against marauders, so the citizens of Keswick had never needed to wall in their town. With the arrival of Arthur, however, activity had increased to house and feed his growing army and to rebuild the more important roads.

The road Merlin and Heather took was one of these.

But soon they left it for an old sunken farm lane running between two stone walls. The hedges and wildflowers that once would have softened the stark gray stones had long ago vanished. Their climb brought them into the mists again, and Heather clutched her hood around her. Her thoughts were as dismal as the setting.

"Here we are," Merlin said. Heather jumped, realizing this was the second time he'd said that. Dutifully she looked around, and her heart nearly stopped. Ahead of her on a bleak hilltop, hulking gray shapes seemed to move in and out of the mist. Her throat went dry.

"I thought stone circles were . . . dangerous," she said hoarsely.

"You're remembering the one on the Devonshire moor. Yes, some are, but they are also places of power. Almost any really old site is. Ancient peoples built where they did to make use of the power. True, it can attract other unsavory things, like the wraith we met in Devon. But I've checked this place out. The only spirits here are sheep."

Heather looked more closely and saw that some of the gray shapes were indeed moving, and one was rubbing its back against a rough tilted stone. She certainly felt no menace about the place.

Slowly they walked forward. Some of the stones were missing, and some had toppled over or were leaning at crazy angles. Most of the unworked boulders were no taller than the two of them.

Merlin stepped into the circle. Heather took a deep breath and followed. He stood, head tilted, as if listening to some distant sound. Then he turned to Heather.

"The power here is a gentle kind—earth power, mostly.

I don't really know what sort of magic you have, but we should be able to tell something here."

He walked off to one side, where an inner rectangle of stones stood. "Ah, this should do," he said, squatting down beside one of the fallen stones. With a sigh of resignation, Heather joined him.

Centuries of weathering had hollowed a shallow depression in the stone, and now it was filled with rainwater.

Merlin patted the ground, and she sat beside him. "Reflective surfaces are one of the simplest magic tools. They help focus the sight.

"Here, put your hands on each side of this pool. Like that—fine. Now just look into it. Let your mind go free. Just look at the surface, at the reflections, and at the depths beyond them."

Heather felt foolish. She looked between her hands and saw a hole in a rock filled with stagnant water. The only thing reflected was the mist and the gray sky above her.

She looked and looked until her eyes ached. Her mind tired of even thinking about what she was supposed to do, and she just stared. Eventually he would tell her to quit, and they'd go home.

The reflected mists swirled and thickened into heavy clouds, then suddenly parted, revealing a scene below. She cried in alarm, but the cry was the cry of a bird, a graceful gull with pure white wings.

Bright, clear sunlight sparkled on the water below. The estuary of a great river, it was dotted with boats, some small and active, some huge and quiet in their docks, others sliding majestically along the water.

The gull tilted its wings and soared away from the river, over a great city. The city stretched in all directions, its buildings towering into the blue sky. Windows glinted like jewels in the sun. The noise of rumbling activity rose muted and distant as the gull glided on.

Below, trees replaced buildings. Grass swept in a green wave over the crest of hills. Tiny figures moved over paths and open space. Suddenly their faint voices were drowned under a discordant wail, a piercing cry that swelled to fill the world with its alarm.

The gull veered from the noise and rose up and up, upward toward the sun. Abruptly the sun's brightness and heat consumed the sky and the bird and all creation.

Dizzyingly the brightness faded, and the wings that seemed to carry her were black, a dusty, sullen black. The cry was the hoarse cry of a crow as it glided through the cold gray air. Below, the plain was bare except for wisps of snow harried by an icy wind.

Under a shrouded sun, the bird circled. Below now were two great clusters of figures. There was little movement— a time for scavenging. Lower and lower the crow dropped. Figures sprawled motionless on the ground, upturned faces blank with terror and death. The bird screamed.

And screamed. Heather found arms around her, shaking her as her own screams faded from the air.

"Heather! Come back!" Merlin's command quavered with worry. She sagged in his arms.

"I'm all right, I think," she said faintly as he helped her lean back against a stone. "Oh, Earl, is it always like that?"

"It depends on what you see. The more alarming the vision, the more alarming the experience. But tell me what you saw, that is, if you're up to it. I don't want to—"

"No, I can tell you. Only the end was really awful, and the middle, maybe. But mostly it was beautiful—and confusing. I really don't understand what I saw."

With Merlin huddled beside her in the misty cold, she

described her vision. At last she drew toward the end. "The armies were spread out over the plain, but when I . . . when the crow flew lower, the warriors were lying still as death, all over the ground. Earl, I knew some of them! People from here, part of Arthur's army."

She began sobbing again against his shoulder. "Oh, Earl, what did I see?"

He frowned, shaking his head. "I don't know. These things can be so confused. Past and present and future, or simply allegory, all muddled together. But . . ."

He was silent until Heather prompted him. "Yes?"

"There's something about it. Somehow it's the same sort of thing I've been sensing. A feeling, a foreboding that's been growing ever since we came out of Avalon with Arthur. It's as though the same cycle is beginning again. An endless, compelling, fatal cycle."

"I don't understand."

"Heather." He sat forward, looking at her tear-smeared face. "Once before, Arthur worked and fought to build a united, peaceful world. He succeeded for a while, until hatred and warfare tore it apart. Later, others built on what he had done, and civilization grew—but so did the wars and hatred until they blasted us back to this." He swept a hand angrily across the shrouded sky.

"The world is different now," he continued. "There are new forces moving it. Still, much is the same, too much. I have this dread that the end will also be the same. We will build and create, and in the end, it will all be destroyed. Maybe this time with no remnants left."

Heather shuddered, haunted by snatches of her vision. "Earl, with your power, isn't there something you can do?"

Frustrated, he slammed a fist against the stone. "I don't know! In this new world, magic has changed somehow, too. My spells and tricks seem to work, yet it's as though I am using an old, dying language, an archaic dialect. I can make myself understood by yelling loud enough, but there's a new language, a new magic abroad, and I don't understand it.

"Once I could prophesy, as Arthur said. I had a silver bowl that I made myself, working spells and power into the design. In it I could sometimes glimpse possible futures and help direct the present to the right course. If I had that bowl now, perhaps I could do that again. But it's long lost, and I don't even know if it would work in this new world. Yet I don't know what else to try! My ideas are as old and dead as the world they came from."

He huddled into his cloak, resting his hands dejectedly on his knees. Now Heather found herself comforting him.

"Come on, Earl, you'll work it out. You're young now, just like this world. I haven't any idea how to deal with whatever magic I have. I'm not sure I even want to. But I know you can use your power. You'll find something."

He looked up, smiling gratefully, then shook his head. "Here I am, Merlin the Wizard, just as insecure as any other teenager." He squeezed her shoulder, then stood up. "Well, we did find out one thing."

"We did?"

"The nature of your magic. You didn't see those visions, whatever they were, by yourself. You saw them through the eyes of animals. The events with the horse and the sheep, those were tied to animals, too. What about the other times you mentioned?"

"Oh, well . . . yes, maybe so. I found where the rats were

nesting, and I knew that the gatekeeper's horse was dying, and I really found the necklace only because of a spider."

Merlin was stamping his cold feet, trying to bring some life into them. "That's it, then. Unfortunately, I'm not very adept at animal magic. I'll help where I can, but you'll have to pick up a lot on your own, I'm afraid."

Heather stood up, turning her head to hide her scowl at that suggestion. Sighing, she brushed the dead grass from her trousers and followed him out of the stone circle.

Mists now hid only the peaks of the surrounding fells. A cold, damp wind carried the contented sound of sheep talking to each other and tearing out mouthfuls of coarse grass.

As they passed the last tilted stone, Merlin looked at his companion, then glanced away shyly. "I am sorry, Heather. I know this still must be very upsetting. Power always is. I wish I could make it easier for you. But I have to confess, I am glad to have someone to share it with."

Heather tried to smile in reply, but she was too confused to bring any words with it. She wasn't convinced she wanted loneliness, whether shared or not.

20

WINTER'S TALES

Before winter fully cut off Cumbria, closing its passes, word came to Arthur from two distant trouble spots. Messengers from the Duke of Carlisle reported that Queen Margaret had led her troops south from the frigid borders of the Scottish ice fields. After rampaging through Northumbria, they now threatened Newcastle. And Carlisle, which also bordered Scotland, was nervous.

The other news traveled with a group of traders from the Midlands. Arthur invited them into the great hall the afternoon they arrived. Throwing skins on the floor, the merchants spread their merchandise temptingly upon them. There were bolts of finely woven linen, dyed red and yellow, and costly carvings of wood from the southwest, where enough trees still grew for such. But the most treasured items were from the olden times.

Heather was particularly intrigued by ancient glass bottles of amber or green, while others looked over pieces of china and a few scraps of rare plastic. Merlin was drawn to a stack of pre-Devastation books.

The metalworker, though, drew the most attention. On the cold hearth, he set up his forge and blew a bowl of carefully conserved coals into life. "I search for scraps of metal everywhere," he told those around him. "Ruined cities are best. But you've got to be careful about what you take—nothing too rusty, mind. And you mustn't mix most metals. They melt at different temperatures, see. Sometimes I just heat and rework scraps into spear- and arrowheads." He clattered a handful onto the stones, and Arthur and the others looked them over appraisingly.

"Or I make new beautiful things, like this fine copper necklace. Look at the delicate patterns, at the red glow of the old sun itself. Now, Your Majesty, surely a treasure like this deserves to adorn a royal throat. You're a single man, I understand, but I can't believe you haven't some young mountain beauty you're thinking of making your queen."

Arthur stood up abruptly. "I am not giving any thought to queens! Being a king is quite trying enough without them."

The metalsmith knew he'd made a blunder. He was a clever man but not a learned one and was unaware that this particular king had, millennia earlier, bad experiences with one queen. So as not to lose his royal audience completely, the man quickly changed the subject.

"We also, of course, carry news along with our merchandise, and to men of affairs like yourselves, it is often more valued."

"So, what can you tell us of happenings in the Midlands?" the King asked gruffly.

"Well, Cheshire and Manchester still glower at each other, and there's talk of a full-scale war between them. Manchester wants more land; it's never had much besides old ruins. But Duke Geoffrey of Chester says it can just look elsewhere.

"Now, let's see ... oh, yes, there's the Duke of Staffordshire, who married the King of Nottinghamshire's daughter a while ago. All their children were born muties, and he's just sent his wife back. There's trouble brewing between those shires, that's for certain.

"And as for Wales, the old Duke of Glamorganshire died just a couple months past, and now his son's upped the rank and taken on the title of king."

Three in the crowded room suddenly looked at each other and laughed. "King Nigel!" Welly exclaimed. "A royal pain."

The merchant nodded. "Yes, Nigel is the gentleman's name, though as to his personality, I cannot say."

"We can." Heather giggled, thinking of the last time she and Welly had seen the heir of Glamorganshire—tied up on the floor of her bedroom while they made their escape from Llandoylan School.

Merlin cleared his throat. "We three had the opportunity to make the gentleman's acquaintance in school. I think, Arthur, if you're considering forming alliances in Wales, you'd better look elsewhere than Glamorgan at present."

The glass merchant spoke at this. "Well, if it's alliances you're wanting, there are some shires that'll be seeking ties with anyone, what with the goings-on in the East and South."

"You mean Morgan?" Arthur asked sharply.

"Yes, that's the witch who's been leading them. Kent's been hers for a couple of years now, but her army's grown. Mostly muties from the Continent, they say, them and other things best not talked about. Last year they gobbled up Essex and this year Suffolk. The shires nearby are plenty worried, I can tell you. Her army's worse than most; they pillage and murder something awful."

An old cloth merchant pushed his way into the knot of listeners. "Aye, there's strange doings all over the South. There's a boy with us now, come all the way from Devonshire, what has some pretty rum tales to tell. You ought to talk with him."

"Yes, perhaps we ought," Arthur said thoughtfully. "From what I'm hearing, I fear we may have to deal with Morgan before we'd planned. Have him brought in."

A guard slipped out the door and returned with a boy who looked no more than eight or nine. One arm was shriveled, and he walked with a pronounced limp. But his eyes were held high as he approached the King.

"Well, young man," Arthur began, "I'd like you to have a seat and tell us—"

"John Wesley Penrose!" Heather suddenly jumped up and ran to the boy, followed closely by Welly. Merlin looked up from a newly made silver bowl he was examining and hurried to join them.

The boy's somber face lit with a smile. "I thought maybe you two would be here. And you, Mister Earl, I knew you would be."

"You did?" Merlin asked. "How?"

"Well, when you stayed at our farm, you told me such exciting stories of King Arthur that when I heard he had returned, I was sure you'd try to join him, too."

The King grinned at Merlin. "And you, John Wesley, you came all the way from Devon to join us?"

"Yes, sire. I hadn't anyplace else to go, and from what Earl said of you, I was sure you'd take me in."

Arthur looked amused, but Merlin frowned. "What do you mean, John Wesley? Where are your parents?"

The boy's face clouded, and he looked down at his hands. "They were killed. Remember that bird-cat that attacked our farm? Shortly after you all left, three more came. They killed everything—my mother and father and most of the sheep and cattle. I hid in the barn under the manure. But they tore up nearly everything."

Heather knelt beside the boy and grabbed his hands, too upset to say anything. Welly could do no better.

Merlin's face rippled with anger. "Those were Morgan's creatures," he told Arthur. "She couldn't abide the Penroses being kind to us."

"It's not your fault," the boy said, his voice thick with suppressed tears. "When I was trying to find my way here, I saw other things like that and worse. Not regular muties, but really awful things. They make the air feel dirty."

The King frowned. "You were right, Merlin; she is calling things from the other world. Hasn't changed much, has she? If there's anything filthy Morgan can deal with, she will."

"And her forces are getting stronger, it seems," the wizard said flatly.

"Yes, as ours must before we confront her."

"Sire," an adviser said, "do we really have to confront this Morgan person? I mean, all her conquests so far are to the south. Surely we aren't threatened by her."

"We are *all* threatened by her. At some time, Morgan and I must meet. Our ambitions for Britain are too much at odds. Ask Merlin. He knows."

But the young wizard was paying no attention. He was once again staring at the silver bowl in his hand and fighting off a sudden wave of dizziness. The bowl seemed to grow and become entwined with interweaving snakes. A vision stirred deeply in its depths, swirling and forming just out of sight.

He gasped and dropped the bowl. It lay on the floor, small and unadorned. Arthur grabbed for him as Merlin swayed over it. "Are you all right? What was it, a vision?"

"No, a vision of a vision. And yes, I'm fine. It's over." He put shaking hands on John Wesley's shoulders and managed a smile. "Well, young man, it looks as if we're going to live some of those stories for real now." He looked around. "Heather, why don't you and Welly see that our new recruit gets something to eat."

Late into the night, by the smoky light of torches sputtering in wall sconces, Arthur and his advisers talked of future strategies and alliances. But Merlin's thoughts kept straying to the past, to a good Devonshire couple murdered for their kindness, and further back, to a silver Bowl of Seeing lost two thousand years earlier.

As winter closed around the lakelands, people and animals huddled together in houses and pens. In hearths, fires were sparingly lit, scarce logs supplemented by dried sheep dung.

Last year, Heather had found this season boring and confining, but at least she had felt part of a whole. Now she wondered if there wasn't some slight difference. Was she imagining it, or were some people avoiding her? Certainly, *some* were paying her more attention than she wanted. She wished she had a place tending the sheep and horses, as John Wesley now did. But instead, she found herself with three eager tutors and too much to learn.

Merlin taught her magic, but not the spells he knew, for he said their powers were too different. Rather, he tried to teach her how to open her mind to her own power and be sensitive to its messages.

Heather was not an eager pupil. She loved her tie with animals, but the power itself frightened her. Sometimes when she felt it welling up inside her, she would shrink away as if from a venomous snake.

Even Merlin seemed discouraged. "I don't know," he told her once as they sat bundled up in the snowy garden. "You have power; I can feel it. But maybe I'm just not the one to bring it out." He sighed. "And it's not only that our powers are different. I'm simply not attuned to this world's new magic. It has a different source, a source I can't quite see yet. My old powers work technically, but more and more they feel dry and out of place."

He frowned until his dark brows met. "Not that any of this brooding is helping you. At least your power, whatever shape it is, is right for your world. But I wish I could at least get some gauge of it. You might be an ordinary village witch, or you might be something more. I just can't tell."

"Then don't try," Heather muttered, then quickly looked up, glad he hadn't heard. She didn't want to hurt him, and it seemed to mean so much to him that she had powers, too.

Other times, Kyle tried to teach her music. She was flattered that the handsome young harper took an interest in her, but she could not respond with much interest in his lessons. He said she had a pleasant voice and could carry a tune, but he seemed to believe it should carry every tune he knew. She liked music well enough but didn't want to live with it every moment of the day.

Kyle, too, was less than content with her progress. "If you'd open yourself to it more," he complained once, "and let it flow through you, you'd be really good." Frustrated, he ran a hand through his blond hair. "It's all that magic you're fooling with. It closes you off, poisons you for honest things. It isn't natural, you know, Heather. You should lead a normal life, with music, a family, pleasant things. A pretty young woman like you shouldn't darken herself with magic."

"I'm not a pretty woman, Kyle O'Mara! And magic isn't dark. It's just difficult, like music. I'm not sure I'm meant for either."

Whatever spare moments Heather had left, Welly slipped into with weapons instruction. Overweight and nearsighted, he had not been good at weapons in school. But in these last two years, he'd become quite skilled with the sword, though his spear aim wasn't what it could be. At least, he thought, his martial name of Wellington no longer seemed quite so ludicrous.

And what he learned, he wanted to share with Heather, his companion in a good many adventures already. Admittedly he had heard people say that Heather McKenna was getting of an age to stop adventuring and think about marriage. She was, after all, fourteen, and with the difficulties women had bearing live healthy children, girls were encouraged to marry and start becoming mothers as soon as possible. But Welly cringed at the thought of independent Heather's reaction to that idea were it ever mentioned to her.

Welly was surprised to discover that one of the cook's helpers had such thoughts about him—the marriageable part, anyway. Of course, the idea was absurd. He wanted to stay as he was, with a few girls as friends only. Still, it puffed him up a little to know that a pretty thing like the cook's assistant should think of *him* as a good catch.

At long last, even in Cumbria, winter began losing its hold. Heather, as anxious as anyone to ride on the first sortie, was even happier that her three-part tutoring was tapering off.

One morning, John Wesley ran to her to say that the herd's first foal had been born. He still treated her as an old friend and was not put off by rumors of her odd powers. Grateful always for that, she followed him eagerly to the enclosure. The air held a thawing mildness. It carried the sound of trickling meltwater mixed with the pawing and snorting of horses restive at the promise of spring.

The new foal was small and dark, but already it was up on its spindly legs, butting its head under its mother's shaggy belly and gulping down milk. Heather watched the scene with lazy contentment. She could reach out and feel the foal's warmth and security, its simple pleasure in the milk and in the presence of its mother. And she felt the dam's love, pride, and happy surprise. Heather refused to look at this awareness as magic.

She spent the day helping John Wesley fork hay or shovel horse droppings into drying pans. Soon she smelled of horse and sweat. Her thin hair, wisping free of its braids, was studded with bits of hay. She was thoroughly happy. No dark musty halls, no conflicting voices inside and out. Just a job to do and the freedom to do it.

In midafternoon, she was scouring a stone trough. Raising her head to shove back a strand of hair, she caught sight of Merlin walking down from the hall. Almost at the same moment, she saw Kyle heading up the road from town.

A wave of guilt at having avoided their tutoring was swiftly followed by anger. What right had those two to make her feel guilty about what she did with herself? If she never hummed another tune or gave another thought to magic, it was her life!

Angrily she threw down her tools and, crouching low, scuttled along a wall, almost colliding with John Wesley as he limped around a corner with an armload of rope.

"If anyone asks about me," she hissed, "I haven't been here for ages. And tell them it's none of their business anyway!"

Sprinting off behind cover of outbuildings, she cut into town, then took the back way up to the manor. Feelings of triumph were muddled with disgust—disgust that even this petty evasion should give her such a sense of freedom.

Dirty, disheveled, and angry, she crept into the lower garden to find Welly hurling spears at a straw target. He turned and smiled at her, his plump open face showing no signs of inner turmoil.

"Heather, why don't you come here and try—"

"No! I'm not going to. I want to do something of my own for a change!"

"Huh?"

"I'm getting fed up with you people! Earl wants me to become a sorceress and a hermit, Kyle wants me to stay away from magic and be a singer, and you want me to be some sort of Amazon warrior!"

"Hey, I never said anything like that. You can just be what you want, as far as I'm concerned."

"Oh? Then what should I be? With everyone after me, I can't think. What's your advice?"

"I don't know, Heather. Just go your own way."

She stamped her foot. "Welly, I asked for advice, not wishy-washy philosophy. Why are you always so middle-of-the-road?"

"The middle of the road's often the safest place to be."

"Bah! You're no help. All right. I'll go my own way. I'll do exactly that!"

She stalked off toward the hall. Bewildered, Welly looked after her. What had gotten into her lately? He'd heard Cook say, after watching her fly into another such rage, that Heather was just growing up. It looked more like blowing up to him. And it worried him. He didn't want her to do anything stupid.

He picked up another spear and threw, missing again.

Heather did not go down to supper that evening. She said she had a headache. But actually she felt calm with resolve. She was sorry, though, that she'd lost her temper with Welly. It wasn't his fault. It wasn't even Earl's or Kyle's. It was hers.

Everyone *was* making demands on her. But she couldn't even try to answer them because she didn't know what she was anymore, or what she wanted or needed. All right, she would find out.

The first step had to be the magic. She couldn't deny it any longer. Whether she wanted it or not, it was hers. Maybe, though, she could control it, channel it into ways that wouldn't ruin her life. But she couldn't do that until she knew its strength. And Earl couldn't seem to discover that. All right, if he couldn't, she would have to. And she'd do it tomorrow.

21

DISCOVERIES
ON A MOUNTAIN

The sky was just pearling with gray when Heather, dressed in fleece-lined trousers and jacket, slipped out to the royal stables. The guard gave her a surprised nod but said nothing. She was one of the royal household and was free to come and go as she wished. If the hour was odd, it was no more so than the girl's reputation of late.

Heather ignored him and the sleepy stableboy. She could no longer doubt that a strained distance had sprung up around her as word of her powers had spread. The answer, she'd decided, was to pretend she didn't care. That's what Earl did, though she suspected it was more pretense than he'd care to admit.

Feeling bitterly alone, she swung onto her sturdy little horse. The misty predawn silence was broken as she clattered through the courtyard and out past the gatehouse. Turning right, she rode down into the sleeping town and out to the lake.

The air was cold and needle sharp. Her breath and the breath of her horse rose about them in white plumes. But signs of thaw were already around. The snow on the road had melted and refrozen into a slippery crust. On

Derwentwater, the imprisoning ice was beginning to break up. Cracks and dark patches spread over the surface, and mists rose from them, veiling the far shore and the lake's shadowy islands. Along the beach, sheets of broken ice had been thrown up by the waves, looking in this uncertain light like jagged teeth tearing at the mists.

As the road climbed above the east shore, Heather looked over the misty expanse of water toward a distant valley, the "Jaws of Borrowdale." Her goal lay there, among the dark, hunched shapes. She hoped some answers lay there as well.

Her power, Earl said, was something she would understand in time. But she didn't have time. Too much was tearing at her *now*. Was hers the power of a garden-variety witch, meant for healing and foretelling storms? Or was it something more? She hardly cared which; she just needed to know so she could start taking control of her life.

As she rode on, the shape of Castle Crag, dark against the graying sky, loomed more and more forbidding. Yet it was the best place she could think of to go. Earl had said that the ancients built in places of power, and from a shepherd she'd learned that this spot held one of the oldest sites around.

The lake came to an end, and on both sides the fells crowded into a narrow valley. Ahead of her, the crag loomed like a supernatural watchtower guarding the route to Borrowdale and beyond.

She stopped at a crossroads, trying to recall the old map she had studied. The best route should be to the right. She urged her horse across a humpbacked bridge into the tumbled stone ruins of an abandoned village. Turning south, she headed along the River Derwent, still shrouded in its icy winter silence. It seemed that the only sound in the whole world was what she brought with her, the jingle of bridle and the steady clop of horse hooves on frozen ground.

In the deep, sheltered valley, rare trees grew—a grove, almost a forest, like those in ancient tales. Wind moaned coldly in the branches, and the dark, towering pines seemed alive with the hostile spirits of those same tales. She was relieved when her trail began rising again, leaving the trees for the open fells.

The path, steep and rocky now, cut along the base of bare cliffs, their surfaces scarred with the white of frozen waterfalls. As she looked up, one ice cascade seemed to shimmer and flow with fire. Over the eastern fells, a huge reddened sun broke free and sent a tide of ruddy light down the opposite cliffs.

Her horse plodded on, bringing her closer and closer to the pass. Perplexed, she reined in. The map had shown the ascent striking off before the pass. Of course, it was an old map, pre-Devastation, but surely the landscape hadn't changed that much.

Standing in her stirrups, she looked around. Then she saw it. The distinctive pattern of sheep walls lay behind her in a hidden side valley. Feeling like a successful explorer, she headed the horse back until the narrow valley floor ended in a tumbled wall. Beyond it, the crag rose sharply. With a pang, she realized she would have to leave her horse here. Even his throwback three-toed agility couldn't manage this trail.

Dismounting, she tied the reins to a rock and patted his shaggy flank. He was uneasy; she could feel it. He didn't like being away from his fellows. Suddenly she wasn't sure she did either. This idea had seemed fine in Keswick. Now she was less enthusiastic. True, the people and pressures she sought to escape crowded her like this horse's stablemates, but they were protective, too. And familiar.

She looked up at the starkly unfamiliar mountainside, then frowned angrily. She was never going to learn about herself if she huddled in a herd! Scrambling over the wall, she began climbing.

On the crag's face, wind had scoured away most of the snow, exposing bare earth and rock. It was the rock that proved difficult. In times past, this place had been used to quarry slate, and the tailings from the quarries now spilled down this whole side of the mountain.

The slate scree ranged from blue-gray slabs to tiny chips, all shifting and clattering under her as she climbed. It was a nightmare climb. For every two feet she advanced, she slipped back one. The rattling, tumbling noise of her passage seemed an outrage in the icy morning stillness.

Finally, panting for breath, she reached a plateau. Below her, cupped in its mountains as if in the palm of a hand, lay Borrowdale. Stone walls veined the snowy fields and led to a distant cluster of farm buildings. It all seemed safe and familiar and infinitely more rational than this scarred, windswept crag.

Pulling her hood tighter around her face, she looked up and groaned. There was still farther to go to the summit. But at least she had reached the level of the quarries. The hillside above would have proper rocks set in soil. Wearily she continued climbing. If there was a place of power anywhere here, surely it would be on the highest spot.

Finally she staggered out onto the summit, then

looked around in confusion. There were no signs of ancient fortifications here. To one side was a cairn of piled stones, but that was the type left by climbers in pre-Devastation times, when people did this sort of thing for fun.

Discouraged, she sat beside the scant shelter of the rocky mound. The wind sang mournfully over the cold, bare rocks. Behind her, Borrowdale was obscured by the shoulder of the hill, but to the north, Derwentwater stretched beneath its fells like a shattered mirror. At the lake's north edge, light from the rising sun was finally sliding over Keswick. Above the huddled gray buildings, smoke from cookfires blended with the fading mist.

In the great airy gulf between her and her home, a single bird soared. She smiled with delight. Birds were so beautiful, with their grace and their achingly precious freedom. How wonderful if the air and hillsides were filled with them! Earl had told her that once summer days had danced with their song. She longed to reach out and touch that bird, to share its soaring flight, to . . . No. She hadn't come here for that, but to touch whatever ancient power still ran in this hill.

With a businesslike frown, she looked around the summit again and noticed that there was something unnatural about it. The surface had been flattened and was cupped up evenly at the edges. It was a perfect circle, except where quarries had chewed into the hilltop. Standing up, she walked to where the slope dropped steeply from the built-up rim.

So this *had* been an ancient site, though she hardly felt it bubbling with power. But then, she instructed herself firmly, she was not really trying. She walked to the center of the hilltop, thought a moment, then moved farther west to what would have been the center before the quarries left a gap, like a wedge cut from a cake.

Bracing her feet apart, she closed her eyes, spread out her hands, and tried to think of nothing. Earl had repeatedly showed her how. But it was so hard. Stupid little thoughts kept sliding in, silly phrases people had said yesterday or pictures of meaningless, ordinary things. Closing her eyes tighter, she tried to drive these fragments away. But the more she fought, the more willfully they sidled in.

She simply had to succeed! Maybe if she tried to stay cool, cool like the snow around her. Cool, pure, untouched. Slowly she relaxed. Coolness and rest spread through her body. She could feel a faint tingling, a faint distant movement like blood throbbing through arteries far, far below her. It was so far, so faint, and other things kept coming in the way.

Ants moved in the darkness, feeling and smelling the earth, grain by grain moving and shaping it, clearing tunnels in age-old patterns of comfort and purpose. They tunneled and crawled past the den of a sleeping mouse, its pulse slowed, its furry chest scarcely rising and falling, its mind drifting in a single summer thought.

Little things, little lives. Heather felt them first with pleasure, then with annoyance. Where was the power? Where was the power they hid? Eyes clenched shut, she wrenched her body forward to another, perhaps better, spot and threw open her mind. This deeper power—when would it find her?

Wildly she flung back her arms, tilting her head to the sky. Suddenly she was slipping, arms flailing like bird wings. Her eyes flew open to see the snow-mantled rock at the quarry's edge buckling and sliding beneath her feet. Her mind screamed. Blue slate and white snow spun past her and up to meet her. A rumbling avalanche of snow and rock poured into the quarry. Then mindless silence settled over the hillside.

Wellington Jones never claimed to have a magical bone in his body. But he was certainly good at worrying. He woke up just as worried as he'd been the night before. Heather was his best friend, and it worried him that she'd blown up at him like that. It worried him even more the way she'd stomped off threatening . . . what? He didn't know, but she was always one for madcap schemes.

When she hadn't come down to dinner, he had been really worried. To anyone who enjoyed food as much as he did, missing a meal meant a monumental crisis. Her not appearing for breakfast was the last straw. She was being ridiculous now.

He stormed upstairs to her little room in the west end of the building. One of the few girls in Arthur's "court," Heather had a room of her own, whereas Welly slept in one of the men's common rooms. He hammered at the door. No answer.

"Come on, Heather, open up! I'm sorry if you're mad at me, but at least you could tell me why."

Still no answer. Hesitantly he turned the knob and pushed. The door opened onto a small, silent, and very empty room. He looked at the rumpled bed. It had been slept in, but on the wall behind it, the peg that usually held her outdoor jacket was empty. "Little silly," Welly muttered. "She's off doing something crazy—and without me!"

In moments, he was down the stairs and running toward

the stables. Heather's horse was gone. The stableboy re-ported she had saddled it before dawn but hadn't said where she was going. Useless lump, Welly thought, not even to ask her. But then, he reflected, if Heather had been in the same mood as yesterday, the stableboy had been well advised to lie low.

A thought struck Welly as he was saddling his horse. He hadn't paid much attention to something Heather said the other day. But was it true? Were people really avoiding her because she had some sort of magical powers? The idea boiled into anger. His two best friends, and people treated them like muties!

As Welly trotted across the courtyard, Otto called out from a doorway, "What you up to, Welly?"

"Important business," the boy answered, throwing him a serious frown. He didn't want to draw any attention to Heather until he learned exactly what craziness she was up to. That could just make things worse.

The guard at the gatehouse remembered Heather heading down into town. Welly did the same. Threading through the narrow twisting streets, he bashfully nodded at occasional smiles and waves. All the people of Keswick knew the plump, bespectacled boy and the skinny, intense girl as being Arthur and Merlin's first two companions. They'd become something of folk heroes, and that made Welly acutely embarrassed. Fame sounded all right in the-ory but was proving surprisingly silly in fact.

As he neared the edge of town, he stopped uncertainly. But unless Heather had ridden down to the lake to skip rocks on the ice, she'd probably taken the east-shore road. He turned his horse and was soon rewarded with the sight of fresh tracks in the crusted snow. Of course, they could have been made by another rider, but it was worth taking a chance they were hers.

Farther down the road, Welly realized that there were several sets of tracks. His confidence faded. But he plodded on until he came to a spot where a single set left the others and crossed the River Derwent on an old stone bridge.

Most farmers with horses had given them over to the King. Just his luck, Welly thought, if he was following one of the holdouts. Thinking again about wild geese, Welly urged his stocky mount across the bridge.

There was cold and emptiness and then a hint of pain. It felt like nothing worth waking up to. Heather's mind tried crawling back into darkness, but there came a slap on her cheek, wet and warm. A very odd sort of thing, considering that she lay dying in a frozen quarry. Curiosity lifted a single eyelid.

She stared straight into the face of a dog. Wonderful, she thought. Instead of bleeding or freezing to death, I'm going to be eaten. She hadn't the strength to make even basic frightening-away sounds.

But if he wasn't to be frightened, the dog wasn't very frightening either. His fur was black with white splotches, and his mouth, which should be striking her with terror, was grinning, a pink tongue lolling stupidly to one side.

Heather opened her other eye. Correction, there were two dogs. Both equally ridiculous-looking. One seemed intent on washing out her ear with its tongue.

"Enough!" she gasped as the other's tongue slurped across her face. Obediently they stopped, and, whimpering happily, both dogs grinned down at her.

Well, she'd have to get it over with, she thought, and moved one arm. No searing flash of pain. Slowly she tried to sit up, struggling out of a deep drift of snow. Snow, not rocks, she realized. That's why she wasn't shattered over the hillside.

She looked down at the dogs and almost screamed. It was one dog—two heads, two tails, but one dog.

Weird, really weird. But suddenly she wasn't afraid of them, or it. It clearly wasn't a fell-dog but some sheepdog pup that had been born a mutie and abandoned by the disgusted herder. Its ribs showed through the matted fur, but the eyes, all four of them, looked at Heather with trustful confidence. The two tails wagged steadily.

Cautiously Heather reached out a hand and rubbed behind one set of floppy ears. The other head set to washing her hand.

Who was that dog in mythology, the one that guarded Hades? Cerberus. "You're like him, aren't you?" she muttered aloud. "Only I guess you fall a little short. He had three heads. So I won't call you Cerberus, just Rus. You like the name Rus?"

Both tails wagged furiously.

"I wonder if I can stand up. If I stay down here, you'll lick me to death."

She flailed about in the snow, trying to bring her legs under her. Then came the jolt of pain. Her left ankle. Had she broken it? Twisted it?

She tried again and almost retched with pain.

"Oh, Rus," she said angrily, "just when I thought I was going to live after all. Now I guess I'll die out here."

The dog whimpered, an odd two-part harmony, and began poking her with a forepaw.

"Quit it, Rus. I can't get up, and you're not big enough for me to ride."

He was whining now and looking at her with such pathetic grins she couldn't help laughing. "All right, I'm not giving up that easily. I'll try again."

Cautiously she pulled her good leg under her, and slowly putting her weight on it, she tried to stand. Swaying, losing her balance in the deep snow, she instinctively stuck out her other foot to steady herself. The pain shot up her leg in a sickening wave, knocking her down into blackness.

Whining, the dog poked around the unconscious heap in the snow.

Several times Welly thought he had lost the trail. The road was getting rocky, often without enough snow for tracks. But he was following a road, at least. The rider before him, he guessed, would probably have done the same. The road climbed out of a gloomy pine grove, then rose steeply along the fringes of the fells. A rocky island-mountain, Castle Crag, towered on one side. Cliffs glistening with frozen waterfalls rose on the other.

Finally he made the pass and, shifting in his saddle, surveyed the scene beyond. Borrowdale opened out below him on the left. The old road continued ahead along the base of the cliffs. No tracks led anywhere.

Suddenly his horse shied, and he felt something leap against his leg. Alarmed, he looked down, and the thing barked and leaped again. A fell-dog, an awful mutie, trying to tear him right off his horse!

With a frightened squeak, he struggled to pull his sword from under his heavy jacket. But the enemy was sitting in the snow, smiling with both of its jaws, wagging both of its tails.

Gods, it was ugly, he thought. But at least it wasn't lunging at him anymore.

The creature barked doubly. Jumping up, it ran several feet away, then stopped and looked back expectantly.

"That's right; you can leave, as far as I'm concerned," Welly said, lowering his sword.

It ran at him again, barking, then spun around and ran off a few feet. Welly just stared at it. Was this incredible creature rabid, too?

The dog repeated the performance several times to the accompaniment of multiple barking. Welly shook his head. "I actually believe you want me to follow you. But I can't; I'm looking for someone out here and I . . ."

His gaze had gone beyond the dog, down the direction it seemed to be pointing. At the head of a small, nearly hidden valley, he caught a flicker of movement. A horse switching its tail. Heather's horse! "She went off that way!" Welly spurred his own horse down the road again with the dog prancing and barking ahead. Reaching the old wall, he dismounted and tied his horse beside Heather's. The two animals nickered happily at each other and rubbed noses.

The dog was already through the gap in the wall and peering back at Welly with both heads.

"All right, I guess I *am* going your way. But go on, keep your distance. I still don't like the looks of you."

The dog shot on ahead, occasionally stopping to bark impatiently as the stout boy struggled up the slope behind him. On the shifting hillside of shale tailings, Welly alternated his puffs and gasps with colorful curses he'd picked up from Arthur's troops. Despite the cold, the climb soon had him itching with sweat. It was made doubly awkward by his having to clutch his sword in one hand in case that bizarre dog attacked again.

Finally, gasping and shaking with exhaustion, he stood on the open plateau staring out to Borrowdale. Wearily he looked around and groaned. The summit still rose above.

"Heather *would* go up there." He sank down on a pile of stones. "Well, I can't. Not another inch, not just yet."

The dog was beside him again. Welly was too tired to shake it off when it grabbed his jacket cuff in one mouth while barking with the other. He stumbled to his feet and was relieved to see that the crazy dog wasn't leading him upward but along the level, back into an open gash in the mountainside.

The quarry opened out. Above him, raw slate jutted in jagged slabs against the sky. Snow lay in white splinters among rocky chinks and crevasses and piled loosely over the huge stones at the quarry's base. In the center lay something else, dark and heaped.

"Heather!"

Through the deep snow, Welly ran clumsily toward the figure, but the dog got there first, poking and licking with both tongues.

Heather groaned as Welly stumbled up. "Enough! Let me die in peace."

"Heather, what on earth . . . ? Never mind. Let's get you out of here."

"Who? Welly! How did you . . . ?"

"Your funny-looking friend fetched me. Can you stand?"

"No."

"Then I'll try to carry you. If we take that same awful route, you can probably slide most of the way."

Heather was fully awake now. Her ankle was too cold to feel much. "Uh, Welly . . . ?"

"Yes?"

"I'm sorry I blew up at you. I'm a really mixed-up jerk."

"True. But at least you're not a dead one. Come on."

22

RIDING FORTH

Welly pushed open a narrow window. Oily lamp smoke coiled out while cool tendrils of evening mist slipped in. He turned back and looked at the sleeping blanket-mounded figure on the bed.

Beside her, Merlin finished his work and gently pulled the blankets back over her left ankle. Having wrapped her with bandages and spells, he now sat down beside his patient.

The flickering lamp cast odd shadows and angles over his face. Heather moved her head restlessly on the pillow. Her hair had wisped free of its braids. Groggily she opened her eyes. She smiled vaguely. "It feels better already, Earl. But it shouldn't. I don't deserve it. I should be lying up there on that snowy mountain being eaten by fell-dogs."

"No, you shouldn't!" Welly objected. The dog lying beside the bed whined and began licking Heather's limp hand with one of its tongues.

The wizard laughed. "These two would never have let you. You have some good friends, Heather."

"I know I do. All of you. But I don't deserve you. I was such a self-centered, headstrong idiot going off like that."

After a silence, Welly said, "I don't suppose you'd tell us why . . . ?"

Heather blushed and tossed her head. "Oh, Welly, I'm not even sure why. I was trying to . . . trying to find out about myself, I guess. I wanted to find out what was in me, what sort of power I have. I was tired of everyone but me knowing what I should do with myself. But it was just a big stupid failure."

"A failure?" Merlin questioned.

"Yes, totally. I went up there because I thought it would be a place of power. Maybe it was, but I could scarcely feel it. All I could sense were the little animals in the dirt below me. Hurrying ants, sleeping mice. I'll bet even village witches do better than that. And they wouldn't be so blind as to stagger around the snowy edge of a quarry."

Merlin stood, looking sternly down on his patient. "Heather, you *are* blind, but not in that way. Sensing those small lives, talking with them, that is not small magic. It's not something great magicians learn as babies, then go beyond. Yours is a large power, I believe that now, but it's a different track of magic from mine. I could have stood on that mountain sensing the major lines of power and completely missed what you felt."

"Earl, if you're just saying that to make me feel better . . ."

"No, you little twit! Look at this ridiculous animal here. Do you think he just happened on you accidentally? And if he did, do you think a half-starved pup would have led a rescuer to this convenient hunk of meat instead of dining on it? No, you had your mind open to that power, and when you fell, you called out for help. He heard and came."

With both tails wagging vigorously, Rus slipped one head under Heather's hand and allowed Merlin to pat the other. A thoughtful smile played over Heather's face. "Well, if I do have to have power, I guess this isn't such a bad kind. That is, if you're right about all this."

He frowned theatrically at her. "You dare question the judgment of the ancient wizard?"

They laughed as he dropped into his chair and continued. "Anyway, I do have a royal command to convey. You are to get well as soon as possible. I tried to work that into my little healing spells. Arthur has decided to head east to join Carlisle against Queen Margaret and her Scots. We'll be leaving in a fortnight, and you and your battlehound here might want to join us—unless, of course, you've decided it's time to stay behind and sew like a demure young lady."

Ducking back from her flying fist, he raised an eyebrow. "That's the message I'm to convey to His Majesty?"

"Phrase it however you want. But I'll be riding with you."

Their once-quiet town now bustled with activity. Word had spread like smoke that the King was assembling a warhost. Farmers and shepherds took up whatever weapons came to hand and marched proudly through the passes and valleys toward Keswick. They came from fell and farmstead, from Grassmere, Ambleside, and Windermere, and from the coastal villages of Ravenglass and Whitehaven.

While recovering, Heather watched the flurry of preparation. Excited half-wild horses were trained, metal scraps were hammered onto leather armor, and in the clanging glow of the smithies, weapons were forged or repaired. All the while, provisions for the growing army were gathered and stowed away in wagons and packs.

On a cold day, when snow had turned to drizzling rain, Arthur gave word that they would march on the morrow. News had come that Queen Margaret had conquered Newcastle and forced a shaky alliance on Durham. It seemed likely she would move next against Carlisle, and they could wait no longer.

The morning dawned clear and dry, with the sun rising like a bronze shield behind its pall of ancient dust. The hillside camps were astir early, and soon the valley resounded with protesting horses, creaking wagons, and yelling men.

Excited children ran underfoot, some attempting to slip off and join the assembling troops, only to be dragged away by scolding mothers. Youngsters who had passed into their teens proudly joined the warriors' ranks, their eyes glistening with pride and the reflected adulation of their younger comrades.

There were young men, too, and old, and some women as well. Some were veterans of skirmishes between shires, and others had never lifted a weapon. But all felt the lure of fame and adventure, the promise of fighting a grand war as in days of old, and of fighting for a king who came from the heart of legend itself.

At last the army was ready to move. From the manor on the hill, the King's troop issued forth and took its place in the lead. Above them fluttered the banner of Pendragon, the winged gold dragon against a field of black. People who had flocked in from miles around lined the road, pointing out personages of note.

At the head of the troops, clutching the King's standard,

rode John Wesley Penrose, his pride as bright as the banner he carried. Just behind, on his large gray stallion, rode Arthur himself, the faint sun glinting off his armor, his helmet, and his golden hair.

Near him rode the Duke of Ambleside, Kyle the harper, Otto Bowman, and others of the King's companions. With them, but in a large island of space, rode a pale young man, his hair the same midnight-black as his horse. Strapped to his saddle was a twisted wooden staff. Knowingly, locals told newcomers that this was Merlin the Enchanter. Even if he appeared far too young for the role, his dark look of brooding seemed suitably daunting.

But while their friend was brooding and remote, Welly and Heather were thoroughly enjoying themselves. From the small troop of musicians marching behind rose the compelling throb of drums, the haunting call of pipes, and the ferocious, challenging blare of ram's horns. The towering fells echoed with the cheers and music, and Welly decided it wasn't all that essential that one ride a tall white charger to feel heroic and glory-bound.

Gradually the troops pulled away from Keswick. The road was soon lined with rocks, not cheering people, but the drumbeats still rolled back from the hillsides, and the soldiers laughed and talked among themselves.

In time, the drummers tired, and the army, concentrating on marching, was accompanied only by the sound of its own passage: the stomp of hoof and boot, the creaking of harness, the rumbling of wagon, and the casual scrape and clang of weapon against armor.

Heather looked back at the glinting body of warriors winding dragon-like under the bare fells. Excitement was settling into contentment. With little effort, she could feel the determined, purposeful thoughts of the horses and the more distant annoyance of sheep as they scattered from the army's noise. She was still unsure of how she felt about her power or of the effect her having it made on others, but for now she willingly laid the question aside.

Rus trotted happily beside her, both heads full of curiosity. There was a great deal to smell, see, and chase along the route, and he constantly ran back and forth, dodging horse hooves and marching men.

Only one thing troubled Heather, and that was the brooding cloud that seemed to hang over Merlin. Finally she urged her horse up to join his. He turned in his saddle with a weak smile but said nothing.

"All right, Earl," she said after a long silence. "What's the matter? You have a toothache or something?"

He laughed dryly. "You know, it is rather like that. Something keeps nagging at me about . . . about all this." He swept a hand through the air along the line of march, and Heather noticed several soldiers duck, thinking the wizard was casting a spell.

She frowned, then pointedly ignored them. "You don't think we should move against Margaret now?"

"No, that's not it, not in itself. Strategically this move makes sense, though in the long run it's Morgan, not Margaret, who is the greater danger. No, certainly, to unite Britain, Arthur must deal with the Scots first. But somehow, setting out today with the crowds cheering for the glory and honor of war . . ." He slammed a hand against his thigh. "We've been on this road before, Heather. And look where it ended!" He jabbed a hand upward at the shrouded sun. Again, nearby soldiers flinched.

Heather shook her head. "But what other route is there?"

"I don't know! That's what's eating me. I feel there

must be another, one that doesn't lead us off a cliff. But I can't see it! If I could glimpse the future as once I could, or maybe if I could get some grasp of this new power . . ."

He rode on, silent for several minutes. The cold wind ruffled his hair and the fur of the hood thrown back over his shoulders. Sighing, he looked up at the gray fells. "Yes, the new magic might be the key, or one of them. This world is new, starting again. It's no wonder things are different."

He pointed to a tumble of rocks on a bare hillside. "There's one of the differences now. Do you see?"

"No, where? What . . . oh, yes, I see something. It's . . . it's a band of muties! Watching us."

"Yes, muties. Some are mutated only in body, you know, not in mind or spirit. They are part of this new world. It's theirs, too, whether we're comfortable with that fact or not. Some will work against us, no doubt, but not others, and in the end, Arthur must be *their* king as well.

"And then there are the creatures of the other world, from Faerie. Doors are opening again to all its many parts. They'll be having more and more stake in what's happening here." He laughed dryly. "When I lived before, I saw those doors closing; magic was drawing to the end of its cycle. But now the powers are coming again; they're new and growing. If only I wasn't so tied to the old world, maybe I could help change the outcome this time, both in the long and the short run. Otherwise, what is the point of my being here?" His last words came as such a shout that even his horse shied. But the wizard hardly noticed.

The army camped that night near Penrith, picking up another eager contingent of volunteers. Next morning they marched north and by the middle of the third day had reached Carlisle. The town's newly constructed walls showed the people's fear of the impinging Scots.

Arthur camped his troops outside the walls, not far from Carlisle's own army. In the center of the sprawling camp, a large tent was erected and the Dragon standard stuck into the ground before it. The smoke of cookfires was rising into the dusk when a ram's horn blared from the gate, and a small troop rode forth, led by Clarence, Duke of Carlisle.

When the riders reached Arthur's tent, Duke Clarence swung with arthritic care from his horse and bowed to his High King. Then, smiling, he slapped the younger man on the shoulder.

"By the gods, Arthur, this army is even more impressive than the one you marched against *me* last year. I think even my hotheaded young generals are thankful now for this old man's wisdom in forming an alliance."

"So are we all, Clarence. You make a far better ally than enemy, particularly considering the enemy we face at the moment."

"Speaking of which, I received a message this morning from Queen Margaret, or as she styles herself, 'Queen of Scots and the Lands of the North.' A little presumptuous, I think, since Carlisle is as far north as one can get without crossing Hadrian's Wall."

"She sounds like a very presumptuous lady altogether," Arthur observed. "But let's discuss this sitting down."

The flaps on the King's tent had been raised awning-like for the war council of Cumbria and Carlisle. Crowding in, the nobles and generals seated themselves on animal skins. On a stool in the center, Arthur sat near a pile of ancient maps, with Dukes Reginald and Clarence beside him.

The tent was crowded, but the space around the King's young wizard was left free until two even younger figures appeared on the edge of the crowd, and Merlin patted the spot beside him. Welly, Heather, and the girl's alarming dog worked their way through to join him.

Shifting on his stool, Duke Clarence pulled a rolled parchment from his jacket. "Before proceeding any further, Your Majesty, I should pass on Margaret's message, arrogant as it may be."

"Certainly, read it to us all."

The old man unrolled the message and squinted at it closely. " 'To Clarence, Temporary Duke of Carlisle.' " The phrase brought gasps and angry muttering from the crowd. " 'From Margaret II, Queen of Scots and the Lands of the North. In pursuance of the pledge taken by Myself in ascending the throne of My fathers, I have led My people from their lands of ice and snow to the heart of English plenty. It is My will that the ancient wall that once divided the Scots from England's northern shires now unite us as a backbone. Northumbria is Mine. Newcastle is Mine. Carlisle must be Mine as well.' "

Again, outraged muttering in the assembly. "But there's more." Clarence raised a hand, and the group quieted. " 'It has come to Our attention that you have formed an alliance with a young upstart from Cumbria falsely calling himself Arthur Pendragon. If you persist in refusing generous offers to submit to Our dominion, We must move against you and any demented allies that creep from their hills. We urge your surrender now. Obstinacy and fairy tales cannot prevail against the might and majesty of Scotland.' "

The Duke let the parchment roll close and handed it

to the King. Arthur smiled thinly. "Well, it seems that centuries of ice have done nothing to cool Scottish arrogance. Now, shall we see what we can do?"

From around him came cheers and laughing boasts of what they would do to Margaret and her Scots. Before the noise subdued into earnest planning, Merlin stood up, his face more pale and drawn than ever.

"Sire, a word. I leave war plans to you and your generals. But remember, our goal is not vengeance or simply to have one shire win against another. It must always be to unite those shires, to unite them for the future against the threat in the South. Defeat of that common enemy must be uppermost. Any strategy that furthers that is wise; any that weakens it is foolish."

"Have you any specific advice, then, Merlin?"

The youth hung his head. "No. I cannot see the answers, only the dangers." He looked up again, his face sickly pale. "Too much eagerness for bloodletting may be one of them."

Abruptly he turned and left the tent. The silence was broken by muttered questions about who this pushy brat thought he was and by hushed answers from those who knew. As talk turned to the coming battle, Heather left her place and slipped out.

Cold night had fallen, its stars shrouded by the usual high dust. In the distance, the darkened bulk of Carlisle glimmered with scattered lights. On the surrounding plain, the shapes of men and horses were dark smudges, illuminated here and there by the ruddy glow of campfires. Acrid smoke from burning dung twisted through the chill air along with the sounds of men and horses and the muted clatter of equipment.

Heather asked a guard outside the tent if he had seen Merlin. Making a quick sign against ill omen, he pointed to a thin figure standing alone on a nearby knoll. She frowned as she left the guard. These people, she thought angrily, were willing enough to benefit from magic. They might even use a little about their farms. But they still feared it and those who worked it for them.

"Earl?" she said, approaching the shadowed figure. As he turned toward her, the glow of a distant campfire lit his haggard face. Suddenly she wasn't sure why she had come. She certainly didn't want to talk about magic. No, it was he who worried her.

"Earl, you looked awful in there. Are you sick?"

He sighed in the darkness. "I might as well be. It's the same thing, Heather, getting worse. Sometimes it tears at me so, I can hardly stand it."

"But surely you don't think we should abandon this battle? Carlisle's an ally. What respect would people have for Arthur if he didn't help his allies when they needed it?"

"I know, I know. But look at the whole picture. Here we've gathered the best warriors and some of the best farmers and shepherds from all of Cumbria. We'll join the same sorts from Carlisle and march against more of the same from Scotland, Northumbria, and Newcastle. And what will happen? Oh, there'll be a 'glorious victory' for someone. But hundreds of people will be dead. There'll be that many fewer farmers and shepherds to work this land and that many fewer warriors to hold out against Morgan and her forces in the South."

Heather shivered, remembering her own past meetings with Morgan. "But what can we do? I mean, right now? You said yourself that Arthur must unite all these little quarreling shires. If they don't acknowledge him voluntarily, how can he do it except by war? If you tell those generals of his not to confront Margaret's army, they'll tear you apart."

"Oh, we can confront her, all right. But maybe . . ."

A long silence. Impatiently Heather broke it. "Maybe?"

"Heather, I may need your help, and Welly's, too. Can I have it?"

"What kind of help?"

"Nothing you can't do."

"Yes, but *should* we do it? No, don't answer that. If I can, I'll help. But what is it?"

"I'm not sure yet. Just an idea. If I only had my Bowl of Seeing, we could get some inkling of what this battle has in store. But we may have to act nonetheless."

He laughed and gently squeezed her shoulders. "Thanks, though. I'm suddenly feeling better. Maybe you should play around with healing magic while you're at it."

With dawn came orders to break camp and prepare to march. During the night, word had come that Queen Margaret was on the move, marching west from Newcastle along the course of the ancient Roman Wall.

Heather crawled from her frost-stiffened bedroll. After three days in the saddle, every muscle in her body ached. She was moving so much like an ancient crone, she was almost surprised to see that her hair hadn't turned white. Gingerly combing and rebraiding it, she soon joined the bustle around Arthur's tent.

Duke Reginald, his short, squat body planted firmly in front of the King, was arguing vigorously. "You're a stubborn man, sire, if you'll excuse my boldness. But it's a mistake to march out to meet her. We know where she's heading. Stay put, I say, and let her troops tire themselves marching to us."

Arthur ran an exasperated hand through his hair. "That makes sense, Reggie, but think of it from Clarence's point of view. He doesn't know how this battle is going to go. We could lose it or reach a stalemate. Every foot the Scots move into his territory is land they might hold."

"True, but . . ."

"Rest assured, friend, no forced march. We'll move just fast enough to limber ourselves up."

The other laughed, but beside him, one of his serious-faced young generals shook his head. "Sire, you said we couldn't know how this battle will come out. But we could, couldn't we, if we asked that wizard of yours?"

Merlin, who had been struggling nearby with the bent clasp of a saddle girth, turned toward them, but Arthur waved him back. "It would be nice, wouldn't it," the King said. "I admit I don't understand magic, but Merlin tells me prophecies are out." He smiled, thumping the general on the shoulders. "Besides, half the fun of these things is the suspense."

But the man persisted. "Well, then, how about improving the odds? Couldn't he throw thunderbolts at the enemy or make them fall asleep or turn us all into forty-foot giants?"

Merlin sighed and, leaving the saddle, walked toward them. With a wry smile, the King deferred to him.

"Arthur knows just how often we've had this conversation, and the answer's always the same. Magic's not much use on a battlefield. If you'd been with us these last few years, you'd know that magic used simply to frighten tends to scare both sides equally. If I used it as a weapon and started hurling spells or flames at an enemy, it'd likely hit our people as well. And as for turning us into giants, one magician, even a troop of them, couldn't maintain an illusion like that for long, not with several thousand pseudo-giants running around.

"No, Arthur and I have an arrangement. I understand magic, and he leaves that to me. He understands warfare, and I leave that to him. I'll go along, but only to help here and there."

Arthur nodded. "What this smooth-faced kid is saying, gentlemen"—he dodged a good-natured kick from Merlin—"is that we have to win this ourselves—which is as it should be. How are we going to win and hold a kingdom unless people know we have the strength to do it on our own?"

Heather caught Merlin's eye before he headed back toward his heap of stubborn horse trappings. "But I thought you said . . ."

"Hush." He looked furtively around, then pulled her aside. "I meant that. There's no point in throwing magic indiscriminately around on the battlefield. But if we are very, very discriminating, we might turn one thing at least in the right direction."

"Earl, stop being an enigmatic wizard! What do you mean?"

He smiled infuriatingly. "You'll see."

23

CLASH ALONG THE WALL

I n three days' time, Heather was to learn what he meant. The land around them now was bleak and wild. From horizon to gray horizon, it stretched in a rolling plain, bare except for rock outcrops and coarse grass ruffled by loud, cold winds. To the north, the land swept upward, rising into a long chain of ridges, like waves frozen seconds before breaking. Dark along the crest ran the remains of the Wall.

Millennia earlier, the Romans had built that wall to set off their civilized empire from the barbarian north. But the empire had fallen, and in time so had much of the Wall. Yet now, on the sweeping ridges above the army, a crumbling spine of stone still spoke of ancient order.

As Arthur's army made camp that second night, the sky clotted with thick gray clouds. Before dark had fallen, snow sifted from the sky, sizzling into cookfires and settling wetly on waiting bedrolls. By dawn, the whole landscape was dusted with white. Dark stones standing out starkly now, the Wall snaked silently over the ridgetops to their north.

Heather had no eyes for scenery as she tied heavy leggings over her trousers and fastened on the stiff leather

breastplate. As she moved, its fish-scale metal plates tin-
kled like sinister wind chimes. Every few seconds, she
looked up at the dark smudge that spread slowly toward
them from the east. The Scottish army. The enemy.

Nervously she buckled her short Eldritch sword about
her waist, recalling the first time she had used that weapon
after they'd found it in the ancient shipwreck. Then she
had faced an uncanny army of Morgan's. This Queen
Margaret, however arrogant, was at least leading a human
army. Still, she reflected uneasily, those Scots could kill her
just as dead.

With Rus jumping excitedly beside her, she made her
way to where Welly was standing by the horses. Everyone
was too intent on his own fears and preparations to bother
avoiding a young magic worker and her mutant dog. She
hardly noticed the others but smiled when she saw Welly.
He looked impressively martial in his metal-studded armor.
But already there was a sheen of sweat on his face, and one
plump hand was fidgeting with the horse-head hilt of his
own Eldritch sword.

Over the steady howling of wind, horses neighed, men
shouted orders, and metal clattered on metal as soldiers
swung into saddles and hurried to their positions. The
cold air smelled of horse, leather, and sweat.

"Farther east!" Arthur shouted to Otto as a groom
brought up the King's gray horse. "Keep to the high ground
but move farther east. The drop-off on the Wall's far side is
too steep here. We can't risk being driven against it."

The King swung onto his horse, and Welly, Heather,
and the others did the same. Already, John Wesley, seated
proudly on his shaggy brown mare, had raised the Pendragon banner. It snapped above them in the sharp,
icy air.

With Arthur and his standard in the lead, the King's troop pulled out. Merlin rode up beside Heather and Welly. "Stick with me," he said over the din of horses and men, "and stay uphill from the King."

To the blare of horns and roll of drums, the army began flowing eastward. Heather looked ahead at the enemy advancing to the eerie wail of bagpipes. They were closer now but not close enough to pick out individuals. She wondered if the smudge of their own army looked as large and daunting to the Scots. There were a lot of people on both sides. Earl was right. Once they had finished fighting, no matter who won, there'd be a lot of people dead.

Heather squelched the thought and, like many others, strained for a glimpse of Queen Margaret. Riding beside her, Welly pointed. "There she is, on that big red horse. Guess that's her banner in front."

Heather kept her eyes on that distant figure. Even from so far away, she could see the Queen's flaming red hair. The banner was a splash of red on gold, but she couldn't make out the device.

Suddenly Merlin was beside them, working his black mare like a sheepdog to cut them off. "Higher. We don't want to get swept up in the charge." Rus yapped eagerly, and Heather shot him a hushing look.

Both armies slowed, seeking favorable positions. Arthur held the north ridge, while across a shallow swale still scarred by Roman ditches, the Scots took a lower swell of ground.

Heather could see the Queen better now. She looked young, not the brutish veteran everyone seemed to have expected. The banner was clearly a rearing red lion blazoned on gold.

Merlin maneuvered his horse between Heather and Welly. "When the charge is sounded, head for those rocks." Welly opened his mouth to protest, but Merlin cut him short. "No, I'm not asking you to hide. Look, this is the plan."

After his instructions, Heather felt twice as scared as before. "I don't know if I can do that, Earl. I've never tried to—"

A challenging horn brayed over the hills and was answered by another across the swale. Voices rose in growling shouts, and like water bursting from dams, the two armies poured toward each other, yelling and brandishing weapons.

"There!" Merlin shouted as the three galloped toward the rocks. "Margaret's holding back at first, directing things from that knoll. You can always find her by the banner. Now, Heather, the Queen's horse!"

But Heather was already looking at the horse, a big red stallion. His ears pricked forward eagerly, and his mane bristled along the proud arched neck. He snorted and pawed the earth. He had known many battles and would wait for command, but not patiently. He wanted to run with his fellows, to carry his mistress into the exciting chaos, to strike with his hooves at any who faced him.

"Closer!" Heather's voice was strained. Welly, his hand on her horse's bridle, had been steadily leading her while she concentrated. The three were now east of the battle. On a rise above them and to their west were the Queen and her guard. The shallow valley vibrated with sound, the sound of screaming horses and men and of weapons clashing on armor.

"Now, Heather," Merlin urged. "Now!"

Heather followed the path she'd forged, reaching into the red horse's eager, battle-hungry mind. *This is the way. Now is the command. The only way, the only time to join the battle. This way. Now!*

The Queen's horse screamed and bolted sideways, his rider struggling to stay on his back. Heather stared at the joyous, tossing head. *Yes, that's right, this way, faster! Let no one stop you. This is the way, the only way to battle.*

The horse veered east and then plunged down the slope. Confused, the Queen's guard watched a moment; then, seeing her in danger, they prodded their horses after her.

Suddenly a mounted warrior sprang out of nowhere in front of the guards, a stout young man waving a fabulous sword. Then there were others, many others, all alike, brandishing identical swords. Alarmed, the soldiers pulled out their own weapons.

The young warriors laughed, sun glinting off their spectacles. Eerily they laughed as one, and as one, they turned and rode on ahead, surrounding the Queen and her runaway mount.

Now at the feet of the pursuers, warhounds appeared, dozens of them, all hideous. With two heads each, they snapped and snarled, and the guards' horses plunged in terror.

Surrounded by unearthly dogs and warriors, the Queen's horse continued its mad flight behind enemy lines. Closer and closer they drew to the gold and black banner of Arthur Pendragon.

The battle slowly faltered. "They've captured Margaret!" came the word. "Arthur's taken the Queen!" Fighting slowed under a weight of confusion, and in places, the Scottish line wavered and broke.

On the hillside, Queen Margaret had given up trying to control her horse or turn it back from its insane flight. She cared now only to stay on with dignity, but that had already been shaken by the sudden appearance of the strange identical warriors and their horrid two-headed hounds. Surrounded, she could scarcely see where this mad charge was taking her. Then her eye caught a flutter of black blazoned with a snarling gold dragon.

Suddenly the host around her shimmered and shrank into one boy and a single grotesque dog. At her other side rode two more warriors. No, these two were hardly more than children, a wispy-haired girl and a pale, scrawny boy. Confusion and indignation threatened to choke her. Then she looked ahead.

A tall, fair man sat astride a stallion as large as her own. He took off his helmet, and golden hair glinted in the pale sun. His smile was broad but bewildered. "Your Majesty, to what do I owe this honor?"

She stared at him in silent anger, but the thin boy beside her spoke up. "Her Majesty, Queen Margaret, is here to discuss a truce and an alliance."

She turned savagely on the youth. "I'm here to do nothing of the sort!"

"Oh yes you are, Your Majesty," the pale boy said softly. "What other choice have you?"

From his horse, Arthur smiled in comprehension and signaled to his trumpeter to sound a blast. As the echoes faded, the skirmishing below lessened.

The King stood in his stirrups, his voice booming over the battlefield. "I, Arthur Pendragon, hold Margaret, Queen of Scots, as my . . . guest. To assure her safety and yours, let all hostilities between our two forces cease.

"Your Majesty"—Arthur turned to the Queen as a babble of voices broke out below—"let us and some of our aides retire to a quieter spot. It seems we have a good deal to discuss."

Margaret's face had turned an angry red, almost the shade of her hair. But her voice was like ice. "Am I to have aides at this 'talk' as well?"

"Certainly. Give us the names, and we will send for them."

Arthur directed their horses up the hillside toward scattered rocky ruins. Behind them, Heather suddenly swayed in her saddle. Merlin quickly reached over and steadied her.

"Oh, Earl," she said weakly. "I feel as if I've been flayed on the inside."

"It will pass. But need I say you did splendidly?"

"You certainly did, Heather," Welly chimed in. "But I almost forgot to look ferocious when those copies popped up, all looking as terrified as I did. There were an awful lot of me."

Merlin chuckled. "And all played their parts beautifully. So did Rus. I threw him in at the last minute. It was a pretty good touch, though, wasn't it?"

"Brilliant," Welly agreed. "One of him is enough for most folks. But let's catch up with the others."

Higher on the slope, a small assembly was dismounting and finding seats among the weed-choked ruins. The red-haired Queen sat by herself, tall and erect, with a face as cold and stony as the wall on which she sat. However, when Heather, Welly, and Merlin rode up, her face kindled with anger.

"So now this travesty of a council is to be joined by children? I won't have it!"

"Madam," Arthur said calmly, "these 'children' not only persuaded you to join us, they battled their way through great evil to fetch me out of Avalon. Their swords are Eldritch and their rights unquestioned."

The Queen jumped angrily to her feet. "Avalon and Eldritch swords, bah! Maybe you can delude your simple hill folk with such fancies, but not me! I'll talk to you about armies and land—I have no choice. But I will not talk about fairy tales!"

Arthur took an angry breath, but Merlin held up his hand. Dismounting wearily, he faced the Queen. "Your Majesty, may I point out that a woman whose horse has been called from her by the power of magic and whose guard has been threatened by spectral warriors is hardly in a position to question fairy tales."

The Queen's sputtering reply was cut short by the arrival of four of her lieutenants. Looking confused, angry, and worried, they reluctantly turned over their swords and joined their Queen.

The King nodded at the newcomers. "Thank you for joining us, gentlemen. Now, let us begin. We should have a neutral mediator, but as none is available, I suggest that Merlin begin the discussion. The idea for these talks was, I believe, his."

Queen Margaret raised an eyebrow when the same skinny boy stood up. This was the fabled Merlin? Nonsense. Even in fairy tales he was an old graybeard. Still, there were all those phantom warriors. . . .

"Your Majesties"—Merlin bowed to each—"and nobles of Scotland and the North, this truce provides an opportunity to reevaluate our situation." The Scottish generals snorted, but Merlin ignored them. "We have below us the fighting forces of all northern Britain. Between us we've achieved more unity than this island has seen in five hundred years. But if this battle continues, a chance for greater unity is shattered. Both armies are strong; there would be no easy victory." This time generals on both sides snorted. "No matter who won, hatreds would last for generations, and the fighting forces of these lands would be devastated. Half, maybe more, of our warriors would die."

"That's the hazard of war, boy," one of the Scotsmen called out. Merlin could see grizzled veterans on his own side nod in agreement.

"Perhaps you are right. Perhaps Britain should remain a pack of barbaric states snarling and biting at each other. Perhaps we don't want the peace, prosperity, and unity these lands once knew. If so, we should continue this battle and let the carrion eaters claim victory.

"But even were that our goal, we would not enjoy it long. Because there is another form of unity alive in these islands, a unity of evil. You all know mutants have been crossing the diminished Channel from the Continent, but these are not aimless destroyers. They have found a leader, someone with power enough to turn them to her will. And her will is to conquer Britain, all of Britain, for herself."

Uneasy muttering broke out in the assembly.

"Look at the start she has made. Five shires already are in her hands! And her armies number not only conscripts and foreign muties but also creatures from another world. Morgan is an enchantress." Angry scoffing sounds. "This is no fairy tale! It is as real as the little magics emerging around your own lands." Merlin looked around at the uneasy nods. "Magic is returning, and there is none who can wield it for greater evil than Morgan Le Fay.

"Every day that we fight among ourselves, she grows stronger. Every loss we suffer is one less obstacle for her. And what can stem her conquest of this divided island if we are busy licking our self-inflicted wounds?

"But if instead we unite, we could move south and spread our unity. The size of our combined forces would convince many to join rather than resist us. And when, in time, we faced the real enemy, we might hope for the strength to triumph."

Merlin sat down to scattered cheers from both sides. A black-bearded Scotsman spoke up. "You are suggesting we unite our two armies, but under whose command? We're not buying your claims that this golden puppy is High King of Britain."

Several Cumbrians jumped up angrily. Merlin stood, raising his staff. "The command would be a joint one, the King of Cumbria and the Queen of Scotland sharing equally, along with a council of their choosing."

The Scottish Queen now jumped to her feet. "If you are asking me to share command with this arrogant young play-actor . . ."

Arthur, purpling with rage, stood as well. "Madam, if you think I want to share anything with an uncouth, snarling fell-bitch like yourself—"

Merlin stomped his staff against the ground, producing a shower of purple sparks. "Shut up, Your Majesties! I am not asking that you like each other, only that you lead your armies away from self-destruction to possible victory. Surely both you youngsters are mature enough for that!"

"Well!" Margaret said indignantly. "You're hardly the one to talk, you nasty little beardless brat!"

Arthur laughed gustily. "Madam, that nasty little beardless brat is several thousand years your senior. But I admit, age hasn't made his meddling any easier to take—particularly when he's right."

Arthur turned and jumped onto a wall. "All right. I accept the proposal." He looked coldly at the Queen. "My army is as ready and anxious for battle as yours. But we are even more anxious for lasting victory. If that can best be found by uniting forces and moving south, then let us do so. I will share command with Scotland's queen, but I ask that our advisers do their utmost to keep us out of each other's way!"

The Queen rose with disdainful dignity. "I, too, accept the proposal. The forces of Scotland will gladly conquer any southlands laid before us. And if to do so I must accept joint command, I will. But on one point I agree with this pale upstart. Councillors be warned—the less we two have to do with each other, the better!"

Heated discussion began over the details of the alliance. Heather and Welly joined Merlin where he sat by himself, looking tired and depressed.

"What are you so down for?" Welly asked. "That was a stupendous speech. It really seemed to do the trick."

Merlin smiled wanly. "A bit flowery, I'm afraid, but it worked. No, what worries me is that the 'beardless brat' line could rankle me so. Last time I was this age, it took me forever to grow a beard, and that drove me absolutely crazy. Now my body's doing the same thing again. You'd think I'd have the sense not to let it bother me. But it does! I guess it just shows that the age shifting was complete. I'm a teenager again, inside and out. What an ordeal!"

The following evening, the leadership of both armies joined for dinner. It began as an awkwardly stiff affair, but after the barley beer made several rounds, a semblance of camaraderie spread through the group. Arthur and Margaret sat on opposite sides of the fire sharing good-humored chatter with those around them but having nothing but glowers for each other.

After Scottish pipers had screeched for a while, Kyle launched nervously into a newborn song of his own. He had worked on it frantically all day, trying to make all participants in the recent battle sound equally dignified and brave. He finally avoided the problem of whom to glorify most by playing up the magic element instead.

Afterward, when less tuneful songs were being belted out by the diners, Heather slipped over to the harpist.

"Kyle, that song was terrific." She smiled wryly. "But I couldn't help noticing how much you made use of the magic and all. I thought you hated it."

"One can't hate magic any more than one can hate fire. But that doesn't mean I want nice people getting hurt by it."

"If you're going to lecture—"

"I'm not. I'm a harper, and magic is a natural for songs and stories. But did you like the way the song showed you?"

"I . . . well, it wasn't anything like me—a cool, magical heroine, ha! But you've told me often enough how an artist has to mold raw mud into something lovely."

"Yes. But the hearers don't see the trick. If it's artfully done, they take it for truth. Soon they'll see you not as Heather McKenna but as that cool, magical heroine. They'll leave a wide space around you just as they do with Merlin. They'll be afraid if your hem brushes against them. Think, Heather, is that what you want? Because, slowly, that is what you are choosing."

Heather paled and turned away. Kyle had jabbed into her deepest fears. She didn't want to make that choice, not yet. She needed time to think, to decide!

Just then, Otto bawled something and swayed drunkenly to his feet. With relief, Heather turned toward the commotion.

"A toast!" he repeated. "To the alliance of King Arthur and Queen Margaret!"

A portly Scot jumped up as well. "Aye. An alliance started on a battlefield may end in a marriage bed!"

Otto laughed and swung his mug high. "Now that's diplomacy. I'll drink to that!"

"You shall not!" Margaret shrieked, and jumped up, flinging her mug into the fire. "None of you shall, or I march out of here tonight! I've had enough of my 'advisers' trying to marry me off to any princeling who doesn't fall off his horse. I am Queen. And I am not sharing my throne with any arrogant English madman. The next person who suggests I do gets my sword through his throat!"

Arthur was on his feet now, glaring across the fire at her and the whole assembly. "Save your sword for your own men, Queen. The next man of mine who so much as thinks of mating me with an uncouth wild woman will feel my own blade. Now, all of you, do this lady and I make ourselves clear on this point?"

The shocked mumbling was broken into by the sound of horsemen on the hillside above. Moments later, one of Arthur's guards rode up and, dismounting, hastily bowed to the King.

"Your Majesty, there's a man here with a message from the Duke of Cheshire. He's sought you in Keswick, Carlisle, and now here. Will you see him?"

"I will. Anything would be preferable to the insanity I've just been hearing."

The guard motioned into the darkness. A spent horse stumbled forward, and a man dismounted and walked wearily toward the King. He bowed and looked up at Arthur with a moment's awe. Then, composing himself, he stammered, "You are Arthur Pendragon?"

"I am."

"Then, sire, I have a most urgent message for you from His Grace, Geoffrey, Duke of Cheshire."

"Deliver it, then. These are allies; we have no secrets."

The young messenger straightened himself and unrolled the parchment clutched in his hand. " 'To Arthur Pendragon, High King of Cumbria and Carlisle, from Geoffrey, the third of that name, Duke of Cheshire.

" 'Sire, having heard much of your prowess, both in olden times and of late, and having heard that you seek alliances among the shires, let me extend the offer of such. We are in dire need. Chester, our chief city, has for weeks been laid siege to by the armies of Manchester. Our supplies grow short, but the enemy shows no sign of tiring. We are an ancient and proud people, but we would rather lay our allegiance at the feet of one known for his openness than have it wrested from us by the greedy hands of old enemies. In hopes that soon I may offer you my gratitude in person, I am yours, Geoffrey III, Duke of Cheshire.' "

"Thank you, young man," Arthur said to the courier. "Someone fetch him food and drink." He turned to the others. "What do you say, Your Majesty? We must try this alliance out somewhere."

The Queen smiled coldly across the fire. "I say we march to Chester."

Cheers broke out and cries of "To Chester, to Chester!" Quietly Arthur turned to Merlin. "I'd ask a prophecy if you'd give it, old wizard. But have you at least some feeling on this plan? Is it right that we march to Chester?"

Standing beside Merlin, Heather looked at her friend

anxiously as his face creased with pain. His voice was low and strained. "It is right, and it is wrong. But it is the way you must go. I know nothing more."

"Well, that's enough for me," Arthur said, turning back to the others.

Merlin gazed at Heather, his eyes blank with anguish. "No, it is not enough!" he rasped. "I should be able to tell him more."

She reached for his hand, but there was nothing comforting she could think to say. Above them in the dark, she felt the passage of a lone night bird. It soared on winds of cold foreboding. Fear and terrible emptiness slid beneath its wings. She shivered and clutched the wizard's hand tighter in her own.

24

THE ROAD TO WAR

When the armies marched south from the Wall, it was with Dragon and Lion banners fluttering in the lead. John Wesley had struck up a friendship with the young Scot who carried Margaret's standard, and the two rode close abreast.

The farther south they moved, the grimmer the landscape became. Heather was surprised at the desolation. Since only London had been bombed during the Devastation, she'd assumed that most old cities would not look greatly shattered. But with massive deaths from cold, radiation, and plague, their social and economic order had quickly collapsed. The few survivors had fled, and the once-great cities had fallen into ruins. They were inhabited now only by scavengers and bands of mutants.

Between these ruins were scattered farms and small settlements from which supplies were taken for the advancing army. But when their route took them past the hollow cities, an oppressive silence fell over the company, as though a cloud of dead dreams still hung about the ruins.

The roads they followed were straight and wide, but under the weeds, the pavement was cracked. Overpasses were collapsed, and tall metal lightposts sprawled beside the roads like dead giants. On every side, skeletons of buildings and smokestacks stood silhouetted against the dust-gray sky.

Of all those in the southward-marching army, the King's wizard seemed most deeply sunk in gloom. Whenever Heather tried to talk to him, he muttered something about roads cycling back and continued staring at the dead landscape.

By the time they crossed the Cheshire border, Merlin's tension was so apparent, no one rode anywhere near him. Even Heather and Welly were afraid to speak to him for fear he might shatter like a figure of glass. Instead they rode with Kyle or trotted forward to exchange words with John Wesley.

After many long, gray days, the vanguard finally climbed a low rise and saw, in a glinting bend of the River Dee, the ancient walled town of Chester. The besieging army from Manchester clustered like ants outside the wall. But warned of the North's coming, they were already redeploying their forces.

Margaret and Arthur consulted briefly with their generals, and word was given to fan out along a low ridge. Turning her eyes from the deployment, Heather glanced to where Merlin sat, hunched dejectedly on his horse. Appalled at how ill he looked, she spurred her horse over to him.

"Earl, I don't want to disturb you, but you really don't look well. Maybe you should just stay back here. They probably won't need magic in this one."

He shuddered and glanced at her as if suddenly coming awake. "It's wrong! Every step we take and every road I see is wrong. They lead in huge circles. We ride past ruins on our way to war. There'll be little wars, then bigger wars, until we build cities of our own and blast them into ruins to crawl past once more. There must be somewhere to turn aside, but I can't see it!"

He cried that last with such despair that those nearby sketched hand signs against evil and moved away. "Earl," Heather said, "if you think we're going to lose this battle . . ."

"No! No, it's two separate things. Both connected, though . . . somehow. But I can't see either very well, the long-term doom or the short-term battles. With the battle at the Wall, I was just fumbling in the dark. It seemed to work, but it led us here. And what will happen today? Who will die, and where will it lead us? A wizard worth the name should be able to tell. But without the new magic or even the use of my old tools, how can I?

"And then there's the big battle, the one with Morgan. It's coming; it lies before us as surely as tomorrow's dawn. But what is she planning? What is her strength? Have we any hope of defeating her? It we don't, then all my brooding about mankind's future is just empty thought. The future she'll bring can only be one of servitude, torture, and evil. Better that the Devastation had wiped the human race out entirely and cleansed this planet than leave us to drown like that."

Merlin's head hung over his horse's bowed neck. Then he began shaking with silent laughter. "I'm sorry, Heather. I really do sound like a demented old wizard. To answer the question that I think you asked somewhere back there:

No, I won't sit it out. I may be useless as a prophet, but I can still wield a sword."

Heather had understood only part of his words, but the suffering behind them was clear. She almost wished that he was plain Earl Bedwas again. If magic and its responsibilities could eat at a person, a person she cared for, like some terrible disease, then how could anyone want it?

Suddenly horns blared. Movement erupted around her, and Heather instantly lost sight of any military tactics. She concentrated on keeping astride her horse as it pounded over the plain, on watching where her crazy dog was getting to, and on keeping close to the King's standard. She hoped that as long as she thought of mechanical things, she'd forget to be afraid. She was wrong.

Nearby, Welly employed his own and, he discovered, largely useless device for ignoring fear. He watched patterns unfold from mental plans to the actual battlefield. The King's and Queen's guards had pulled up on a rise, while below, the front line formed into a shield-protected wedge to drive through the Manchester line. The cavalry was taking positions on the flanks, waiting to trap the enemy in tightening pincers, while the mounted troops around their leaders fidgeted in anticipation of their own final drive through the center.

Suddenly, right around them, all became noise and chaos. Nothing was as it should be. Welly and Heather craned their necks to the right, looking for the cause of the turmoil. Then it was all too clear.

A troop fresh from Manchester had come upon the battle and attacked the Northern forces from the rear. Like a spear, they were driving toward the banners of the two war leaders. Their plan was simple and obvious: kill or capture those two, and the Northern attack would crumble.

The sudden disturbance shocked Merlin out of his lethargy. With grim determination, he pulled out his own gleaming Eldritch sword and sent power flickering along its blade so that it slashed with strength far beyond his own. But the enemy seemed everywhere. No sooner had one fallen than another took its place.

In the center of it all, Queen Margaret, her hair flying about her like flame, cast her spear at one foeman, then drew her sword. Beside her, Arthur's great sword swung through the air, sun glinting off its ancient blade. It slashed down into an attacker, spraying the air with blood. He raised his sword again when suddenly the gray stallion rose, screaming, onto his hind feet, a deep gash from a war ax streaming blood down his neck. The horse pawed the air, then tumbled over, throwing the King to the ground. Dazed, Arthur struggled to his knees as a bloody axe cleaved the air toward him. The axman's face, snarling in victory, suddenly contorted as the Queen's sword drove deep between his ribs.

Warrior and axe thudded to the bloodied earth, and Arthur staggered to his feet beside Margaret's horse. She reached down, and he swung onto the saddle behind her.

Several horse-lengths away, Merlin watched this scene with horror as he automatically fought off attackers with his own sword. Now he wrenched himself away and plunged through the skirmishing warriors to defend his King.

But Arthur and Margaret were doing a capable job of defending themselves, each wielding a sword on a different side of the great red horse. Suddenly Merlin heard an odd cry behind him, high like a young bird's. He spun around to see John Wesley clutching the King's banner, his face blank with surprise as he looked down at the quivering spear shaft protruding from his chest. Slowly his hands slid down the pole, and the boy toppled sideways off his horse.

"No!" Merlin roared. From the tip of his sword, he shot a bolt of flame that incinerated the spearman. Before the ashes had drifted to the ground, Merlin was off his horse and holding the dead boy in his arms.

Welly, fighting nearby, had heard Merlin's shout and turned to see the Dragon standard waver and slide downward along the now-riderless horse. Driving his own horse toward it, Welly reached out and grabbed the pole. Awkwardly he wielded his sword with one hand while clutching the standard with the other.

Battle tides surged back and forth over plain and hill. Below, the Northern wedge finally broke through the Manchester line and scattered the besieging forces. When they saw their main army routed, the reinforcements wavered, then called a retreat. Northerners cheered their departure, vengefully pursuing stragglers.

When relative calm had returned to the battlefield, Heather looked down at her sword to see it red and sticky. Sick horror rose in her throat, and she hastily dismounted to wipe the blade on the grass. Distrusting her wobbly legs, she mounted again and looked over the battlefield.

On a hillside littered with dead and dying, she saw Merlin's black horse riderless and alone. Fear sliced through her like a spear. She spurred her horse to a gallop. As she neared, Welly, having turned in the standard, rode up as well.

Heather felt faint with relief when she saw Merlin

kneeling, apparently unharmed, but her joy shriveled at the sight of what he held in his arms. She and Welly dismounted.

"He died," their friend whispered. "He was nine years old, and he died."

"He died nobly," Welly said, his own voice strained and tearful.

"Oh, yes, nobly!" Merlin laughed bitterly. "That makes it all right, then. He died nobly clutching the standard of the King. And you nobly saved it from being trampled in his blood, and Kyle the harper will compose a ballad about how noble we all were and how tragically and nobly the crippled boy from Devon died, and we'll all feel sad and somehow better about it." The bitterness in his voice was as sharp as a sword.

Angry now, Welly snapped, "And I suppose you'd rather I'd let the standard fall?"

"No! No, I'd rather you'd never had to save it. I'd rather this whole bloody waste had never happened!"

"But, Earl," Welly objected, "you said we had to unify the country and face Morgan. . . ."

"I know. And we do. That is right. But something is wrong, too, very wrong. If only I could see what!" He laid the limp form gently on the ground. "If I could have seen this battle, if I could have seen the relief column from Manchester, then this boy wouldn't be lying here now. If I could see further, we'd know what we faced with Morgan; or further still, and maybe I could keep us from plunging down that same long, deadly road. But I can't. I can't see any of it!"

Hesitantly, Heather placed a hand on his shoulder, tears streaming down her own face. "Earl, we loved John

Wesley, too. But this isn't your fault. None of it is. You're doing the best you can."

He reached up and grabbed her hand. "No. I am *not* doing that. That's one thing I do know."

The wind froze the tears to her cheeks as Heather looked down at Earl's ashen face and the sad dead boy beside him on the grass. This world, she thought, was harsh enough without the demands of magic. That was an added curse, one no one should have to bear.

The siege of Chester was broken. Duke Geoffrey rode forth from his city to thank the liberating army and its leaders. He invited them to enter as victorious allies on the morrow. The remainder of that day and evening were spent tending to the dead and wounded.

The battlefield was strewn with the bodies of soldiers and horses. They were gathered up, friend and foe alike, and placed in a large, freshly dug grave. A great stone was erected on the raw heaped-up earth, but no writing was placed upon it. The pain was still too fresh to have distilled into words.

The following morning, Duke Geoffrey rode out again and presented to Arthur a rare throwback, a tall white warhorse, to replace the horse fallen in battle. Those who knew Arthur knew he'd feel nothing could replace his gray. But the King accepted the gift; it was a magnificent animal.

A dawn drizzle had given way to pale sunshine. To the throb of drums and the peal of pipes, the victorious army marched toward the city they had saved. First, under Lion and Dragon banners, rode Queen Margaret, a blaze of red, and King Arthur, hair and sword gleaming gold. Their great horses pranced and tossed their heads. Behind them came their warriors, battered weapons and armor hastily polished and flashing in the sun. People who had poured out of the city for the first time in weeks cheered wildly and strained for a glimpse of their deliverers.

As the host neared the city, Duke Geoffrey proudly pointed out how Chester had strengthened its defenses by pulling down structures that had sprawled beyond its medieval wall. People lined that wall now, cheering, waving, and throwing down bits of cloth and anything bright. Chants of "Arthur" and "Margaret" filled the air as the two rode under the gate. The streets were crowded with jubilant people who stood amid a crazy mixture of buildings: medieval half-timber, Georgian stone, and twentieth-century concrete, all patched with rubble for modern utility.

Triumphantly they rode on, finally clattering into the Duke's ancient castle, built into the city's south wall. Soldiers found welcome and lodging among celebrating townsfolk, but the King and Queen and their closest followers were lodged in the castle. That night they dined as royally as the town's scanty provisions, augmented just that day, would permit.

It was a noisy feast, noisy with the relief people feel after having lived through a victorious battle. In a smoky, torchlit hall, dancers whirled while Kyle and other musicians played pipe, harp, and drum. Heroic events of the previous day were already elaborating into legend.

Seated apart at one corner of the King's table, Merlin alone seemed immune to the jollity. Silently he picked at the food before him or stared desolately into his cup of ale. The cup was a simple unadorned one, beaten from some salvaged metal. With the noise and torch smoke swirling around him, he stared unheeding into the cup's brown depths.

Foamy bubbles and shapes were there. Shapes of warriors marching toward a city, a walled city by a river, besieged by enemies. The warriors spread out to attack, and as they did so, an unguessed-at enemy drove toward them like a spear, taking them by surprise. Surprise as the troops rallied around their King and Queen. Surprise on the face of a young boy clutching at a banner, dying with a spear thrust through his chest.

Merlin clenched his hand around the cup. It felt wider now, polished silver carved with intricate designs. In its depths, the boy's face still held surprise, eternal dying surprise. But there should have been no surprise! He should have known. He should have known!

Leaping up, Merlin hurled the cup across the room. In sudden silence, everyone turned toward him. Slowly his vision cleared, and he looked down the table at the King. "Arthur, help me!"

"Tell me how."

In the crowded, breathless room, there might have been only these two.

"Arthur, I must know what happened to my things after . . . I disappeared."

"After Nimue took you from Caerleon?"

"Yes."

The King sat back and stared, unseeing, across the room, stared back through centuries into another life. "We didn't know what had happened to you," he said slowly. "They said Nimue had enchanted you, had entombed you in some mountain. But we didn't know where. If you'd been dead somewhere, we would have buried your things with you. But . . . what are you thinking about in particular?"

"My silver bowl."

"The carved one that hung at your belt?"

Merlin nodded, and again the King thought. "I think I told Bedevere, my squire, to take care of all those things. I don't remember what happened to the bowl particularly. Since it was silver, I imagine it was treated as part of the royal treasury."

"And what would have happened to it?"

"I don't know. It could have been kept in the store-room at Caerleon or moved on to Camelot, or I suppose it could eventually have been given out as a reward to some loyal vassal or maybe even melted down for coinage. I really don't know, Merlin, but obviously it's important."

"Yes, it is." He nodded at the King. "If you will excuse me, sire, I need to think."

Arthur nodded back, and Merlin left the room. The others in the room were silent in awe, as if a window had just opened onto an ancient mythical past.

Looking around, Arthur sensed the mood. Sighing, he closed that window. "Now, ladies and gentlemen, to the concerns of our own time. Let us have a toast. A toast to Duke Geoffrey of Cheshire and his welcoming city and to Queen Margaret of Scotland and her most welcome sword."

The people in the room cheered and raised their cups. Their King was back.

After the banquet, Heather was shown to the room she would share with several ladies of Cheshire's court. They were eager to know about Arthur, about the strange, frightening Merlin, and about beautiful Queen Margaret. Restlessly Heather chatted with them a while, but as soon as she could, she slipped a cape over her borrowed dressing gown and said she had to say good night to someone. Rus, told to remain behind, woefully obeyed.

She found Merlin on the battlements. There was no mistaking his thin, gangly figure or the pale smudge of his face in the darkness. Above them, the moon, through the high dust, cast misty light on the Welsh mountains rolling darkly to the southwest.

He turned as he heard her approach but said nothing.

"Earl, what are you going to do?"

"Go find it."

"The bowl? But Arthur said it might be anywhere or even melted down by now."

"I know. But I have to try. Without it, I'm of no use to him or anyone."

"That's silly. That trick with Margaret—"

"Yes, but it was just that, a trick, and one that counted on luck. Yesterday, Arthur won without tricks, but the luck ran out for John Wesley, didn't it? I should have been able to foresee that."

"Earl, you couldn't—"

"Heather, I could have. I've been so submerged in worry over the new magic and the far future that I've neglected the present, and that's our only sure link to the future. What happens if Arthur is defeated in our next battle? What happens to the future then? At the stone circle, you had a vision. You saw a battlefield strewn with Arthur's warriors. When is that a possibility? Will it come after meeting Morgan? That is the big confrontation, and she knows it's coming as well as we do. She'll be planning for it—something diabolical, no doubt—and I want to know what. That Bowl of Seeing is the only way I know to find out. It may not work in this world; it may not even still exist. But I've got to try something!"

"So where will you go?" Heather asked after a moment.

"To Caerleon first. Arthur moved his court around a good deal, but that was where we were when Nimue . . ."

"I know. You don't have to talk about it."

"No, but oddly I want to. Tonight raked up all those memories. It's hard to believe a wise old wizard could have been so blind. But Morgan wanted me out of the way, and she had learned my weakness. All my years of magic had cut me off from simple human caring. I was bitterly lonely, and Nimue filled that loneliness. With Morgan's guidance, she learned enough of my secrets to trap me in my own enchantments."

He sighed quietly, then turned and looked at Heather. "I know what Kyle's been saying to you, Heather, and he's right. I haven't wanted to admit it. I'd hoped that this time my life could be different, that I could let myself be close to people. I was so happy when I thought that you and I could . . . share the working of magic. But it's no good. Having this power and letting it grow controls your life. It cuts you off. People come to fear or hate you. I have no right to lead you away from a normal life into that."

"Earl, you're not . . . it's just that . . . Oh, I don't know. I don't know what to think."

"Yes, you do. You know I'm right. You've been a good friend, and that's more than I should have hoped for. But I'm fooling myself to think there is any choice. This road I must go alone."

The silence stretched on and on. There was so much Heather wanted to say. Yet her mind churned with confused thoughts that she seemed powerless to mold into words.

On the battlefield, she'd felt part of herself crumble when she'd thought Earl had been killed. She ought to tell him now that she'd go with him, help him, share the exile of power. But her mind recoiled from that. She had a whole life to lead. Could she bear to lead it like that— shunned, feared, self-tormented as he was? The taste she'd had of that was chilling enough.

Choked by fear and indecision, she said nothing.

At last Merlin broke the silence. "I'll leave tonight. Arthur will know I have to go, but I'd rather not face any more leave-taking. If . . . when I find the bowl or learn what became of it, I'll return. Tell him that for me, will you?"

She nodded bleakly.

"And, Heather . . ."

"Yes?"

"No, nothing. Yes, maybe there is something. I'll be taking the route past your family's home in Brecon. Do you want me to stop with any message?"

"Oh." She looked away. "Yes, I suppose so. You know my mother and I haven't had much to do with each other since she remarried. She'd rather produce heirs for Lord Brecon than bother with her homely firstborn. But still, she is my mother. If you stop, let her know I'm all right. At least they should give you a warm meal and a bed. Knowing my stepfather, he wouldn't offend anyone important."

She tried to think furious thoughts about her uncaring family, but her mind was too numb for real emotions of any sort.

Merlin looked down at her, his own face tight against unspoken feelings. "I'll try to stop at Brecon, then. Good-bye, Heather."

"Good-bye."

He started to turn.

"Earl . . ."

"Yes?"

"I . . . Please come back."

He smiled tautly. "I'll try."

As he walked away, the words she wanted to cry after him fell silently down inside her. She leaned against the parapet, wishing she could be as cold and hard and unheeding as the stones.

25

In Quest of Vision

I t was several hours before dawn when Merlin rode his horse down to the city's main gate. The guards halted him, then, seeing who it was, blanched and hurried to open the gate. Merlin smiled wryly. The reputation of the King's wizard must have spread rapidly. The guards probably thought that if they questioned his doings, he'd turn them to stone or disintegrate their guardhouse.

The great gate creaked open, and the lone figure on a black horse rode out, hoofbeats echoing hollowly in the cold and silence.

The hazy moon was near to setting in the west. He rode toward it along the dark, lonely road, his thoughts equally dark and lonely. It had been right, what he had said to Heather, but he felt as if he'd just torn out a part of himself and left it on the walls of Chester. His had been a false hope, he knew, but it had sustained him these past two years. Now he felt empty.

The sky grayed toward dawn, and he tried turning his thoughts ahead. As he passed the first dragon-tooth peak of the Welsh mountains, his mind told him he was coming home. But his heart did not. Too much had changed. The mountains of his Wales had been green and fair, clothed in forest and in rich grazing land. Now the rocky slopes were bare of all but dry, gray grass. A few trees huddled in the valleys where rivers fell in wild tumult over rocks, unsoftened by fern and moss.

He passed abandoned farms and villages and an occasional inhabited one, where he stopped for provisions. He traded for Arthur's newly minted coins or more often for news from the outside world. These rugged folk had little dealings with the world beyond their mountains, but they were always hungry for news and tales that could be repeated around an evening's fire.

The wizard concealed his name, calling himself Earl Bedwas, a traveler from King Arthur's court. But though hospitality was always extended, at night he chose to camp by the wayside. He had no wish to depend again on human companionship. Not that he found his own very cheerful, but it was less demanding. And he knew he had nothing to fear from brigands or muties. His few encounters of that sort ended in a flash of power that sent his assailants fleeing back into the rocks and hills.

One morning, Merlin rolled from his blankets to find that instead of frost there was a light dusting of snow. Not unusual for July, but it depressed him. He wanted the wildflowers and chorusing birds of those ancient mornings. Looking up, he wished for a lightly blue sky, a sky with honest clouds, not atmospheric veils of soot and dust. He sighed. This world, he knew, was slowly improving, but it would never be the same. All that seemed the same were the ways of people and his pain in dealing with them.

Thoroughly dejected, he walked to his saddlebags, near

where his mare was cropping at the short grass, and fumbled around for a chunk of bread and a turnip. Taking these to the stream, he sat on a flat rock and began sluicing the turnip through the cold, clear water. He was just pulling it out, clean and white, when a pale, clawed hand shot from the water and grabbed one end.

Startled, he gripped the turnip and tugged back. For a moment, two pairs of hands struggled back and forth for their prize. Then, with a sudden jerk, Merlin found himself flying off his rock and into the icy stream. The cold slammed his breath away. Letting go of the turnip, he flailed at the water, slipped under the surface, then gasped and sputtered into the air again.

Through strands of dark hair dripping over his face, he saw another face bobbing before him in the water. Yellow skin drawn tightly over a misshapen skull made huge ears stand out even more. Little, close-set eyes stared at him in alarm.

Suddenly the thing lunged, grabbing him around the chest with long, hairy arms. Swallowing water as he sank beneath the surface, Merlin struggled with his captor, managing only to hit his own head against a rock. Vaguely he realized he was being dragged out onto a boulder.

He lay gasping and coughing in the cold air while a whiny voice muttered beside him. When he'd regained his breath and coughed out most of the water, Merlin sat up dizzily. His assailant squatted near him on the rock, wringing long hands and looking miserable.

"Great Wizard turn me into toad now. Troll nearly drown Great Wizard. Spend rest of life as toad."

"Troll," Merlin said weakly. "You're the troll from the Severn Bridge."

The creature hung its head. "Me was. Me be toad now."

"I'm not turning anyone into toads at present." Merlin shivered in the icy air. "But I've got to get out of these wet clothes."

The troll brightened. "Yes, change clothes. Troll help, like loyal servant. Wizard can turn Troll into toad later."

He scurried like a spider over to Merlin's pack. The horse gave him a sideways stare and shuffled aside. As soon as Merlin had peeled off his wet clothes, the troll eagerly handed him dry ones. He'd clearly had little experience with clothing and presented everything in the wrong order, but soon Merlin was dressed and relatively warm again. "Well, Troll," he said as he looked through his other pack, "since you brought the subject up, would you care to share breakfast with me?"

The wispy beard twitched, and a broad smile spread above it. Then the creature dropped his eyes. "Me still deserve to be toad."

"Perhaps, but we'll put that off for the moment." Handing him a turnip, Merlin pulled out another for himself. He broke the chunk of bread in half. Sitting on a rock well away from the stream, Merlin took a bite of his turnip. "Tell me, Troll, what brings you so far from the Severn? You had a pretty good arrangement there, accosting travelers on that bridge. Did you change over from threats to riddles, as I suggested?"

The troll smiled through a huge bite of bread. "Oh, yes, me very clever riddling troll. Not big enough to scare folks with 'grind your bones' lines."

"So why did you leave? There're not as many travelers in this part of the world."

The little troll shook his head sadly. "Spot too good. Bigger troll take it. Many folks come from Faerie, from all parts of Faerie, now that things get better here. Little runts like me not keep good spots."

"So you thought you'd find a small, untenanted bridge in Wales?"

His breakfast companion smiled broadly. "Oh, no. Me clever troll. Me remember once meet Great Wizard and friends. Hear they find Avalon and High King. Me go join them. Troll be fierce warrior!"

Merlin laughed. "Yes, I guess you could be, as long as we're not fighting larger bridge trolls." He sobered again. "If you want to find Arthur and . . . the others, I can tell you where they are."

"Great Wizard not go there?"

"No, not now. Maybe later. I need to find something first. Something I lost a long time ago."

The troll thought a moment, head nodding violently on his spindly neck. "Then Troll stay with Great Wizard and help find lost thing."

Merlin felt a jab of happiness, which he quickly suppressed. "No, you should go on. I've no way of knowing if I'll find it or if I'll ever rejoin the others. Besides, it may be dangerous where I'm going."

"Then Great Wizard need Troll for guard. We find lost thing and go back to friends. Nice Lady who feed Troll there, too?"

"Heather. Yes, she and Welly are with Arthur."

"Then must get Great Wizard back safe. Troll help."

Merlin smiled—for the first time in weeks, it seemed. "All right, I'll take you on as a traveling companion and guard. We'll forget all about the toad business."

Grinning from ear to huge ear, the troll leaped to his feet and began wadding up the wet clothes and cramming them into a saddlebag. Merlin winced. A traveling companion, maybe, but a valet, never.

The Northern armies stayed in and around Chester while wounds were tended and emissaries sent to negotiate a truce with Manchester and perhaps an alliance with York and Lancaster.

Welly, Heather, and the ever-eager Rus explored the old walled city. It was the largest settlement they had ever seen, though parts were still uninhabited. The natives took pride in pointing out features of interest, such as the canal and the ancient red-stone cathedral. Welly enjoyed these excursions and the training of new recruits, but Heather's thoughts kept drifting off. She spent more and more time on the castle walls looking out to the purple mountains of Wales.

She stood one afternoon on a favorite spot above the spreading branches of Chester's famed oak. Somehow the ancient giant had survived the rigors of the Devastation and continued growing against the castle's sheltering walls. Now in brief summer, its gnarled branches were in leaf. Heather thought that looking down on it was almost like being a bird in flight.

Just then, a real bird flew into view. It was a small hawk and soared with effortless beauty, gliding between herself and the tree below. She reached out her mind and felt the peace and purposefulness of its flight. It circled once, then settled itself on a branch below her, calmly folding its wings.

There was sudden motion. A large snake, which had

been stretched along the branch, whipped a coil around the bird. The hawk shrieked, flailing with wing and claw. Both creatures fell from the branch, disappearing over a ledge.

Heather gasped, staring in horror at the spot. But she heard or saw nothing more. Suddenly she was buffeted by a cold wind, a wind of fear and terrible certainty. She wanted to scream, to tear the vision from her mind, but it persisted. And, real or illusion, she knew its meaning. Earl had once shown her a picture of a merlin hawk. It had been like this one.

She leaned against the stone parapet as her world swirled around her and suddenly fell into place. If she hadn't been so worried, she would have laughed with strange relief. Earl was in danger, and in an instant, all her uncertainties vanished.

Her power had warned her of Earl's danger, and now perhaps she could help him. Yet this was the same power she had feared would cut her off from the normal world. Well, if it did, then let it. It was Earl that mattered. Until now, she'd been too blind to see that! She'd let him go off alone while she'd crouched, undecided, behind useless shreds of "normality."

She laughed, feeling as if great weights had fallen from her. Then, recalling the vision, she hurried down a series of stone steps. In the courtyard, Arthur and Margaret were just riding out to inspect the troops camped beyond the city walls.

"Your Majesties!" Heather called. "Wait a moment, please!" They turned in their saddles and watched her run toward them, braids flying.

"Please," she gasped, "I would like your permission to leave, to go into Wales."

"You, too?" Arthur said. "What is it about Wales that's calling away all my sorcerers?"

"I'm not much of a sorcerer, Your Majesty. But Earl, Merlin, is in danger. I . . . saw it."

The King frowned. "What sort of danger?"

"I don't know. But I know there is danger waiting for him where he least expects it. I have to warn him."

Queen Margaret spoke up. "I should think young Merlin could take care of himself. I've seen a sample or two of his powers."

"Yes, Your Majesty, I'm sure he could if he were prepared. That's why I must warn him."

"Mightn't he have received a warning as you did?" Arthur asked.

Now it was Heather's turn to frown. "I don't know. But if my help wasn't needed, why did I have the vision?"

The King shook his head. "I don't know, Heather, and I've learned enough not to meddle in affairs of magic. Yes, certainly you may go. Merlin means a great deal to me, adolescent troublemaker as he may be at present." He smiled. "How many should I send with you?"

"Oh, just me, sire."

"No. Too dangerous."

"Perhaps," the Queen suggested, "the young warrior who was so effectively multiplied at our . . . alliance?"

The King nodded. "Welly. Yes, of course. I doubt that he could be kept back anyhow. But wouldn't more be advisable?"

"No, sire. It's speed, not force, that's needed, I think."

"Well, then, take two of the faster horses, not your hairy barrels on legs. That will please Welly, I imagine. And, Heather . . ."

"Yes, sire?"

"Whether he finds that trinket or not, bring my wizard back to me."

Welly, when she told him, was indeed pleased with the chance to ride a tall, slimmer horse. He couldn't begin to understand why Heather knew she had to go; but if Earl was in danger, then he, too, was determined to help.

They set out at dawn the next day, Welly and Heather on tall, swift horses with Rus trotting beside them. They took the road they supposed their friend would have taken. Stops at inns and farmhouses confirmed that a gangly, pale youth on a black horse had passed that way. Each day, Heather urged them on to greater speed. She saw no further portents, but her sense of danger and urgency increased.

For days, Merlin and the troll traveled south through Wales. On and off, the wizard was annoyed with himself for deriving pleasure from such simple companionship. But since that was the best he could probably ever expect, he decided he might as well enjoy it.

The troll clearly did, sometimes catching fish for their supper and always making a big production of guarding while the wizard slept. Merlin quietly set up additional guarding spells—a wise precaution, he realized, since whenever he woke in the night, he found the troll asleep sitting up.

As they neared Brecon, Merlin considered whether to stop at Heather's home. He wasn't anxious to do so since it meant revealing who he was. But whether she admitted it or not, he knew Heather had some feelings for her mother and would like some news of her. Besides, the thought of stopping with Heather's kin made him feel somehow closer to her. Angrily he tried to dismiss the feeling. He had no right to any special closeness with her. Still, he had said he would try to stop.

After asking directions at the Griffin Inn, he took a side road to Lord Brecon's manor. The building had clearly started as a sturdy farmstead with house and barns forming an open courtyard. Over the years, it had been added to and fortified into an imposing residence.

It was twilight when, advising his companion to spend the night outside, Merlin rode through the courtyard and up to a heavily barred door. Dismounting, he pounded on the metal-studded wood. A hatch slid open and a squinty-eyed guard peered out.

"I am Earl Bedwas," he announced, "friend of Heather McKenna, daughter to Lady Brecon. I request entry to convey messages between daughter and mother."

The little window slammed shut, leaving Merlin to stand impatiently on the stone steps, wondering if, after all, it wouldn't have been better to pass the night with Troll in some quiet ravine. Nonhuman company was usually far less stressful.

He had almost given up hope that his message would be delivered when the door was flung open and torchlight poured out over the steps. Against it, a woman stood silhouetted.

"Young sir, welcome. Heather mentioned you in her letters, and I am pleased to meet you. Come in."

He followed the woman inside and down a long stone corridor. The place smelled of age, but even in the hallway, woven tapestries hung from the walls. Clearly Lord Brecon was as wealthy as his stepdaughter had said.

They entered a large paneled room. With boastful

wastefulness, a fire burned in the stone fireplace, even though it was the middle of summer. In the center of the room stood a carved oak table set with pre-Devastation china. The colorful mix of patterns gleamed softly in light from tallow lamps.

A large, broad-shouldered man stood by the fireplace. He was completely bald and had dark, severe eyes, which lighted in a semblance of welcome as he walked across the room.

"Mr. Bedwas, is it? I understand you are a friend of my stepdaughter's. As such, you are welcome. My wife and I were about to dine. We have no other guests this evening and would be honored if you would join us."

"The honor is mine."

Servants appeared from another door and set a third place. Lord Brecon took his seat at the head of the table and motioned the guest to his right. As Merlin sat, he looked carefully for the first time at the woman seated opposite him. He was struck with painful similarities.

Everything about her recalled Heather, but it was as if the mother was the model after which the daughter had been inexpertly copied. Where Heather's hair was dark blond and thin, the mother's was pale gold, full, and wavy. Where Heather's eyes were a muddy gray, the ones across from him glinted like pure sapphires. And Heather's face could only be described as long and thin, while this woman's was slender and delicate. Yet for all that, he couldn't find this person beautiful. She was like an ancient porcelain figurine, perfect in every detail yet cold and hollow inside. There was none of the life and warmth that bubbled up around Heather.

"Well, Earl," Lady Brecon was saying. "I may call you that, mayn't I? Tell us how our dear girl is doing. We've heard from her twice since she left Llandoylan School. Once from Devon saying she'd gone on some important mission with you and another friend, and then a year later from somewhere up in Cumbria saying she'd fallen in with this new King Arthur. I do hope you can tell us a little more."

"Yes, madam, I will try." Merlin launched into an account of Heather's activities since leaving the Glamorganshire school. It was carefully edited for parental consumption, playing down the hardships and dangers and highlighting the girl's important roles and her place in Arthur's court. He also glossed over the magical elements and their confrontations with Morgan, feeling most people weren't ready to take magic too matter-of-factly.

As he talked, servants brought out a meal that was notably better than most he'd had with Arthur recently. There was rich barley beer as well, and toward the end of the meal, Lord Brecon had a green glass bottle brought out.

"An occasion worth celebrating, I believe. This wine, all the way from Kent, is made from carefully cultured gooseberries. I think you'll like it."

Servants carried out rare glass goblets and poured into them the pale gold contents of the bottle. Merlin sipped at his appreciatively. He hadn't tasted anything calling itself wine in two thousand years. This could hardly compare with the grape wine he had known when Britain was still on the fringes of the Roman world. But it was heady and sweet and had a pleasant fruity taste. He had several glasses while Lord Brecon talked about weather and farming and about their border clashes with the dukedoms of Dyfed and Gwent.

As the man droned on, Merlin began to feel slightly

unwell. Maybe it was the heat of the firelit room, but he could feel himself breaking into a clammy sweat. The voices around him sounded distant and tinny, and a fuzzy heaviness began settling over him. He wondered if his body was currently too young to deal with that much wine.

It was with relief that he heard Lady Brecon say, "But, my dear, I do believe our guest looks tired. I'll have the servants show him to his room."

Gratefully Merlin stood up. Suddenly he was wrenched with a violent dizziness. The room spun like a cartwheel, and the table rose up to meet him. As he smashed to the hard oak, he saw the precious glass goblet roll past him and crash to the floor. That, and a laugh, were the last sounds he heard for some time.

26

A Visit Cut Short

When Merlin's mind finally struggled to consciousness, it was with the sense that a good deal of time
had passed. He seemed to be lying on a thin straw pallet.
He could feel its prickliness along the length of his body
and the cold rising through it from the stones below.

He tried to sit up. Nothing happened. He tried again,
but there wasn't the slightest twitch from any muscle. His
head would not turn even a fraction of an inch. He was
completely paralyzed. Though his eyes were slightly open,
he wasn't able to raise the eyelids farther.

Through the fringe of dark lashes, he could see a stone
wall glistening with damp. Ten feet from the floor was a
small barred window with the grayness of daylight beyond.
He could see nothing else.

For several more hours, he lay trapped in his cold, motionless body. Only the involuntary muscles of heart and
lungs seemed to work at all. He drifted in and out of consciousness until he heard distant voices coming his way.

The sound of a heavy door opening, then the voice of
Lord Brecon. "Well, she was certainly right about that
drug. Three days now, and he hasn't twitched."

Lady Brecon answered, "I wasn't certain about the dosage when I saw how young he was. But I guess I cut it enough. If we'd killed him, she would have been furious. This should keep him out long enough for your message to reach Cardiff and for Nigel to send someone to fetch him."

Lord Brecon stepped closer, the torchlight gleaming off his bald head. He poked Merlin roughly in the shoulder. There was a slight rattling of chains. "I still don't know why we had to do it this way. A swift blow on the head would have been easier."

"That's what you know! Morgan said he's a powerful wizard, despite his looks. If he could even move a finger or mutter a charm, he'd turn your chains to grass."

"What superstitious rot! You've been taken in by that Morgan woman and her parlor tricks. She's just someone who wants power and found that an alliance with King Nigel is a way to get it."

"Then why do they want this boy so badly?"

"On Nigel's part, a personal vendetta, perhaps; and that woman, I believe, wants to use this kid in some power play against your Heather's precious King Arthur. But that's none of our affair, so long as Nigel comes through with the troops and weapons we need against Dyfed."

Lady Brecon moved into Merlin's line of sight. He was struck again by her distorted resemblance to Heather. "Are those chains fastened securely?"

"Afraid of this pip-squeak? I thought you said we didn't even need chains."

"Yes, but who knows how long it'll take those soldiers to get here. If he got loose, he'd turn us into worms."

"Will you shut up about magic! I've put up with your

petty witch tricks, but I won't have that woman dazzling you with her blather about 'high powers.' The only power we need is swords and swordsmen."

Footsteps out in the hall and a gruff deferential voice. "Begging your pardon, Your Lordship, but there's a party at the door to see you."

"Ah, maybe they're here," Lady Brecon said. "Now this brat'll be someone else's headache." The pair hurried out of the room, leaving cold and silence behind them.

But when they reached the front door, it was not soldiers from Glamorganshire awaiting them.

"Mother," said a slim girl in a hooded jacket. "May my friend and I stay the night?"

The woman stared at the two with blank astonishment, only slowly pulling herself together. "Heather . . . what . . . ? That is, of course. Come in."

She turned to her husband standing behind her in the shadows. "Look who's here, dear. It's Heather."

The man muttered something and disappeared down the hallway. Lady Brecon led the newcomers to the room with the fireplace.

"My, Heather . . . such a surprise. Whatever brought you here?"

"We're looking for a friend of ours. He was coming this way and said he might stop here. Calling himself Earl Bedwas, maybe. Have you seen him?"

Turning away, the woman took a small log from beside the hearth and threw it into the fire. "Why, yes, dear, he was here. About three days ago."

"And where did he go afterward?"

"I don't know. He didn't say, dear. Just south, I suppose. You'll be wanting to go after him right away, then?"

"Yes, but I thought we could spend the night here. We're awfully tired and so are our horses, and it's raining rather hard."

"Certainly, certainly. I'll see that you're awakened early, in time to make a good start."

Just then, a servant poked in his head. "My lady, are those persons staying?"

"Yes, Clive, just for the night."

"I'll tend to their horses, then, but I'll not deal with that dog!"

"Oh, Rus," Heather said. "Yes, send him in here to me. He's rather leery of strangers."

"He's not the only one what's leery, miss. You can have him."

Dinner that night was a strained affair. Lady Brecon chattered nervously, and occasionally Heather pretended to listen. Welly concentrated on eating. The food was excellent, but the atmosphere was so tense that it hurt his digestion. Lord Brecon scowled silently throughout the meal and excused himself before it was over. Only Rus seemed to enjoy himself, sprawling over the hearth, each head chewing a meaty bone.

When the servants had cleared the table, Lady Brecon said, "Now, I'm sure you're both tired. Heather, you can have your old room, and Wellington may take the little one next to it. I'll have you awakened early."

Heather stood up. "All right, Mother. Thank you for putting us up." Briefly she glanced at her mother's tense face. There was something to read there, but it certainly wasn't love.

"Good night, then." Hurrying out of the room, Heather was followed by Welly and then Rus, a bone in each mouth.

Lord Brecon returned to the room after they had left. He held a green glass bottle in his hand. "Perhaps a little bedtime wine for our guests?"

"No! Morgan didn't say anything about wanting those two. She did give me some trinket for Heather if I should see her. I'll give her that, but I won't have her harmed."

Lord Brecon snorted disdainfully and left.

When Heather had shown Welly his room, she went into her own and sat on the bed, dejectedly twisting her braids. She wished they hadn't come here. They'd had to, of course, following Earl, but she had also hoped in the back of her mind that maybe it would feel like home. It didn't.

She had moved to this house after the death of her father, when her mother married Lord Brecon. But it had been clear from the start that this plain, awkward child of a Scottish refugee father was an embarrassment to the household, and she'd been sent off to Llandoylan as soon as possible. Sighing, she looked around at the cold stone walls. She'd actually spent little time among them, and they certainly exuded no feeling of home-coming now.

She began undressing, angrily tossing her clothes on an old, ornate chair. Her mother seemed anxious to have her out of here. Well, she was no less anxious. Get some sleep and go. The less time she wasted in this cold dump, the better.

A knock on the door startled her. "Yes?"

"It's your mother, Heather. May I come in?"

Mechanically Heather walked to the door and opened it. The woman stepped in, looking around distractedly. Then, moving Heather's wet clothes to the bed, she gingerly sat down on the chair. "I . . . I'd like to talk a moment."

Heather felt herself tensing up, inside and out. Resignedly she sat on the bed.

Her mother smiled awkwardly. "I'm sorry we haven't been quite as close as we might have been, Heather. There are things we really don't know about each other, aren't there?"

Heather said nothing.

"I mean, for example, over the years I've discovered I have certain . . . talents. I picked up little skills, you know. And since I understand such things are often hereditary, I was just wondering if you'd found you had any?"

Heather frowned at her. "Magic, you mean?"

"Yes, I suppose you might call it that."

The girl was silent a moment. "Yes, I guess I do have a little power."

"Good. Well, you see, I have something for you, then. It's an amulet. An old heirloom, really. It sort of helps with those things. I don't use it much. Lord Brecon doesn't approve, you know. And I'd like you to have it."

She reached into a pouch and held out a lump of black stone, trailing a fine gold chain. When Heather looked at it closely, she could see it was not shapeless but roughly carved like the head of some beast. Two shallow depressions formed its eyes.

"Take it, dear. It's old and I'm sure quite valuable, as well as useful. I do want you to have it. After all, I've never given you much, have I?"

Heather reached out and took the amulet into her hand. It felt cold and smooth.

"Here, let me help you." Her mother quickly slipped the chain over Heather's head, disentangling it from her braids.

"Yes, it's right for you. I can see that. Well, I'd better let you get some sleep." She moved quickly to the door. "Good night, Heather."

"Good night, Mother."

Heather stood staring at the closed door. Her mother had some powers, too? And she'd given her a gift, an old family thing. Maybe she should have tried to know her better. Unexpectedly she felt a trickle of regret.

She fingered the worn amulet. It was pretty enough in an odd sort of way. And it did feel as though it had something to it. But she was too tired to experiment now. Sighing, she moved to the window to check that it was fastened against the rain—and almost screamed. A horrible yellow face was plastered against the glass panes. Bald, with a scraggly yellow beard, it had close-set eyes and two enormous ears. And it was saying something through the glass.

Curiosity vied with horror, and she moved closer. She could just make out the whiny words.

"Nice Lady. Glad you come. Help Great Wizard. Me show."

"Wizard! You know where Earl is? He needs help?"

"Plenty help. You bring other friend, too?"

"Other friend? Oh. Oh, I know you! You're the troll from the bridge."

"Yes, Nice Lady. But Troll not good at sticking to walls. Let in, maybe?"

Hurriedly Heather opened the other half of the window, and the troll scuttled in like a hairy yellow spider, rain dripping from his bedraggled fur. Rus jumped up and smelled him with both noses, then wagged his tails approvingly.

"Where is Earl? What happened? Oh, wait, let me get Welly."

She rushed to the next room where Welly was already

asleep. Soon he was standing beside her, staring with sleepy amazement at the troll.

"The little fellow from the bridge. I can't believe it!"

"Me not little fellow. Me fierce troll warrior, companion to Great Wizard!"

"Last I remember," Welly said skeptically, "that great wizard threw you off a bridge."

"Oh, that's water under bridge now. Hee hee!" For a moment, the troll curled up, laughing at his own pun. Then he straightened proudly. "But we good friends now. Great Wizard needs help."

"Where is he?" Heather asked anxiously.

"Downstairs. Way down in old cold dungeon. Troll look in window. Wizard not move for days."

"Oh, no!"

"He alive, or why they chain him?"

"Good thinking," Welly said. "But who are 'they'?"

"Lord and Lady here. Bad people. Trolls never nasty to guests."

Heather was already throwing on her clothes, a look of grim determination on her face. "Maybe not. But some people can be."

Minutes later, the two were fully dressed with sword belts around their waists and, with the troll, were moving down a darkened flight of stairs. Rus, having been admonished to keep quiet, slunk along behind like a nightmare shadow. In a room below, they could hear Lord and Lady Brecon talking. Heather wanted to listen, to catch them in their treachery, but she knew she had to hurry on.

She had led the party through several passages when a servant suddenly stepped from a doorway. They threw themselves back around a corner. After a breathless moment,

Heather peered out, then scurried across an open space to a small wooden door, hurrying down the narrow stairway beyond. Shadow-like, the others followed.

Smoky, widely spaced torches lit the stairs and the dank passage beyond. Jumping anxiously about, the troll pointed to the end of the corridor. "Great Wizard there. They not lock door."

But when they cautiously peered into the far room, they could see no sign of the wizard.

Summoned to the manor door, Lord and Lady Brecon had hurried out of the cell, leaving Merlin gripped by despair as well as paralysis. In minutes, he thought, Glamorgan-shire soldiers would throw him over a horse and haul him like a sack down to Cardiff for that poisonous little Nigel to gloat over.

Still, it did seem as though his hostess had given him slightly the wrong dose. His mind was fully alert even if his body remained like stone. Perhaps if he tried focusing his mind.

He slipped into relaxed coolness. Like rivulets of water, his thoughts ran through his body, feeling out the poison and flowing around it. It was everywhere, stretching its barbs into every fiber of his body. He tried gripping his thoughts around it, seeking to pry it loose. But the poison tendrils were too thin and widespread. There was little to get hold of. He struggled on and on until his mind, too, was exhausted and numb. Weakly he floated back to the surface.

The room around him was still empty, and his body was still motionless. Yet there was a certain tingling about his face and hands. Maybe he had pulled something loose. But it would never be enough, not to work an escape before the troops came, even if that hadn't been them arriving.

No, without some control of his body, he could not work the proper spells. Yet his mind . . . There were certain personal magics that didn't use the body, or even speech, that worked instinctively without deliberate action. He'd learned that several years ago before regaining the memory of who he was. Maybe if he couldn't escape, he could appear to have escaped.

He sank back into his mind. Unfettered by paralysis, his thoughts raced over his body, changing the way it reflected light. Lying motionless on the pallet, he slowly faded from sight until nothing but the dented straw was visible and the empty-seeming manacles.

Now if they came, they'd think he was gone. But suppose they searched, suppose they touched the pallet? They'd feel him there even if they couldn't see him. There must be some other clue he could lay.

The small, high window was dark now with night. And it was still latched shut. But if they were to find it open, they might think he'd escaped that way and search the room no further.

He concentrated on the vague tingling around his face. If he could just get out one word. His thoughts battled with the heaviness of his lips and tongue. He tore at it, shred by shred, like clinging vines. Slowly, slowly, it began to drag away. Inside his mouth, his tongue twitched. Painfully his lips tingled, feeling less and less like stone.

He tried to form the word, tried again and again. Slowly he came nearer. There was a noise in the corridor. It must be now!

Like a spear, his thoughts shot across the room, dragging with them a word. Poorly formed and faint, still it was spoken. The window unlatched and blew open, letting in a cold, wet gust of wind.

Outside in the corridor, several pairs of eyes peered through the half-open door. "Great Wizard gone!" squealed the troll. "Not understand."

"Hush!" Welly whispered. "Someone's coming. Quick, in here."

The four ducked into an unused cell, tearing aside sticky sheets of cobwebs. A guard shuffled around a bend in the corridor. He muttered as he passed. "Why I got to check a prisoner what's chained to the wall and out cold . . ."

He shoved the door fully open and stomped into the cell. "Wha—? Chains still fastened, and look at that window! Great gods, he *is* a wizard!" The man rushed from the room, yelling for help as he pelted up the passage.

Welly, Heather, and the troll looked at each other in the gloom of their cell. They were about to step out when more voices and footsteps were heard.

"How could he be gone?" Lady Brecon demanded shrilly. "That drug shouldn't have worn off for days."

"If you've bungled this, my dear, and we've no one to send to Nigel . . ."

They burst into the end cell. "Gone, all right!" Lord Brecon roared. "Slipped free of the chains and out the window. That's what comes of fooling with magic."

"It wasn't my idea to—"

"Shut up, woman! We've got to call out the guard and find him. Hurry!"

The footsteps rushed back up the corridor, while behind

them four figures slipped from the neighboring cell and into Merlin's. They looked about the empty room.

"Well, at least he got away," Welly said, polishing his glasses on a dirty sleeve. "Now we've got to do the same."

There was a faint noise behind them like a whispering mouse. They turned and stared as the empty pallet and manacles slowly appeared to hold someone.

"Earl!" Heather rushed to the inert form.

"Can't move," he whispered faintly.

"Great Wizard fooled them!" the troll chortled.

"Yeah," Welly said, "but he's got to get out of here for real, before they check back."

"Earl, can you melt those manacles or something?" Heather asked.

He tried to shake his head but failed. "No," he mouthed.

"What'll we do?" Heather said, examining the solid-looking iron rings to which the chains were fastened.

"Heather, use your magic," Welly urged. "They may be back soon."

"But I can't deal with iron. All I'm good for is animals."

"Right," Merlin whispered.

"What? Animals? But how . . . ?" Slowly Heather turned to look at the only animal in the room. Rus's fore-paws rested on the straw pallet as he whimpered mourn-fully.

Heather grabbed the furry paws in one hand. With the other she reached out for Merlin's cold, lifeless hands, bringing them together with a clatter of chains. Then she fell silent, her eyes closed, her body tense and rigid. She wasn't at all sure she could do this, but she had to try.

Very slowly at first, there came a change. The furriness

she felt in one hand was gradually matched in the other. At last, the changing forces stopped passing through her. Drained, she opened her eyes, then laughed with delight.

The hands in the manacles were no longer hands but sleek furry dog paws small enough to easily slip free of the iron. Merlin's lips twitched in a smile.

"Heather, you're terrific!" Welly exclaimed. "Troll, check the window."

Toes and fingers finding every chink in the stone, the troll swarmed up the wall and peered out. "No people," he announced.

"Good. Heather, go get that chair from the other cell."

She slid Merlin's paws free of the manacles, then hurried out of the cell. Returning in seconds with a rickety chair, she placed it under the open window. Welly was already staggering to his feet with Merlin slung over his shoulder.

"Good thing he's so scrawny."

Welly climbed carefully onto the chair and passed his limp burden up to the troll. Once the wizard was dragged through the window, Heather handed Welly her squirming dog. Next came her turn, and finally with Troll and Heather each grabbing an arm, they hauled up Welly. He jammed firmly in the window. His legs flailed the air, and he groaned piteously as the others renewed tugging. Suddenly he popped through, tumbling them all onto the rain-wet grass. Scrambling to their feet and supporting Merlin between them, they moved quickly through the dark to a clump of low bushes. The earth smelled of mold, and the branches around them drooped with cold raindrops.

"We're outside the courtyard here," Heather whispered. "But we can't get very far with Earl like this."

"Me get horses," Troll said, and, scurrying out of the

bushes, he slipped through the open gate of the courtyard. Running about and shouting, the men with torches failed to notice one more shadow.

Then one guard searching the walls of the manor squatted down by the window they had just crawled through. "He came out here, all right. See how the grass is all trampled down?"

"Idiot, we know that!" another called. "What we want to know is where the skinny brat is, not where he was."

"Maybe you do," the other muttered. "If he's a wizard what can melt through chains, *you* go find where he is."

Still squabbling, the two returned to the courtyard and soon joined a mounted search party that clattered off down the road. A few minutes later, three dark horse shapes slipped out through the gate with the troll prancing in front of them.

"Troll good with horses, like Nice Lady. But not know how to do dog-paw trick."

"Oh, the paws!" Heather gasped. "I'd better try to change them back."

Merlin grunted agreement.

Welly looked at his friend and chuckled. "Good old Puppypaws the Wizard."

Heather clutched the hairy paws in her hands and closed her eyes. Frowning, she tried to remember how they ought to look. Why didn't she notice these things? Long, thin hands, she thought, very, very pale, with bones and faint blue veins showing through. For good measure, she tried visualizing dog paws as they should be on the end of long, furry dog legs.

She opened her eyes and squeaked with alarm. Merlin's paws remained the same, and his arms were now distinctly furry.

Scowling, she tried again. Just concentrate on hands this time, she told herself. At last she felt, then saw, the familiar hands in hers. They even moved in a weak squeeze, which she gratefully returned.

"Can you stay on a horse?" Welly asked anxiously.

"I'll try," Merlin whispered.

They boosted him onto the black mare. He sagged forward over the neck, feebly twining his fingers into the mane. Heather laid a hand on the horse's neck, urging it to go gently. Then she and Welly mounted up, and with Rus and Troll loping along beside, they trotted swiftly down the darkened road.

Behind them on the gate, someone saw and called out the alarm. But the dark was with them now. They had escaped.

27

REUNION IN THE RUINS

Using side roads and south-tending valleys, the escaping party eluded their pursuers. But with a proven wizard as the quarry, the pursuit was less than enthusiastic.

They rode through a cold, raw dawn and into morning, finally stopping at an abandoned farmstead. Moving more easily now, Merlin still felt appallingly tired. He gratefully slid off the horse and was content simply to sit in the weak sunshine against an old stone wall.

Welly happily noted that Troll had also brought their packs, which they'd not taken to their rooms, including, most importantly, the food. The wizard's staff and sword, which he'd left with his horse, had come as well.

While Welly doled out some food, Heather hesitantly explained to Merlin what had brought them after him. Surprised, he didn't say much for fear that somehow a wrong word would send her back. His happiness at that moment felt too fragile even to question.

"Where to now?" Welly asked finally as he broke a large, greasy slab of cheese into five parts. Reconsidering, he split the dog's share into two, one for each head.

"I am still heading to Caerleon," Merlin said quietly.

"But I would be honored to have more company . . . if you two would like to come, that is."

"Of course we would," Heather said. "We didn't come all this way just to visit my miserable family."

"Troll honored with company, too. Great Wizard needs many guards."

"It certainly looks that way," Merlin laughed.

As they shared the welcome meal, Welly said, "You came from around here, didn't you, Earl? Originally, I mean."

Merlin nodded and swallowed a bite of bread. "Southwest of here, actually. I was born in Carmarthen." He glanced at Welly and chuckled. "Why are you looking so surprised? Even wizards are born, you know, not hatched."

Welly blushed as his friend continued. "My mother was daughter of the local chief. But she wasn't married to my father. She wouldn't even tell most people who he was. He was Eldritch, you see, and that sort of thing was rather frowned upon. Rumors spread instead that my father was a demon, and needless to say, I didn't have the easiest of childhoods. Once I started learning how to use my powers, it was sore temptation to pay back my 'little playmates.' But I moved away, and sort of fell into the business of advising kings."

"Did you go back to Carmarthen often?" Heather asked.

"No, not often. But that was where I thought I was taking Nimue that last time." He was silent a moment. "We stopped on the way at a cave near Bedwas. They trapped me there. Nimue and Morgan."

Uncomfortable for his friend, Welly tried to sound matter-of-fact. "It was lucky those Gwent raiders spilled their salvaged dynamite where they did, or you might still be in that mountain."

"Lucky, perhaps, or fated. Like the age change. Was it just chance I was at the low end of that spell cycle I was using? If I'd been at the extreme old end, I wouldn't have been of much use to Arthur now. Though I've got to admit"—he rubbed a hand ruefully over his smooth chin—"I wouldn't have minded a few more years of maturity."

Heather laughed, but Welly was still pondering fate. "But what about Morgan? You said we're bound to fight her. Is that fate, too?"

Merlin frowned and closed his eyes. "Morgan. She's part Eldritch, too, you know, but the power she cultivated is different from mine. It has other, darker sources. She used those to sustain her life, and she'll use them, if she can, to win control of this world. Arthur's goal of peace and unity never suited her, because the kind of power she wields works best in chaos and ignorance. She can dominate that kind of world.

"And she's making another try at that now. That's why I must find that bowl. It might give us some glimpse of her plans; it might give us a fighting chance."

Heather shook her head. "And Morgan's not the only enemy we have, it seems. Not with Nigel as King of Glamorganshire."

Merlin snorted. "Nigel's just a petty tool. Dangerous, yes, but not smart enough to be a major actor." He was about to add something about Morgan's role in the plot to poison him, but a glance at Heather's strained face silenced him. She'd clearly been feeling bad enough about her mother's betraying him to King Nigel. It would hurt her needlessly to learn that her mother had also been dealing directly with Morgan.

He changed the subject. "Welly, are you thinking of dropping by and seeing your folks at Aberdare?"

"I was, but we'd better skip that. Nigel knows that I'm from there, and he won't be any too happy when his bounty hunters report that you've gotten away."

Merlin laughed. "I hope never to be in a position to make Nigel happy. Let's get on our way."

As they continued south, the weather varied between cold and dry, and cold and wet, with rain occasionally turning to sleet in the evenings. In three days' time, they reached the outskirts of Caerleon.

Merlin shook his head in bewilderment as he looked at the sprawling town. The fifth-century settlement he had known had been a small, affluent Roman town, only slightly decayed after the withdrawal of the legions. Now, later centuries of buildings sprawled over the landscape, most abandoned and fallen into weedy ruin.

In gray midmorning, the companions rode through the town gate. Troll, hidden under a blanket, rode behind Welly, steadily grumbling to himself. In front of an inn, a little girl was walking along a low wall, balancing herself with much flailing of arms. Merlin pulled his horse up beside her.

"Young lady, would you be so kind as to direct us to the really old part of town, some Roman ruins, maybe?"

The girl looked him and the others over, taking in their good horses and the swords at their belts. Then she jumped down and ran toward the inn. "Grandpa, there's a bunch of rich tourists here who want to see the old Roman stuff."

In seconds, a bald old man bustled out, wiping his hands on a stained apron. He smiled as he saw the travelers. "Well, well, young people out to see Caerleon's claim to fame. Afraid there's not much left, but if you poke around some, your trip'll be worth it, I dare say. A big Roman city and fort there was. Golden domes, the books say. Very grand.

"Now the old baths, what's left of 'em, are right down there. Turn to your left where the road jogs. Then the theater, that's off to the right at the next crossroads. There's a field they say used to be barracks, just humps in the ground mostly now. But the theater's pretty impressive still."

"Thank you, sir," Merlin replied. "But what about houses, those golden domes you mentioned?"

"Well, I daresay they were all over the place once. But they've been built on since, you see. Why, just last year we dug up some old tiles in our cellar. It's the same all around here, but not much to see unless you're a mole." He laughed heartily.

Merlin nudged his heels into his horse. "Well, thank you, innkeeper. We'll just keep to things aboveground."

"And after your sightseeing, young sirs and madam, you won't find a better beer or finer victuals than we serve here."

"Thank you. We'll keep that in mind."

As they trotted on, Welly said, "This bowl of yours, would anyone have left it in a bath?"

"I shouldn't think so. Those were big public baths. Let's start with the theater. Arthur used to hold court there when the weather was good. I ought to be able to get my bearings and figure out where the houses and villas were."

The theater proved to be a large oval depression. Brittle weeds filled the center arena and climbed over the stone mounds that once had been seating.

"How do you expect to find an old bowl in a place like this?" Welly said when they'd dismounted and walked into the amphitheater.

Merlin sighed. "I've no vision of where it is, none at all. But I'm sure that if I'm close, I'll feel it. I put so much of myself into it, there must still be some link."

Slowly he began walking around the remains of the theater and the area nearby. The troll trotted along eagerly, occasionally stopping to dig in places of his own, exclaiming over whatever bits of rubbish he unearthed. Rus happily helped the troll dig, while Welly drifted off to explore the barracks' remains. Heather was left alone in the theater.

After looking halfheartedly about, she sat on a grassy mound and thoughtfully twisted a braid. Was there any way she could use her powers to help find Earl's bowl? Probably not. Her magic seemed totally linked with animals. And unless a mouse was curled up in the bowl, she'd probably never see it.

But what about the amulet? She had tried to forget that. After what had happened at Brecon, she wasn't sure she wanted anything of her mother's. Still, if the amulet was a family heirloom, it was rightfully hers now. And maybe it did have some powers, ones she could use that weren't tied to animals. She touched the chain at her throat and slowly pulled the amulet from under her shirt. It was worth a try, anyway.

Heather studied the black stone. What sort of face was carved there? It could be either human or animal. In its sunken eyes, high cheekbones, and pointed chin, she saw no expression at all, only a sense of cool power.

She stood up. The stone felt smooth and cold in her

hands. All right. She'd look for silver. Closing her eyes, she filled her mind with thoughts of silver, bright and smooth, gleaming like unclouded moonlight.

As she walked slowly around the amphitheater, the amulet tingled in her hands. She walked on, and it burned like cold fire. Suddenly excited, she dropped to her knees, scrabbling in the dirt. Her fingers tore through grass and damp soil, then touched something small and hard.

Eagerly she pulled it out and scraped off the dirt. A small disk, and it was silver! She rubbed and spat on it but couldn't quite make out the inscription. A coin showing some ancient queen. It wasn't Earl's bowl, but it was silver.

This was exciting! She tried again, and before long, she had recovered another coin, a badly tarnished thimble, and a silver ring. The ring was far too big for her. She could give it to Earl. But no. Somehow she didn't want to tell him about the amulet. He was probably just as bitter as she was toward her mother. And anyway, this was *her* magic. She'd work with it on her own for a while; then maybe she'd tell him once she could handle it better.

She dumped her treasures beside a rock, where Troll found them almost as soon as he returned to the theater. He jammed the ring on his thumb and jumped about proudly showing it off. But Merlin, when he rejoined the others, was too discouraged to show much interest.

"Well, it certainly isn't around here." He sighed and sat wearily on a pile of stones. "Of course, it may not be anywhere near Caerleon now, but I'd better check the rest of the town. There was a big villa Arthur used as his residence when he stayed here. I should be able to find that site. And there're several other possible spots as well."

Welly groaned. "Can we eat first, maybe at that inn?"

"Yes, why don't you all rest and get something to eat. It'll be quicker if I do this on my own. But better stay away from the inn. We are in Glamorganshire, after all, and the less public notice we draw, the better."

"Troll go, too. Great Wizard need guard. May find more poison wine."

Merlin laughed, holding a hand to his head. "No fear. I think I've sworn off wine for the rest of my life. But come along; you're a first-class digger."

The wizard set off with his staff and his troll companion. It was beginning to rain in earnest now, and taking some food from a pack, Welly and Heather crowded into the ruins of a little building beside the theater. Staring out into gray sheets of rain, they ate in silence, sharing tidbits alternately with Rus's right and left heads.

After a time, the rain let up, turning at last to fine mist. Bored with doing nothing, Heather walked again into the center of the theater, and Welly followed.

"What sort of theater do you suppose this was?" she asked, looking around the enclosure. "The kind they fed people to lions in?"

"Maybe," Welly guessed. "But I bet they did real plays, too. Those ancient Romans and Greeks had a bunch of famous playwrights."

Heather struck a theatrical pose. " 'Friends, Romans, countrymen, lend me your ears'!"

"That's Shakespeare."

"I know, but that's the only old playwright I've read. 'To be or not to be, that is the question'!"

"Bravo," a sharp voice said behind them. "But there is no question about you being my prisoners."

The two spun around. A rank of horsemen was standing in the misty rain beyond the rubble walls. Foremost among them was Nigel Williams, King of Glamorganshire.

"Nigel!"

"What a pleasure to meet old schoolmates again," he said dryly.

"Eh, yes," Welly said, recovering. "A lot's happened since Llandoylan, hasn't it?"

"Yes, it has, Frog Eyes, and I still remember our parting. Actually, I'm quite pleased to find you both. When I rode up to Brecon, I had hoped to lay my hands on only your pallid friend, a present for a certain ally of mine. Of course, I do have my scores to settle with him as well, but I'll have to leave that to her. You two, however, are all mine."

With a gesture from Nigel, several of his warriors dismounted and stalked toward Welly and Heather. The two drew their short Eldritch swords.

Nigel snorted. "The little vermin have sprouted stings. Careful, boys, I want them alive—for now."

In the low hills above Caerleon, Merlin stood on a bare knoll, kicking dejectedly at featureless stones.

"It's no use, Troll," he said, more to himself than his companion. "I thought maybe here, where they had a little summerhouse . . . Arthur and Guenevere came here sometimes. There were always some bits of treasure about."

He stamped his staff angrily onto the ground, ignoring the scorched hole it left. "Oh, Troll, it was so lovely here! At sunset in summer, the air was soft and warm, and there were birds in the sky and flowers in the grass, rich green grass. It's such a loss, such a horrible, senseless loss!"

"Your bowl?"

"No! No, this world—or what it was. How could people have become so filled with hate that they were willing to destroy that beautiful world?"

The troll frowned, furrows rippling over his bald head. "Me only know this world. Not even seen much of Faerie. But Mama's seen lots; say it pretty place. Like this place once, maybe?"

Merlin smiled. "Yes, they were very much alike. But maybe it's better to know only one world. Then you don't break your heart comparing."

"Troll's heart not broke. But stomach empty. Go back to Nice Lady and Brave Warrior?"

"And full saddlebags? Yes, let's."

They had almost reached the theater again when the troll, who had been eagerly scampering ahead, came slinking back, eyes wide as saucers.

"Trouble, Great Wizard. Bad men with horses catch friends. Tie up like rabbits."

Cautious now, Merlin hurried forward. Nearing the theater, he crawled onto an old wall where he could look down into the stone-circled depression. Welly and Heather, tied hand and foot, lay on the wet grass. Beside them, the dog was totally swathed in ropes with particular attention to his muzzles. Merlin could tell from the sword slashes and bites several of the soldiers nursed that the capture had not been easy.

There were few soldiers to be seen now, but he could sense others out of sight, probably waiting to ambush him. He slid quietly off the wall, whispering for the troll to stay back.

Down in the theater, Nigel sat on a stone, cleaning his

fingernails with a dagger. "Pity you wouldn't tell me where your washed-out friend's gone," he said to his bound and gagged prisoners. "It would have saved this tiresome wait. But I expect he'll be back soon. You three dears seem so inseparable. Morgan tells me you've all taken service with that Northern upstart who calls himself King Arthur. Sounds like the sort of mangy charlatan you *would* take up with. Though, frankly, what you three misfits could offer anyone, I don't know."

He got up and sauntered over to the bound dog, kicking it roughly in the ribs. "Except maybe this warhound of yours. He has possibilities; he's mean enough."

Strolling back to the wall, he casually threw his dagger into the turf. "But to be equally frank, I can't understand what the lovely Morgan wants with that scrawny troublemaker. She gave me some song and dance about his being a dangerous wizard. Ha! The day Earl Bedwas is a dangerous wizard is the day I grow donkey ears!"

"Better get some new hats designed, then, Nigel."

The young King spun around. His former schoolmate was standing inside the theater.

"How did you get—? Well, never mind." He motioned down the soldiers who were scrambling to their feet. "I'll take care of you myself. I suppose you've acquired a pretty little sword like these children here?"

"I have, yes. And a few other weapons. But I think we should talk, Nigel. You, after all, are King of Glamorganshire now. And I am adviser to the King of Cumbria."

"Yeah, yeah, I know. King Arthur Pendragon riding out of legend! Just your sort of madman."

Merlin struggled to keep his voice calm. "Regardless of your opinion of his historical claims, he does hold the kingship of Cumbria and alliances with Carlisle, Newcastle, Cheshire, and the Scots. You may find yourself dealing with him someday. And in any case, your current alliance with Morgan is most ill-advised."

"For you, yes, since I'll be turning you over to her; but she is just the sort of powerful friend Glamorganshire needs."

"Powerful, yes. But Morgan is nobody's friend but her own. I'm simply warning you, Nigel. Beware of her."

"My, how I appreciate your concern." He looked around to see the rest of his troops moving back into the theater. "But now that we've had our friendly little school reunion, it's time to get on with business. Take him, men!"

The soldiers charged forward. Swiftly Merlin brought up his staff, pointing it at his three captive friends. Their bonds suddenly writhed with life and slid off. Like snakes, the freed ropes twisted in the air, stretched out, and multiplied, until a swarm of wriggling ropes swept toward the astonished King and soldiers.

They raised their swords against them, but for every rope they hacked, two slithered down their sword arms and twisted around their bodies. The soldiers and their King yelled and struggled, but within moments they all lay on the damp grass like flies enwebbed by a spider.

Lowering his staff, Merlin walked over to the feebly struggling bodies. He looked down at Nigel, who glared at him through the web of ropes. "The day Earl Bedwas is a dangerous wizard is the day you grow donkey ears? Whatever you say, Nigel."

He flicked his hand toward the bound King's head, and two long hairy ears sprouted up between the entwining ropes.

Welly and Heather were now on their feet, helping each other off with their gags. Heather looked at Nigel and could barely keep from laughing. "Earl, I've had enough of Caerleon. Can we leave now? People look a little odd around here."

"I think that's a splendid idea. Welly, why don't you get our horses. I've a few details left here."

As Welly headed in one direction, the sounds of neighing and thumping hooves came from another.

"Reinforcements?" Heather said in alarm.

Looking through openings in the stony banks, they saw the soldiers' horses in panicky flight away from the town. The troll bounded in through one of the gates.

"Great Wizard tie up bad men. So Troll tell horses go away."

"Good work," Welly said, leading in their own mounts.

As they mounted, Merlin held up his staff again. "We don't want the neighbors setting this lot free too soon."

He swept the staff through the air around the perimeter of the theater. On four opposing banks, mist curled up, purple-red mist. It spread and thickened and began to take form—the form of four good-sized griffins. They stretched, then folded their wings along their lean lion bodies. With beaks open and tongues flicking, they fixed glowing eyes on the suddenly quiet captives.

"Let's go," Merlin said, turning his horse toward one of the theater entrances. "Glamorganshire's a lovely place to visit, but I believe we've outstayed our welcome."

He paused, then looked back at Nigel, who couldn't speak for the rope running between his clenched teeth. The King's donkey ears twitched angrily.

"Regardless of what you may think of us, Your Majesty,

I strongly advise that you stay clear of Morgan. Alliances with her are very one-sided."

He kicked his horse into a trot, and the three humans and one troll left the ruined theater. Rus gave his former captors a parting chorus of growls, then followed after the others, his tails wagging jauntily.

28

PURSUIT

They rode swiftly out of Caerleon, then stopped to consult the old maps Welly had brought.

"Those ropes were real enough, but the griffins are just illusion," Merlin said as he examined the map's tracery of pre-Devastation roads. "A nice touch, I thought, but they'll fade. Somehow, though, I don't think we need worry about being followed."

"Speaking of nice touches," Heather said, "I did like those donkey ears."

"Oh, they'll last only a month or so, but I probably shouldn't have done that. Arthur's wise old adviser deliberately humiliating the king of another shire. But Nigel's such an ass!"

Welly laughed. "Well, you can't deny he asked for it."

After a steady ride eastward, they came at last to what once had been the estuary of the River Severn. Under a great steel bridge, it had fanned out and emptied into the Bristol Channel. But now the ocean had receded, its waters locked up in northern ice. The bridge spanned an empty valley, dry except for the now-narrow Severn, doggedly cutting its way through the ancient silt. As they followed the old road, the bridge towered above them. Five hundred years of neglect had left it rusty and twisted. The soaring cables, which had once linked the twin towers, coiled down like dead snakes, and the shattered roadway sagged toward the water.

The troll, however, was enthralled. "Ooh, look at bridge! Look at bridge!" he chanted in ecstasy. "Troll dream of bridge like that!"

"You'd have to be a mighty large troll to defend that bridge," Merlin pointed out. "Besides, I don't think the tolls would be very good. Looks as if it's not used much."

He headed his horse along a dirt track that cut through the old estuary to cross the diminished river on a make-shift bridge of stone and scrap metal. The troll rushed ahead and, sticking his head over the side of the bridge, shouted out several fierce-sounding phrases. Then he trotted cockily back to the others.

"Safe to cross now. Troll lead famous wizard and warriors. Nobody bother."

After they'd crossed, Heather rode up beside Merlin. "Doesn't he have some name besides 'Troll'?" she asked. "I mean, what would we call him if he were among a bunch of other trolls?"

"Oh, he must have a personal name. But folk of Faerie are awfully private about such things. There's a great deal of power tied up in their names. I suggest that if we ever find ourselves among a bunch of trolls, we give him a name of our own."

Welly had ridden up beside them. "Maybe something like Clancy or Wilberforce or . . ."

Heather wrinkled her nose. "I think 'Troll' is just fine."

Having crossed into the relative safety of Gloucester,

they camped for the night and started south again early the next day. As Heather rode along, the amulet kept swinging into her thoughts. She could feel it, a cold, exciting weight against her chest. She wished she'd thought to use it when they were attacked at Caerleon. But she really didn't have any idea of how to work it. It seemed to be some kind of focuser, a conduit of power that freed her from having to go through animals. The idea made her oddly uneasy but excited as well. The countryside about them was drab and uninteresting, and each of her companions seemed wrapped in his own thoughts. She'd experiment.

Letting her horse fall slightly behind the others, she slipped the amulet from under her shirt. She thought about a focuser, focusing power the way a lens focuses light. All right. Thinking about flames, she gazed beyond the black shape in her hand to the dry, brittle-looking bushes along the roadside. For minutes of monotonous riding, she kept at it until suddenly she saw a wisp of smoke rise from one of the bushes. She turned in her saddle as they passed and saw the twigs burst into pale flame before being snuffed out by the cold breeze.

An excited thrill of achievement—and guilt. Quickly she looked ahead, but no one had seen her. She was unsure why she felt a need to keep this secret. But the cold stone clutched in her hand gave her a heady feeling of control and independence. And somehow its secrecy was part of that.

She practiced with the amulet through the day. Each time, her tie to the thing seemed to strengthen so that working it became easier. The day's ride now seemed a good deal more interesting.

But while Heather's mood improved as the day

progressed, Merlin seemed to become more and more uneasy. Occasionally he stopped his horse and looked about or stood in the stirrups, head tilted as if listening to something just out of hearing. Finally Welly asked what the trouble was.

"I'm not sure. I've just a vague sense of being watched, of being followed, maybe. It's very indirect, as if the observer's either far away or cloaking itself somehow."

Uneasily Welly scanned the gray landscape. "What do you think it is?"

"Well, there's no doubt that there are folk from Faerie about. They could be watching us out of curiosity. But somehow, I don't think it's quite that innocent."

"Oh?"

"There's a faint whiff of Morgan about this."

Heather shivered as if hit by a cold wind. "You think she's after us?"

Welly said, "Nigel could have sent her a message that we'd escaped."

Merlin nodded. "He probably did. And I'm sure she wants me as a prisoner just on general principle. But for now, as long as she doesn't know what we're after, I don't think she'll interfere. She seems to be keeping some sort of tabs on us, though. Can't say I like it."

The three rode closer together. Picking up their uneasiness, the normally far-ranging dog and troll closed ranks as well.

At the small town of Cheddar, Merlin turned them from the main road. "This route heads our way," he explained, "and it used to be one of the loveliest in Britain. I almost hate to see what's happened to it, but surely the cliffs are undamaged."

The ancient crumbling road narrowed as it climbed,

sheer cliffs rising on either side. Before long, buttresses of stone towered above them. Looking upward, they could see jagged rocks tearing against gray sky. Mostly the rocks were bare, the elemental bones of the earth exposed in a deep raw wound. But here and there, dampness trickled out of a cliff face and ivy cascaded down in a shower of dark, wind-ruffled green.

Welly and Heather found the place stark and slightly daunting, but Merlin was enthralled. "Look, there's still some ivy, even some ferns. I'm willing to bet they don't survive here just by chance. Troll, would you say there are any folk of Faerie hereabouts?"

"Oh, yes, Great Wizard. Think so. This strong place. Me see." Before they could say a word, he had leaped off into the rocks and bracken.

"Shouldn't we wait for him?" Heather said as they rode on.

Merlin looked around. "He'll catch up. Beautiful as it is here, I don't think we want to linger. There is something . . . something wrong."

The silence in the rocky gorge weighed down upon them as much as the glowering cliffs. Muffled clomping of horse hooves echoed and reechoed between the rock walls, but that was the only sound save the trickle of an occasional spring as it seeped out of the rock like blood through wounded skin.

With a sudden rustling and clattering, Troll appeared before them. "Great Wizard right. Plenty rock sprites here. But they not talk much. They afraid."

"Afraid of us?" Welly said, surprised.

"No, no. Happy see Great Wizard and friends. Afraid of something else. Something coming."

Whatever it was, the horses seemed to sense it, too, and quickened their pace on their own.

Heather slid a hand under her shirt and felt the amulet. Perhaps this would tell her something. It tingled under her touch. The longer she held it, the colder it became, yet she could learn nothing from it. Maybe she should ask Earl how to use it. The thought filled her with reluctance. This was nothing she wanted to share just yet. Perhaps if she—

A screech sawed through the air. Fearfully they looked up. A winged black shape darted through the narrow band of sky above them. It cried again, then banked sharply and headed back, joined by another. More like flying snakes than birds, they shot along the gorge. Then, with wrenching screams, they dove toward the riders.

The horses neighed in terror. Merlin's bolted off in one direction and Welly's in another. Heather's mount reared so suddenly that she was flung from its back. Lying half-stunned on the earth, she grabbed at her amulet, trying to work it against the flying things. It did nothing. One creature veered and dove directly at her. She scuttled to the shelter of a boulder just as the screaming shadow whipped by her.

Regaining some control over his horse, Merlin was working back toward Heather, filling the air with bursts of fire. But in the narrow confines of the gorge, these kept missing the dodging targets.

There was a sudden silence as the attacks ceased. Holding his staff high, Merlin looked anxiously about to see why. Silently one of the creatures dropped from its perch on the clifftop. Wings outstretched and jaws open, it hurtled like a spear toward the wizard. But as it moved down, a tendril of ivy uncoiled from the cliff and ensnared the creature in midair. Wings entangled, it jerked sharply, snapping the vine loose and plunging out of control to the rocks below. Sprawling beside Merlin's shivering horse, the thing twitched once, then lay still. From above came a single mournful cry, and the second creature shot away like a black arrow.

Heather did not want to crawl from her shelter and look at the thing. Closing her eyes, she concentrated on her horse and on Welly's. In a short time, both animals plodded up the road, with Welly limping behind.

When Rus found her and began licking her face with both tongues, Heather finally abandoned her hiding place and joined Welly and Merlin by the dead creature. It was black and long, a scaly snake body with wings, and it stank as if it had been dead for days.

The troll slipped from rocks at the base of the cliff. Merlin looked up. "I believe we have your friends, the rock sprites, to thank for snaring this thing."

Troll nodded, smiling broadly. "They happy to. Say snakes belong in rocks, not sky. These bad."

"Well, they smell bad, too," Welly said, covering his nose. "Let's get going."

"Right, but just a minute." Merlin got off his horse and, walking to the base of the cliff, piled several stones into a rough pyramid. Then he yanked three black hairs from his head and placed them on the top stone. Kneeling, he muttered a few words, then got up and returned to the others.

"What was all that about?" Welly asked.

"A thanks offering," his friend replied. "A token of friendship and trust. The folk of Faerie generally don't take part in the battles of men, but when enemies of their own are involved, they can be very useful allies. That thing does stink. Let's go."

They passed out of the gorge without further incident, though somehow the cliffs seemed less hostile and lifeless than before.

The following day, they sighted what might be flying snakes several times, distant black specks against a pale sky. That evening, five streaked like poison darts across the crimson sunset.

Camping in flat, open land, the travelers felt uncomfortably exposed. Merlin conjured a large fire and they huddled around it, eating their meal and flicking occasional glances up into the darkness.

Finally Welly, Heather, and Troll wrapped themselves in blankets and curled up on the ground to sleep. Rus snuggled in beside Heather and was soon snoring with both muzzles. Wrapped in his own blanket, Merlin leaned against a rock by the fire and kept first watch.

Heather could not fall asleep. She closed her eyes, but visions of flying snakes darted vividly through her mind. The occasional real shrieking of one in the high distance sent shivers through her. Shifting restlessly, she rolled over and watched the firelight play over Merlin's gaunt features. He seemed lost in thought. She sat up.

"Earl, where are we headed next? Camelot?"

He looked toward her, his eyes slowly blinking back into focus. Sighing, he rubbed a hand over his face. "I had planned that, yes. In the daylight you could see the hill south of here. But now . . . I think we'll try somewhere else first."

"Why? Didn't you say that's where the bowl would have been taken if it weren't at Caerleon?"

"True, but it might not have stayed there. Once Arthur

was gone and his kingdom falling apart, the royal treasure would probably have been moved somewhere safer. Glastonbury, I should think."

"Glastonbury? Where's that?" Swathed in her blanket, she shuffled closer to him and the fire.

"West of here. It was a village, a small one, but it had a church and monastery, probably the oldest in Britain. The monks there were good friends with us at Camelot, particularly a Brother Joseph. He was a young fellow and used to come over to gossip and play chess." For a moment, the wizard seemed lost in a dreamy distance. Then he focused on Heather again.

"Arthur's told me that after that final battle—it was fought right around here by the River Cam—the wounded, himself included, were taken to Glastonbury."

"Is that where . . . ?"

"Yes. It was from there that he was taken off to Avalon. A hill there, Glastonbury Tor, was a main entrance to Faerie."

He was silent a while until Heather asked, "And you're certain all of the King's treasure would have been taken to those monks?"

Merlin shook his head. "No, I'm not, but . . . but frankly, Heather, I don't want to go to Camelot if I can avoid it. It will be a bare, weedy hilltop, and I'll remember it with wooden palisades, banners snapping in the wind, laughing people, faces I knew. I would . . . rather not deal with that now—unless I have to."

His voice cracked. Hesitantly Heather placed a hand on his but could find nothing comforting to say. Finally he continued. "That's my problem, you see. I'm too tied to the old world, to its memories and ways of magic. Even now I'm circling through the old sites, searching for an old tool that might not even work in this world."

The desolation in his voice was unbearable. Heather struggled to change the subject. "Earl, there's something I've been wondering about. I know how you survived all those years enchanted in that mountain. And you've said that Morgan probably survived by having some unscrupulous dealings with death. But she wasn't locked up in a mountain. What did she do all that time?"

"Morgan?" He smiled bitterly. "Oh, make trouble, I imagine. Of course, her powers would have weakened as the strength of magic did. But come to think of it, I suspect she was quite comfortable in some of those later centuries."

"How so?"

"Well, her magic was always very cold, very 'thing-oriented.' And from what I've read, those last pre-Devastation years were quite thing-oriented as well. They must have been, I suppose, for people to allow their things to destroy them."

The two sat for a while in silence, cold pressing on them from one side, the fire's heat from the other. Heather looked at her friend. "And that's what you're trying to stop from happening again, isn't it?"

"Yes, that and whatever Morgan is planning for our immediate future." Angrily he crushed a twig he'd been toying with. "But the question is, *how* do I stop it, any of it? If that bowl doesn't work, what then? That's the only sort of magic I know. Sometimes, despite all our 'power,' I suspect that both Morgan and I are irrelevant in this world. We have our little magic toys and play our little magic games. And they work, in their way. But still we don't quite fit in this new world with its new magic."

"But, Earl, remember talking about how all this might be fated? If there is some overall pattern, then—"

A nerve-tearing screech sliced down at them. Heather dove to the ground as Merlin hurled a hasty fireball into the air. The creature's gaping mouth glowed red as the flames flew past. It veered away. Shooting upward, it joined a half dozen others circling overhead.

"What was that?" Welly cried, sitting up and groggily groping for his glasses.

"One of Morgan's little toys," Merlin replied.

"Ooh, me saw!" Troll said, jumping about excitedly. "Great Wizard singe nasty snake's wings. Next time shoot one down in flames."

"Next time?" Heather questioned, huddling closer to the fire.

Merlin sighed, looking up at the black forms circling in the darkness above. "I can see that this is not going to be a particularly restful night."

29

TREASURE LONG KEPT

When dawn finally came, the snakes broke formation and drifted eastward, at last disappearing into the orange smear of sunrise.

"What a night," Welly groaned as he unwound himself from his blanket. "How many of the little beasts did you incinerate?"

Wearily Merlin started to answer, but Troll piped up, "Three, me count!"

Merlin nodded, yawning. "Yes, though I think the last one was just singed. But I don't believe that Morgan sent them to seriously threaten, just to harass. Right now, I think she's more curious than dangerous."

"Well, I feel plenty harassed," Welly said. "I can put up with a lot of abuse, but a good night's sleep is sacred."

Merlin laughed. "Once we get going today, everyone had better keep an eye on each other so no one falls asleep and gets left in a heap by the roadside."

The road that day proved to be a long and dreary one. The land was featureless with distant hills, dark against a gray sky. A few stone buildings huddled beside fields of muted green crops.

Once more, Heather's thoughts were dragged to her amulet. Last night when the flying snakes were attacking, she'd felt a nagging urge to grab and use it. But part of her kept warning that she didn't know how, that it had worked badly in the gorge, and that, anyway, Earl could handle things. It was her comfort in Earl's presence that finally shut out the nagging. In the end, she'd tried to lie so that the cold black stone couldn't touch her skin. She was reluctant to take it off altogether, but when she couldn't feel its tingling cold, she was more at ease.

Now, however, anything seemed better than the boredom of the trip, and she tried experimenting with it again. Rippling the grass as from an unseen wind or making rocks roll along the road behind them was great fun. But after what Earl had said last night, even this play made her a little uneasy. If this was some magic tool from the old, old days, maybe it really ought not to be used now. And besides, anything her mother had used . . . No, that was probably unfair. Still, the power didn't feel quite right for her.

The sky lowered as the day wore on. Clouds tumbled over one another, turning darker and darker shades of gray. Against them, the shape of Glastonbury Tor grew steadily larger. Occasionally they saw black things slipping between the clouds. And at times they caught glimpses of movement among rocks and ditches as they passed.

"Earl," Welly said uneasily, "that hill you mentioned, is it still an entrance to Avalon?"

"No, not to Avalon. That is the home of the Eldritch, and they've closed most of their doors to this world. But there are many parts of Faerie, all very different, though some share doors. What do you say, Troll?"

"What, Great Wizard?" The creature bounded up on its spindly legs.

"Those little shadowy things we've been half-seeing, are they out of Faerie?"

The troll sidled closer to Merlin's horse and looked around nervously. "Yes, from Faerie, but not from Troll's part. Other parts—dark things there."

"And are they coming through the Tor?"

"Me think so, yes."

Merlin frowned. "Which means we're heading into a hornet's nest. If Morgan wants to cause us trouble, she's got ready-made helpers. And whatever happens, she mustn't get that bowl. That would give her far, far too much power." He thought for a moment, then looked down again at their small yellow companion. "Troll, is there any chance that the Tor also opens onto your part of Faerie?"

"Don't know. Maybe." Suddenly he sprang up excitedly. "Oh! Great Wizard wants Troll to go on secret mission. Fetch help. Be hero!"

"Well, if we have to face an assortment of Faerie's darker folk, it might be useful to know if there are any willing to rally to the other side."

"Yes, yes. Troll go. Fetch help. Big hero!" Quickly he jumped over a roadside ditch and disappeared into the gray landscape.

"Do you think he'll bring help?" Heather asked.

"Hard to say. Most folk from his part of Faerie aren't strongly committed one way or another. But they're not averse to fighting if the mood strikes them. Like those rock sprites at the gorge. Actually, this area was once full of swamp sprites, and they made powerful friends if you could interest them."

"Swamp sprites?" Welly looked around. "It's dry as a bone around here."

"Yes, now. But it used to be all swamp and lakes. Glastonbury on its hill was almost an island, with a little dock down near the base of the Tor. People must have drained it later for farmland."

As they approached the town, their road climbed out of the lowlands. It passed ruined outskirts and entered finally through recently refortified city walls.

The arrival of three mounted warriors and their extraordinary dog caused quite a stir. Market booths clustering around the old stone cross were beginning to shut down, but there were still plenty of people about to point and ask questions.

One stout, authoritative-looking man walked up to Merlin. "You young people on your way to join the King?"

"That depends on which king you mean."

"Why, Edwin of Wessex, of course. He's called for all able-bodied fighters to rally to him at Uffington. I'd go myself if I were a bit younger, that I would."

"I'm certain you would. But, you see, my companions and I have recently ridden here from Wales and are rather out of touch with events in these parts. What is the threat that causes your good King to head for Uffington?"

"Indeed, you must've been under a stone of late! Take no offense, none was meant. It's the armies of the East under that witch woman of theirs. Rumor has it they are ready to move on Wessex."

"Rumors!" scoffed a second man. "We've had rumors of those Easterners for months and not seen a one."

A short gray-haired woman bustled up. "Oh? What about the muties attacking flocks down near Salisbury?

Those aren't rumors, and they say the witch controls them, too."

The first man nodded his head. "And if it's rumors, then King Edwin takes them mighty seriously, because I've heard he's called on those two in the North, the Scottish Queen and King Arthur himself."

"More rumors! And if you believe that King Arthur story, you're more of a doddering old fool than I thought!"

"Huh, that shows how much you know, Jedediah!" the woman said. "That King Arthur is as real as these three youngsters here. Why, he's united half the shires in the North already."

"Maybe so. But you can't pretend he's the real King Arthur."

"Who else but the real one could have done a thing like that, I'd like to know. Besides, they say he's brought back his old wizard, too, and they work magic—a lot bigger magic than Sam the tailor or the old henwife do."

"Bah! You're not going to catch me believing in a fairy-tale king and a crazy graybeard wizard. I've got sense!"

"Jedediah, if that old wizard were to hear you say a thing like that, he'd turn you into a centipede. What do you say, young people? You've been traveling."

All three suddenly developed a cough. But finally the eldest recovered and said, "Ah, yes, I suppose he might. Though maybe into something less nasty—a goose, perhaps. But, friends, you say Arthur is to join your king at Uffington?"

"That's what they say," the stout man replied. "Will you be going there, then?"

"Yes, I think we might. But first we have some business here. Could you tell me where the church is?"

"Which church is it you want? There's Saint Mary's and Saint Michael's, the New Zoroastrians, the Armageddonites, the—"

"I mean the old church, the very old one."

"You mean the abbey? That's supposed to be the oldest church in England. It's nothing but ruins now, has been since way back."

"No matter. That's the one we want. Where is it?"

"Just down the road and beyond those walls. But if it's praying before battle you're looking for, there's no clergy there."

"Thank you, but we're looking for something else."

As they rode down the street, Welly and Heather were still quivering with laughter. Merlin shot them a squelching look, then chuckled. "Maybe once I finally start growing a beard, I'll dye it gray, just to live up to expectations."

The dark afternoon was slipping into a darker dusk. Yet as they passed through the enclosing walls, there was still enough light to see the ruins of the once-vast abbey. The building was a great shattered shell. Roofless now, it was paved only with weeds. Remaining segments of wall soared upward, holding empty windows against the sky. Here and there among the ruins crouched rare hawthorn trees. In the dusk, their blossoms shone a ghostly white.

Merlin shook his head. "This place certainly grew after I saw it last. Then it was just a couple of wattle-and-daub buildings with a fenced-in churchyard. Now the trick's going to be finding just where that old church was."

He dismounted and, clutching his staff, wandered toward the east end of the sprawling ruins. There the roofless span was widest. Suddenly uneasy in the growing dark, Welly and Heather hurried to join him.

As Merlin walked slowly about, concentrating on stones and weedy soil, the attention of the other two kept shifting to the darkness beyond the walls. Shadows seemed to flit there, just out of sight. Whimpering, Rus crowded up to them, both tails stuck between his legs.

"Earl," Welly whispered, slowly pulling out his sword, "I don't think we're alone here." But the wizard, poking at some stones with the end of his staff, didn't seem to hear. Shrugging, Heather unsheathed her own sword. The two followed their friend, keeping eyes on what they couldn't quite see.

Deliberately they crisscrossed the open space, then passed through an arch in a lone fragment of tower. Suddenly something snapped out of the darkness. Wrapping a scaly paw around Heather's ankle, it yanked her to the ground. She slashed at it. Her sword met something solid, and the air was sprayed with rank liquid. Shaking, she scrambled to her feet to find Welly struggling with some dark, entwining shape.

Spinning around as if suddenly awakened, Merlin slammed his staff on the ground. Purple flame shot from its top, illuminating the scene. The creature wrapping itself around Welly shrank back, but not before they clearly saw its many hairy arms and bulbous head.

Heather nearly gagged at what the light showed of her own attacker. Her sword had slit open its scaly hide, and entrails now lay steaming on the bloody grass. Turning away, she took several shaky breaths and walked to where the wizard was now kneeling beside a dip in the ground.

"Please, Earl, let's come back and look in the morning. This place is . . . occupied at night."

Earl stood and headed off in a new direction. "I don't think it is normally. They're here because we are. All the more reason I must find that bowl now. Morgan's getting much too interested in us."

"But suppose it isn't here either?" Welly said anxiously.

"I . . . I think it is. Somewhere." He continued walking westward, questing like a hound following a scent. As he walked, his staff shed a heatless pool of light about him.

The others stayed near but kept turning around as they walked. Where the light faded into darkness, it reflected back from watching eyes. Some were low to the ground, some high up. A sudden shriek and something dove at them from the sky. Annoyed, Merlin raised his staff, searing the underside of wings. It veered off, screaming.

Fearfully lowering her gaze, Heather saw eyes again. Their numbers had grown. "Earl, could we hurry? We're attracting a lot of attention."

"Yes, yes," he said absently. "Keep them back; I've got to concentrate. We're closer now. I know it."

"Well, keep your light going!" Welly begged as the flame on the staff faded. It flared up again, but, emboldened by numbers, the things in the dark were closing in.

Something all teeth and claws darted toward them. Welly swung at it with his sword. It dodged back, but another scrambled in from behind. Heather spun around, nicking it with her blade.

Suddenly cries and the sound of fighting erupted around them. But who was fighting whom? Even Merlin noticed the change, and his staff shot out a new flare of light, showing a battle raging on all sides. Constant motion confused the picture, but clearly none of the combatants were human. Among them jumped a yellowish creature, jabbing and thrusting with a great pike.

"Troll!" Heather cried. "He's brought reinforcements!"

Desperately now, Merlin continued his search as the strange battle surged around them. Suddenly the noise of fighting shrank under a new sound, a flapping of giant wings. Cowering, Heather and Welly stared into the dark sky.

Great black wings hovered overhead, then lowered slowly to one of the central towers. Now, above the third tier of arches, something crouched like a living gargoyle.

"Merlin!" a clear voice called from above. "Stop poking about in the dirt. I wish to talk with you."

High in the wall, an empty stone niche glowed with green. In its center stood a pale woman, black hair flowing about her shoulders. A hideous creature sat hunched on the wall above her.

Angrily Merlin looked up. "Perhaps, Morgan, but I don't wish to talk with you." He moved quickly to where an arch led to a smaller, more intact section of the ancient building.

"Such a rude child!" The woman laughed coldly. "I've been keeping an eye on you, you know, ever since you slipped away from that incompetent Nigel. You are obviously looking for something, Merlin dear, and I've decided the time has come to see what it is."

Motioning the others to follow, Merlin hurried down some weed-choked steps beyond the arch. "If I am looking for something, it is nothing of yours. So you can just take your misbegotten pets back to wherever you crawled from."

"But, Merlin, your interest is recommendation enough. Whatever it is, I intend to make it mine!"

She thrust forward her hand, and a spear of green light shot toward them. Merlin flung up his staff, deflecting the assault. "Troll!" he yelled. "Get your people in here. Now!"

On the fringes of light, the shadowy forms shifted and creatures scuffled toward them. Merlin jerked up his staff and shot a gob of purple flame toward the figure on the wall. It smashed against the glowing green stone, shattering into a shower of sparks.

"Poor aim!" came the taunting reply. "But I don't want to play games, little boy. I want what you are looking for."

By now, an assortment of creatures had slid down the stairs to join them. Some were thin, wispy things, and others were as chunky as stone. One looked something like Troll, only much larger.

Merlin leaped again to the top of the steps and shouted something, staff raised high above his head. Snakes of purple flame jumped from the staff to the sides of the arch, then rapidly crawled upward. Spreading along the tops of the walls, the flame encircled the western end of the ruins. Every empty window and broken wall glimmered with purple light.

Beyond the barrier of light, Morgan screamed and hurled a mass of green flame. It shattered harmlessly against the purple wall. Enraged, she rained down volley after volley, but the barrier held.

"That had better hold long enough," Merlin muttered as he turned away. "Now, I must find it!"

The air crackled with light and choked them with the stench of ozone and sulfur. Half-blinded by the glare, Merlin suddenly stepped into nothing. Crying out, he plunged into the ancient crypt, gashing his forehead on a stone at the bottom. Blood ran down his face as he dizzily pulled himself to his knees.

Still stunned, he stared down into the growing pool of his own blood. Something was there, moving beyond the surface. A figure running through the darkness, running through a fenced churchyard. A guttering torch showed the worried face. Brother Joseph. The now-elderly monk hurried on. Saxon raiders attacking the town. He must hide the church treasures, especially those that had been Arthur's. The Saxons must not desecrate them!

The robed figure came to an alcove of stones and hurried down the worn steps. At the bottom lay a stone slab and a crude wooden cover. He yanked the cover aside and from his bulging robes pulled out clattering handfuls of things. They glinted briefly in the torchlight before dropping into the darkness of the well.

The pool of water shimmered and changed into blood. Whose blood? Merlin passed a hand over his eyes. Had Brother Joseph survived the attack? But that was over, long over. And at last the secret had been passed.

The wizard staggered to his feet. The barrage was still heavy about them, but the defensive purple glow seemed fainter.

Heather was calling from above. "Earl! Earl, are you all right?"

"Yes," he croaked.

"The barrier's weakening!"

Already he was running to the left. "Yes. I'll be back soon!"

He found what he sought, an opening in the crypt wall and steps leading down. By the light flickering along his staff, he saw a carved stone arch at the bottom. It was later work, but below it was the same stone slab. The hole in it, glinting slightly from damp, was choked with trash and stones. Dropping to his knees, he frantically pulled at the rubble with both hands. Some was jammed firm. He could hear shouts and fighting again from above.

Desperately he rammed the point of his staff into the stones; letting power flow down the shaft, he pried the fill away. Then, dropping the staff, he reached into the well's cold water, down to the mud beneath. His fingers groped about, touching various objects. But they sought only one and tingled with kinship when they found it. Scrabbling at the smooth, round shape, he pulled it free of silt and water.

In trembling hands he held it. Its intricate designs were obscured by mud and tarnish. But he knew it, and it him. They remembered so much.

The shouting from above called him back. Rubbing at the blood still trickling into his eyes, he scrambled up the stairs and emerged into the night. The purple light had faded to a flicker, and all about him creatures were fighting.

Morgan took no part now, content to watch her minions win from her perch on the broken wall. But when she saw Merlin again, she shouted her triumph. Holding both hands above her head, she drew power about her into a pulsing green mass more potent than anything she had launched before. She hurled it now toward her ancient enemy.

Merlin recoiled. His staff was below, out of reach. Instinctively he raised a hand to shield his face. The bolt of power slammed downward, striking the bowl. With a deafening blow, it rebounded back. Sorceress and gargoyle screamed as the reflected power sheared off the top of the tower, leaving smoke and silence behind.

Groggily Merlin sank to his knees, looking at the now-gleaming bowl in his hands. "Well, that's one way to clean old silver," he muttered before slumping, unconscious, to the ground.

30

THE HILL OF THE WHITE HORSE

The predawn light was gray and cold. Merlin stared up into it, wondering chiefly about the pain in his head. Slowly he raised a hand to find bandages wrapped around a throbbing forehead. As he struggled to sit up, the jacket that had been thrown over him slid from his shoulders.

"Well, welcome back," Heather said, limping toward him. The whole left side of her body was burned, the boot on that side nothing but a few sooty shreds.

Others hurried toward him. Welly's right shoulder was wrapped in a bloody rag. Rus was missing half of one tail, and a ragged gash running across Troll's forehead ended in a severed ear. Looking absurdly unbalanced, he grinned from ear to former ear.

"Great Wizard find bowl and blow away nasty witch. Troll proud."

Merlin found his voice. "We'd never have lasted long enough without your recruits, Troll. Where have they gone?"

"Oh. Some hurt, some killed. They go back. No like to stay around humans. Some muties they not mind. But plain humans scare them."

"They don't like us," Heather said, "yet they fought and died for us?"

"They not like humans but like to fight! And like witch and friends even less. Besides"—the troll proudly straightened his squat body—"folk of Faerie very learned. Know Great Wizard. Happy to help."

"Well, I was happy to have their help."

After they had breakfasted, Merlin tied the bowl to his belt by one of the three metal rings at the rim. Welly looked at it, then frowned slightly.

"Earl, we haven't found any trace of Morgan. Did that blast completely incinerate her?"

"I doubt it. That bolt did carry most of the power she could muster, but it probably weakened in the reflection. I imagine she's off somewhere nursing hurt body and pride.

"And speaking of hurt bodies, let me try a little healing magic, at least for the burns and cuts. I can't do much for missing tails and ears, I'm afraid."

Soon Heather's burns and the gashes Troll and Welly sported were reduced to tender redness. The painful cut on his own forehead became an angry scar, which Merlin tried vainly to hide behind his ragged black hair.

When they finally rode away from the abbey ruins, they found fearful, curious faces staring from windows and doors. The events of the previous night could hardly have been missed, and the group's appearance now was particularly impressive due to the presence of the troll.

Merlin recognized several citizens from the conversation of yesterday. "I'm afraid, sir," he said to the stout, authoritative gentleman, "that we have ruined your ruins a little further. But King Arthur and your own King will be grateful."

"Ah"—the man nodded knowingly—"so you do have

something to do with Arthur. All the rumors are true, then? The real Arthur has returned?"

"Indeed. As has his graybeard wizard. But tell your doubting friend I won't turn him into a goose after all." He ignored the openmouthed stares and furtive hand signs. "Now, if you want to help defend this fine town of yours, I suggest you send all able-bodied fighters to Uffington. The Kings and Queen may well need them."

Their ride eastward from Glastonbury took several days. On the way, they encountered parties of Wessex warriors rallying to their King's call. They also noticed occasional shadowy forms flitting along the roadside, but they felt none of the uneasiness such sights had brought earlier.

"Troll, are these friends of yours?" Merlin asked one night as they were setting up camp in a ruined farmstead.

"Don't know most. Faerie is big place."

Welly unfastened the saddle girth under his horse's shaggy belly. "But I thought you said your people didn't care much about wars between humans."

"They don't," the troll agreed, looking hopefully at the food bags Heather was unloading. "But this not just human war. Something big coming. That witch call up folk from dark parts, folk we not like."

Merlin was squatting down, arranging rocks for a fire circle. "What Troll means, I believe, is that if Morgan's forces have netherworld allies, so do we. Not as many, perhaps, nor as visible. But they're coming from all over. I can feel them."

Heather felt them, too, an occasional mist blowing across field or streambed, or dream shadows flitting by while they slept. But she didn't probe at the feelings. And despite its nagging, she firmly ignored the amulet. It had burned at her during the fight, but she hadn't taken the time to try using it. Now she felt she'd seen enough of high magic, and to stifle the stone's stirrings, she took it off and stuffed it in her pack. She was content to be with Earl and the others and to touch at the thoughts of passing animals.

Merlin was enormously relieved to have the ancient bowl swinging at his side again, but he hesitated to put its old powers to the test. Better to wait until they were back with Arthur, where he could concentrate on it. In the meantime, there would be several days' riding with his friends.

Friends. He was surprised at how happy that term made him. Heather and Welly and even Troll were here not simply because they wanted to help in what he was doing, but because they wanted to help *him,* to be with him. The idea was so new it frightened him, though he dared hope that somehow in this new world it might last. Sometimes as they rode along, he and Heather exchanged smiles. He wondered what she was thinking and feeling but couldn't bring himself to harden things into words.

The villages they passed while riding eastward were alive with rumor. It was said that a great army had arrived from the North led by Arthur Pendragon and the flame-haired Queen of Scots. They had joined with King Edwin of Wessex at the ancient hill fort above Uffington. From everywhere, would-be warriors, both men and women, were streaming to join them.

The eagerness of these people to fight and face death awakened Merlin's uneasiness. He saw again the startled face of John Wesley, bloodily clutching the King's banner. How many other such faces would haunt them in the end?

His somber thoughts lifted slightly when the chalk

downs came into view. For miles, they formed a bold southern wall along the Vale of the White Horse.

As they rode up the shoulder of the downs, Heather looked eagerly about her. A fresh, cool wind rolled in pale waves over the grass and blew wisps of hair about her face. "Did they have a lot of white horses here once?" she asked.

"Maybe," Merlin replied. "But the name comes from one horse in particular. It was so old, people had forgotten its origin, even in my time. I wonder if, after all these years, it could still be there?"

"A horse?"

"Yes." Then his voice quickened with excitement. "Yes, look! Look at that hillside."

Heather squinted ahead. "I don't see anything, just some scars in the grass."

"But they form a pattern. Don't you see it?"

She stared again. "Well, maybe. Oh, yes. Yes, I see it. A prancing white horse!"

"Thousands of years ago, people cut that figure through the turf down to the white chalk. And ever since, others have kept it from growing over. I imagine no one knows why anymore, just keeping faith with the past."

Welly's gaze rose to the slopes above the stylized animal. "Is that the old fort up there where those people are?"

Merlin's sigh was tinged with regret. "Yes, we're almost there."

As they rode up the steep hillside, what had appeared to be a natural plateau resolved itself into a large enclosure surrounded by a ditch and two massive banks. The ancient fortress's command over the sweeping countryside was dramatic. Only to the east did the shoulder of the downs obscure the view, and there a rock and turf watchtower was already being built.

As they rode through the camp, only a few heads turned. Many recruits were new since Chester. But then a tall young man with a golden beard came running their way, and attention swiveled onto them.

"Merlin, you old truant, you're back! You wouldn't believe how I've missed you, prophecies or not." The King smiled at the others. "I knew your friends would bring you back safe." Then his gaze stopped at the troll. "And you have a new friend, I see."

Merlin nodded toward his one-eared companion. "Troll here is my loyal bodyguard. And"—he lowered his voice—"you may have noticed a few more recruits of his general sort in the shadows."

Arthur nodded. "They seem to be gathering in the hills beyond the Ridgeway. Most of our troops are keeping well clear of there, trying not to see anything. But I, for one, welcome the help."

"For one?" Merlin questioned. "And how are you and the fiery Queen of Scots getting on these days?" Merlin had seen the lady in question striding toward them, red hair tied back with a golden band.

Arthur turned and addressed her. "My lady, this old wizard asks how you and I are getting on at present."

She smiled as she walked up to them. "About as well as two captive fell-dogs, always at each other's throat and lost without each other's company."

She deftly ducked Arthur's mock cuff, and Merlin smiled. He didn't need a bowl of prophecy to see how things were developing there.

In the days that followed, they settled into camp life

with the army growing around them. Merlin finally turned his attention to the bowl. He spent hours sitting by himself at the edge of camp, the bowl filled with water and swinging on a tripod before him.

He saw visions, but they were confused, oddly removed and displaced, as though glimpsed through a distant window. The more he tried to look at them squarely, the more they slid away, fleeting visions at the edge of sight.

What he did see was distorted and strange, twisting currents of time coiling through past and future toward a blinding blast of white hate. It had to do with Morgan, he knew, and with battle, but the only message he could extract was a vague compulsion, a need for movement to the southeast.

Day after day he spent by the bowl, trying to drag the vision closer, to shake it into focus. He scarcely ate or slept, and when Heather brought him meals, she often found the last one untouched.

Sometimes Heather would simply sit with the wizard, though he seldom pulled himself away from the elusive vision to note her presence. She was surprised at how content she was simply to be near him, to sit on the turf bank watching the wind silver the grass or watching the cloud shadows chase each other across the land below.

One afternoon, as she left in an effort to find Merlin some tempting food, Kyle came up to her. They hadn't spoken a great deal since her return. He had been busy with his music and the attentions of young ladies of the camp. But now he stepped deliberately in her path.

"Heather, I don't like to meddle. But you're too good a

person to sink into some dark, useless sort of life. Why don't you leave the wizard to his brooding and join the rest of us?"

Her frown deepened. "Kyle, a while back you were telling me I had to choose. Well, I suppose I have chosen. I know where I belong, or at least with whom I belong. Now please let me be!"

She stomped away, anger smoldering. But in one thing she knew Kyle was right. She might be less torn by indecision now, but she *was* rather useless. Welly, when not with the cook's assistant, was spending his time training new recruits. Even Troll was busy with the growing troops out of Faerie. Earl, she felt, did need her, but she really wasn't being of much use to him.

Wandering dejectedly back to her campsite, she decided there was still one way she could help him. Reaching into her pack, she pulled out the amulet. Despite an occasional itch to use it, she hadn't put it on since Glastonbury. Slipping the chain around her neck, she knelt down on her blanket. She might not understand or fully trust its powers, but she had to try something. If only she could figure out how to channel it.

But it was difficult. The power of the amulet was of a cold and alien sort, nothing like the animal-tied magic that came so easily to her. Clearly it was closer to Earl's high magic, so if she could just use it, surely she could be of some help to him.

Suddenly, like a bolt of lightning, fear blasted through her. She wanted to help Earl, and he was indeed in terrible danger. Bathed in sweat, she gazed at the shiny black surface of the amulet. It sank away like a dark tunnel. She fell through it, and pictures rushed past her. Massive rocks in a sunlit circle, their patterns ancient and meaning-ful. Mounded earth over the cold and decay of a stone tomb. The pictures were clear and precise and reeked of threat. Threat that only she could save him from.

Welly, walking by to fetch his sharpening stone, no-ticed Heather crouched on her bedroll, shaking as if in a fever.

"Heather?" He walked over and knelt beside her. "Heather, what is it? Are you all right?"

He noticed the amulet and her frozen gaze. Covering its riveting blackness with a plump hand, he shook her shoulder. "Heather, come out of it!"

She fell back with a cry. Looking wildly at him, she slowly realized who he was. "Oh, Welly, I've got to help him!"

"Help who? And what is this?" He raised his hand from the black stone.

"It's a magic amulet." She no longer felt a need to hide it, not from Welly. "My mother gave it to me; it's an old family piece. It showed me . . . Welly, Earl's in terrible dan-ger, and I have to go right away and save him from it!"

"Earl is sitting by the north wall brooding over that bowl of his. He's not in any danger."

"Not now, but soon. If I leave now and go where I've seen, I can still save him from it."

"Why don't you just go to Earl now and tell him about it?"

"No!" She closed her fist possessively around the amulet. "Then he'd want to see and go there, too, and that would be the greatest danger."

"I don't see that."

"But I do! I *see* it. And I'm going right now." She stood up and fastened her sword to her belt.

"You can't go alone."

"I'll have Rus."

"Don't be crazy; that's not enough!" He looked after her as she strode off to the horse corral, her dog padding behind her. "Aren't you even going to tell someone or leave a note?"

"No time."

Furiously he pulled off his glasses and started to polish them on his shirt. Jamming them back on his face, Welly ran to catch up with her.

"You coming, too?" she asked matter-of-factly.

"I have to. Earl would turn me into a swamp rat if anything happened to you. But this whole thing is crazy, and you know it."

She smiled grimly and picked out a tall, fast horse for herself.

A few minutes later, Heather and Welly, with Rus at their side, rode out of the south gate and along the ancient trackway that ran over the crest of the downs. Shortly afterward, a gray shape slid from the ditch that encircled the fort and glided from shadow to concealing shadow until it reached the campsite of Merlin the Wizard. From folds of misty clothing, it pulled a scrap of folded parchment and pinned it to the bedroll. Then, like a puff of acrid smoke, it slipped away.

Hunched by his bowl near the north wall, Merlin sighed and sagged back with fatigue. Again, visions had danced and jibbered at him just out of reach, leaving him with only a sense of dread and a vague compulsion for the southeast. Shuddering, he looked up to see Arthur standing over him.

"Merlin, I've been standing here talking to you for five minutes. You've been somewhere else entirely, and by the looks of you, somewhere you're better off away from."

Merlin sighed wearily. "Yes, but somehow I've got to make this work. There's danger out there, terrible danger, and maybe a solution. Morgan has some dreadful plan. I can feel it. But this Bowl of Seeing is the only way I know to see it."

"Maybe, old friend, but don't kill yourself in the process."

The King squatted down beside him. "And I'll tell you something else—less mystic, perhaps, but also important. We need water. Those two springs on the hillside aren't enough any longer for this horde. When the old Celts used this place as a fort, they must have had a well. Can you find it for us?"

Arthur stood up, pulling Merlin shakily to his feet. "Come on. Put your wizardry to some down-to-earth use and find us some water."

His friend laughed ruefully. "You're right. Maybe I should give up on prophecy and concentrate on removing warts and divining water. Then at least I'd be of some use."

He looked about, really seeing the fort for the first time in days. It bustled with soldiers and horses, and the turf ramparts were steadily rising. He turned his thoughts to wells. "I'd better use my staff; wood has an affinity for water."

"I'll send someone for it. You still look a little tottery. Heather says you haven't been eating enough." The King waved a beckoning arm at Kyle, who was walking by, talking with a Scottish piper.

"Kyle, would you trot over to Merlin's campsite and bring us his staff? Don't look so alarmed; it won't turn into a snake. Will it, Merlin?"

"Not if I don't ask it to."

Despite this assurance, Kyle could think of a good many errands he'd rather be sent on. Near the King's tent, he found the spot where the wizard had stashed his things. Among rolled-up blankets, a saddlebag, and several cooking pots lay the slender staff. Its wood was pale and smooth except where it knotted into a clawlike root at the top.

Gingerly Kyle reached for it, then saw the note pinned to the bedroll. On the outside, "Earl" was written in Heather's distinctive round script. Kyle picked up the staff, which felt reassuringly woodlike, then unpinned the note, deciding he'd take that to the wizard as well.

He returned to where Merlin and Arthur had been joined by several of the King's engineers. Merlin took the staff with a nod of thanks, while one engineer was saying, "It really ought to be within the banks, but we haven't found any stones or depressions."

Merlin stood still, closed his eyes a moment, then slowly began walking toward the southwest. The others followed at a distance.

Kyle stayed behind, watching. He hadn't had a chance to give Merlin the note. Well, he would when they'd found the water. But now he wished he'd taken no part in this sending of notes between the two. He had to admit that the wizard was a good enough fellow, but his kind shouldn't get mixed up with regular people. And despite Heather's few tricks, Kyle felt she belonged in the normal world.

He wondered what message she had sent. Making some assignation, perhaps? Or asking about some mystic formula? Maybe Merlin was having her act as his agent with those outlandish things lurking about south of the fort.

Curiosity vied with courtesy. The note wasn't sealed. He'd take a quick look.

"Dear Earl," the note began. That very familiarity annoyed him. He read on. *"I want you to know that I am leaving with Welly. The time has come for me to make a choice. Welly is of my world in a way you can never be. Your world is right for you, but it frightens me. I want a simple, normal life somewhere, and I am going off to find it. Please don't follow us. This way is better."* Signed, *"Heather."*

Astonished, Kyle stared at the note, quickly rereading it. So that was the choice she'd meant! He hadn't given her enough credit. It was a shame, though, that she'd have to leave them all, and for that he blamed the wizard. But Kyle guessed that Merlin would pay for it. Cold fish that he was, he seemed genuinely fond of Heather—of Welly, too. He might take this pretty hard.

Kyle folded up the note and looked guiltily about. The wizard, King, and others were gathered around a spot near the southwest wall. The harper walked toward them.

"Dig here," Merlin was saying as Kyle approached. "There'll be stones two feet down where it was filled in. Another three feet, and you'll hit water."

The engineers looked doubtfully at one another. Merlin shook his head wearily. "It's there. Do you want me to do the digging, too?"

The others smiled sheepishly, but Arthur said, "In this army we specialize. Wizards find water, and engineers dig for it. Come on, Merlin, I want you to get something to eat before you go back to glowering at that bowl."

As they walked off, the King's arm over the wizard's thin shoulders, Kyle stepped up. "Merlin, I found this note pinned to your blankets when I went for the staff."

Merlin flushed slightly when he saw the handwriting. "I'll be with you in a minute, Arthur. I want to tend to this first."

The King nodded and walked briskly away. Kyle had already left, almost wishing he'd torn the thing up. He didn't like to see people hurt, not even odd magical people.

Merlin opened the parchment and read it. He felt as if he had stopped breathing. Each word cut him like ice. He tried to read it again, but his eyes blurred. Slowly he folded the note, slipping it into his shirt. Inside him, cold spread into numbness. Quietly he headed for the north gate and walked out into the gathering night.

31

EMPTINESS AND PERIL

Through that evening and into the night, Heather and Welly rode along the Ridgeway. When Welly wanted to stop, Heather urged them on, finally allowing a few brief hours of sleep before prodding them on again.

Welly knew how attached Heather was to Earl and could understand her worry over some mysterious danger to him. But there was something odd about her now. When they had left Chester, spurred by her vision of the hawk and the snake, she had been worried but otherwise her usual self. Now, after whatever she had seen with the amulet, she seemed obsessed. Saying nothing, she kept her eyes intently on the road. Needing no map, she drove them along roads and over the countryside as if on the end of an invisible line.

By midafternoon, the horses were staggering with weariness, and Welly urged that they stop. It wasn't like Heather, of all people, to be so inconsiderate of animals. Rus was so tired, Welly carried him for a while across his saddle. Heather's only response was, "Not now; we're almost there."

They were off the downs now, heading through fields

of dry grass. Sheep bleated their annoyance and scattered out of their way. After a distance, a road they had joined cut through a wall-like mound of earth. As they passed through, Heather sighed, letting her weary horse stumble to a halt.

"This is it. This is what I saw exactly."

Welly looked around. They seemed to have entered a huge earthen ring with a ditch running around the inside of the high bank. Inside that encircling ditch, the circle was repeated by a ring of massive upright stones. In places, the circle was incomplete, but one could see where it had once run.

"Look at the size of those stones," Welly marveled. Running off in both directions, the unworked boulders jutted out of the earth like gigantic decayed teeth. Even Welly could feel the awesomeness of the place. But the locals seemed undaunted. Not only were sheep grazing beside the stones, a small village nestled inside their circuit.

Heather looked around as well, but with an air of scientific detachment, as if trying to read a pattern in the stones.

"Ah, I think that's the way we want to go," she said, pointing to the right.

"No, it is not." Welly was looking straight ahead at a rambling thatched building signed "The Red Lion." "What we really want is a break at that inn."

"Wellington Jones! Here Earl is in mortal danger, and all you can think about is eating and drinking!"

"That's not fair, Heather! I've gone with you all this way. The horses are exhausted. Even your crazy dog is tired out. It's nearly sunset. Why don't we stay here and head off to wherever else in the morning?"

"Because that may be too late. Come on, it's not far now."

"That's what you said before. Isn't this the place you saw?"

"I saw it, yes. But it's only the first part of the pattern. There's an avenue of stones that leads from here. We follow it to . . . to wherever it points."

"And where is that?"

"It's . . . a place. I don't know for sure. But I have to see the pattern before the light fades, or I might miss it."

"Oh, all right, all right. I'm just along as a trusty sword arm. But take it slowly, will you, for the horses at least?"

As they rode by the Red Lion, Welly gazed longingly at the half-timbered building, looking cozy and welcoming under its thatch. Through a window, he glimpsed a snug little room with low-beamed ceilings and a large fireplace. Then he wrenched his eyes away toward the brooding stones, their shadows stretching long and cold in the late-afternoon sun.

Soon they rode out of the circle. Before them marched an avenue of stones leading off to the southeast. Right again, Welly thought. Uncanny. He preferred it when Heather talked with horses and sheep, even fell-dogs.

They followed the double row of stones over a rise and down into a swale. There the markers disappeared.

"Well, where to now?" Welly asked grouchily.

"Just follow this bearing as if the stones continued. We'll see it from the top of that rise."

Welly sighed wearily, but already Heather was urging her tired horse upward.

A cold evening wind grated harshly against their faces. At the top of the rise, Welly looked about. To their right was an odd-looking conical hill. He figured that was peculiar enough to be their goal, but when he glanced back to Heather, she was looking straight ahead.

"There it is. You see that bump? Right on the horizon, a long, low hump."

He looked where she was pointing. Barely discernible along a distant ridge was something resembling a raised scar.

"That?"

"Come on." Riding down into a valley, they passed through the tumbled ruins of a long-empty farmstead. After they had forded a small stream, their way began rising again. When the long mound appeared on the ridge above them, Heather halted her horse.

"Let's walk from here."

Welly groaned. He was too tired to walk an inch. Then guiltily he patted his shaggy horse. The poor beast must feel the same, with far better reason. He slid from the saddle, fixed the reins to a stone post, and trudged up the hill after Heather and Rus. Grass rustled in the cold breeze, and a lone bird called forlornly from the grayness overhead.

Ahead of them, the western sky was stained red with sunset. Silhouetted against it, the long mound looked dark and ominous. As they drew closer, Welly could see several large stones looming up sharply at one end. The whole thing seemed extremely unwelcoming.

Once they'd reached the mound, it was clear that the stones marked some sort of entrance.

"Are we going in there?" Welly asked dubiously.

"Of course."

"What sort of place is it?"

"An old tomb, I think."

Welly shook his head. "No, Heather, we really don't want to go in there."

"It doesn't matter whether we *want* to or not, we *have* to."

Rus, however, clearly shared Welly's doubts. Sticking his one and a half tails between his legs, he flopped down by the farthest stone and whimpered.

Ignoring him, Heather walked through a narrow gap in the stones into a small open courtyard. Then, bending down to clear the lintel, she stepped into the dark of the tomb itself. Very reluctantly Welly followed.

Light filtered through ragged gaps where ceiling stones had fallen through, but it failed to penetrate the blackness of several chambers that branched off from the main passage. Welly was relieved when Heather passed these by.

The passage itself was narrow and low. Its stone walls felt cold as death, and the chill air smelled of earth and damp decay. The mass of rock and soil above seemed to weigh heavily down on them. Despite the bone-numbing cold, Welly felt sweat break out all over him. He wanted fervently to be elsewhere. Abruptly the passage ended, much sooner than the length of the mound had suggested.

The final chamber was small and round. On its earthen floor lay a large flat stone. A hole in the roof let in a thin mist of light. By it they saw a black lump on the stone.

"There's nothing in here," Welly said anxiously, feeling very much that there was something in there. "Let's go."

"No, wait. What is this?" Heather knelt down and examined the black thing. She reached out her hand, but then drew it back. "Why, it's a piece of charred wood."

Welly squinted at it in the fading light. It did look like a sooty piece of old root. "Yeah, probably part of someone's campfire. Please, let's go."

"But I think this is important."

"It is, my dear," said a voice from the passage behind them.

Welly squeaked and leaped over the stone. Spinning around, he saw a woman standing in the passage, a woman with long black hair and green eyes. A ball of green fire glowed coldly in her hand.

"Morgan!" Heather gasped. She clutched at her amulet, then snatched her hand away as the stone seared her palm with cold.

"Ah, you brought back my amulet. Good. I'll take it now."

"*Your* amulet? It is not! My mother gave it to me. It's a family heirloom."

"Oh, is that the story she told you? Resourceful woman. She has promise, even if she did muddle the drug in the wine. No, my dear, I told your mother to give that to you in case you should come her way. I thought it might be useful."

"You . . . you mean . . ."

"I used it to keep tabs on you all. Every time you played with it, the ties strengthened. Finally they were strong enough for me to call you here."

"To call me? I came here because Earl was in danger!"

Morgan laughed. The chilling sound bounced back and forth in the tiny chamber. Heather and Welly huddled back against the cold, damp stones.

"And so he will be. But I need you out of the way first. Now, give me my amulet."

Reaching up, Heather snapped the chain and hurled the amulet against the fallen stone. It cracked sharply in two. "I should have known it was evil. Only animal power is right for me. I should have guessed."

Morgan stared at the broken amulet, her mouth compressed into a thin, hard line. "Breaking that means nothing, fool! It was an old thing, just a tool, and it's done its work nicely. Now, pick up that wood."

"No!" Heather glowered back at the sorceress.

"Don't put on airs with me, brat! I'm not playing at a battle of wills with some barnyard witch. Pick it up!"

Heather shrank back against Welly. Laughing contemptuously, Morgan hurled her green flame at the stump of wood. The flame smashed on the stone, rocketing the wood up toward the two cowering figures.

Heather thrust up an arm to ward it off, and the wood grazed her. Everything shattered apart. Her splintered mind screamed for help.

The world was loud and filled with terrible sensation. Blades of cold seemed to slice their bodies into strips, strips of being that stretched impossibly thin. The strips twisted and coiled, suddenly wadding together and hurtling into bottomless darkness.

When Merlin failed to join them that evening for supper, Arthur was annoyed. But when the wizard was nowhere to be seen the following morning, he became concerned.

After questioning several people, he learned that Merlin had been seen climbing down the Hill of the White Horse early the evening before. The King was just considering whether or not to set out after him when his harper stepped hesitantly forward and told him about the note.

Arthur's face shadowed in remembered pain. Abruptly he turned from the harper and strode out the north gate. Scrambling down the steep hillside, splayed with its giant white horse, he stopped for a moment by the animal's single eye. Below he saw a lone figure, no, two figures, on distant Dragon Hill. The odd square hill rose abruptly from the fringes of the chalk, a last assertion of the downs before giving way to the wide vale below.

Arthur half ran, half slid to the bottom of the slope. Crossing an ancient road, he struck off toward the flat summit of the hill. Once there, dirty and out of breath, he saw Merlin seated on the ground staring vacantly across the valley. The troll huddled miserably nearby.

When he saw the King, the creature hopped up and scuttled to him. "Glad King is here. Great Wizard very sad. Not talk, not even eat."

Slowly Arthur walked over to his friend and sat beside him. The other never blinked.

"Merlin, it's me, Arthur. Please come back; please listen to me."

As though pulling his mind from some distant dragging sea, the wizard turned a blank, expressionless face to the King.

"Merlin, I know about Heather and Welly. I understand what you feel. Remember, I was betrayed, too—by a woman."

Something flickered in the other's face. "She didn't betray me! I betrayed her. She was a friend, and I demanded more. I dragged her out of the normal, comfortable world and into mine. A young, kind girl, and I dragged her into the cold just to share my loneliness."

"No, Merlin, I'm sure it wasn't like—"

"Oh yes it was. I wanted this life to be different. I wanted not to be alone. I wanted someone to love me honestly this time. And what did I do? I drove the most loving person I've ever met away from me!" The wizard stood up angrily and paced the top of the hill.

"How could I have been so blind, so egotistical as not to know what would happen? There's nothing human left of me. I'm just an empty shell. Anything that might once have been worth loving in me was eaten up by magic long ago."

Now the King jumped to his feet. "That's not true, you crazy old man! Remember me? I'm your friend, aren't I? I've found a few lovable scraps in you."

Merlin smiled thinly. "But you're different, Arthur. You've been touched by Faerie since your birth, stubborn human that you are. But to the rest of the world, to the real world, I'm a hollow, useless specter."

"You are not useless, not unless you sit out here and let yourself starve to death! We need you, Merlin. Come on back with us. Who knows, perhaps in time there may be other—"

"No!" The wizard spun around, glaring. "Never any others."

"All right, no others. I'm sorry. I'd almost forgotten how I felt about Guenevere . . . before I met Margaret." The King blushed and turned aside. "But I do need you, Merlin. And besides, you did promise us something of a prophecy."

Merlin looked down at the bowl hanging at his waist. "Yes, I did. Though whether I and this . . . this toy can still do that I just don't know. I'll try again." He sighed, rubbing a weary hand over his face. "Have some food sent out if you want. I'll try the bowl here. This is an ancient Hill of Seeing, you know."

"No, I didn't."

"You wouldn't, lucky, ignorant child!" He smiled wanly. "Maybe I can't read the future, Arthur. But you do deserve a better one this time. So does our world. I'll do what I can." Arthur laid a hand on his old friend's shoulder, then without a word turned away, beckoning Troll to follow. Once, the King turned and looked back. The thin figure on the hill seemed painfully alone.

32

EXILE

When Heather opened her eyes, it was to bright light and kaleidoscopic color, a dizzy riot of blue and green. She jammed her eyes shut hoping something would settle. Cautiously she opened them again, but the light and colors remained and began forming into shapes.

She was lying under a tree, a huge oak tree in full leaf. It was lit by brilliant, unfiltered sunlight, and beyond it arched bright blue sky.

Beside her, Welly's voice said, "Are we dead, do you think? Or in Avalon, maybe?"

Heather propped herself onto an elbow and looked around. This tree wasn't an isolated giant. There were others, many others, on the hillside around them. All were lushly green, touched here and there with a splash of orange or yellow. And the hillside itself was covered in grass, not coarse gray stuff but long, deep green blades. She combed her hand through them, feeling their cool softness glide between her fingers. Scattered through the grass were tiny white flowers.

Heather sighed and lay back again. "Well, it sure isn't our world. But I don't think it's Avalon either. When we were there before, it was different somehow, like this but . . . more so."

Cautiously Welly sat up. "Well, then, where are . . . Look at that, will you!"

Heather sat up quickly. "A city. Look at the size of that city!"

"The buildings, they're so tall!"

"And there are no ruins. Welly, do you see that?"

"I sure don't see any from here."

They both stood up. Heather turned around to where the hill rose toward the blue sky. "Let's climb up and look from there. Maybe it'll make more sense."

Scrambling up the grassy slope, they realized just how warm the air was. Both were soon sweating under the fur lining of even their light summer jackets and had to stop and strip them off. A warm breeze blew over them in a soft unfamiliar caress.

When they reached the top, they didn't notice the view as much as the activity around them. People were every-where on the grassy hilltop, people in bright colors and light, almost skimpy-looking clothes. And there were dogs. Heather felt her stomach tighten, remembering fell-dogs. But these looked very different, both from the dogs they knew and from each other. They barked and ran about in pursuit not of prey, but of balls and sticks people threw for them.

And children ran among them, laughing children, un-afraid of dogs or anything else, it seemed. Several women walked by, pushing smaller children in odd four-wheeled carriages.

A faint flapping sound came from overhead. Both in-stantly crouched and looked fearfully to the sky. Sunlight shone through the rainbow streamers of a kite as it dipped and soared through the air. They looked sheepishly at each other, then stood up laughing with relief. They could see now that there were other such specks in the sky, while people below tended their thin, barely visible lines.

Something else moved through the sky, something much higher. Silver glinted from outstretched wings and thunder trailed behind it. "An airplane," Welly breathed. "An ancient airplane! Great gods, Heather, where are we?"

They looked back now at the city. To the south, buildings stretched as far as they could see, their multiple windows glinting with sunlight.

"What is that?" Welly asked.

"What is which, young man?" said a voice behind them.

They turned quickly and saw a pale old man, lightly dressed, with a little curly-haired dog on a leather strap beside him.

"Ah . . . those buildings." Welly pointed vaguely to the mysterious city.

"Well, that funny-looking one there is the old Post Office tower, and the square tower beyond it, the one with the spires, is part of the Houses of Parliament. Now over there by all those tall new buildings, you can just see the dome of St. Paul's."

Heather looked confused. "Eh, I guess we mean, what are they in general?"

"Well, those there are in Westminster, but the ones around St. Paul's are in the City."

"What city?"

"The city of London, of course."

"London!"

"From Hampstead Heath you're not thinking to see Paris, I hope?" The man seemed slightly annoyed.

"No. No, certainly not," Welly mumbled.

"Thank you," Heather squeaked out as the man and his dog, eyeing them curiously, continued their walk.

Speechless, Heather and Welly looked at each other. London. Fallen, fabled London!

"This is too incredible," Heather whispered at last. "But why did Morgan send us here? This is hardly durance vile."

"Maybe it's a mistake. Maybe she meant to send us back to some dinosaur swamp and ran out of oomph."

"Yeah," Heather said dreamily, then became suddenly practical. "And she might realize her mistake any moment and blast us on again. Let's get a look at old London while we have the chance!"

Together they ran down the hill toward the distant buildings. But soon they were diverted by the natural beauty around them. Strange flowering bushes. And trees, a whole forest of them. They wandered off among the huge trunks, wondering at their height and the luxuriant greenery below.

They met other people on the paths, walking with dogs or whizzing by on alarming two-wheeled vehicles. People nodded at them in a friendly, if curious, way. Even with their fleecy jackets slung over their arms and hiding their swords, they felt hot and out of place in leather trousers and heavy wool shirts.

Emerging from the trees, they entered a lane lined with houses, impressively big houses, two or three stories of brick. All of the windows were glass, and in front of each was a little walled garden brimming with flowers. The colors were dazzling in the bright sun.

Whistling with delight, Heather saw what could only be a rose, a huge pink flower with delicate open petals like she had seen in pictures. Gently she touched it, tipping it down to her face. Soft wet petals brushed her cheek, and an intoxicating aroma seemed to fill her body. She felt she could spend the rest of her life smelling that one rose.

Welly gripped her arm. Reluctantly she turned away and saw a motor-driven vehicle rumbling down the street toward them. It pulled up beside the walkway. Doors opened and two people carrying bags made of paper stepped out, then walked into one of the houses.

"Look at that car!" Welly exclaimed when they had gone. "A real ancient car. And see, there're others down the road there. Fantastic!"

He walked over to the car and cautiously ran a hand over its smooth red surface. Heather started to join him when she saw something else. On one of the garden walls, an animal lay asleep in the sun. It had thick golden fur and a long tail that drooped off the wall like a fluffy snake. As Heather watched, the creature opened one eye, gave a paw a few quick licks, and rubbed this across its whiskered face.

Tentatively Heather reached out a hand. Surely this was a cat, but the only ones she had seen were the shadowy feral cats that roamed the wildlands. Those were dangerous things, silent, fierce hunters. She touched the furry side, soft and warm in the sun. Lazily the cat turned its eyes toward her, then began a low contented rumbling.

"Welly, look at this! A domestic cat, and it's purring."

A woman walking by in a yellow dress smiled at her pleasantly. "Old Tom's a good cat, he is. A fine mouser, right enough, but he does like his afternoon nap."

The two children smiled self-consciously at the woman.

Heather gave the cat a parting rub; then they headed down the lane, which opened into a large, noisy street. Vehicles of all descriptions roared by, and people bustled along the sidewalks. The traffic was alarming, not just the sight of it but the unfamiliar raucous noise and the hot chemical smell. The two stayed well back from the curb. Soon, however, they found that the buildings lining the sidewalk were fascinating enough.

Huge sheets of glass covered displays of things they had seen only in pictures. Some of the objects they couldn't even imagine a use for. Heather looked at the clothes and wistfully imagined herself wearing them. They were ridiculously impractical, of course—but beautiful. The two progressed slowly down the street, barely pulling themselves away from one window only to be fascinated by the next.

Outside one shop stood several tables mounded with mysterious fruits and vegetables. The aroma was enticing. For minutes, Heather looked longingly at some round pinkish-yellow fruits. Her mouth was watering so hard that her cheeks hurt. Suddenly Welly appeared beside her again and dragged her to a small shop on the corner. Its window was filled with candies, a dazzling variety. Sweet smells drifted out the door and pulled them in. Inside the cheery shop, glass counters were heaped with candies of rich brown and every possible color.

"May I help you?" a plump white-haired lady said from behind a counter.

"Oh," Heather sighed, "they all look and smell so good. But . . . I don't know if we have any money."

"I have," Welly said, pulling a leather pouch from his pocket. Pouring several coins into his palm, he looked at them doubtfully. Two were ones Arthur had minted in

Keswick, and one was Wessex coinage showing a rough profile of King Edwin.

"Will any of these do?" He handed the coins to the shop lady.

She looked them over curiously. "Foreign, aren't they? But I should have guessed from your accent and clothes. Where are you from, then?"

Heather thought frantically. Geography class. What had the pre-Devastation world been like? What countries might be near Britain yet cold enough to explain their clothes? And what about their darker skin?

Welly had the answer first. "Newfoundland. We're Eskimos here on a visit."

"Eskimos. Well, fancy that. You'd better ask your hosts to give you some of our money if you're going to be visiting shops. But my grandson's a coin collector. I'll sell you some sweets for one of these with the animal on it. What is it?"

"A dragon, ma'am."

"A dragon, how nice. Now, what would you like, duckies?"

They looked at each other helplessly, overwhelmed with indecision.

"Suppose I give you a sampling of several?" At their eager nods, she took a white paper bag and began scooping a few pieces from many piles. Finally she handed the bag to Heather and the two remaining coins to Welly. "There you are, duckies. Enjoy your visit."

"We are," Welly said as they slipped out the door.

Outside, standing on the sidewalk, they eagerly opened the bag and went into ecstasies over every new bite. Heather particularly liked the brown ones. She wondered what they were.

"We'd better not eat them all now," she said at last. Tucking the bag into a pocket, she tried wiping the stickiness from her face, only smearing it further.

After working up courage to run across a street, they looked at shop windows in the next block. The one that most fascinated them had boxes with moving pictures behind glass sides—colored pictures, and with them went voices and music, muffled behind the shop window.

"I've read about these," Welly whispered. "Televisions. They run on electricity."

"Are those things really happening?" Heather asked.

"Somewhere. They have machines that send pictures through the air."

Several people had stopped in front of the shop now. Welly wandered down the street, but Heather stayed and watched a box showing people on tall horses riding through a beautiful countryside. They stopped in front of a big white building, and several women ran out, all wearing gorgeous colorful dresses, incredibly wide and long.

Most of those crowding around were watching one of the other boxes where a man was talking. Boring, Heather thought. Then abruptly the story stopped on her box, and a man was talking there as well. The shopkeeper reached an arm through the back and turned up the sound.

"... about the crisis. The Prime Minister's warning was issued at eleven forty-five this morning. So far there has been no reply from the Russians. But in Washington, the ultimatum issued by the President yesterday has spurred an emergency session of Congress. We switch now to our Washington correspondent."

Another face appeared on the screen. Heather glanced away and noticed the worried looks on the faces around her. She wished they'd show the people with horses and long dresses again. She picked another candy from the bag and began licking off the brown coating.

Suddenly Welly was tugging at her arm. "Come here. I want you to see something." His voice was strained, and he looked ghastly. Heather wondered if he'd eaten too many candies.

"Look at that!" he said when he'd dragged her down the street. In front of them was a shallow wooden stall with folded piles of printed paper on the counter.

"At what?"

"Those are newspapers. They were printed out every day. Look at the date on these."

She stepped over and examined the papers. It took her awhile to find the dates above big black words like "Latest Crisis" and "New Ultimatum." She looked from one paper to another. Suddenly she understood. Fear slammed into her like a club.

"Oh, no! That's the date!"

Welly nodded. "The war, the bombs, the beginning of the Devastation."

"And we're in London! The only bomb that fell in England fell here."

"Now we know why Morgan—"

His words were cut off by a horrible scream. The wailing rose like a banshee's cry, filling the air with high keening.

The effect on the people around them was intense. There was a second's pause, then everyone began running somewhere. Children cried, and mothers scooped them up and ran off. Customers poured out of stores, and shop-keepers locked up immediately after them. People everywhere were yelling and screaming, car horns blared, and the streets were clogged with hurrying vehicles.

In the midst of the mounting chaos, Heather and Welly stood frozen with horror. Everyone was running, but there was nowhere to run. Death was hurtling toward them, and there was no escape.

33

CALLED TO DOOM

Seated on the lone hill, Merlin slowly chewed the food Troll had brought him. He scarcely tasted it, but he knew his neglected body needed the strength. His movements were cool and mechanical. He felt emotionally empty and hoped that if he could stay that way, the pain might fade.

He finished eating, then stood up, unfastening the bowl from his belt. Deciding against using the tripod, he walked to where bare chalk showed like bone through the grass. Raising the gleaming bowl above his head, he turned slowly, exposing it to all four directions. Then, seating himself on the earth, he held the bowl at eye level, tracing a thin finger along the interweaving patterns and murmuring the invoking spell. Setting the bowl firmly into the chalk, he took up a waterskin and filled the bowl nearly to its snake-entwined rim. Whispering a final phrase, he hunched over, blew on the surface three times, and stared into the liquid. He focused his mind on the upcoming battle, on the need to see Morgan's plans.

Timelines and shadowy images swirled in the depths. Careless now of personal safety, he hurled the whole strength of his mind at the vision. But again it jiggled and sidestepped. He felt distantly the waves of power, hearing them like great music, but cracked and oddly out of tune. Briefly he caught the distorted image of a battlefield and felt a sense of place and of incredible importance. But before he could grasp even that one vision, it danced away from him and vanished in the familiar enigma, the explosion of white hate.

With a despairing cry, he smashed a hand against the bowl, staring blindly as it spun away, splashing water over the bare earth.

Clearly it was useless now—an outgrown toy, a thing hopelessly tied to the past. As was he! Was there no way he could fit into this world, to find, to understand its new strain of power? Was there even any reason for him to care anymore? Torn by despair, his mind pulsed like a raw, open wound.

Suddenly a new force hit him. Human need, a frightened cry for help. It sliced into him like a knife, and with it came a brief flash of understanding. Abruptly its plea was cut off by an alien blast of energy. It swept the call away and smashed into his own mind with incredible pain.

The wizard cried out and pitched forward to the ground.

Instantly the worried troll was beside him, slapping his face with cold flat hands. "Great Wizard! Not be dead. We need Wizard. Troll need Wizard. Please, wake up!"

Slowly Merlin began to hear and feel again, but his mind still throbbed with pain. It was minutes before he could speak even a whisper.

"Troll, I need your help."

"Anything! Wizard say, Troll obey."

He struggled to sit up, dizzily resting his head on his knees. "I felt it. Before I was attacked, I felt something new. I think, yes, I think I understand now. A little. But I must go somewhere, help someone first. It has nothing to do with Arthur or future battles. I'm useless there. So is that old hunk of silver." He looked at the bowl lying lifeless on the grass. "Still, it did give me one thing, and it's important I pass that on. Troll, you must take a message to Arthur."

His companion looked confused. "Great Wizard be better soon; he go."

"No, I have to go elsewhere. You must tell him. Here, get me the map from the pack you brought."

The troll scuttled off. When he returned, Merlin spread the ancient paper on the ground beside him and marked a spot with a lump of chalk.

"Take this to Arthur. Tell him he must move his army southeast to that spot immediately. I don't fully know why, but it is very important that if he is to meet Morgan's army, he do so right there. You understand all that?"

The troll nodded eagerly. "Yes, yes, Troll understand. Can tell King. But what Wizard do?"

"If I can, I'll try to join him there, though I don't know of what use I'd be. Now go on, Troll, hurry with the message. They must leave right away."

Obediently the troll trotted off, but he kept stopping and looking back, reluctant to leave the wizard. Merlin smiled encouragingly and waved until the other was out of sight. Then he sat on the ground in a weary heap.

Yet tired as he was, a tremulous smile played over his lips. True, the bowl was dead, a thing of the past. Magic tied to it had failed to bring anything but an infuriating, veiled sense of the future.

But that first blast of power, that was new. That was the

new magic in all its force. And it had come to him when his mind had been torn open to human feeling, without any "thing" transmitting it—anything except the links of friendship and need. As if a curtain had finally been torn aside, Merlin began to see how this new magic must work.

Eagerly now, he stood up. With that pleading cry had come a brief picture, and a fearful one—places of power, places he knew. Heather might not need his companionship, but she needed his help. He would go there.

But that would mean a hard day's ride, and time was short. There was one other way, though he hesitated to take it. It meant using a sort of magic he had never liked. And now, exhausted as he was with his fast and his efforts at seeing, he relished it even less. He wouldn't even be able to take his staff. But perhaps he didn't need that, and there really was no choice.

The sun had already set, leaving a bloody smear against the western horizon. The evening air was cold and fresh. Breathing deeply, he looked up into the wide, beckoning sky. Like dry leaves, whispered words blew from him.

Slowly his shape began to shrink and thin. He stretched out his arms and they spread into wings. With a shrill cry, he launched himself into the air.

The hawk flew off toward the sunset, the last rays rippling his feathers with gold. With powerful thrusts and long, soaring glides, he sped on and on. The land below him darkened into night, but the sky was his world now. Cold wind slid beneath his wings. Smoothly he rode the wind, climbing the sudden warm gust that wafted up from the earth, that lifted him nearer to the stars. Starlight glimmered faintly on his wings; it glinted in his black eyes; it called to his mind.

His mind was a hawk's, and only with a struggle could
he hold to any sense of human purpose. He had a goal and
he flew there, but his thoughts were of the flight.

There were thoughts, too, of a hawk's body. He fought
them, but inside the small, feathered body, hunger grew.
He needed food; he needed warm flesh. Slowly he dropped
lower and lower to the earth, his course veering into a
wide circle, sweeping back over a field. He hovered motionless in the air until there came a twitch of movement
below. Like a stone, he plummeted to the earth, talons extended. He heard the squeal, felt claws sink into fur and
flesh. Then he was eating, beak splattered with blood,
warm gobbets of meat sliding down his throat. Refreshed,
he preened his feathers, then rose into the air again. Only
the tiniest corner of his mind felt revulsion.

He headed straight to the southwest. The waning
moon rising behind him cast a watery light over the land
below. It transformed his feathers to purest silver. The ecstasy of flight could carry him on and on.

But there was somewhere he was supposed to go,
somewhere below. He cared nothing for that now; he
wanted only to fly. Yet the thought dragged at him, drawing him closer to the earth.

He shifted his gaze downward to shapes that the
moonlight showed sliding beneath him. There, below him
now, that was what he sought. His flight circled back,
echoing the shape below.

A great circle of earth and stone. The standing stones
were far fewer than when his human mind had known
them, the buildings more plentiful. He circled again. One
ancient stone avenue was gone entirely, but another struck
off to the south and east. He swooped along its course

until it, too, petered out, and he glided up over a ridge. His mind's vision faded, and the strength of his small bird's body was fast failing.

He must land, touch the earth. Ahead to his right rose a tall cone-shaped hill. With weary wings he flapped toward it; no goal now but to rest. The flat summit rose toward him, and he stretched out his feet to meet it. Weakly he fluttered to the grass. Sleep blew over him before he could fold his wings.

It was the rising sun that finally roused him, brushing warmly against his eyelids, coaxing them to open. When they did, he looked at the appendage stretched out on the grass and wondered why it had no feathers.

Shivering, he remembered and sat up. He hated shape-changing. Others had more of a knack for it and could slip in and out of bodies, always staying in control. It was the sort of skill Heather might well have.

Heather! It was her call that had brought him here. Here?

He looked around. Yes, Silbury Hill, and before that the Avebury circle. But this surely had not been his goal; it had been . . . His gaze wandered over the horizon, then stopped at a dark grassy scar on a ridge below. The Long Barrow!

He scrambled to his feet. His legs wobbled beneath him, and he was hungry. But his stomach churned at the memory of his last meal. Shunting the thought aside, he hurried to the edge of the hill and clambered down. The ease of flight did not even tempt him now. The earth felt wonderfully solid beneath his feet.

From the foot of the hill, he struck off across fields to the barrow-topped ridge. At its base he found two horses tied to an old stone gate. Grimly he looked up and began to climb, following a faint trail in the weedy grass. Halfway up, something leaped at him. Two paws slammed against his chest; two tongues licked his face.

"Rus! Down, boy. Glad to see me, are you? Where's your mistress?"

Immediately the dog calmed down. Whining, he walked slowly up the hill looking frequently over his shoulders as Merlin followed. When they reached the stones at the barrow's entrance, the dog stopped and, slinking up against Merlin's legs, began whimpering.

"I know, Rus. I have no desire to go in there either."

"And you needn't bother to, Merlin. She's not there."

Startled, he looked up. A woman stood on top of the mound, gazing down at him with cool green eyes.

"Morgan," he said resignedly. Beside him, the whimpering dog pressed harder against his legs.

She laughed. "Merlin, you are so predictable, it's funny. Each time, I trap you with the same bait."

"Bait?"

"People, Merlin. Love." She walked lightly down the mound and sat on a flattened stone, swinging her legs like an innocent young girl.

"You need people, Merlin. You may spend lifetimes denying it, but you do. That's why you've never been as good a magician as I. I need only power. I feed on it, grow strong on it. But you need to love and be loved. It weakens you—to say nothing of how easy it makes you to trap."

"To trap? What do you mean? That attack might have been yours, but not that first call."

Frowning thoughtfully, the woman plucked a gorse sprig and crushed it in her hands. "No, that was hers, all right. And stronger than I expected. She does have an odd sort of power, that one. But when it comes to dealing with people, she's as weak as you are."

Laughing, she scattered gorse over the ground. The cold air turned briefly tangy with its scent. "I admit, the amulet didn't work as well on her as I had hoped. After Brecon, she should have been drawn to use it until it ensnared her. She kept fighting it, even ignoring it. But then, it was old and I suspect its powers had gone a little flat. It worked in the end, though."

"Amulet? What did . . . ?"

"The best part is that what finally brought her was thinking she was coming here to save you from dire danger. Ironic, isn't it?"

"To save me? But she . . . but the note . . ."

"Ah, yes, the note. A nice little frill of mine, don't you think? I couldn't resist. A chance to twist the knife and let you wallow in self-pity while I laid the trap."

For all his long life, Merlin had hated this woman. Suddenly, forgetting all his powers, he lunged at her like an animal. Startled, she fell back, slapping him away with a blast of power.

"Temper! Don't lose your subtlety, Merlin dear. Oh, I will miss you! This time I really must dispose of you permanently. But then there will be no one to appreciate the finesse of my powers."

Merlin had been shaking with anger, but suddenly he laughed until great gusts of laughter battered the cold evening air. "Powers? No, Morgan, your powers are nothing! They're tattered, dying relics. I've only just seen it, but surely you've feared as much. Your amulet, my bowl—they are things, cold, lifeless *things*. In this new world, trying to channel power through them is like using stone tools when iron is at hand. I don't know what you tried with that amulet, but Heather, novice that she is, was able to resist because she is part of a new power."

"You're quite mad!" Morgan's eyes flared with anger; then she leaned back and laughed derisively. "I almost hate to put you away now, because that would be a mercy. And you deserve much, much worse."

The wizard's smile was grim. "You said a moment ago that your power was greater than mine because you had no need for people. Perhaps that was true once, Morgan, but not now. The strongest new magic comes from *people,* not things. It comes from their hopes, their fears, their ties with each other. Your amulet worked in the end only because it used Heather's need to help . . . to help someone she cared for."

His look was pitying now. "You are still a person of power, Morgan, as am I. But keep trying to use it in the old ways, and it will prove a sterile power. You will be helpless."

"Helpless?" She jumped up, glaring at him. "In a short time, your precious Arthur will see just how helpless I am! I will defeat him and his army utterly. I've worked for years, Merlin, wedging a crack in time, and through it I will call an army, an army of the dead. They will come in such numbers, wreaking such despair, that Arthur's mere human army will freeze in horror, freeze while my forces seize the victory!"

Merlin recalled his persistent vision, the twisting time-lines, the blast of white heat and hatred, then that one glimpse of a battlefield. Nothing made sense. "A crack in time? Where could you—?"

"Enough, Merlin! It's been fun all these years, having

an opponent almost worthy of myself. But your time is over!"

Reaching behind a stone, she pulled out a charred lump of wood. "Go join your puny friends, if they mean so much to you." She tossed him the wood. "Catch!"

Instinctively he did. It was like clamping down on an explosive. His self shattered apart, its shreds spinning over an immensity of collapsing time.

Like a leaf, he was swept down an endless dark stream. Eternity flowed past. Then, after timeless time, he seemed to be caught by a web of roots, washed up against the base of a great tree.

Slowly the world stopped rocking beneath him. He felt the softness of grass, the solidity of earth. The air was gentle and warm. He opened his eyes. A massive oak tree spread above him. Beyond it was bright blue sky.

Dizzily he sat up. Beside him, Rus crouched on the grass, both faces looking bewildered. From behind them, a shrill barking shattered the air. Quickly Merlin looked around to see a small curly-haired dog yapping and straining at a leash. On its other end, a pale old man was holding him back and looking thoroughly aghast at the sight of Rus.

"Oh." Hastily Merlin waved a hand over the mutant dog. One head and one tail became invisible.

Startled, the old man now shifted his gaze to Merlin and his fur-lined clothing. Then he yanked his dog away and went off muttering, "More of those crazy kids. What is the world coming to?"

Unsteadily Merlin got to his feet, looking around in vague recognition. Their world somewhere in the past. Then he glanced down at Rus and laughed. The visible head and tail were offset, leaving room for their invisible companions.

"Come on, you lopsided mutt, we've got to find Heather and Welly. Go on, find your mistress."

Excitedly the dog jumped about; then, smelling the ground, he suddenly shot off down the hill. Fur coat flying and sword banging against his leg, Merlin raced after him.

They ran over the grass, then cut to the right, following winding paths among a forest of trees. Merlin wanted to stop and look around, but more than that he wanted to see Heather. She hadn't written that note! She'd wanted to help him, not leave him! He paid no attention to the startled looks that swept them as they raced past.

Rus slowed when they came out into a lane. His long nails clicked on the unfamiliar pavement. Nose down, he moved steadily along. A startled yellow cat bristled at him from atop a wall, but the dog spared it only a passing snarl. The noise of traffic grew until they reached a large busy street.

Suddenly a distant wailing rose and filled the air. Rus sat back and howled with both throats, visible and invisible. Puzzled, Merlin looked about. Then he caught something of the fear and urgency swirling around them.

"Go on, Rus, find them. Hurry!"

The dog took off down the sidewalk and Merlin followed, dodging around rushing, panicky people. They crossed another street, and then he saw them. Standing like an island in a sea of chaos, Heather and Welly huddled together against a building, fear and hopelessness written on their faces.

Rushing madly toward them, Merlin grabbed Heather in his arms and kissed her on her chocolate-smeared mouth.

Welly looked on in happy surprise. "Well, it's about time you did that." Suddenly he sobered. "But it's not the *right* time—the world's about to blow up!"

Merlin looked at him, confused.

"The Devastation!" the younger boy yelled over the noise of people and sirens. "Morgan sent us back to the day it began!"

"And this is London!" Heather added, clutching his arm.

Realization dawned on Merlin. "Of course, a way to really destroy me." His look of horror slid into excitement. "But no . . . the crack in time. Her 'army of the dead.' From here, of course! The dead of the Devastation! The crack she created will still be open for them."

Urgently he grabbed Heather's shoulders. "Heather, the new power, the new magic . . . If we can use it, we have a chance. Hurry, back to the tree! The opening must be there."

"How?" Welly protested. "We don't know where—"

"Rus does. Follow him!"

Crazily the three pelted after the dog. Everyone else, intent on their own panic, ignored them. Sirens wailed on and on throughout the vast city. The park was nearly deserted as they ran, gasping, up the hill.

Suddenly Heather slowed. Looking up, she scanned the blue sky. A graceful white gull soared overhead.

"Earl! The vision I saw at the Keswick stone circle. I just realized . . . This is the City! Look, there's the bird!"

He turned back and grabbed her arm. "Of course, yes. Your vision." He pulled her after him. "Then use it, Heather! Use the new power. Focus through that bird, the dog, the tree, through every living thing around."

"But you . . . you haven't your staff."

"But I have you!" His smile shone. "I'll focus through

you and Welly . . . and through Arthur. Arthur back there needs us desperately. Now, quick, grab Welly's hand. Welly, hold Rus."

They flung themselves against the rough bark of the tree. As Merlin chanted phrases beside her, Heather felt the touch of his love and his power, new and strong as she had never felt it before. Reaching into new depths of her own, she let her power rise through her, stretching out to the others, binding them in strength and need. Visions of their time, their King, and each other formed in their minds.

Suddenly around them the sirens stopped. All sound stopped. A blinding whiteness filled the world, and a searing heat. Its horrible power slammed behind theirs as they hurtled through time.

34

To the Ends of the Earth

The army led by Arthur Pendragon was nearing its goal. It had not been an easy matter, arriving where they were. The order to abandon their strategic position had been hard for some of the allied leaders to accept, particularly on the word of a demented boy wizard brought by a scuffling one-eared troll.

But to Arthur's surprise, Margaret of the Scots had been Arthur's staunchest supporter. "If that skinny kid says we must do something," the Queen had said, "and Arthur believes him, then we must do it. This King Arthur of ours has led us through a good many improbable situations already. I, for one, am ready to follow him to the ends of the earth."

Arthur treasured that statement and what it reflected. In the end, the others had agreed with her. And now, shadowed by forces out of Faerie, they followed behind him toward the site of ancient London. But as they rode on, their route became more and more daunting.

At first there were the usual abandoned buildings. Then there were ruins that seemed to come from more than neglect, empty stone shells and buildings that lifted only twisted metal skeletons to the sky. Finally there were no ruins at all, only an empty glassy plain. Ghosts of snow twisted and whispered dryly across its surface.

Londinium, Arthur thought sadly. A sleepy little town on the River Thames, then later, it seemed, the capital of a great nation. If there was anything left of even that river now, it was the faint dry scar that seamed the desolate plain below them. On a hollow wind, snow blew across the wasteland like drifting sand.

It was almost with relief that they saw Morgan's army approaching. Any life and promise of action was better than this. The enemy poured over the plain in a black wave, while the armies of the West and North watched and felt relief turn into growing uneasiness.

Arthur squinted against the glare of snow and patches of mirror-like earth. Of the human warriors marching toward them, most, he imagined, were not volunteers. Once Morgan's forces won a land, the locals had little choice but to do her bidding. But it was the other soldiers who were more worrisome. There were mutants from beyond the Channel, and most chilling of all were the allies from beyond this world. Arthur had never seen their like in such numbers. For his own army, bred in a different age, he knew this must be unimagined nightmare.

He looked to his right, smiling encouragement at Margaret. Grimly she returned his smile, her face unusually pale against her crown of red hair. Sighing to himself, Arthur wished that Merlin rode at his other side. It wasn't the magic he needed so much as the well-tested companionship and counsel. But he could spare little time at present to wonder about his friend. A battle lay at hand, a decisive battle. The King needed no prophecy to see that.

As the enemy neared, their ranks parted and one rider came forward, halting on a bare rise. Black hair blew about her shoulders, and her restive mount hissed and pawed the hard earth with its claws. The woman's voice rang powerfully over the shifting silence.

"Arthur Pendragon. After two thousand years, we meet again. It was very thoughtful of you to come this far to meet me, but hardly necessary. You could have lost this battle just as well where you were."

"I have no intention of losing this time, Morgan."

"But you will, just the same. Your army is large, but it can never equal mine. You haven't even your pathetic little wizard with you. Of course, you are right; you need not lose. You could join with me. We could conquer the rest of this wretched world together. Think of it, you as High King again, and I as your Queen. You don't need that red-haired Scottish harpy any longer."

Beside him, Queen Margaret snarled and hurled her war spear toward the enemy. Arthur laughed heartily. "This is a queen after my own heart. You have your answer, Morgan." He turned in his saddle. "Sound the charge!"

Trumpets, horses, and the battle cries of men and nonmen—the sound of warfare broke out on the long-dead and silent plain.

But Morgan did not engage in the fighting. Instead, she clothed herself in flame and power and worked a terrible invocation. Dragging forth power long prepared, she reached back into time to a day of empty horror, to a day when this plain was peopled neither with warriors nor with city dwellers, but with the restless spirits of countless newly dead. She called forth these spirits. Held by power and their own aimless misery, they came.

Amid Arthur's army, a gray cloud began to swirl. It formed into shapes hardly more solid than mist. Images of death—creatures seared into ashes, vaporized into shadows on a wall. Into the midst of living warriors came specters whose skin hung off them in rags, whose bodies were blistered like scorched meat, whose hollow eyes ran with blood.

They floated by in anguished, unspeaking torment, and the living around them went mad with fear. Brave warriors threw down their weapons and ran. Horses twisted under their riders and stampeded off. Even among those from Faerie, many quailed and slipped away like smoke.

Those around Arthur tried to hold their ground, but fear rose in a choking cloud, gripping both horses and riders. Some closed their eyes and huddled together. Squealing, Troll rolled on the ground, throwing hairy arms over his head.

Suddenly there was a deafening crack, as if the world had split open. Three young people and a dog stood before them, beside a stump of charred wood. Overhead, a black crow screamed and flew off over a plain that was littered with fear-stunned bodies.

Merlin leaped forward. Above the moaning and wailing he shouted, "Morgan, go! You are defeated! The spirits of once-living people cannot be our enemy now. It is *things* we fight against!" Chanting, he thrust his arms into the air. "By the power of human pity, I send these spirits back to their rest!"

The gray shapes churned and thinned like windblown smoke. Morgan shrieked in fury, then cried out, "You cannot win, Merlin! In the end, your side will lose as it has before."

"Perhaps, but I think not. The world has changed, Morgan. And now I would have it change more!"

Turning, he strode back to the tree stump and raised his voice so it echoed over the plain. "You opened a crack, Morgan Le Fay. Now I call through it other things. I call forth the picture of our real enemy, a vision of soulless things gone mad. May its image burn into every soul here, and through them onto the furthest generation! And I call forth, too, the human cry of its victims. May its echoes haunt mankind for all eternity!" He stomped a foot down on the charred wood.

It seemed that heat filled the plain, as if a giant oven had been flung open. There came a concussion of sound like the scream of dying suns, and with it came millions of screams from severed lives. Blinding light burst upon them, searing into the very cells of their bodies. The memory of what had been and what could be again was sealed there forever.

A cold wind of their own world revived them at last. People staggered to their feet, all military order gone. Morgan had fled, and her followers, shaken and abandoned, were slinking away.

The soldiers of the West and North, seeing their leaders still among them, rallied to the Lion and Dragon banners snapping in the cold, clean wind. All were subdued and quiet.

Arthur Pendragon surveyed the field, then turned to his oldest friend. "Even as a vision, that weapon and its effects . . ." He broke off, struggling to control a new wave of shuddering. Then grimly he smiled at Merlin. "But still, you saved us, old wizard. Now will you finally prophesy for us? Is Morgan gone for good? By what you have done, will we finally live in peace?"

Merlin put a hand on the King's shoulder. "Arthur, you were always a dreamer. No, Morgan or others like her will surely be back. And as for peace . . . we are dealing with human beings, creatures that fight among themselves and want what the other has. Changing that will not be easy. Though with this new sort of power, there may be some hope."

The wizard looked at the crowd growing around them. He grinned at Troll's bouncy greeting, then jumped onto the old charred stump. "But here I will prophesy. The nature of humankind may linger, but the memory of this ultimate horror will be carried with each of us as well. By the new powers, it is sealed in every one of the thousands who were here today, friend and foe alike. Their descendants will carry it in their bodies and spread it, a racial memory to pass on for all time.

"Perhaps people will still fight and make weapons, but this one scorching memory may turn them back from that final horror. They may gallop wildly down the same road, but now, perhaps, they will turn aside before the precipice. And, Arthur, perhaps this time you and your queen can lay foundations for a world that will not topple. There is strong, new, *human* power in today's magic. We can use it to build a world of hope.

"There! You wanted prophecy, and you have it!"

Laughing, the wizard spun around and pointed at Kyle the harper. "Now make that into a song if you will, a song to ring through time. But don't forget the verse about how this world's sorcerers—and sorceresses—are human, too, and will be part of the new world as well!"

He stepped down from the stump and hesitantly reached out a hand to Heather. Running to him, she threw her arms around his neck and kissed him joyfully. Then she drew back.

"Earl Bedwas, I thought so! Or perhaps I should start calling you Aged Merlin."

"Huh?"

"It's just that I do believe you are finally growing a beard!"

Startled, he raised a hand to his slightly scratchy chin. "Well, it's about time!"

PAMELA F. SERVICE grew up in Berkeley, California, and spent three years in England studying archaeology. She, her husband, Bob, and their daughter, Alex, lived for years in Bloomington, Indiana, where Pam worked as a museum curator, served on the city council, and wrote. Now back in California, she has published over twenty children's books, works as a museum director in Eureka, acts in community theater, and is still writing. She is delighted to have a couple of her earliest and favorite books available again.